JORDAN DANE

THE ECHO OF VIOLENCE

A SWEET JUSTICE NOVEL

AVON

An Imprint of HarperCollinsPublishers

This is a work of fiction. Names, characters, places, and incidents are products of the author's imagination or are used fictitiously and are not to be construed as real. Any resemblance to actual events, locales, organizations, or persons, living or dead, is entirely coincidental.

AVON BOOKS
An Imprint of HarperCollins*Publishers*
10 East 53rd Street
New York, New York 10022-5299

Copyright © 2010 by Cosas Finas, LLC
Excerpt from *Reckoning for the Dead* copyright © 2011 by Cosas Finas, LLC
ISBN 978-0-06-147414-9
www.avonbooks.com

First Avon Books paperback printing: September 2010

Avon Trademark Reg. U.S. Pat. Off. and in Other Countries, Marca Registrada, Hecho en U.S.A.
HarperCollins® is a registered trademark of HarperCollins Publishers.

Printed in the U.S.A.

10 9 8 7 6 5 4 3 2 1

To my brothers, Ed and Ignacio.
I grin because you're my brothers,
but what really cracks me up is that
there's nothing you can do about it.

ACKNOWLEDGMENTS

This is the fourth book in the Sweet Justice series and is an Alexa Marlowe story. Many readers have written to say how intrigued they are with her, and as you might imagine, I love hearing from my readers, so thanks for writing. Alexa is a strong, resilient woman who has found a way to thrive in a covert world without sacrificing her feminity . . . too much. But with something missing in her life, she questions what her future holds. Her journey has been an intriguing one to write. She is much braver than I would ever be, but she's a woman who would be great to have as a friend. And speaking of friends . . .

Even though writing is a solitary course, I have been blessed with a wonderful support group of friends who help with the process. For their continued support and invaluable input, I'd like to thank Dana Taylor, Tom Radcliffe, and Joe Collins for their help with this book. I feel lucky that our paths crossed and that I didn't scare you away. And to the real Deacon, Mrs. Torres, and my dear, sweet husband, who continue to color my life. Who knew such nice people could inspire such devious thoughts? Pass the ginger-snaps.

Special thanks to my editor, Lucia Macro, for your spot-on insight into this book, making the story and the characterizations stronger. As always, you rock. And thanks to all the staff at Avon Books who had a hand in this project, with a special shout-out to my terrific agent, Meredith Bernstein. It's great having you in the trenches.

Last but certainly NOT least, I would like to thank all of you crazy readers who have written me about this series and my other books. I especially love getting e-mails through my website at *www.JordanDane.com*, written in the wee hours of the morning after you've finished one of my novels and feel the urge to send me your thoughts in your jammies. You really make my day and I love hearing from you. So please, keep it up. You are the reason I write. And I hope you enjoy Alexa's story as much as I did writing it. Jackson Kinkaid still haunts my dreams—in a very good way.

THE
ECHO OF
VIOLENCE

CHAPTER 1

Near Haiti

Not even the mesmerizing beauty of the sea at night calmed Luc Toussaint.

The moon dappled undulating waves with shimmer as his slow-moving trawler navigated the Atlantic toward the Canal de la Tortue. Haiti and Port de Paix lay dead ahead. The crew of the *Aquilina* made ready for docking and had left Luc at the helm, alone with his thoughts. As captain of the commercial vessel, he normally took pleasure in the solitary feeling at this hour and drew comfort from being one with the sea. That feeling of serene isolation reminded him of the old days when he was a younger man—but not tonight.

He had other things on his mind.

To settle his nerves, he had smoked far too many cigarettes as he kept an alert eye on the horizon. He peered through the dim glow of the wheelhouse and beyond the reflection of the boat's running lights on the water, searching for police on patrol.

Earning extra money for his family, he carried additional cargo in a special compartment known only to him and the men he worked for on the side. He played a small part in a smuggling operation with a splinter faction of a drug cartel, and his crew had no idea. His men knew nothing about any contraband on board.

For that matter, he didn't know much more.

For the sake of his wife and children, he only cared about the money and merely played his part as blind courier between South America and Miami, Florida. What had been stowed below was none of his concern. And even though the Dominicans had cut into his action and ramped up their role by becoming wholesaler to many cities on the East Coast of the United States, Luc wanted no part in that.

On most nights, the limits he'd set made him feel absolved of the crime. A more palatable rationale.

When he first saw the city lights of Port de Paix—a distant glow that had robbed the skyline of stars—he had called in his position and estimated time of arrival using the special cellular phone he'd been given. As an agreed-upon security measure, he avoided using the high-frequency radio transmission, the equipment he had in the wheelhouse. Luc blew smoke from his nose and glanced at his watch one more time. When he looked up, he spotted a searchlight on the water dead ahead. The Haitian national police were about to intercept him.

After speaking to his South American contact, he had expected the marked patrol boat; but making it through an inspection at sea always made him nervous these days.

Luc only hoped his part would be over soon.

He breathed a sigh of relief when he spotted the familiar face of a Haitian inspector as the man boarded his vessel, an official he'd seen before and knew by reputation. The hulking man in uniform lumbered across the deck—Gerard Heriveaux—a big man with a pronounced slouch. He and his men knew how to look the other way. And knowing that allowed Luc to relax until the man pulled him aside.

"We must break protocol," the inspector said in French. "I'm here to intervene on behalf of our mutual friends. Contact your man and confirm this. I will wait."

One of the inspector's men handed him a duffel bag. Luc had no idea why Heriveaux would need it.

"I do not understand," he said. "What is happening?"

The Haitian officer looked over his shoulder and kept his voice low. "We've received word that the counternarcotics unit will raid your vessel when you dock. If you want to be held harmless, you will contact your man to confirm and let me do my part. Now is that clear enough?"

Luc stared at the older man, unable to control the escalating beat of his heart. Nothing like this had ever happened before. The threat of a raid would put him in the middle, between dangerous drug smugglers and an unforgiving Haitian government. Even the hint of an illegal operation would mark him by local officials. He had not been so foolish as to deny this possibility, but being faced with it turned his stomach sour.

God help him.

"Yes, very clear," he nodded. "I will make the call."

Luc headed for the privacy of the wheelhouse to use his cellular phone. When the man on the other end of the line made it easy for him to explain—offering his take on the raid—it made him more confident he would be doing the right thing and reinforced that he'd not be held accountable. His contact told him what to do.

When he returned to the Haitian inspector on the leeward deck, Luc made sure his crew was distracted by the official inspection and delegated the paperwork to one of his men before he waved the officer forward. "Come. Follow me."

In privacy, he led Heriveaux to his personal cabin below. Behind a large wooden panel on the back of his bunk, he yanked at one side and opened a secret compartment. Bolted down and welded, a large combination safe was secured inside.

A safe he didn't know how to open.

"If you have the trust of my contact, you will know how to access what's inside. I do not," Luc told the man. "And I have no wish to be involved. I'll be outside my cabin until you have secured . . . whatever is in that safe."

As he opened his duffel bag, Heriveaux acted surprised by his reaction, but smiled. "You are a smart man, Captain. Go. Do what you must. I will be with you shortly."

Luc shut the door behind him and stood outside his cabin, waiting for the inspector. With the trawler adrift on the sea, the *Aquilina* pitched in the rolling waves, forcing him to widen his stance for balance. His stomach roiled with the motion, the start of nausea more attributable to the sudden change in plan. He wiped both hands over his face and waited.

Luc Toussaint prayed he'd done the right thing.

Once the *Aquilina* was moored to the pier at Port de Paix, Luc's crew got to work unloading the documented cargo. But a familiar face on the dock below caught the eye of the captain. He quickly disembarked down the gangway and walked toward Inspector Gerard Heriveaux. The man barely glanced at him, as if nothing was the matter.

"Why are you here?" He shrugged as he stood before the Haitian official. "Has something else happened?"

"What are you talking about?" the inspector questioned. "I'm here to inspect your vessel and collect your port fee."

Heriveaux scribbled on a document clipped to a board and prepared another inspection form—a form Luc already had signed and had in his possession, stuffed into his pocket. He retrieved the executed document, unfolded it, and pulled the man aside.

Lowering his voice, Luc said, "But I already paid you. And don't you think it's unwise to duplicate the paperwork? Someone might notice."

With a confused look on his face, Inspector Heriveaux knitted his brow, cocked his head, and opened his mouth to speak. But the ringing of the private cell phone clipped to Luc's belt distracted him.

When he recognized the number, he raised a finger and said, "Please . . . I must take this. Excuse me."

Heriveaux grumbled and turned back to his paper-work with a show of indignation as the harsh voice of his South American contact stole Luc's attention.

"Why have I not heard from you? You were sup-posed to call by now. What's your position?"

Luc's eyes grew wide and his jaw dropped. But as he stared at the annoyed inspector standing in front of him on the pier, it did not take long for him to realize—

He'd been pirated and put out of business by a slick operator.

"I c-can . . ." He choked on words he'd never believe himself. ". . . explain."

The Haitian patrol boat set course for Tortuga Island, the historically infamous Pirate Island across from Port de Paix. En route, every decal, flag, and uniform that designated the identity of the boat and its personnel would be removed, bagged, and thrown overboard with weights. No evidence of their piracy would remain.

In his cabin belowdecks, Jackson Kinkaid stripped out of his uniform to his skivvies and stared at the age-ravaged face and thinning gray hair of Inspector Gerard Heriveaux in the mirror one last time. Being a chameleon, he admired his work. His best disguise to date.

What had taken him hours to create would be gone in minutes.

Kinkaid removed his brown-tinted contact lenses and dug his fingernails into the skin at his cheek, tear-ing at the latex until his own face emerged, dotted with adhesive. He bent over a small sink to scrub off the last remnants of the disguise and wet down his dark hair. When he looked into the mirror again, familiar green eyes stared back. And he straightened his spine and shoulders to regain his youth . . . and attitude.

"You won't have to worry about old age, Kinkaid," he smirked at his reflection. "You won't live that long."

Before he dressed, he sat on his bunk with eyes closed and listened to a digital recording on an iPod. He needed to hear it like he was compelled to breathe, and he'd made this special time a ritual—a self-inflicted reminder of how much he had changed. The recording also never let him forget that his life hadn't always been empty.

While he took his personal downtime, his team headed for Tortuga Island, where his men would separate, and a helicopter awaited him. Not too long ago, the island had served as the filming locale of a sequel to *Pirates of the Caribbean*. Kinkaid appreciated the irony, especially considering what he had just pulled off.

Forty-five minutes later

"Boss, we're here." The voice of his number one man, Joe LaClaire, called to him from on deck.

Kinkaid knew from the plan that they would be docking in a discreet cove on the island, away from curious eyes. For security reasons, they randomly selected the location, but this spot had a unique attribute. A helipad was nearby, and a Bell 210 helicopter awaited his arrival.

By the time he emerged topside, Kinkaid garnered his men's attention when he came out wearing a navy Armani suit with a light gray shirt and burgundy-striped tie. The stark contrast of dress attire on board generated a flurry of whistles and verbal abuse he found hard to ignore.

"Cut the crap, you bastards," he yelled. A rumble of good-natured laughter from his men made Kinkaid smile. He gripped the shoulder of the short, dark-haired man standing in front of him and lowered his voice. "Get the cash where it needs to go, Joe. You're in charge now."

He trusted Joe with his life, so relying on him to secure what they had plundered wasn't an issue. The drug money taken off the trawler had been easy pickings, especially with an inside track to the drug cartel. Eavesdropping on the international maritime satellite communication network helped determine what cargo to hit and the level of risk involved—all part of their usual meticulous homework. And the anxious trawler captain had given him plenty of time to break into the safe when the man left him alone in his cabin.

But commandeering the trawler's private cell phone—pretending to be the captain's smuggler contact—had been a stroke of genius Joe had orchestrated. It had saved the trawler crew from having to face Kinkaid's plan B if anyone had resisted.

"I'll see you at the rendezvous point tomorrow morning. Eight sharp," he said.

These days he had few friends. He'd severed ties and kept moving to avoid dealing with the baggage. Friends expected too much. And they knew when he was lying and called him on his shit. LaClaire understood the way things were. He rarely pushed and didn't take it personally when he drew the line. And that was okay, most days.

"Just watch your ass." Joe narrowed his eyes. "I don't want to dip into my hard-earned funds to bail you out." He leaned in and whispered, "There was close to a half million in that safe."

"Good haul." Kinkaid forced a smile. "I gotta go."

"I hate not leaving together after an operation. You sure you won't need me to stick around?" Joe asked.

"No, I have obligations." Kinkaid adjusted his cuff links, thinking about the second half of his evening. He was already late.

After his helicopter touched down, he had arranged for a taxi to get him to his next stop. A taxi service in Port de Paix was a high-risk sport. Most vehicles were nothing more than unmarked junk heaps without meters. But given his timetable, he didn't want to risk not finding one.

The charity event he'd be attending was an affair put on by a determined Catholic nun.

"People are waiting for me, Joe." He raised an eyebrow. "Hell, I'm the damned guest of honor."

CHAPTER 2

Port de Paix, Haiti

When Kinkaid arrived late to the party, the fund-raiser for the St. Thomas Aquinas Academy was in full swing, an occasion that marked the tenth anniversary of the missionary school. With its aqua stucco walls and red-tiled rooftop, Dumont Hall was a civic building on the fringe of town and near the academy.

Port de Paix was not much more than an impoverished village with dirt streets, but the school was situated close enough to the children who really needed it and was bordered by growing commercial establishments that might support the academy.

The town had seen a growth spurt, and the organizers had done well to have their event at one of the newer civic buildings. Partygoers could be seen through the windows and on the front steps of the building. Women in fancy dresses accompanied men in suits with children playing dress-up. And the music of a small quartet wafted into the night air as Kinkaid's taxi pulled to the curb.

He cringed at the thought of walking into an event at which he knew he didn't belong. And if he believed in divine intervention, the course that had led him to this fiasco had a real hinky vibe to it, like an unavoidable retribution for his sins.

Four years ago, he'd crossed paths with a very persistent Catholic nun, Sister Mary Katherine, when her need for cash outweighed her common sense. Their meeting had been a surprise for both of them. It had not been their first. After his arrival in Haiti—under the guise of an American businessman traveling the islands—the woman had tracked him down, looking for donations. How she'd found him, she never said. And she'd followed his lead in not talking about the past. She had left that up to him, which meant the topic never came up.

The nun had no idea what he'd become. And he never told her otherwise, but being with her was a constant reminder for him. *Deserved penance.*

Standing on the curb with the taxi driving away, he delayed making his entrance. He took a breath of fresh air to dispel the smell of the taxi from his nostrils. Despite his usual swagger—a product of the flamboyant public image he had cultivated out of necessity over the years—he hated being the center of attention. But tonight he'd have to put up with it. If Sister Kate hadn't specifically asked him to attend and made such a big deal about it, he would have turned her down flat.

"Only for you, Kate."

Killing time, he avoided the main hall and headed for a spot in the garden to the left of the entrance. Dirt and gravel crunched under his shoes when he entered a courtyard. The pungent aroma of flowers mixed with the scent of the ocean off a warm breeze, but something more lingered in the air. His eyes trailed to a far corner of the garden, where he searched the shadows for what he knew he'd find. He had taken a gamble that he wouldn't be alone, and he was right.

In the dark, under the dim glow of moonlight, he saw Sister Mary Katherine. Her dark silhouette stood out against the stonework behind her. A faint yet ghostly twist hung low around her head like an aura, and he grinned at the faint impression of a halo. Sister Kate was too grounded in the reality of life to ever be mistaken for an ethereal saint, despite the fact that he couldn't think of anyone more deserving.

The nun was sneaking a cigarette—her one true vice—and billowing smoke like a flume. She smoked when she was nervous. Socializing at the fund-raiser had her on edge, too. When she saw him, she didn't bother to hide her smoking.

"Come here." She waved her free hand. "Let me get a good look at you."

"Okay, you got me at this shindig. Now what?" With arms crossed, Kinkaid slouched against the stone wall next to the nun, who was dressed in a traditional black tunic and veil with starched white collar.

Sister Mary Katherine flicked her cigarette away to glance at him, top to bottom.

"You clean up real nice, Jackson. You change the color of your skin to suit the occasion."

"You have no idea, Kate." He crooked his lip into a

smile until he noticed that Dumont Hall had uniformed guards with weapons at key locations, not exactly low-profile. "This event is supposed to be about the kids. What's with all the firepower?"

"Now that's where you're wrong," the nun argued, waggling a finger. "What we do at the school is for the kids, yes. But this event? It's about you, Jackson Kinkaid. I'm proud of you. And people are curious about the wealthy American, my dear. I'm afraid I've been bragging about you again. I caught the local media on a slow news day, and they gave me a feature to promote the event and our new programs."

She cocked her head. "And I've invited other regional school administrators to see the programs you've generously funded. Some have flown in for the occasion, and if local contributors like what they see, they might make a donation, too. So play nice, will you? Do it for the kids. A few of the children will be attending with their parents. They're excited about playing dress-up, like real grown-ups."

Over the years, he'd gotten a bit of a reputation in certain circles. Partly due to his involvement with Sister Kate's pet project, the media had initially placed the spotlight on him, but when other more influential people took notice, he had to invent a persona that people and the police would buy. One thing led to another, and things got out of control fast. He'd been mistaken that the local media would get tired of covering his story—and now he was stuck with the consequences. No good deed went unpunished.

He'd never told Kate that she'd brought trouble to his

door the day she'd found him in Haiti and brought the
past colliding with the present for him. She thought she
had done him a good turn—drawing attention to what
she believed to be his philanthropic nature—and the
academy's kids had benefited from it. The choices he'd
made in his life were not their problem.

Sister Kate walked with him toward the main building, but not before she wiped stone dust from the back
of his jacket like a nervous mother hen. With her arm
in his, the nun explained that since the local papers had
circulated the news of the charitable event for the St.
Thomas Aquinas Academy, the local police thought it
would be wise to add security. She told him that she
had little to say about it.

"In truth, the police are here for you, Jackson."

"That's not funny, Kate. Armed men in uniform
aren't my idea of a good time," he protested.

"But an armed man who is well dressed in designer
threads is perfectly acceptable?" She reached over and
tugged at the lapel of his suit. "I noticed you were packing heat."

Under his jacket, he wore a .45-caliber Glock 30 in
a holster.

"Packing heat?" He laughed. "You've been watching too many Bogart flicks."

"And you're ignoring my question." She crossed her
arms and stood in front of him. "You're a man with
secrets, Jackson Kinkaid. You always have been. Don't
bother to deny it."

"Wouldn't if I could," he agreed.

"You've always struck me as someone I can trust

when it really counts, but I have a feeling I'd never know you in a lifetime. Why is that?"

"Why you trust me?" He smirked. "Good question."

"That's not what I meant, and you know it." She poked his arm.

"I could say the same about you." He shrugged. "I trust you, but I haven't scratched the surface of understanding who you really are. You're not exactly an open book."

"I'm a nun. What's to know?" She brushed off her habit. "Being trustworthy comes with the uniform."

"Not in my world, Kate." Kinkaid grinned. "You're a complicated and uncompromising woman who respects secrets. And I like that." He looked away and broke the hold she had on him. "Besides, you don't want to know who I really am. Men like me are the reason you pray."

"You're not the only reason I pray, Jackson. Not by a long shot."

"I remember the day we first met at the hospital. Sometimes that day seems like a lifetime ago." He stared into the night sky and sighed. "Other times, it feels like only yesterday. Some wounds never heal."

"I'm surprised you remember that day at all. You weren't in any condition to recall much of anything." She stroked his arm. "I do pray for you, Jackson. And I have faith that one day you'll find peace."

"Pray for someone who deserves it, Kate. Your odds would be better."

He caught the glint of her eyes in the moonlight and

knew she was staring at him. When she didn't say anything more, he knew that she understood not to ask questions. If she ever did, he would tell her the truth, about the man he'd become, and that might change everything between them. She had accepted him into her life, and that was good enough for him. And for a reason he didn't want to think about, it mattered what she thought of him. But that didn't mean he wanted to risk crossing the line—to tell her the truth about his life.

"Come on. Let's get this over with . . . for both our sakes."

She took his arm again and headed for Dumont Hall, muttering under her breath, "Who invited the likes of you and me anyway?"

"Someone with exceedingly low standards." He smiled. "But remember. This is all for the children."

"That it is, my dear." She patted his arm and grinned at him. "That it is."

New York City
Lower East Side
9:30 P.M.

Alexa knocked on the apartment door and peeked through the peephole. From the outside looking in, nothing was very clear through the lens, but she spied a light on inside. That was good enough for her to decide that someone was home, although that didn't ensure her knock would get answered. Straightening her blond hair, she took a step back into the hall so she'd be visible through the peephole—and waited.

Jessie Beckett opened the door without a hint of whether she was pleased to see her. And she didn't feel the need to break the ice by talking either. Dressed in faded jeans and a black Chicago Bulls tee, the former bounty hunter could play poker with the best, yet she'd never make a good politician since she spoke her mind, short and sweet—one of the reasons the woman had grown on her. And the pronounced scar over her eyebrow hinted at the darkness in her past.

"You don't call . . . you don't write." Alexa leaned a shoulder against the doorjamb with her arms crossed. "Can I come in?"

Jessie stared at her a moment, then backed away to let her in. Alexa entered the small apartment before Jessie had a chance to change her mind.

"I've been busy, that's all," she said. "You didn't tell me what hard work it would be. Garrett's people have me jumping, but it's all good . . . I think."

"From what I hear, you're a star," Alexa replied, unbuttoning her light tweed jacket and putting her hands into the pockets of her khaki pants.

She glanced around the tiny living room, sparse with cheap rental furniture and worn cardboard boxes stacked in a corner. The mundane room was colored in varying degrees of brown and looked like something anyone would scrape off their shoe. And it smelled a little musty, with the faint scent of pine and ammonia.

Although it was clear that Jessie had made an attempt to clean, she barely looked like she lived there. No personal effects could be seen, only the essentials for her to eat and sleep in the apartment that Garrett Wheeler—the liaison to the Sentinels—had leased for her after she'd picked it. The woman definitely gravitated toward the simpler life, having no tolerance for the more-upscale lifestyle he would have provided.

But that only made Garrett peeved that he hadn't gotten her total buy-in. Lavish gifts and posh living quarters were more his style. Yet she had refused his usual ploys to make her feel obligated to him—and to add insult to injury—the woman could pick up and go in a heartbeat. Garrett didn't like that. So knowing Jessie had worked late, Alexa had been sent to check on her even at this hour, a task she would have done on her own without his prompting.

She had something personal on her mind, and she had to get it off her chest.

Alexa turned to face her and get a closer look at her new partner. Jessie looked tired, and the spark of her usual defiance had been dulled. Alexa knew about going stir-crazy until that first assignment came along. Living in luxury had made the wait tolerable for her, but Jessie didn't have such a distraction. Plus, the Sentinels' instruction program for its operatives was consuming, a twenty-four/seven schedule that had kept them apart until this week, when she'd be officially assigned her new partner.

Jessie was ready, and they both knew it.

"Rumor has it that you're the one to beat. You had top honors," Jessie reminded her. "I'm just trying to make a good first impression."

"Spoken like a true overachiever who's been smacked

by the humility stick." She chose a chair across from the small sofa and sat.

"Can I get you a beer?" Jessie asked.

Beer was not Alexa's drink of choice, but for Jessie's sake, she said, "Sure, as long as you don't take me to a monster-truck rally after."

"And here I thought you were a Monster Jam groupie."

"Just hearing you say that scares the hell out of me."

Alexa had gotten various reports from Jessie's trainers as her instruction progressed. Top marks on all levels except when it came to a consistent concern. Her instructors had agreed that Jessie was both physically and mentally tough and would make a gifted operative, but she was a definite loner. In the world of the Sentinels, this was not a bad thing, but not everyone was convinced she'd make a good partner until Alexa spoke up for her.

That helped Garrett make up his mind. He needed to test her with the real deal. Soon they'd be assigned a case, another reason for Alexa to make contact with Jessie.

"Garrett told me we'd get one of the next assignments. You up for it?"

"Hell, yeah." Jessie handed her a beer without a glass. "I'd take my urine test over just to feel I'm making progress."

"I'll mention that to the HR Department."

Jessie plopped onto a sofa across from Alexa and took a long pull from her bottle before she spoke again. "I mean, it's not that I'm ungrateful for all Garrett's done for me. The training has been interesting. And

I've never been in such good shape physically. The first few weeks were killer. But lately I've been pulling longer hours to stay . . . focused. Just hanging out like this is driving me crazier than usual. Without a bail-jumping scumbag in sight, I'm going through arrest withdrawals."

"Yeah, I figured."

Alexa knew that Jessie hadn't been back to Chicago since her training started nearly six months ago except to pack a few personal belongings. Garrett was maintaining her Chicago apartment in case she changed her mind. Plus he'd given her the option of flying back on a few occasions—at his expense—but she'd never taken him up on the offer. She hadn't even gone back to see her cop friend, Sam Cooper. Although Alexa didn't know her well, that behavior smacked of avoidance and seemed out of character, even for someone as detached as Jessie.

That left Alexa with questions. And before they worked together, she had to clear the air by testing a theory she had for the reason Jessie had severed her link to Chicago.

"What are you doing tomorrow morning?"

"Not much. Why?"

"I thought you might want to ride with me to the airport. I invited your friend Seth Harper to town for the weekend."

The alarmed look on Jessie's face told her everything she wanted to know. Alexa knew her plans with Seth and her playful weekend of seduction had gotten complicated.

Port de Paix, Haiti
10:00 P.M.

"And are you single, Mr. Kinkaid?" In a coy gesture, the older woman stroked the stem of her wineglass, not taking her eyes off him. Before Kinkaid replied, she added, "My daughter is studying finance back in the States. I'm sure she'd love to meet you . . . to discuss your . . . assets."

He forced a polite smile and downed a full martini, wishing he had a second one on deck. He took a deep breath and gazed across the room to catch Sister Kate smirking. She stood with a small group of guests, holding the hand of a little Haitian boy. And whenever she could, Kate glanced his way, watching over him. Kinkaid could tell that the nun took devilish delight in his uneasiness, mostly because she shared it with him. Misery did indeed love company. He narrowed his eyes and shook his head at her, but Kate had supplied him with all the excuse he'd need.

"Best wishes to your daughter in her studies. But if you'll excuse me, Sister Mary Katherine is calling."

He made what he hoped was a diplomatic exit and went looking for a drink. But as he walked away, he caught the matchmaking woman checking his assets head to toe. She smiled and waved, without any sign of embarrassment. And from a distance, Kinkaid raised his empty glass in reply.

Sorry, lady. For your daughter's sake, you shouldn't troll in these waters. You've got no idea what lurks deep.

Kinkaid took a detour to the nearest cash bar as he listened to the music and took in the room. The musicians weren't bad, especially after a few drinks. And the food looked great. Sister Kate and her organizers had put on a fine spread, with everything donated from local businesses, so the full ticket price could be donated to the school. Sister Kate never wasted an opportunity to raise money.

When he crossed the room, dodging partygoers and avoiding eye contact, he shifted his gaze to the exits. At first nothing seemed out of the ordinary. And he would have let the nagging sensation go, except for one thing.

It wasn't what he saw, but what he didn't see that bothered him. He stopped and turned. Not one local policeman was at his post. The uniforms were gone.

"What the hell . . ." He turned toward Sister Kate with a look of concern on his face. She noticed his expression right away and shrugged to convey she didn't understand.

Neither of them saw what happened next until it was too late.

A blast of automatic gunfire erupted and echoed through the room. A deafening sound. He reached for his Glock as plaster rained down on his head, and he ran for cover. Complete and utter chaos followed. People ran screaming and jammed the exits. Gunmen dressed in black grabbed the guests. Men, women, and children were ordered to the floor, facedown. The assailants wore masks. Only their eyes and mouths were visible, making them appear more sinister.

Kinkaid caught a glimpse of Sister Kate across the

room. She herded children toward the door to help them escape. Her black habit was hard to miss. And for the first time, he'd seen terror in her eyes when she stared back—although he knew her fear wasn't for her own safety.

But the gunmen shut down the mass exodus, and Kinkaid was too far away to help Kate.

"Jackson . . . Kinkaid. We want the American!"

He heard his name called out. The armed men were looking for him. *Damn it!* But why? Had he brought this down on Sister Kate? Or were these men just looking to abduct a wealthy American businessman?

"Kinkaid," a man yelled, and searched the cowering people on the floor. No one looked the man in the eye as he raged and spat at his hostages. "We came for the American . . . where is he?"

Kinkaid stayed hunched behind a column, considering his limited options. By his estimation, he'd be the only guest with a weapon. If he guessed wrong on what to do next, people could die, and he'd be taken out of the equation, unable to help.

Yet he had to do something.

Slowly he wedged his gun at the small of his back and hid it under his jacket. If one of the men got close enough to search him for a weapon, they'd find an empty holster. And that small diversion might give him time to pull his handgun and get some answers. Risking his neck might be worth the gamble if he found out what the men wanted and stopped the gunplay. He stood and raised his hands, ready to come out and identify himself.

But before he could, more shots rang out. This time the bastards aimed into the frantic crowds who packed the exits—a cruel, sadistic show of power meant to terrorize already helpless victims.

"No, no." His lips moved, but his voice sounded muffled in his head. His hearing was trashed from the gunfire. And all he could do was watch. Everything happened too fast.

Two bodies fell. A man in a suit got shot in the back. The round hit his body with a meaty thud and sent him sprawling to the floor. And a gray-haired woman in a blue dress snapped her head back and tumbled. A crimson mist hung in the air as her body fell. When she hit the floor, the back of her head slammed hard, and a pool of her blood seeped onto the carpet. Her vacant dead eyes stared accusingly at a young girl who stood over her. The kid couldn't have been much more than eight years old.

"Oh, shit," Kinkaid muttered.

For a split second, everything in the room stopped as he watched the girl. He tuned everything out. Complete tunnel vision. He couldn't take his eyes off her, but the instant was gone in a flash.

A shrill scream rose above the panicked cries of men and women as they fled. The sound of the pitiable wail triggered a dark memory. He shut his eyes and tried to shake the past, but nothing would break him free until the blond girl screamed again.

His eyes fixed on her and grounded him in the moment. Even from a distance he saw the little girl tremble. And her face had turned a vivid red as tears streaked her cheeks. She stared at the woman's body in shock, unable to move. One of the attackers turned toward the crying child and yelled something in a language Kinkaid didn't understand. The masked man raised his weapon and aimed at the little girl.

The bastard was going to shoot.

CHAPTER 3

He had no time to think, only react.

Kinkaid came out from behind cover and yelled, "Over here, asshole."

He took deadly aim and fired. One shot. Two.

The hooded man staggered back with his chest glistening in streaks of red. With a surprised look, he dropped to his knees and collapsed to the floor, face-first. But the fight was far from over.

In the confusion and gunfire, hostages leapt off the floor and raced for the exits. The gunmen were losing control. Kinkaid ran to grab the little girl, sidestepping the bodies and dodging the panicked crowd. Everything turned into a blur, and the air was thick with the sharp smell of gunfire. Something punched his side. And the skin of his stomach burned.

When he got to the terrified child, he lifted her off the floor and held her in his arms. Whispering in her ear, he wasn't sure what he said or what she heard, but it didn't matter. Bullets whizzed by his head as he shielded the kid. He made it to a set of stairs down a hallway and ducked behind them, listening for sounds that someone had followed.

He covered the girl's mouth with his hand, being careful that she could still breathe. When he was sure that he was alone with her, he brushed back her curly blond hair and stared into big blue eyes brimming with tears.

Holding her, he didn't want that to mean anything—but it did.

Her tiny body trembled in his arms. Seeing her so scared was like taking a hard punch to the belly. She was the child of one of the missionary teachers. Kate had introduced him to her parents earlier in the evening, but he couldn't remember their names. His gut wrenched at the thought that she could already be an orphan. And all he wanted to do was hold her.

His brain demanded objectivity. Other people needed him, too. Yet when he looked at the kid again—a part of him he thought had died years ago—made his normally detached reasoning impossible.

"Shhh," he whispered. "You're safe now, honey." He lied, but he didn't have a choice. "Tell me your name. Can you do that?"

She didn't answer. The kid grabbed for the sleeve of his jacket with tiny white knuckles in a death grip. Her face was pale and slick with perspiration.

"It's okay." He yanked off his tie and undid buttons on his shirt. "You don't have to say anything. Not until you want to."

When he reached for her, the pain in his side got worse. He winced and looked down under his suit jacket to see that his gray shirt was covered in blood. His blood. He'd been shot and couldn't tell how bad it was. Was it a through-and-through or only a graze—or was the bullet still inside him? Not to alarm the kid, he shut his jacket and pulled her toward him. She clung to him and burrowed into his chest.

Kinkaid rocked her until her heaving sobs turned to whimpers. With the child in his arms, old memories of a different kind washed over him like a cleansing rain. And he would have welcomed them, but now wasn't the time. He had to move.

"I'm getting you out of here, honey."

Down the hall, he heard the muffled sound of men shouting orders and the cries of women. Hostages were being moved. As long as he had the girl, he couldn't afford to draw fire. He had to get her to safety before he could help Sister Kate and the others. Moving hostages would slow the armed men down. Maybe he would have time to maneuver ahead and stop them. An open door to his left looked as if it might get him to the courtyard and the garden. Still gripping his weapon, he picked up the kid and carried her from Dumont Hall.

Kinkaid stuck to the shadows and sheltered the girl with his body. Outside, the air was muggy, and the breeze had died. A few hours ago, the courtyard had been beautiful in the moonlight. Now every shadow held danger, and his mind played tricks on his eyes.

And memories of Kate plagued him with guilt. One way or another, had he brought this down on her? He gritted his teeth, dealing with the pain of his wound and a deep regret he'd be cursed to endure.

Until a dark silhouette against a stone wall forced him to stop.

He shielded the girl and raised his weapon to take aim at the dark shape until he realized what it was. A policeman in uniform lay slumped against the wall. Kinkaid covered the kid's head with his hand, his fingers entwined in curls.

He knelt by the man's side to check for a pulse, but stopped when he saw his throat had been cut. A savage attack. His question about what had happened to the on-duty cops had been answered. And a wave of nausea hit him. The sensation mixed with chills and dizziness, adding blood loss to his list of adversaries tonight.

"Please . . . get us through this," he whispered, and clutched the girl tighter. Whoever had assaulted a fundraiser at Dumont Hall had killed the guards in a bold plan to take hostages. But one aspect of the brutal attack stood out from all the rest.

These men had known his name—and they'd come looking for him. *Why?*

The uneven terrain and loose rocks made it hard to navigate in the dark. Kate kept her head down, focused on the four children who clung to her. Andre was an eight-year-old Haitian boy. She'd bought his first dress slacks and tie. He was wearing them now. And Daniel and Faye were brother and sister, the children of one of her teachers. A single mother. Kate didn't think Daniel and

Faye's mother had been taken, but the woman would be worried sick. And Joselyne was the oldest child at age ten, the daughter of a local Haitian fisherman. None of these children should have been here. Their families didn't have money.

Why had they been traumatized like this? What were the assailants after?

She avoided making eye contact with the angry men who shoved them down the dirt path to a street behind Dumont Hall. In the dark she stumbled, but she never gave the men a reason to punish her. She had to stay with the children. And judging by the behavior of the other hostages, she knew they understood the importance of sticking together and the gravity of falling behind.

One of the armed men grunted and pushed them, the international language of intimidation. They appeared to have limited English and no French. The weapons in their hands spoke for them.

"Where are they taking us?" one of her missionaries asked.

"Do as they say. And don't ask questions," Kate kept her voice low. She hated to deny the woman an answer, but now was not the time. If they survived, they'd have to play it smart.

"My little girl . . . I don't see her," the woman cried, clinging to her husband. "Where is she?"

Count your blessings, she wanted to tell the woman, but she kept her mouth shut. To insinuate their plight would not end well wasn't what Kate wanted to convey, even though she harbored dark feelings about why they'd been chosen. Hope would be a fragile commodity, given their circumstances.

Once they got to the dirt-covered street, the men led them toward two dark vans and a couple of sedans. Neither van had windows. And three more armed men stood watch over the vehicles. When they approached, the men opened the van doors, and the hostages were separated into two groups. Her fellow teachers and members of the generous Port de Paix community who supported her school were taken from her sight.

They were led to the second vehicle, leaving Kate to face her fate with those nearest her. Without ceremony, they were shoved inside the first van. And almost from the start Kate realized they wouldn't all fit, but she didn't want to think about what the men would do if that was the case.

"Please, Lord . . . have mercy," she offered a hushed prayer and drew the children close to her, putting them first. If anyone were forced to stay behind, she vowed it would be her.

"My wife is inside. I gotta be with her." A man dressed in a suit nudged Sister Kate aside and crawled into the van ahead of her kids.

Kate made the sign of the cross for the desperate man. Fear made people do terrible things they wouldn't normally do. She wanted to give him the benefit of the doubt, hoping that he hadn't thought about what would happen to those left behind. Judging by the shamed look on his face, she knew better. The man knew exactly what he'd done.

From inside the dark van, hands reached out for the

children. One by one they were lifted inside and squeezed into every spot. In the end, two adults remained standing outside the van, with no room remaining—Sister Kate and an elderly woman from town.

Kate clenched her teeth and prepared herself for what would happen, but the other woman cried and tugged at the shirtsleeve of the nearest armed gunman.

"Please . . . I won't take up much room," she begged. "I can fit. Please let me try." The woman was pleading to stay with them.

Kate shut her eyes and filled her mind with prayer. Her lips trembled with the effort and her heart pounded. Two other men came forward and laughed, amused by the older woman's begging. They exchanged words that Kate didn't understand, and time slowed to a painstaking crawl while she waited to see what the men would decide.

In her heart, Kate had a feeling the news wouldn't be good.

The little blond girl hadn't spoken. She only clung tight to his neck as he looked for a safe place for her. Off the stone courtyard, Kinkaid saw a dim streetlamp below where he crouched. He used the light to guide him through terraced patches of ground, the foundation used for a series of shanties made of stucco. The glow from the street lit a side door to a shack. The house wasn't much, but he noticed that a torn window curtain moved.

Someone was inside.

He wasn't sure he should risk investigating the match-box-sized shanty, yet he had to try. Whoever was inside might be scared, and he couldn't blame them. If they kept the girl from harm, at least long enough for him to help the others, it might be worth the gamble. Avoiding the light, he crept through the shadows near the back of the house. He approached the window where he'd seen the curtain move and spoke in French.

"Please . . . I know you're in there. A little girl needs your help," he pleaded. "Please open the door."

He wouldn't leave the kid if the people in the shanty didn't look trustworthy. The only way to find out was to get them to open the door. He reasoned with them in French and in English until the door at the side of the house opened with the creak of rusty hinges. Kinkaid gripped his weapon, ready to use it.

What he heard next caused him to stop.

"Mr. Kinkaid," a woman's voice whispered. "It's me. Susan Winters. I have my husband and my kids in here."

At first Kinkaid couldn't place the voice, yet the woman's name brought back a memory. He had met her with Sister Kate at the school. Susan Winters was one of Kate's missionary administrators.

"Thanks for speaking up. That took guts," he said.

Kinkaid carried the girl inside and shut the door behind him. In the dark room, with only the pale light of the moon shining through the curtains, he saw the silhouettes of Susan and her family.

"I have to get back out there. Can you take her?" he asked. "I don't know who or where her parents are. And she hasn't said a word, not even her name."

"Sure. We can take her." Susan reached for the little

girl, but the kid wouldn't let go of him. He lowered her to the floor and knelt beside her.

"I need to find Sister Kate, honey. I have to help her and the others. Can you be brave for a little longer?"

He could tell that the kid wanted to cry. She touched his hand, and said, "My name is . . . Caitlyn."

Kinkaid smiled. He reached for her tiny fingers and kissed them. Her hand felt so small in his. "You've been a very brave girl, Caitlyn. Susan will take care of you now."

The girl nodded and took a step back, clinging to Susan's leg. A part of him—the man he used to be—was sad to let her go. Kinkaid took a deep breath and stood. He touched Susan's shoulder and looked at her husband, who stood beside her.

"Stay put," he told them. "Even until daylight if you have to. And keep watch. Trade off on guard duty."

After they both nodded, he headed out the door in search of Sister Kate. And in the stillness of the night, he heard voices dead ahead. Kinkaid gritted his teeth to fight the pain as he navigated through the dark. It had to be them.

In a move Kate didn't expect, one of the armed men shoved her and the older woman aside to haul out the man who barged into the van to be with his wife. Both the man and his wife were removed and stood next to Kate. The man's mix of fear and indignation had vanished.

"Please . . . what are you doing?" the man asked.

"Don't . . . please don't do this. I've got money. You don't need to do this."

"George, I'm scared. What's happening?" His wife reached for his arm, but one of the masked men yanked both elbows behind her, holding her in place.

Kate watched as one of the armed men came forward, the one who had given the order to remove George from the van. The hooded man walked with the assurance of a leader, and his amusement with the situation gave him away. Kate thought she'd play a hunch.

"Why are you doing this?" She watched the man, and he gave her nothing. Under the hood, his dark eyes were a chilling blank slate. She held her breath and stood firm.

When he turned to a comrade and spoke in his own language, Kate fixed her eyes on his, and interrupted, "Your fly is open. Better zip up."

The masked man looked down at his pants before he realized that he'd given himself away. He spoke English. And now everyone knew.

"You speak English?" George's voice cracked as he touched the arm of his wife. "Let me do the talking, Joanna."

"No, you do enough talking." The leader glared at Kate as he spoke, but eventually turned his full attention to George. "As you see, we have no room," he reasoned as he toyed with him.

"But I can pay," George argued. "For me and my wife, I can pay you."

"What about these?" The leader pointed at Kate and

the older woman standing next to her. "And this one, she is a servant of your God. No?"

George took a deep breath and didn't answer.

"Then it is for me to decide." The leader smiled at Kate, his lips and teeth showing through a hole torn in his mask. The image raised the hair on her neck. "Does your God listen to your prayers?" he asked. "Perhaps we shall see."

And with one gesture from him, the horror began.

Kinkaid still heard voices. Trusting his instincts, he peered through the dark to track the sound. Behind Dumont Hall, the steep hillside was terraced. He knew there would be a path down, but he didn't have time to look for it. Shoving through brush and crawling over boulders used to reinforce retaining walls, he gripped his weapon and made his way down the hill. Sharp branches cut his hands and face. He pushed on, thinking only of Kate and the others.

The moon cast a bluish haze over trees and boulders and shanty houses with tin roofs crammed next to each other. The dense setting obscured his view. He still heard voices and followed the sound.

Although he tried to be quiet, he made noise as he went. It couldn't be helped. Kinkaid hoped the sounds of the hostages would cover his movement. When he got closer, he slowed his pace to be more careful. With gun raised, he braced his back to the wall of a shack encircled by a worn picket fence. He inched toward a corner to get a better view.

The voices of men and women were clearer, but still a

distance away. When he peered around the stucco wall, he saw a man dressed in black near a tree. His AK-47 leaned against a stone wall. The man had been too occupied with his full bladder to hear Kinkaid coming through the brush.

He was relieving himself, dick in hand.

Kinkaid pulled back and grimaced, leaning his head against the wall. He stalled until the bastard finished before he tossed a rock into the brush and waited. He focused on every sound and heard the gunman pick up his rifle. Kinkaid held his breath and listened. In a stupid move, the guy let the streetlamp below telegraph his move. A long faint shadow emerged and became more distinct as the man edged toward the shanty.

Kinkaid had to play this right. Any noise would bring the others. And he wasn't in any shape to play the tough guy. When the masked gunman came around the corner, Kinkaid racked the slide and aimed his Glock at the man's head.

"You gonna waste a good piss?" He had no idea if the guy spoke English, but he let the universal language of the Glock translate his intentions.

After the man raised his hands, Kinkaid took his rifle. He leaned it against the wall behind him and kept his gun pressed to the man's temple, but a chilling scream erupted in the night and shattered the stillness. The pitiable wail gripped him, especially when it came to an abrupt stop.

Kinkaid couldn't help it—he turned toward the sound.

With the distraction, the masked man took advantage

of his carelessness. The man shoved him to the ground onto his back and leapt on top, wrestling him for his weapon. The weight of the heavier man made it hard to breathe. And as they scuffled, they kicked up dirt. Kinkaid sucked dust into his lungs, choking on it. Sweat stung his eyes and made it harder to see in the dark.

Still, he wouldn't let go of the Glock.

He rolled down an embankment and his spine collided with sharp rocks. The blows nearly knocked the wind from his lungs. And his wound felt as if it had been torn open. It stung like acid. Blood loss had made him weak. He struggled for consciousness.

And when the masked man thrust an elbow against his throat, Kinkaid saw stars. He felt his muscles give way when his air ran out. And the moon flickered to nothing.

Up the hill, Kate heard a faint noise coming from the shadows, but too much was happening for her to worry about it. The older woman who had stood next to her, trembling, was pulled from her grasp. The terrified woman scratched Kate's hand with her nails in desperation.

"Please . . . don't let them do this." With eyes wide, the woman begged the others in the van to save her, but no one moved. She screamed when one of the gunmen grabbed her by the hair and dragged her off. She was hauled into the brush—along with Joanna, the wife of the man who tried to buy his way into the van. The two women would pay a price that had nothing to do with money.

"George, no! Tell them you'll pay, George," Joanna cried out, and reached for him.

"Stop this, please!" he pleaded for his wife.

George and Kate had lunged for her hand, but armed men held them back. Others threatened to shoot into the van. Not even the hostages in the vehicle were safe. And for the first time, she noticed that one of the masked men held up a video recorder. He pointed it toward the women to record what would come next. Kate's eyes trailed back to the scene, unable to look away.

She watched as one of the abductors unsheathed his machete, mere feet from where she stood. He grabbed the hair of George's wife and raised his weapon. The moonlight glinted on the blade. Joanna bucked and fought and begged. Her eyes bulged in terror.

But the man held firm—and made his first cut.

"Oh, God. No." Kate made the sign of the cross and shut her eyes, yet she couldn't stop her ears from hearing the garbled screams, the weighty strikes of the blade, and the aftermath of blood splattering the foliage in a nightmarish rain.

Kate retched as their captors cheered. George fell to his knees, weeping. And the video cam had recorded everything.

They had all been forced to watch the beheadings of two innocent women. And in that instant, every hostage glimpsed a fate no one had wanted to imagine. Their survival would be left in the hands of men they would never understand—men who had no respect for life. Tears filled Kate's eyes, and she tried to swallow, but couldn't.

She was shoved into the van, along with George, both of them too weak and numb to resist. George sobbed and rambled incoherently, calling his wife's name. She had no doubt the man was in a deep state of shock.

After the vehicle door was shut and locked, she heard voices outside, but they soon faded.

In the dark vacuum of the van, the sounds of weeping and the stifling smell of fear almost suffocated her. Kate kept her silence, struggling to find solace in prayer. The women's screams and the hacking sound of the blade replayed in her head, over and over and over—a torturous echo of violence she'd never forget. She stopped praying and let the darkness and horror close in on her.

She couldn't stop shaking.

Kate knew she had to find a lifeline to God—some sense he was with her—despite the abject cruelty she had witnessed. She wanted to believe that tomorrow would be another day and that God would give her strength. Instead, fear and her own human frailty had defeated her. That's when she let the tears come. Kate wasn't strong enough for anything else.

The deathly quiet outside the van was broken. Angry voices merged with the rumble of engines. The vans lurched forward and picked up speed. They were on the move—and in the hands of brutal killers.

When she heard police sirens behind them, she let herself hope that they would be rescued, but her hopes quickly shattered when the sirens became too loud . . . and far too close. A jolt and a jarring crash sent the hostages hurtling to the front of the van. The police had bashed their bumper to force them off the road. The van sped up and careened out of control.

"My God, please no . . ." she yelled and grabbed for the crying children. Her desperate plea for help was lost in the screams of the others.

Outside, she heard the bumpers break free and the shrill sounds of grating metal sent shivers down her spine. Her heart pounded her rib cage, and fear tightened her throat as the van veered onto the shoulder of the road. Amidst all the chaos, a series of thunderous explosions erupted.

Kate gasped. *No! This can't be happening!*

Bullets slammed hard against the van with a deafening thud. One punched through metal. And the frantic screaming inside the van intensified with an ear-piercing force. Bodies lurched against her, and panic took hold. Kate felt the crush of weight on her chest. She couldn't breathe. And the children were pulled away from her grasp.

The police were firing at them. *The police!*

CHAPTER 4

His lungs burned. And a wailing siren edged his lifting fog. Kinkaid's mind cleared enough for him to find his back in the dirt. And over his head, the shadow of a masked man eclipsed the moon. He felt a hand on his wrist, the one that still held the gun. An elbow was jammed hard to his windpipe. And his side hurt like a mother.

It took him a second to figure out what had happened. At the sound of the police sirens, his attacker had looked over his shoulder and loosened his grip—enough to allow him a breath. The bastard had made the same mistake.

The distraction would cost him.

With the man focused on strangling him, Kinkaid took a chance and fumbled in the dark for anything to use as a weapon. The fingers of his free hand searched the ground as he strained to maintain the grip he had on his gun. He bucked and arched his back to keep the man off-balance and kept his hand moving until he found a jagged rock. And with all his strength, he slammed the stone into the man's head.

Once. Twice.

On the third blow, his assailant lurched forward and released his grip. Kinkaid could breathe again. And with his momentum, he used the man's weight against him. He shoved him hard. The larger man toppled, but he was still conscious and dangerous. The guy recovered too fast and lunged for him again. Kinkaid had enough. Without hesitation, he raised his weapon and shot him in the chest, point-blank. The man grunted, and his body jerked. With his last breath, he collapsed and lay still.

It was over. And he knew he'd come close to dying. *Too close.*

He gasped for air with eyes watering as he knelt near the dead man. No matter how justified, killing always came at a price. And now wasn't the time for a soul-searching tally. Kate needed him.

With police sirens blaring, the sound of his gunshot would not stand out, and he had no need to tread softly. After holstering his gun, he searched the dead man's pockets for ID or a cell phone, anything that might serve as a lead, but came up empty. He grabbed the AK-47 left by the masked man and raced down the slope, heading for the road. Lunging over obstacles, he ignored the growing agony that burned his side. And through the brush he spotted red taillights fading in the distance. He had no doubt Kate was inside one of those vehicles.

Spiraling police lights swept eerie color onto the trees and cast long shadows between the shanties. He ran across a terraced ridge to make up time. When the vehicles sped by him, he heard gunfire coming from the police.

"God, no. No!" he shouted, and waved his arms, frantic to get their attention. He bounded down a dirt path toward the road, yelling, "They've got hostages. What are you doing?"

He fired the AK-47 in the air as the police raced past him. In the barrage of gunfire, he knew they hadn't heard him. The local cops were in hot pursuit of murdering terrorists. They either had no idea these men had taken hostages, or they didn't care. And giving the cops the benefit of the doubt would only leave Kate and the other hostages in the line of fire.

He had to stop the shooting. There was no one else.

"Damn it." He got to the road in time to watch the last taillights vanish over a hill—a blur of red that drifted in and out of focus. He bent over and gasped for air, holding his side. The trees, the moon, the shadows—everything morphed into a jumble. He was losing it, and dizziness was only a fraction of his problem.

Unless he found a set of wheels, he'd be dead in the water—and so would Kate.

"Stay down!" Sister Kate yelled as she reached for the children at her feet, covering them with her body. "Protect the children."

More bullets slammed through the van and ricocheted. There was nothing they could do. The driver made a hard turn, and the weight of bodies crushed her in the dark. She fended the others off for the sake of the children, but gravity worked against her. She was pinned and powerless to help anyone.

The steady shrill sound of sirens had been interrupted by gunfire. She knew the police were doing the firing. Why would they shoot at a vehicle in a highspeed chase with innocent hostages on board? The van driver swerved again and hit something. The collision sent bodies sprawling. Once the driver regained control, the van felt and sounded as if it had a flat tire. With the police so close and taking deadly aim with their weapons, she knew this wouldn't end well.

She was in a fight for her life—they all were. And with the Haitian police firing on them, who was the enemy now?

But the van came to an abrupt stop. And she heard angry voices outside. In seconds, the door was unlocked and opened. Squinting, she raised her hand to block the glare of a flashlight. Shadows of faceless gunmen grabbed them and forced them out of the van.

"Head down. Move . . . Move!" one man yelled in English.

With the commotion, Kate did her best with the children. She only got glimpses of being shoved through a door. The building looked and smelled like a medical facility, and inside it was dark. They were taken to a murky room and herded into a corner and forced down on their knees. Two men aimed rifles at their heads and yelled at them. She didn't understand any of it. Others shoved tables and metal cabinets against the windows in the room—windows with police strobe lights shining through them—a standoff.

On orders, one of their captors punched a hole through the glass with the butt of his rifle. He shot his weapon, and the police returned fire. Kate grabbed the hysterical children and shielded them with her body. Her eyes blurred with tears.

She didn't want to think about dying—but she did.

"Piece of crap!"

Kinkaid peered through a cracked windshield and cursed. Being a beggar didn't give him any right to complain.

If he'd been back in the States, he'd have a much tougher time hot-wiring newer cars with the added security. He hadn't bothered keeping up his car theft skills—a byproduct of a misspent youth—and might have regretted it now except for one thing.

In Haiti, most of the vehicles were old and easy to steal. His vintage skills had been good enough.

With only one of the car's headlights working, he floored the old Toyota sedan he'd "commandeered" and gripped the steering wheel tight, navigating half-blind. Dust from the streets kicked up in his rearview mirror, a red cloud colored by taillights. With the windows down, the dirt made it harder to breathe, but in the distance, he had heard gunshots. He gunned the old car and followed the sound. And without much visibility, he hit every pothole for a bone-jarring ride.

After he crested a hill, he saw the rotating police

lights and heard more gunfire. The terrorists had taken refuge at a medical clinic. Smaller than a hospital, the facility looked closed. No lights were on inside. And from what he saw, even though the cops were positioned for a siege, the hostage takers were taunting them by firing back—a no-win situation with Kate and the others stuck in the middle.

Kinkaid parked the car with the confiscated AK-47 in the trunk. Because he'd hot-wired the vehicle, he left the engine running in case he'd need it in a hurry later. He looked for someone in charge to plead his case. He'd need balls of steel to press his luck with the Haitian police, especially given his unique line of work. And being an outsider, he'd have little chance to stop the shooting, but he owed it to Kate to try.

If he couldn't sway the local cops, he'd come up with a plan B—even if he had to call in markers to do it.

Shattered glass was strewn across the floor. One terrorist lay dead—shot in the face. A dark hole had caved in his nose. And his blood pooled near Kate's feet. Bullets pummeled the walls again. The gunfire intensified as the police escalated their assault, even after their captors, outnumbered, had ducked for cover. Tear-gas canisters were launched through the broken windows.

Kate huddled with the children, covering their faces. Her burning eyes streamed tears down her cheeks, and her nose ran without stopping, making her queasy. The coughing had grown unbearable and made her throat sore and chest tight. A heavy fog of gas filled the room, leaving them nowhere to hide from it. Disoriented from the gas, she had trouble thinking clearly, and her body ached all over.

Yet for her, there was something far more painful to endure than tear gas. Seeing the terrified faces of the children broke her heart.

And the Haitian police were as deadly as their captors.

"Please . . . make this stop!" she cried to no one, more out of frustration—and fear. Her screams didn't stop the violence. She doubted anyone heard her over the deafening noise.

"Sister . . . I'm scared." A child's voice filtered through her muddled brain as a small, dark-skinned hand clutched her veil. Her eyesight blurred and made it impossible to see who had said it. She pulled the children closer and lowered her head to pray.

It was all she had left.

The Haitian police hadn't been very sympathetic. From what he saw, they were poorly equipped and lacked discipline and training for a hostage-rescue operation. And although they made promises to do what they could for the hostages, Kinkaid noticed that didn't stop their siege of the clinic. As long as the terrorists fired their weapons, the police returned fire, shooting at anything that moved. The armed men inside the medical facility had not communicated their demands, nor had the police asked their intentions. Both sides let bullets do the talking.

Not a good sign.

Feeling dizzy and sick, Kinkaid retreated to a spot away from the front line. He clutched his side to stop the bleeding, but it was too dark for him to see. Blood loss had weakened him. His body raged between feverish and an intolerable chill. And even though everything had happened too fast, now he needed time to think. The Haitian police had escalated the violence and posed a bigger problem. He couldn't act on his own. He needed help from someone who had connections in the area. And one name came to mind.

Joe LaClaire. He pulled out his cell phone and made a call. His friend answered with a groggy voice.

"Hey, boss. What's up?"

"Listen, Joe. I don't have much time to explain." He briefed the man on what had happened and where he was. "I don't care who you contact. I need results. Call in some markers if you have to."

An AK-47 punctuated the urgency of his call. Kinkaid ducked for cover.

"Do I hear gunfire?"

"Yeah, Joe. A friend is in trouble. My friend Kate." He plugged an ear and kept talking. "We need to mobilize a covert hostage rescue. People have died . . . and there'll be more. The cops are treating the hostages like collateral damage. Rescue isn't part of their operation."

"Understood. What are you going to do?" Joe asked. His friend knew him well enough to know he wouldn't sit on the sidelines of a fight with innocent lives at stake.

"I'm going to find another way into the clinic."

"Are you insane? Crossing police lines can get you killed. And cornered terrorists don't play nice." Joe raised his voice. "Getting stuck in the cross fire will be a bitch."

"The hostages have no one else, Joe. And if you're only questioning my sanity now, what does that say about you?" He winced, with pain radiating heat across his belly. "Please . . . do like I told you. And with any luck, I'll meet you like we planned. I'm turning off my phone now. Leave a message when you know something."

Without waiting for a reply, he ended the call. Sticking to the shadows, he made his way back to the Toyota and retrieved the AK-47 he'd stashed in the trunk. The Haitian police had the building surrounded, but with any luck, he'd find a way in.

He had to.

Tortuga Island, Haiti

Being awakened in the middle of the night by a troubling call from his boss, Jackson Kinkaid, left Joe La-Claire on edge. Raking a hand through his dark hair, he paced the floor of his motel room on Tortuga Island. Sweat beaded the skin of his bare chest. Even wearing nothing but boxers, he felt the muggy heat close in on him. And although his mind raced with names of people who might help, only one name hit the top of his list and stuck.

Garrett Wheeler.

The man had resources and plenty of them. And he could mobilize a covert hostage-rescue operation anywhere in the world, fast. Joe reached for the fifth of Crown Royal on his nightstand and downed the rest. His throat burned as the whisky went down.

There was only one drawback—Kinkaid had something against Garrett Wheeler.

The two men had a history that had created a rift between them, and Joe knew nothing about the particulars. He only knew Wheeler by reputation and from being in Kinkaid's inner circle. And although men like Jackson Kinkaid were frequently short on details, he respected the man's privacy.

His friend had urgently asked for results, even if he had to call in markers.

If that meant pissing Kinkaid off to get the job done, then fuck it. Mission accomplished. He'd deal with the consequences later.

"Move. NOW!" The leader yelled in English and gave orders to his men in his own language.

Sister Kate felt the sharp jab of a rifle at her back. Metal hit her spine and sent a chilling jolt of pain to her neck and shoulders. One of the terrorists shoved her toward a door. She had no choice but to move. A hail of police gunfire had killed another man and one of the women hostages. And George, the guy who'd lost his wife, was holding a bloodied hand to his shoulder. She had no time to assess the damage. Bullets pounded the walls above her head and sent chunks of plaster raining down on her. And the screams of women and children raised goose bumps across her skin.

Kate prodded the children to stay low and shielded them from the horror. She looked back to see her captors crouched behind her—masked faces with hostile, glaring eyes—but a few of them remained to return fire and cover their retreat.

A suicide mission.

Kate wiped tears from her face—dealing with the aftermath of the tear-gas assault—and resisted the urge to throw up as she scrambled through the door with the children ahead of her. She clutched her habit and pulled up her tunic so she could move. When more bullets pounded the wall behind her, she stifled a scream. She pressed a tight fist to her lips, not wanting to panic the children more. The gunfire made her ears ring, and sounds were muffled in her head. Her captors had them moving in a line and winding through corridors. Kate never looked up. She kept her head down and made sure the children stayed together.

Two men led them to a stairway that took them into a basement. The darkness swallowed them, and she lost track of the children. She whispered for them to hang on to the one in front, but she wasn't sure they heard her. Gripping the shirt of the boy ahead of her, Andre, she held on and kept moving. Crouching low, she stepped down the stairs with aching knees. And when her tunic got in the way again, she hoisted the folds of the garment, and the cross on her rosary beads clanged on a metal railing.

One of the terrorists must have taken offense. In the dark, a hand grabbed her. He groped her body until he found what he wanted and yanked the rosary she wore. Beads fell to the floor. And she felt the force of his hostility to her faith, but she didn't resist or give the man any reason to kill her. For the children's sake, she had to do as she was told.

When she reached the bottom level, she turned a corner and squinted. A dim glow in the basement came from narrow windows at ground level. And a pale gray washed over the cramped space of a storage area for the clinic, where wooden shelves held boxes and other supplies. She peered across the room through sore, watering eyes. In the sweltering heat, a layer of grit covered her skin, and trickles of perspiration crawled down her back and armpits. The smothering stale air and the lingering effects of the tear gas intensified her feeling of hopelessness by making it harder to breathe.

At the first sign of movement at the windows, she ducked and reached for the children, drawing them closer.

"Hold hands. Stay together," she urged them, keeping her voice calm as she looked over her shoulder.

Glaring lights from outside swept across the windowpanes, casting an eerie silhouette on the men who held them at gunpoint. And even though she suspected the police had the building surrounded, there were only a few lights on this side of the clinic. Fewer police had staked out the rear. She had no idea what her captors were planning.

If escape wasn't an option, would they shift gears into a suicide mission? Desperate men resorted to reckless measures. And her gut twisted with a more disturbing thought. From what she'd seen of the Haitian police, all their lives were in danger. And bullets killed no matter who pulled the trigger. Were their captors the lesser of two evils?

In another life, she would have cursed her predicament. Now their survival meant more to her than giving in to her own rage. Every ounce of her energy would be focused on getting the children and the other hostages through this ordeal. And although she found comfort in her objective, she knew these men would test her faith—and her humanity—before this was all over if she survived.

A bolted metal door led to a belowground walkout. From what she'd seen of construction in Port de Paix, a cinder-block wall would give them marginal cover. But once they made it to the top of the outdoor steps, they'd be exposed to gunfire from the police. And she had no doubt their captors would use them as shields.

What would the police do then?

"Oh, God . . . please," she whispered, fearing the answer. She made a quick sign of the cross to stop her body from trembling.

The masked men peered out the windows and kept to the shadows of the storage room. They spoke in hushed voices in a heated debate she didn't understand.

One man pulled another weapon from a pack he carried. She couldn't make out what it was. Kate could tell they'd assessed the danger, same as she had. And when their leader intervened, she held her breath.

Whatever he decided, it would happen now.

CHAPTER 5

New York City
Sentinels Headquarters

Dressed in suit and tie, Garrett Wheeler arrived in the middle of the night at Sentinels headquarters, not an unusual occurrence in his line of work. He was determined to assess the Haiti situation as soon as possible. Committing resources to an urgent rescue mission of this magnitude would be within his authority to sanction. Yet the political ramifications of deploying a covert team from the United States to handle a hostage rescue in Haiti would require that he keep Sentinels' group leaders apprised.

His analysts monitored events over the globe twenty-four/seven. And that meant as operational head, he was on call. The influential and wealthy men behind the covert organization owned his ass, but he wouldn't have it any other way. His involvement had given his life a purpose he never would have imagined. He carried out the Sentinels' objectives and had become the organization's only public face so they could operate in anonymity. And he liked to think he had done his share of shaping the group after he emerged from its ranks to take a leadership role.

Only time and his unflinching diligence would determine his contribution in the long run.

After the ocular- and facial-recognition program scanned a blue light across his face, the private elevator opened its doors and took him to his office on a subterranean level located in an unmarked building on the streets of New York City.

A voice greeted him in the elevator on his way down.

"Good morning, Garrett. I've sent the files you requested. They're on your desk." The Southern drawl of analyst Tanya Spencer came over a speaker, along with her smiling dark-skinned face on a small screen. "And we've been monitoring the situation in Haiti. Satellite images for the region are being sent to you now. Anything else, sir?"

"Thanks, Tanya. I'll let you know."

When the elevator doors opened again, the lights to his office suite illuminated a large room with minimal furnishings of glass, black leather, and sterling-silver fixtures. A bank of monitors gave him a glimpse of news, weather, and other hot-spot situations across the globe. And teleconferencing equipment allowed him to make secured contact with members of the Sentinels. At the touch of a screen on his desktop, he could bring up any view he wanted.

Before he got to his usual morning briefing rituals, he smelled fresh-brewed coffee. A service had been set up on a console table on the far wall. He poured a cup

and replayed in his mind the earlier phone conversation he'd had with Joe LaClaire as he settled behind
his desk. The call had been recorded, analyzed, and
dispatched to him via a Sentinels' security screening
process that wouldn't allow anyone else to trace it to
his location.

Garrett had met Joe LaClaire on more than one occasion through mutual associates. Yet it wasn't until
he discovered LaClaire was a trusted ally of Jackson
Kinkaid that he gave him any serious consideration as
a player in international circles. LaClaire was discreet
and had a reputation for getting the job done in a low-
key way, an attribute Kinkaid would have admired.

Their association made sense. Yet the urgent distress call still surprised him. Why would anyone
close to Kinkaid contact him? The situation had to be
damned hopeless. And other thoughts occurred to him,
driven by his suspicious nature. After all these years,
why now? Why would Kinkaid contact him out of the
blue? The answer could be as simple as the man didn't
know LaClaire had made the call, but what if Kinkaid
couldn't leave the past alone?

What if he had an appetite for payback?

Something else bothered him, too. He hadn't been
able to uncover any real details about how Kinkaid
made a living these days although he hadn't given up
trying to find answers. And for a number of years, the
reclusive man had dropped off the grid. Gaps of time in
his records had gone unexplained. With an operative,
this wasn't unusual. Garrett was certain that what could
be found on paper for the man's tax filings and other

official documents was only a fraction of the story. Kinkaid was rumored to be involved with warring factions of drug cartels in South America, a mercenary working for the highest bidder.

The man had been trained in weapons and combat tactics. He knew how to use force, yet his biggest assets were his intelligence and his preference for subtle mind games and intimidation strategies, something Garrett had always respected and admired. But if Kinkaid was involved with ruthless drug cartels, that meant he had changed for the worse—making him a dangerous man.

"Jackson Kinkaid." Saying the name aloud spawned dark memories he would have preferred not to think about. He couldn't afford to indulge in guilt. To do so would make him ineffective at his job.

When it came to Kinkaid, he hated to admit their past was like a festering wound that had never healed. *His wound.* And he wasn't used to owning up to blame. Over the years, they had kept their distance, both in denial that it would only be a matter of time before their paths would cross again.

"And apparently"—he took his first sip of coffee—"that time is now."

Regardless of the obligation he felt toward Kinkaid, he would not send a team into a rescue operation on foreign soil without doing his research. That was why he had Tanya Spencer indulge his curiosity with an analysis. And for his part, he thought of only one person to lead a covert hostage rescue in Haiti—and his choice was not purely made on qualifications alone.

Garrett knew that at one time Alexa Marlowe had

had feelings for Jackson Kinkaid. He had no idea if those feelings were returned. She'd never told him, but it had always made him wonder. If there was still an emotional tie between his beautiful blond operative and Kinkaid, he could use that edge, although he had mixed feelings about doing so.

On a personal level, it pained him to use Alexa in such a way. Yet if it became necessary, manipulating Kinkaid was another matter. He'd use any means that would give him an edge.

Garrett took another sip of coffee. If he played his cards right, he could bury the hatchet and sever the obligation he felt toward Kinkaid, plus turn the tables in the process. He much preferred manipulating a top-notch operative into believing he owed him many times over.

He gritted his teeth and pushed through the materials in front of him. He had work to do before he gave the assignment to his number one field agent. His choice to send Alexa had ramped up the importance of his decision. And depending on what came of his assessment, Alexa's new recruit, Jessica Beckett, might get assigned, too. From the sounds of the situation in Haiti, Jackson Kinkaid was desperate.

And desperate men—with plenty to lose—could be played to his advantage now and in the future.

Port de Paix, Haiti

Kinkaid cut to the rear of the clinic and kept his distance from the perimeter the Haitian police had set. On a ridge, he ducked into the shadow of a deserted old armory and crouched against a stone wall to catch his breath and watch the action below.

The police had strategically directed lights along the rear of the medical facility. Although it complicated matters, the lights gave him a better view. The clinic where the hostages were being held had a basement. Narrow windows at ground level, two subterranean walkouts reinforced by cinder blocks, and a small loading bay for supplies made possible entry points. The windows were too tight to squeeze through, and the cops had the points of entry covered. He wasn't about to slip by them unnoticed.

On the side of good news, there were fewer cops guarding the back side of the building. If he got lucky, and the cops suddenly went blind, he might have a chance to find a way in. But the bad news far outweighed the good.

He wouldn't kill a cop who was only trying to do his duty as ordered, end of story. Yet the feeling wouldn't be mutual. So long as he carried an AK-47, if the Haitian police caught him, they'd shoot first and ask questions later. Dead was dead. They find his body with the rest of these bastards, and no one would know he was any different. Considering what he did for a living, it would be an easy mistake to make. He'd be fitted for a body bag, no matter what his intentions were. And being the only dead terrorist in a fancy suit wouldn't matter when it came to a body count in a foreign country.

Kinkaid shut his eyes tight to stop his head from spinning. He took deep breaths of muggy air to overcome his nausea. His body's struggle between chills and fever was getting worse. And in his weakened state, he couldn't afford to waste time. He'd get only one chance at helping Kate. He had to make it count.

Before he made himself into a one-man wrecking crew, he checked his cell phone for any messages from Joe LaClaire. After he came up empty, he heaved a sigh in frustration. Calling Joe had been a long shot. The whole thing sucked. The urgency of Kate's predicament made any rescue nearly impossible for a man working alone, and he'd be bucking local cops, who weighed success by a high body count and had the photos to prove it.

"Damn it," he cursed under his breath.

When he hit his speed dial to try Joe one more time, a thunderous blast shook the ground. And the night sky erupted in flames. Kinkaid covered his head as dirt and debris pelted him. When he looked up, he knew what had happened. The terrorists had used a grenade launcher that tore through police lines and cleared the way with deadly precision. Some cops broke cover and ran. Others stayed and fought, even though they didn't stand a chance. The Haitian officers were outclassed in equipment and training.

The terrorists had rushed out a basement door using hostages for cover. A crush of humanity moved as one. Assault rifles erupted with short bursts of flame piercing the darkness. He squinted through the fires left burning from the grenades, unable to see who was shooting. The gunmen cut a swath through the few gutsy police officers who dared to resist. With brutal force, the terrorists showed no mercy as they hid behind women and children.

They were on the move again—and so was he.

Kinkaid tracked the cowards from the shadows on the ridge, weaving in and out of cover as he traversed the rough terrain. Armed with a grenade launcher, the men were more dangerous and better prepared than he had first thought. And coming off a firefight, they'd be wired with adrenaline and a shitload of testosterone. A lethal combo in his line of work. He'd have to be more careful.

And if these men escaped with Kate and the others, the terrorists would be in complete control to carry out their agenda. That was unacceptable.

When blood splattered her face, Sister Kate winced. A scream had wedged deep in her throat though she was too stunned to know if she'd actually cried out. The fierce explosions and the automatic gunfire had muffled any sound to her ears; it seemed as if the only thing she could hear was the pounding of her heart.

One of the gunmen had his arm tight against her neck, choking her. He'd killed a Haitian police officer in front of her. His bullets pounded the young man's chest, the force of the blows staggering him. Her captor stopped long enough to see the body fall before he trudged on, dragging her with him.

The brief encounter forced a gap between them and the rest of the hostages. It isolated her with the man who had her by the neck until they approached a group of small dwellings. Kate caught movement from the corner of her eye. Another man in uniform stepped out from behind a shanty and thrust an arm near her head. She heard a series of thuds and a gasp from deep inside her captor's chest. He arched his back and let her go. Kate turned in time to see that a policeman held the masked man's body. And until the dead man collapsed to the ground, she didn't know he'd been stabbed to death.

The uniformed man held a bloodied knife in his hand. After a stunned moment, he ventured a faint smile and stared at her. Another young man.

"Please, Sister, we must get you to safety," he whispered in French, and waved for her to follow him.

She took a step toward him. It would have been easy to escape her ordeal—to run and not look back—yet something stopped her. The young officer didn't understand, but when he turned to grab his rifle, a single shot rang out. He came to a dead stop. His body stiffened, and he never turned back. He crumpled to the ground at her feet, his face in the dirt. He was dead.

And for a split second, her eyes settled on his rifle. It was within her reach. So very close. She swallowed, hard. Her throat was parched, and she felt sick. She thought about running again, yet something made her turn.

A masked gunman, the leader of the terrorists, stood only yards from her. He was alone with a gun in his hand. He had killed the young officer. In another life, anger would have driven her to go for the rifle, but instead she took a deep breath and waited for what he would say.

"Get moving." His voice was low. And although his words had been an order, he remained composed. She almost didn't hear him.

Kate fell into step in front of him. A mix of emotions made her stomach churn, and tears coursed down her cheek, uncontrollable. She'd had a chance to make a difference, and she froze. Could she have pulled the trigger? If their roles had been reversed, she had no doubt he would have killed her. And yet something in his behavior and his unperturbed reaction to how close she had come to the rifle had confused her.

She didn't have long to think about what had happened.

She was in the dark again, running with the man who held her against her will. And worse, Kate had lost track of the children. They were too little to be spotted in the cluster of hostages up ahead. She wanted to call out their names but was too afraid to draw attention to them. If the children didn't keep up, she was afraid these men would kill them on the spot.

"Move faster . . . or you die," the terrorist leader yelled to those in front of them.

His voice and the sound of his boots made her cringe. Every time he yelled, she thought he directed his abuse at her. Given the life-or-death extremes of their situation, the man had total control over her and the others.

Yet she needed to know one thing.

"You could have killed me back there," she said, her voice cracking. "Why didn't you?"

He didn't answer at first. And she'd begun to think he hadn't heard her until she looked over her shoulder.

"It would have been too easy." He fixed his eyes ahead and shoved her shoulder, forcing her to face forward. "And I have plans for you now. When I could not take your wealthy American guest of honor hostage, I had to settle for you. An American nun. Now shut up and keep moving."

Kate grimaced and fought a lump in her throat. Their lives were in his hands. And behind her, the steady skirmish between the terrorists left at the clinic and the Haitian police had stopped. Even with her muffled hearing, she'd noticed. The police must have overrun the facility and arrested or killed anyone who resisted.

With the deadly force used by the local law in response to the terrorists' aggression, she wondered if any of them would have survived the final assault if their captors hadn't escaped before the police reinforced their lines. Their abductors had used explosions as an element of surprise, but if the local law had known they were so well armed, they might have reciprocated with more firepower to put an end to the standoff. That thought left her feeling a strange gratitude toward the man who'd forced them to leave. And he'd sacrificed some of his men to ensure that they got away.

Why? What plans did he have for them?

She understood that the diversion to the medical clinic had not been in his scheme, but it wouldn't be long before the authorities would learn they'd escaped. They'd be better prepared for round two and hungry for revenge, if only to save face. And following the hostages would be easier since they were now on foot. Their captors must have figured this out. They had picked up the pace and weren't bothering to keep to the shadows anymore.

Kate searched the horizon, looking for clues to determine where they were. She detected the smell of the ocean on the breeze, and it was getting stronger. They were near a beach. Did these men know where they were going, or were they merely putting distance between themselves and the Haitian police?

Cresting a small hill, she saw the faint lights of Tortuga Island in the distance, and the moon glistened on waves that lapped the shoreline of a small cove. She expected the armed men to scramble up the beach or down. Instead, they gathered the hostages together and forced them to their knees. The children spotted Kate and ran for her. Tiny hands gripped her hard as they collapsed to the sand.

"We thought you were . . ." Joselyne sobbed, unable to finish.

"I'm fine. We'll all be fine. We just have to stick together." She held them and kissed their heads, ignoring the twinge of guilt she felt for telling them something she didn't believe.

She wanted to believe these men had a backup plan—that their grand scheme wouldn't end in death on this beach. The grotesque image of dead bodies on the sand—even the children—gripped her mind and wouldn't go away. Her gut twisted, and she couldn't breathe.

The masked men stood between her and the ocean. The undulating waves by moonlight normally soothed her. She focused on the water and imagined other nights when she'd taken a quiet walk on the beach.

Another time. Another place.

A living nightmare ago.

Dark silhouettes of faceless men surrounded her now, and they were armed with weapons that could kill them in seconds. The brutal men had grown edgier. They peered through the shadows, waiting for something.

She started a prayer and hoped she'd be allowed to finish. Shutting her eyes, she clutched the crying children tighter. There was no comforting them. They all knew something worse was about to happen—or it would end here on this beach.

They were in God's hands now—as they had been from the start.

CHAPTER 6

Armed with the AK-47 he'd taken off a dead man, Kinkaid crouched low behind a stand of trees and got as close as he dared. He was positioned on a rise, careful to maintain the high ground and a good view of the scene below.

He watched the terrorists and thought about what he'd seen of their op. Relying mainly on AK-47s, the men assaulted the fund-raiser using low-tech weapons until they resorted to grenades to blow their way out of the clinic. They hadn't employed the usual al-Qaeda tactics of suicide bombers or massive explosives to launch their attack. Yet with relatively few men, they'd been effective, and the op had been well orchestrated. That was what the Haitian police and the media would report.

But from what he was witnessing now, this terrorist cell was far more sophisticated than he'd first thought. One man carried a satellite phone and another had a handheld GPS unit and a laptop. That kind of communication meant they had handlers. They could be aligned with any number of splinter groups. No one had seen this part of the operation except him. The combination of their simpler tactics and more sophisticated gear might mislead anyone analyzing the attack into underestimating them.

And all the Haitian police had were dated walkie-talkies, outclassed weaponry, and virtually no tactical support.

Kinkaid counted heads for the first time. Although he couldn't be certain of what he saw through the darkness, he tallied six or seven armed men and fourteen hostages. One or two of the captives looked wounded, but he couldn't determine their condition. He didn't like the odds. All he had was a rifle with only one magazine and a handgun. He had to face facts. Confronting these men in his condition—and without resources to back him up—would only get innocent people killed.

He searched the frightened hostages, and his heart lurched when he saw Sister Kate. The nun had gathered the children and held them tight. Although she was putting up a strong front for the kids, she looked terrified; but at least she was still alive. He took comfort from that and forced himself to focus on the armed men.

Why had they stopped running? The Haitian police would figure out what had happened at the clinic and track them soon. Why risk getting caught with their backs to the sea?

His eyelids were heavy, and it was difficult to focus. He loosened his grip on the AK-47 and wiped the sweat and grit from his eyes with the sleeve of his suit jacket.

Stay alert, damn it! He took a deep breath and let it out slow to clear his head.

Kill shots would have to be on the money—quick and thorough. Any other day he would have been up for the assignment, but not now. An AK-47 wasn't the rifle for the job. It lacked accuracy and stealth. And he didn't have a knife to pick them off one at a time.

That didn't mean he'd given up. The right tactic might still work. Once he started shooting, the terrorists would know where he was. Muzzle flash in the dark would put him in the spotlight and place a target on him. After his first strike, he'd have to dodge their grenade launcher and keep it from roasting his ass. If he kept the bastards busy, the hostages might have a chance to escape.

Would Kate be one of the lucky ones, or would his interference only get her and the children killed? She and the kids were positioned on the edge and near cover. They might make it if he drew fire and kept the gunmen's attention long enough for them to get away.

"Come on, Kate," he whispered. "I won't get a second chance."

He picked his first target—a masked man standing closest to Sister Kate—and took aim, but a noise forced him to stand down. He raised his head and looked for the source of a steady droning sound. His gaze shifted toward the ocean. Offshore, a murky shadow drifted into view. And a double flash of light from an undulating beacon conveyed a message to the gunmen on the beach. They turned their heads, and one man signaled back.

"Damn," he cursed under his breath. They weren't making a stand. They had called in reserves and were ready for round two.

An old motorized fishing boat anchored offshore, a fifty-foot craft in need of paint and repair. He'd seen the type countless times before, owned by a local commercial fisherman working the waters near Haiti. More men stood on the bow of the boat, rifles in hand and on edgy alert. He had no idea how many men were on board.

A small raft was deployed to transport the hostages. It splashed into the water, and the sound of a small engine revving up could be heard. Two men manned the raft and hit the tops of waves as they sped toward the beach. Judging from the size of the craft and the number of hostages, they'd have to make more than one trip.

Now he had no choice. His marginal plan had hit the skids.

If he waited until the hostages were split up, it would only improve the odds for some and make matters worse for others. And if he hit the gunmen before the raft hit the shore, reinforcements were too close by. Too many hostages would be caught in the cross fire. No way he'd start a fight without knowing what he was up against, not when innocent lives were at stake.

He'd have to be satisfied with providing intel for a rescue mission with Joe LaClaire and whoever he wrangled for help. Kinkaid took stock of the fishing boat and memorized details as he watched the hostages being loaded onto the raft. Sister Kate and the children were the first to be transported. And it didn't take long for the gunmen to board the rest.

He tensed his jaw as the fishing boat pulled anchor and motored into the dark, heading north. Whoever the men were, he had underestimated them.

That wouldn't happen again.

"Next time you're in my crosshairs," he vowed, "I'm pulling the trigger."

Kinkaid stood and retraced the tracks of the terrorists to get a good look at their boot prints and any distinctive footprints of the hostages. Such intel could be invaluable if he had to trail them later.

When he'd done all he could do, he gave thought to leaving the area. He knew he'd have to avoid going back the way he'd come. The stolen Toyota would be off-limits, especially with the police tracking terrorists in the vicinity. To avoid getting caught in an official interrogation, he'd need help to get out.

He grabbed his cell and hit speed dial for LaClaire. When the phone rang, he took a step forward and stumbled. A sudden burst of heat raged through his body as nausea hit hard. He grabbed a tree for support and dropped the AK-47. The rifle blurred on the ground as if it had vanished into a black hole. And when he looked down, he lost his balance. His world spun out of control.

Kinkaid dropped his phone and collapsed. He tumbled down an embankment, unable to stop. And jolts of pain melded into numb oblivion when he finally skidded to a halt with dirt and debris hitting his face.

"Talk to me, boss. What's happening?"

Somewhere in the distance, he heard Joe's voice. Lying flat on his belly, he opened his eyes to a blur of vague shadows. The faint glow of his cell phone came into focus for an instant, then multiplied and drifted from view. He tried moving, but couldn't force his body to cooperate. Hell, he couldn't even feel his legs.

"Where are you, Jackson?" Joe asked.

Good question, LaClaire. It was Kincaid's last thought before his world went black.

Once aboard the vessel, Kate was herded with the rest of the hostages to the rear of the boat and shoved to her knees. She clung to the children and kept her head down, afraid to make eye contact with anyone.

A heavy tarp was thrown over their heads. It stank like dead fish, which made it nearly impossible to breathe, especially with the diesel fumes coming from the boat engine. And once they got under way, the rocking of the boat made some of the hostages sick. She heard them heaving and throwing up where they sat. The muggy stench became unbearable. She held her breath as long as she could.

But their isolation under the tarp soon ended.

One by one, hostages were hauled out and dragged to the front of the boat. Not even the drone of the engine masked the sobs and the screams. She only caught fragments of what was happening and recognized the voice of the leader, the one who spoke English. He asked questions about who they were and who might pay money for them. And for those who resisted, he tortured them until they cooperated.

When it came time for her, what would she tell him? And who would pay enough for the children? Their parents had no money.

She crouched under the heavy tarp until her leg muscles cramped, and her neck ached, waiting for them to come for her. Her mind reeled with what she might say. Eventually, her legs went to sleep, and the tingle felt like a million pinpricks stabbing her. And after hours in the same position, she couldn't force her body to move at all. Her legs had grown numb.

But her captors never came for her. And that scared Kate more.

She stayed under the tarp until the boat came to a stop. Morning had come. She saw a pale light edge the tarp. That was when panic set in. She had to get the circulation back in her legs. If she couldn't walk, she had no doubt they would kill her. Bending her legs and stretching her back, she forced her body to work although the movement sent excruciating pain through her muscles. She made sure the children and the other hostages did the same.

When the tarp was stripped from their heads, the shouting began again. They were shoved toward the small rafts and carried to shore by angry masked men with rifles. A lone stretch of beach and a dense jungle with rugged cliffs lay ahead. She looked for any indications of where they had landed, but there was nothing. No civilization in sight.

Kate had no idea where they were.

New York's LaGuardia Airport
Midmorning

"No, this is my first time here. I've never been to New York," Seth Harper told Alexa as he loaded his bag into the trunk of a car she had rented for the weekend. "I'm looking forward to seeing the city. And maybe we can score some tickets to *Regis and Kelly*."

She had no idea if he was kidding.

Jessie would have known, but there was one thing Alexa picked up on. His crooked grin communicated more than he'd probably intended. No doubt Seth felt the awkwardness of their first few minutes together, so it was up to her to break the ice. This was her town and her invitation.

"I'm sure Regis appreciates the shout-out. I'm glad you're here." She touched his arm, and when he fixed his gaze on her, she had a strange reaction to the sudden intimacy she felt between them.

An electric rush swept through her body. She felt the same link with Garrett Wheeler, but that was only after years of demanding erotic encounters that triggered the feeling. She'd become attuned to the workings of her sensual nature *because* of Garrett. Yet so far, she had only kissed Seth. The potency of the physical connection she had with him stunned her.

Perhaps the feeling centered on the prospect of Seth Harper's accepting her invitation, her first step toward taking on a young lover. She felt naughty, rebellious, and liberated at the same time, yet something else was at play that disturbed her. Seth had triggered an unsettling need—one she had to control for a while longer. She had a hurdle to get around before anything happened between them.

And that obstacle was Jessie.

She cleared her throat and grinned. "You look great. Are you hungry?"

"Yeah, I could eat. What's on the menu?"

You, she wanted to say.

Dressed in jeans, he wore a gray cotton shirt with rolled sleeves and vest. His dark wavy hair looked worthy of attention from her fingers. And as usual, his brown eyes held her in place without mercy. He had no idea what he did to her, but she wasn't a fool. Anything personal that had happened between them came from her pushing the line with him, not the other way around. She'd given him plenty of signals that she was interested. Unlike most men, he'd never acted on them.

Some women preferred the bad-boy thing and would have been frustrated by Seth's shyness. And yes, he was younger. His age, stamina, and naïve innocence played a major part in why she had become the aggressor. Alexa knew what she liked. And her flavor of the day was Seth Harper. The more he played hard to get, the more she wanted him—lust in all its glory. His coy game of cat and mouse only stoked her fire.

"I've got just the place in mind." She slipped behind the wheel and watched him slide into the passenger seat next to her. When she shut the car door, her cell phone rang. "Marlowe here."

"Alexa. I hope I'm not disturbing you." Garrett's low

voice sounded intimate and masculine as if he were in bed next to her. "Are you free to talk?"

His not-so-perfect timing provoked a feeling of betrayal in her. And she resented the guilt, especially after she knew Garrett had not been faithful during the time they'd shared a bed. When she'd first learned the truth, she was hurt and angry but forced herself to get over it. That hadn't been easy. Garrett was the kind of man who branded a woman and left his mark.

She had crossed the line with her boss by having a physical relationship with him, and there had been consequences to her actions. Alexa had hoped to put it all behind her—and not sacrifice their working relationship to do it.

"Sure. What's up?"

With Seth in earshot, she was careful not to mention Garrett's name. Her work would be off-limits.

"I have an assignment. It's urgent, I'm afraid."

She listened to what he had to say. Even on an encrypted cell-phone connection, Garrett was careful not to provide too many details. He'd wait until they met to disclose more. He told her what she'd need to know about a trip out of the country.

"How soon can we meet for a briefing?" Garrett asked.

Alexa took a deep breath, looked at Seth, and forced a smile as she brushed back her blond hair and changed the cell to her other ear.

"Let me work something out. I'll call you back." She didn't wait for his reply. She ended the call and turned toward Seth. "Let's grab that bite to eat. I'm starved."

"Is everything okay?" he asked. "What's going on?"

With a straight face, she raised an eyebrow, and said, "I could tell you, but then I have to dump you in the East River. And I'm running low on cement."

Seth blinked twice with a deadpan look on his face. "Is that your idea of New York hospitality? A double tap to the head?"

"Yeah, if I like you." She grinned.

"Well . . ." He shrugged. "Do you?"

"Come on, Harper. I was kidding. What? TSA doesn't allow humor in carry-ons these days?"

"Only if it fits in a Ziploc." He still hadn't cracked a smile. *Definitely cute.*

When she called him Harper, it reminded her again of the bounty hunter who'd become her friend. She remembered the look on Jessie's face when she told her about Seth coming to town. Jessie admitted not having any better plans for the day, yet she turned down a chance to pick Seth up at the airport. Her reaction didn't feel right, so Alexa had questioned her again. Jessie only reiterated that Seth was fair game, and it was open season. The woman had always struck her as a straight shooter until then. When it came to Seth, however, she sent out mixed signals.

And that wouldn't do.

Alexa didn't like the way that made her feel—as if she were intruding on something she wouldn't understand. She wished she knew more. And maybe one day Jessie would trust her enough to tell her.

In the meantime, she had a guest to feed.

"Come on. Let's blow this place."

Alexa pulled from the curb, subconsciously cursing the bad timing of her new assignment. She'd break her change in plans to Seth over breakfast. And with any luck, the job would be over soon, and she'd convince him to stay at her place until she got back. He'd probably appreciate saving money on a hotel.

When she merged into traffic with Seth on her mind, she missed the dark sedan maintaining a safe distance behind her.

"Stick with them until I tell you to break it off," Garrett Wheeler told the driver, a trusted operative who worked for him. From the backseat of the sedan, he watched the rental car as it changed lanes.

He hadn't planned on close surveillance of Alexa Marlowe, but after he'd seen her meeting a man at the airport, he had to admit that a pang of jealousy had caught him by surprise.

Over the years, he had played countless games with her and arranged for clandestine encounters that had turned sexual. They both enjoyed them. Yet this time on the phone, she had played him as much as he played her. This he knew because he'd seen her do it. He'd listened to her guarded responses on the phone as he watched her from a discreet distance.

What could he expect after what he'd pulled a few months ago? For her own good—and for the good of the Sentinels—he'd let distance grow between them. And later he knew it would take more than that for Alexa to realize their relationship was over. He'd set up a scenario that looked as if he were having an affair with another woman. It didn't take long for Alexa to do the right thing and dump his sorry ass.

Her playing him over the phone today reminded him how he had ended it. A self-inflicted wound. They were no longer lovers. And any future he had once hoped for was over. She had moved on and handled their split with admirable professionalism.

Good for you, Alexa. You deserve more than I can give a woman like you.

And the man meeting her at the airport was Seth Harper from Chicago. He recognized him from the booking photo in the Chicago newspaper after the guy had been falsely accused of murder not too long ago. Jessie Beckett's friend. That piqued his interest, too.

What are you up to, Alexa?

She had promised to call. And he knew her well enough to know she'd take the assignment, especially once she heard Jackson Kinkaid was in trouble. That left him wondering about her out-of-town guest.

What plans had she made with him? Or was he in town to surprise Jessie? Perhaps he needed to rethink who he would send on the Haiti assignment, but there was one thing for certain.

Any man who could capture the interest of *both* Alexa Marlowe and Jessie Beckett was a guy he wanted to know. One way or another, Garrett made up his mind to meet Seth Harper whether Alexa and Jessie welcomed his intrusion or not.

New York City
Sentinels Headquarters

Alexa had convinced Seth to stay at her place while she was gone. And he'd promised to change his return trip to Chicago and leave his itinerary open. That made it easier for her to leave. When she returned from her assignment, she'd press Jessie for the truth about her and Seth. She had no intention of letting a man get between her and her new partner. Now with that settled, all that remained was her mission briefing with Garrett. From experience, she knew to be packed and ready to go after they'd talked.

After Garrett served her coffee, they sat at a glass conference table in his office.

"You were a little vague about getting together on our phone conversation earlier. Did I interrupt something?" he asked.

She wasn't prepared for Garrett's interest in her personal life.

"No, not at all." She wouldn't give in to his prying. "I'm here now. Tell me about the assignment."

He stared at her for a long moment. And with his swarthy good looks and penetrating steel gray eyes, he hadn't lost his touch in grabbing her attention. Eventually, he got down to business.

"A hostage-rescue operation in Haiti. Out of Port de Paix to be precise." He filled her in on the call he'd received and the research he'd done.

In his thorough manner, Garrett laid out his assessment of the situation, starting with the profiles of her team, a layout of logistics and communications for the op, and an overview of the region that included speculation of known terrorist and drug-trafficking activity.

"Haiti and the outlying vicinity have become an integral route of the drug trade. Product and laundered funds are moved between South America and the Eastern Seaboard of the U.S." Garrett pointed a red laser light to a map on an overhead monitor.

"As you know, anything afloat in the Caribbean is watched by DEA, DHS, the Coast Guard, and countless other acronym agencies," he continued. "So you'll have to watch your six on this one. No telling who else might be tracking these bastards. And the wire services have covered the assault and are hungry for more. I don't want our organization to get caught in the limelight. This is an out-and-back mission with no frills."

He clicked a remote and other images came on the screen. He enlarged them.

"I used the time frame of the abductions and tracked the activity in the area. These images came from our satellite. The terrorists escaped with hostages from a fund-raiser, but got caught at a medical clinic. They held the captives there until they used grenade launchers to make their exit. After that, the Haitian police lost track of them."

He used the red laser again to point out a series of dark shapes in the water. Several boats.

"It's my understanding that your contact in Haiti will have better intel," he told her. "You'll have to narrow the timeline and sift through these satellite images to determine which bogey to pursue. Just keep a low profile and get the job done."

He handed her a file that included satellite images as well as maps of other locations in the region. "Take this file. You and your contact will need it."

"And who is my contact?" she asked.

"The man who called me was Joe LaClaire."

She knew Garrett well enough to know he was holding something back. There was more to this mission.

"I don't recognize the name," she said, and pressed him for more. "How do you know him? Why'd he contact you?"

Garrett wasn't exactly in the yellow pages. LaClaire had to know how to get in touch. With Sentinels' security, getting directly to Garrett wouldn't have been easy.

"He works with someone we *both* know. Jackson Kinkaid."

She tried to hide her reaction but couldn't. At one time, she had seen a future with Kinkaid. A lifetime ago.

"I know you've worked with Kinkaid in the past, but he's not the man you used to know." Garrett's somber expression got her attention. "Trusted sources have told me he hires out to the highest bidder in a drug-cartel war out of South America. He's nothing more than a mercenary."

"I find that hard to believe."

"Then get over it. Because if he can be bought, no telling how much you'll be able to trust him. His motives are suspect." He slouched back in his chair and stared at her. "Or maybe he was the reason the terrorists picked Haiti and took hostages at a school fund-raiser in his honor."

"Since when do mercenaries get honored at school fund-raisers? None of this makes sense, Garrett."

"Tell me about it. If I didn't owe him one, I'd tell him to fuck off. But I have confirming police reports that these hostages are for real." Garrett reached for her arm. "If you see that this is too dangerous . . . or that Kinkaid isn't on the level, I want you to pull the plug on the operation and let the locals take charge. A handful of hostages isn't worth it. Don't risk your life . . . and your team for a guy who's a turncoat. You understand?"

"Yeah, sure." She nodded. "I'll assess the situation and make the call."

Even though it was hard to picture a man like Kinkaid selling his services to a ruthless drug cartel, she'd seen it happen before. Greed and burnout made good men cross the line and sell out.

"You'll have tracking beacons and a backup team standing by on your order, Alexa." Garrett clenched his jaw and took a deep breath. Something else was on his mind.

"You're leaving something out. What is it?"

"Two things. I have a history with Kinkaid that's between him and me. Expect hostility. Your link to me will make you a target, but you can handle whatever he dishes out. If I thought he'd lash out at you and put you at risk, I'd call this off."

"Okay. Expect flak. What else?" she questioned. "You said there were two things."

"There may be another reason to make this a quick trip." He turned toward one of the monitors on the wall and hit one with his red laser pen. A swirl of color magnified on the screen. "There's a tropical storm forming in the Atlantic. It may miss Haiti, but tracking these bastards just got more complicated."

She watched the hurricane tracker project a path for the growing storm. The odds were against her.

"We'll be in constant communication with you, tracking this storm," he said. "If I tell you to take shelter, that's an order. You understand me, Alexa?"

Garrett didn't bother to hide the concern in his voice.

"Yeah, I hear you."

"I've got a charter at LaGuardia ready to leave in an hour from my private hangar," he told her. "The jet will be stocked, and your team will be waiting. Once you get to Haiti, call this number." He handed her a piece of paper. "You'll get instructions from Kinkaid and La-Claire on where to meet."

The reality of seeing Kinkaid again twisted her gut into a tight knot. The rescue op would be tough enough without the added complication, especially if he took blood money from drug cartels. She blocked that disturbing thought from her mind to ask Garrett one more question.

"Why wasn't Jessie assigned to this mission? Is she on the backup team?"

"No, I've decided not to send her. I need experienced operatives." When he caught her obvious disappointment, he asked, "Is there a problem?"

"No. It's just that she's ready for an assignment. You know how it is after training."

"Yes, I remember." He fixed his eyes on hers and connected in a way only he could. "But this mission won't be easy. If she's along, you'll be distracted. And I need you focused one hundred percent." His gaze softened. "Take care of yourself, Alexa."

She smiled. "Thanks, Garrett."

Alexa packed up the files and headed out of the building with plenty on her mind. And driving to La-Guardia Airport would give her time to think about the mission and the man who had instigated it. But before she left New York City, she had a loose end to take care of. Her out-of-town guest would need a distraction to keep him busy.

She reached for her cell and hit the speed dial for Jessie. When her friend didn't answer, the call rolled into voice mail. If she'd be out of town anyway, having a backup plan for Seth Harper seemed like a good idea.

"Listen, Jessie. I had to cancel my plans with Seth. I'm heading out of town now. An unexpected trip." She smiled and added, "But I need a favor."

She concocted a story about building maintenance being done at her place and asked Jessie to pack a small bag to stay overnight and make sure the work got done. An apartment key would be in an envelope with the manager. Alexa gave her the address and ended the call, content to let nature take its course. If nothing happened between Seth and Jessie while she was gone, then she'd know for sure that Harper was up for grabs.

And she had a feeling that when she returned from this mission, she'd need a good diversion. The difficult assignment ahead took firm hold and dominated her thoughts, clouded by memories of Jackson Kinkaid. A complicated man. Only now he'd be her assignment.

And someone she shouldn't trust.

Port de Paix, Haiti

Wrapped in a pitch-black world, Kinkaid heard quiet voices in the distance that magnified. *Had someone called his name?*

Faces emerged from the gloom in rapid-fire succession. They warped and twisted and taunted him. Some looked familiar, but all of them made him anxious. And as he tensed, the sound of gunfire erupted. The sudden outburst culminated in a mind-numbing explosion that forced him to run. He struggled to break free of the treacherous dark chasm, but couldn't. Everywhere he turned, it loomed in front of him. And the incessant hum of voices wouldn't stop. They grew louder, more distinct, then dropped off to a vague whisper he couldn't understand.

"What? No!" He heard his own voice. It echoed in his head. "Make it . . . stop."

Strong hands took hold of him. The more he thrashed to break free, the harder the hands gripped him until a sliver of light broke through the emptiness. He focused on it and willed it to stay. And when he stopped fighting, the hands let go.

That was when he felt her presence. He sensed her

near him. Her essence lurked in the shadows beyond his reach. And the familiar smell of her skin and blond hair calmed him—a heady floral scent of gardenias. The details of her face never came into focus until a light pierced the blackness and took her from him. She dissolved in a swirling crimson mist.

"No," he whispered. "Don't go."

A wash of gray swept the remaining gloom aside, and blurred images took shape. His eyes watered as the light intensified, and his face and body raged with heat. His bare chest and arms were slick with sweat. And he ached all over with a fierce pain radiating from his belly.

"Jackson, it's me, Joe. I'm not going anywhere." He recognized his friend's voice. The sound of it forced the cobwebs from his brain, and LaClaire's face came into focus. The man stood over him.

"You've been delirious, boss. Are you with me?" Joe wiped a cool wet cloth across his face. After he nodded, his friend continued, "I had a doctor come here. Discreetly, of course. He's got you on pain meds and strong antibiotics for an infection."

Kinkaid raised his throbbing head to look at his surroundings for the first time. A small motel room with two beds. And a plastic bag of clear liquid hung over his head with a tube connected to an IV in his arm. Dank sheets covered him, and heavy bandages were taped across his belly.

"What . . . happened?" he asked.

"You were shot. It went clean through. Does that ring a bell?" His friend tried to jog his memory. "It sure would with me."

Images of the academy fund-raiser rushed to his mind, an event marred by armed gunmen, a screaming little girl in danger—and Sister Kate. And judging by the fact he was in a motel room rather than a hospital with doctors who asked questions, he realized Joe had done his best to keep a low profile.

"How did you find me? I don't remember . . ." He attempted to sit up and winced in pain.

"Oh, no. Stay put, big guy." Joe held his shoulders until he settled down. "You want some water."

When he shook his head, his friend went on.

"I called in some markers and triangulated your position using the GPS on your phone. Remember? You're the gutsy guy, and I'm the clever one." Joe smirked and sat in a chair near his bed. His amusement eventually vanished. "Can you tell me what happened?"

"Not sure. Too . . . tired." Kinkaid had a hard time staying awake. He heard Joe, but his words faded in and out.

"You lost a lot of blood. And the pain meds are potent," Joe explained. "Police said a group of terrorists attacked that school fund-raiser you were at. They used heavy firepower and got away with hostages. You told me a friend was in trouble. And you wanted my help, no matter who I had to ask. Remember that?"

"Kate. She's in trouble. We've got to . . . help her." Despite his condition, Kinkaid picked up on Joe's hesitance, but he was too weak to stay focused. "Who did you get . . . ?"

He wasn't sure he'd spoken or merely thought the

question. He shut his eyes and sank into the black void again, hearing Joe's voice in the distance.

"Help is on the way, boss. But we gotta talk. Stay with me now."

Kinkaid couldn't open his eyes. He drifted into a fitful drug-induced sleep—an agonizing stupor where he couldn't tell what was real or a nightmare—and he wondered if death felt like this.

If it did, he couldn't recommend it.

CHAPTER 7

Port de Paix, Haiti
10:00 P.M.

"Jackson. Come on, wake up, man." A voice jolted Kinkaid from a deep sleep. Joe LaClaire's voice. "I hate doing this, but you'll wanna hear what I gotta say. Trust me."

"What? What's . . . happening?" He opened his eyes to a dimly lit motel room with another unmade bed and his friend leaning over him. An IV was still plugged into his arm.

"That help I promised you?" Joe winced, looking apologetic. "They'll be here soon. We gotta get you up. And right now, you don't look so good."

Hell, he felt like crap. Why would he look good?

"Who? Who's coming?" Kinkaid struggled to sit up in bed. His side ached, and his head throbbed without letup. Joe slid another pillow under him.

"I have a confession to make. You were so desperate for help . . . to rescue a woman named Kate, that I called someone you might not . . ."

Now he knew something was up. Joe was a straight-forward guy, and he didn't mince words. Apparently he had something in his craw.

"Spit it out, Joe. Who'd you call?"

His friend paused long enough for him to glance up and stare him in the eyes.

"Garrett Wheeler."

"What?" Kinkaid glared at Joe before he tore the IV from his arm with a grimace. He swung his legs off the bed and protested, "I thought you understood. I've got history with Wheeler. He's not . . ."

Before he finished, Joe interrupted.

"The thing is, he's the only one who sent a team. And he's got the resources to get the job done." Joe waved a hand and urged him to get up. "Come on. Alexa Marlowe will be here pronto. We gotta get you looking presentable."

"Alexa? She still with . . . Garrett?"

"That depends on what you mean by 'with' him. He sent her with a team. You know her?"

His mind reeled with memories of Alexa. She was a force of nature. A strong, intelligent woman with passions to match. He had kept his private life a secret from her when they worked together, believing it was the right thing to do. But his reticence only added fuel to her fire.

He'd seen the same thing happen to others. Living life on the edge played havoc on operatives' libidos. And staring death in the face with each new op made it easy to form attachments to those who understood the life. Although Alexa had wanted more from him, he couldn't give her what she needed. And after he cooled things off between them, he later suspected that she found Garrett more willing.

All of this came at about the time his life went to hell. And any feelings he had for Alexa melded into his resentment of Garrett.

"Know her? Not anymore I don't." Wearing only boxers, he stood and toppled over before Joe grabbed him. "I gotta get showered and dressed. I can't let her see me like this. She'll find an excuse to put me on injured reserve and leave me behind."

Now Joe lost his cool. "Oh, like the fact you've been shot? Silly woman. Why would she hold *that* against you?"

"Exactly." He shrugged and took his first steps toward the bathroom, fending off Joe's help with a wave of his hand.

"You're insane." Joe raised his voice. "Doc says you had a nasty infection, and you need stronger antibiotics than pills. If you get off the IV now, you'll be slammed harder. You have no business on a rescue mission in your condition. You'll only slow her down."

Kinkaid turned back to his friend to make his point.

"If that happens, I'll make the call and bench myself, but I'm not turning this over to Garrett Wheeler and his blond surrogate. I can't trust them, not with this."

"I'll be your wingman. Does that count?" Joe argued. "Or don't you trust me either?"

Kinkaid raked a hand through his dark hair and heaved a sigh. He was being an asshole to a guy who didn't deserve it.

"I trust you, Joe. And I appreciate all your help. But . . . I feel like I got Kate into this mess," he admitted, his voice barely above a whisper. "Those terrorists . . . they called out my name before they started shooting up the place. They were looking for me, Joe. I gotta know why. And I gotta see this thing through for her sake. I owe her."

Joe stared at him for a long moment before he backed off. "You can be a real son of a bitch, but invoking your name doesn't usually spark gunplay. At least, not right away."

"Thanks, I think."

"No problem. And I brought your bag off the boat. Let's get you dressed and smelling pretty." He grinned and tossed a duffel bag on his bed. "So tell me, boss. Is Alexa Marlowe as sexy as her name?"

He gave his friend a sideways glare. And even though he didn't answer his question, Joe smirked. "Yeah, thought so."

Port de Paix wasn't exactly paradise by Alexa's standards. And the darkness of a cloudy night kept the place in shadows, the best thing she could say about it. The flight to Haiti had been a long one, and she had more hours to work before hitting the sack.

With file in hand, she headed for the motel room Joe LaClaire had given her over the phone. She'd spoken to him from the plane. Once they landed, her team drove straight to the motel and had already checked into their rooms. She'd done the same and planned to meet with them after connecting with Kinkaid and LaClaire.

A dim light shone around the closed curtains of room 15. The motel was nothing more than cinder block painted in a depressing green. The doors were metal, with rust around the edges caused by humidity off the ocean. Muggy air carried the smell of the sea and the faint stench of manure, a deterrent to taking a full breath of good old Mother Nature. The listless backdrop of windblown palm trees with ragged fronds and spindly banana trees surrounded the motel. Weeds shoved through cracks in the parking lot and worn, dented vehicles lined the narrow dirt streets. With most windows down, the cars weren't locked. Why bother? Who would steal crap on wheels?

What was Jackson Kinkaid doing here? He always had a sense of style, yet this place seemed out of character from the man she remembered. Associating with drug cartels must have left its mark.

Out of habit, she reached beneath her windbreaker and released the retention strap of her holster, making her weapon easy to grab. With the sweltering heat, a jacket was the last thing she wanted to wear over her jeans and tank top. But it covered her .45-caliber H&K MK23, her travel companion.

Standing outside motel room 15, she knocked, and someone doused the light inside. The door opened with a creak.

"Alexa?" When he had seen her blond silhouette, a man spoke from the dark room. "You made good time."

Only a streetlamp shed light on someone standing inside the room. She recognized LaClaire's voice.

"Yeah." She stepped inside the room and closed the door behind her. And with a hand on her weapon, she added, "You want the secret handshake? I'll do you one better."

When they flipped the light on, she held up a gesture both Kinkaid and LaClaire would recognize—the one finger salute.

Joe LaClaire grinned and nodded. "Yeah, you and me are gonna get along just fine."

Jackson Kinkaid stood to her left. Unlike his buddy, he wasn't smiling. She fought hard not to react to seeing him again, but the beat of her heart ramped up a notch. She felt it.

He wore faded jeans with a black T-shirt worn tail out. And he stood taller and looked more defiant than she had expected. Hypnotic green eyes glared at her with a smoldering hostility that Garrett had warned her about. And he smelled of soap, with his dark hair still wet from the shower. He wore his hair longer than she remembered, and it curled at his neck. And although he hadn't bothered to shave, the rugged macho thing suited her fine.

When he saw her middle finger, he raised an eyebrow and said, "*You* haven't changed. Nice to see you, Alexa. Who'd you piss off to score *this* cherry assignment?"

She ignored his abuse.

"Haiti, Kinkaid? Is this your idea of a good time?" She crossed her arms and returned his stare. "I prefer the smell of coconut oil and cute cabana boys serving me umbrella drinks."

"Sorry," he said. "The best we can do is bottled water. With any luck, you can avoid a good case of dysentery."

"There's a good kind?" she asked.

Joe took Kinkaid's cue and lifted the lid to a cooler where they had bottled water. She waved him off.

"No, I'm good," she told him. "But you gotta tell me. How did you end up at a school fund-raiser . . . an event in your honor, no less? And who is this mystery woman, Kate?"

Kinkaid looked unsettled, and he shot a glance at his friend, who shrugged. Guess Joe had told her too much.

"That's not important," he said. "By now Garrett has done his homework and confirmed the assault was legit and the hostages real. I'm not in the mood to have my chain yanked or take a trip down memory lane. Are you gonna help or play twenty questions?"

"Attitude? You're giving me attitude here?" She shrugged. "Look, I don't see anyone else lined up outside. So cut the crap. You asked for help, and I brought a team. Whatever beef you have with Garrett, I don't care. It's not gonna interfere with this mission. *Capisce?*"

His jaw tightened and he narrowed his eyes. Eventually he took a deep breath and gave her an almost imperceptible nod. That was all the concession she'd get from him.

Kinkaid crossed his muscled arms over his chest, and his broad shoulders and narrow hips got her attention again. The man carved out his own corner, leaving little elbow room in the cramped space for her to feel comfortable in. Thankfully, he kept his distance and leaned against a wall. His man Joe backed off and took the corner of a mattress.

She still had one more point to make.

"And while we're setting ground rules, there's another thing we're gonna get straight. I'm in charge of this mission. I make the call on pulling the plug. If I see you or your friend endangering my team, I won't hesitate to take you both out of the equation. Is that clear?"

"Crystal. What else?" His somber expression gave her nothing. Only his gruff tone sent her a warning that he wasn't in the mood for playing nice.

"Garrett said you had intel. What happened after the bastards left the clinic? Are they still in Haiti, or did they get out?"

"They left by boat," he said. "I saw them leave, heading north."

"But you didn't tell the cops," she guessed.

"No."

By the look on his face, he challenged her to ask why. She didn't.

"Tell me everything," she said.

Kinkaid gave her what he'd seen, from specs on the boat to bad-guy head counts, weapons details, and the number and condition of the hostages—a thorough account that not even the Haitian police had. His intel might keep them one step ahead of anyone else.

"These guys had a SAT phone, handheld GPS units, and a damned laptop," he told her. "And they were in and out like they'd run the scenario before and knew where to go. They had to be connected to a handler. Why else would they come with all that high-tech gear?"

He shook his head and continued, "The Haitian cops didn't stand a chance. They were outgunned, and all they had were dated walkie-talkies. Hell, the terrorists were willing to die, Alexa."

"Maybe we can help them with that." She narrowed her eyes. "Anything else?"

"Yeah, I got a good look at their tracks after they left the medical clinic. If we cross their path, I'll know what to look for."

The man had given her plenty of detail. Alexa knew how outraged she would have been if this attack had happened to her, but Kinkaid was taking this harder than she would have believed for a guy who was on the payroll of drug cartels. Something else was at play that she didn't understand, and instinct told her to have patience. A guy like Kinkaid wouldn't be pushed into talking if he didn't feel like sharing.

"This is good stuff, Jackson. I'll feed your account back to Garrett. See if he can ID the terrorist cell. And someone might have claimed responsibility on Arab news. Al Jazeera might have something by now. I'll let you know."

After he nodded, she held up her file and stepped toward a small table near the door. "I've got satellite digitals. If we can narrow down the time, we might figure out where they went."

"That's great. Let's do it." He looked surprised to have satellite surveillance and sat down next to her at the table. He was slow to move and looked beat-up, with bruises on his jaw under the shadow of his day-old beard.

"What's wrong with you, hotshot? You look a little rough."

"It's nothing."

She opened her file and put a series of satellite images on the table. Narrowing the time, they were able to locate the time stamp that worked. Using what Kinkaid had witnessed and her high-tech surveillance, they tracked the boat he'd seen leave Haiti.

The news wasn't good.

"Damn it!" he cursed.

No more doubt. The boat that had taken the hostages landed in Cuba—a communist stronghold, a country supportive of terrorism and a transshipment point for the drug trade. She pulled out a map of Cuba and located the southeast part where the boat had dropped anchor. It was east of the U.S. Naval Base at Guantanamo Bay and south of the city of Baracoa in the middle of nowhere. The terrain was extremely mountainous and rugged, plenty of dangerous places for terrorists to hide. And with terrorist training camps in Cuba, such a remote area would be an attractive location, especially given the region's history of guerilla warfare.

"Our plane won't get us close enough and would draw too much attention. You have access to a boat, or will we need to supply that?" she asked.

He looked at Joe and without a word spoken between them, Kinkaid turned back to her, and said, "We got a boat. What else?"

"We'll be linked to Garrett via tracking beacon and a SAT phone. We'll have additional resources at our disposal. Garrett will make sure of that. And a backup team can be within range if we need them. We'll also have GPS and spare batteries, but depending on how dense the jungle, we could still lose our satellite signal. That'll mean we do it the old-fashioned way, using maps and compass. You good with that?"

"Fine." He nodded. Although his expression softened, he was still all business.

"The terrain will complicate things, especially if we have to hunt them into the mountains." She spoke more for her benefit than his and made a mental checklist of her supplies. "We'll pack water in CamelBak hydration packs, but not nearly enough if this takes more than a few days. That would be too much weight to haul. If necessary, we'll have to purify what we find. And we'll have field rations to supplement what we can't forage on our own. Tracking these bastards, we won't have time for hunting." She rested a hand on her knee and stared at him. "We brought extra food and water for you and Joe."

"Good," he said. "Sounds like you've got things covered, but Joe will stay with the boat and handle getting us out. Does that work?"

Alexa nodded her approval. "You never asked for weapons. Do you have what you'll need?"

"Yeah. Plenty."

Spoken like a true mercenary, she thought. And the expression on his face might have chilled her if she weren't playing on the same team.

"Make sure you and Joe are ready first thing. We're leaving at dawn." She leaned back in her chair. "We'll pick you up. You'll meet the team and take us to the boat."

"We'll be ready. Anything else?" He was done talking and was giving her cues it was time for her to leave.

"There is one more thing. And it's not good news, I'm afraid," she said. That got his attention. "Garrett is tracking a tropical storm that's forming in the Atlantic. It may hit Cuba and mess with our timetable."

Kinkaid dropped his chin and let out a sigh with his eyes shut. He looked tired. It was the first time she'd seen a chink in his machismo armor. Whoever Kate was, she was a lucky woman to have someone like Jackson Kinkaid as a dark guardian angel. Lucky, that is, if you discounted being abducted by terrorists.

Kinkaid's moment of vulnerability came and went.

"Shit happens. We'll deal with it." He stood and waited for her to do the same, not bothering with idle chitchat or pleasantries. He'd provided his part of good intel. Now he doled out the bum's rush. No mixed signals. He wanted her gone.

He turned out the lights and opened the door for her to leave. When she walked by him, he touched her arm, and the scent of his warm skin mixed with soap carried on the faint breeze.

"I want to . . ." His handsome face was outlined by a streetlamp behind her. " . . . thanks for everything, Alexa. What you're doing . . . I won't forget it."

"Let's hope you still feel that way when this is over."

She touched his cheek and stared into those green eyes but didn't linger. She walked away and heard him close the door behind her.

Jackson Kinkaid might have distracted her by the sudden display of intimacy, but it didn't stop her from wondering what else he was hiding. When it came to details of their mission, he was very forthcoming. Yet so much had gone unsaid. Gut instinct told her that.

Whatever he was hiding, she had a feeling she wouldn't like it.

After Alexa left the motel room, Kinkaid collapsed onto the mattress and stared at the ceiling. The room was spinning, and he shut his eyes. When that didn't help, he opened them again to find Joe staring down at him.

"This isn't gonna work, Jackson. You can barely stand," his friend protested. "How are you gonna tackle mountains in Cuba and a fuckin' hurricane?"

"Like I said, I'll pull myself out if things go bad." After Joe backed off, he propped pillows behind him and sat up. "I'm gonna need pills from your doc. Antibiotics, no pain meds. I gotta think straight. Can you swing that?"

Joe pointed a finger. "Yeah, but I'm not happy, just so you know."

"Duly noted. And thanks."

His friend got on the phone to arrange for the boat and the antibiotics. Kinkaid shut his eyes again, knowing his mind wouldn't let him sleep. He had too much to do before dawn.

Most of all, he worried for Kate.

Kate had been right before, when she said she was surprised he remembered the day they met at the hospital. In truth his memory back then was not much more than Swiss cheese, riddled with holes that only merged together in a jumbled mess. What he had recalled might have been more attributable to what others had told him later, but one memory held firm.

He had remembered the heat of the sun on his face and the sudden rush of coolness when her shadow blocked the light and she sat next to him. She was a soothing touch when he needed someone to care. The world had carried on without him in shades of black and white—absent any color and mind-numbingly empty—until one day he heard a woman's voice.

Kate's voice.

She had engaged his muddled brain, even after he had given up.

Later, he learned that she sought him out each day. She read to him and talked with him as if they were old friends. It hadn't mattered that their conversations were one-sided. Little by little, he began to listen to her. And one day, he said the first words he'd spoken in a long while.

It had been a start.

There were days since then that he wondered if her efforts had been worth it. His cynical nature made for a tenacious adversary. But as relentless as Kate had been with him back then, Kinkaid wouldn't give up on finding her now. In his mind, her life tipped the scales in importance when compared to his. Any lifeline she'd given him years ago, maybe it had been for a reason.

He owed her his life, such as it was. The least he could do was return the favor, even if it meant risking any future he had.

Southeast Cuba

With the strain of the day, Sister Kate felt her body shutting down. Her throat was parched and her mouth bone dry. She had climbed rugged mountain trails through a dense, bug-infested jungle. And despite the stress her body had endured, she noticed her sweating had stopped and muscle cramps in her legs and back had grown more painful.

She knew the symptoms. Dehydration had hit her hard. And yet her captors had no mercy. Only now, after a full day of climbing, had they gotten any water at all. She shared her tin cup of water with the children, giving them the rest after she'd taken a small sip and held the moisture in her mouth.

Hunger made her stomach growl as she watched the men eat in front of them at the campfire. On the trail they had discarded their masks and she'd been shocked to see their young faces. Most were under twenty. They looked Middle-Eastern, but she had no more understanding than that. Dark-skinned boys with the hardened eyes of hostile men, obsessed with ideologies she would never comprehend.

Kate held the children. Listening to the sounds

of their breathing, she knew Andre and Daniel were asleep while Faye and Joselyne kept their eyes on the men near the fire. They clutched at her tunic with their small hands. Firm, tense grips. She felt their bodies tremble and could do nothing about it. The ordeal was wearing them down, and she was completely exhausted herself.

Several times she nodded off in the muggy heat, oblivious to the torment of bug bites. Every time she dozed, she imagined the horror happening again. The hacking sound of the machete and the screams would jolt her awake. If such nightmares haunted her, she couldn't imagine what the children were going through.

To stop fear from gnawing at her belly, she turned toward the other hostages. Coughing caught her attention. George was getting worse. He'd been shot in the shoulder during the siege at the medical clinic. Earlier, she had tried to help. There wasn't much she could do now. Infection had set in and with the scent of blood in the air, the bugs had targeted him. She could tell he had a fever and had no way to treat it. She'd done her best to stop the bleeding, but George had been coerced at gunpoint into climbing the mountain trails like everyone else.

The man would not last long in these conditions. He needed medical attention. And she knew that their captors would never allow it.

Voices and laughter near the fire grew louder and more threatening. She turned back toward the flame and watched the young men become more agitated. The blaze deepened the shadows on their faces and made them look more sinister. And as they crossed in front of the fire—becoming more frenzied in their movements—their dark silhouettes eclipsed the light and cast elongated shadows over the hostages.

Kate couldn't understand what they were saying, yet by the looks they gave the women hostages, the young men were working up the nerve to do something wrong. They joked. They laughed. They yelled and coerced. And she feared for what would happen next.

Two boys were hauled to their feet and shoved toward the hostages by other young men with rifles. The boys looked over the women, one by one. When they made their decisions, they grabbed two and grappled them to their feet.

Kate recognized one of her missionary teachers, Susan Fleming, a single woman in her early thirties. The other woman was older, perhaps in her forties and the wife of a local Haitian government worker. Both women kicked and screamed. That only spurred the boys on. The violence escalated until more men got involved. And the one with the video cam followed the horde to record the humiliation.

Kate's eyes widened, and she glared at the leader—hoping he had the decency to stop what was about to happen—but he only watched his men with faint amusement.

God, no! She wanted to scream. *Do you have no mercy?*

After awakening Andre and Daniel, Kate rushed to her feet and confronted the leader, who sat on a fallen tree at the edge of the campfire. She didn't know where she got the strength to approach him, she only knew that someone must.

"Please . . . stop this. Can't you see this is wrong?"

He stood and glared at her, eyeing her up and down in a vile fashion as he walked a circle around her. A few of his men, who had remained at the fire, laughed at her.

"Wrong? Who are you to tell me what is wrong?" he demanded. "Your God will not save you, you know. Your life is in my hands." He grinned, white teeth against dark skin. "I am as powerful as your God now, yes?"

The women struggled against the young men who hauled them away. Kate wanted it all to stop and didn't know how to make that happen. Her breathing escalated, and she thought her heart would burst from her chest.

"I'm sorry if I offended you. I didn't mean to." She lowered her head and fought the hysteria welling in her belly. "These women did nothing to deserve such treatment. You can stop this."

"Yes, I can. But my men have needs." He stopped pacing in front of her and stared down. "And this . . ." He tugged at her tunic. " . . . this will not protect you from what will happen out there. So do not call attention to yourself . . . or my men will be reminded you are nothing but a woman to pleasure them."

She kept her head down and avoided his eyes. A tear slid down her cheek. She had been shocked by his disrespect. Living the life of a nun had sheltered her. She had come to expect civility and deference to her position. Yet here she was nothing.

Less than nothing.

"Tell me," he said. "If something happened to you, what would become of the children?" When she reacted to his threat with a choked breath, he laughed. "Go. Sit down and shut up."

He dismissed her and turned his back. And she shut her eyes, feeling utterly powerless. In a daze, she replayed his words in her head as she walked back to the children. They clutched at her and pulled her to the ground next to them.

"Why did you do that?" Joselyne asked with her eyes watering. "He could have killed you."

She saw it on the girl's face—she was the only lifeline these children had.

"I'm sorry if I . . ." She couldn't finish.

The two women had been taken into the jungle, yet not far enough away to cover up the sounds of their torment—the cries, the beatings, the howling when each man took his turn like jackals with cornered prey. It made her sick. Through the trees, an eerie light from the video camera flickered, casting its light on images she never wanted to see. She shut her eyes, but that only made the reality more vivid in her mind. The boys had been goaded into losing their virginity by rape, an act of violence and degradation no one should endure. The young boys' bodies were pumped full of adrenaline, and the pressure of mob mentality had taken over.

There would be no turning back. And no shame for their actions.

"What's happening, Sister?" Joselyne asked. "What are they doing to those women?"

All the children clung to her. Kate didn't want to

answer Joselyne's question. She only shook her head. The words—and the horror—were wedged deep in her throat. Yet she had to say something to calm them.

"Time for a prayer." She forced a faint smile and felt her lips trembling. "Can you pray with me?"

She touched each of their faces to get their attention and prayed aloud. The children joined in, murmuring low. Kate's body rocked as she held them. She fought the nausea building in her stomach and tried to block out the tortured screams coming from the jungle.

Impossible.

Unable to stop herself, she looked toward the campfire and saw the terrorist leader watching her and the children. His dark cruel eyes held no remorse. He smiled at her and, despite the heat, her body shuddered.

If she'd had any tears left, she would have cried for them all.

CHAPTER 8

The sun seared the horizon and streaks of orange impaled the gray edge of nightfall—that solitary time of morning when words were an intrusion. Kinkaid had met Alexa's team at the motel as promised. They all knew what to expect and got down to the business of tracking killers.

When they got to the pier where LaClaire had moored the boat, Kinkaid headed belowdecks and loaded his gear, taking over the cabin that had been his from the prior voyage. He wouldn't need overnight accommodations, but old habits died hard, and he liked his privacy. And having a cabin with a door and a bed would ensure that he had sack time on his way to Cuba if he needed it. Once they landed, there'd be no luxuries like a mattress or downtime. And the last thing he needed so early in the trip was for Alexa to get curious about why he was moving slower than the rest of her team.

He heard the heavy footfalls of Alexa's men on deck, and the boat engine kicked in. They'd be under way soon, and Alexa would expect him up top. He'd have precious few minutes to himself before the mission to rescue Kate and the others would consume him. And he knew exactly how he wanted to spend the time. Kinkaid took his iPod from its canvas pouch and put in his earplugs. He listened to the digital recording he always brought with him. It centered him, yet not always in a rational way.

With his back to the half-opened door, he sat on the edge of his bunk and shut his eyes. He steadied his heart to a slow rhythm and imagined a different time and place, then pictured him there. He felt the boat lurch as it left the dock, and the water rocked the hull. Nothing distracted him—until a sultry woman's voice pulled him from where he was.

"I was wondering who had the choice digs."

When he opened his eyes, Alexa stood in the doorway to his cabin. He saw her blond reflection in a mirror and turned. Before last night, it had been a long time since he'd seen a woman like her. Tall and lean, she filled out her camo BDUs in all the right spots. Her Nordic good looks blessed her with flawless pale skin, full sensual lips, and blue eyes the color of glacier ice. A well-trained, intelligent woman he could trust with his life.

But the life of Sister Kate was another story. He'd learned long ago. Never be the middleman to trust.

"Sorry. I didn't know you were there." He pulled out his earplugs and stowed his iPod in a side pocket of his bag. "You need something?"

"Didn't know you were so into your tunes. You've . . . changed."

He stared at her a moment, trying to figure out how to respond. He decided this mission was too important to get sidetracked.

"So I've been told." He gave her no explanation. Nor did he make excuses for the man he'd become. "What's up?"

"Garrett sent an updated weather report. Lady Luck is not with us." She narrowed her eyes and looked around the cabin before her gaze settled back on him. "Come up top. See for yourself."

She shut the door behind her and gave him privacy to wash down more antibiotics and check his bandages one more time. He was dodging a fever and knew it. He felt the heat under his skin.

A little time, that's all I need.

On deck, he spotted Alexa alone at the bow of the boat and went to join her. The breeze buffeted her blond hair as she stared dead ahead. Her team was in the stern. Each man prepared for the mission in his own way. Some men needed to talk out the adrenaline rush and others only wanted solitude. She'd brought five men. All experienced hands.

Joe was at the helm in the wheelhouse and gave him an anxious nod as he walked by. He'd seen that look before. The salty air was thick with humidity. Not even diesel fumes off the back of the boat masked the impending storm. The wind had picked up. And a dark bank of clouds menaced the horizon to the northeast.

His friend had a right to be concerned.

Once they got by the breaker wall, and the boat hit cruising speed, the swells pounded the hull and sprayed a mist onto their faces and clothes. It cooled his skin. Kinkaid stood next to Alexa, widened his stance for balance, and held on. For a long moment, they both watched the darkening horizon in silence, each rapt in thought.

"That tropical storm has been upgraded to a hurricane, category one." She turned toward him, her blond hair edged in fiery red from the sun. A surge of dark clouds welled up behind her, a somber warning. "Garrett tells me the experts are predicting it'll get worse. We may have another Katrina on our hands, a category four with winds up to 150 miles an hour."

"You gonna pull the plug?" he asked, staring toward Cuba.

"What if I did?" She crooked a corner of her mouth. "You'd dump me off on Gilligan's Island and still head to Cuba, wouldn't you?"

"Yep."

"And you wouldn't respect me in the morning."

"Nope."

"Then it looks like we'll have a ringside seat to the first hurricane of the season," she told him. "You think they'll name it after me?"

"If they knew you, they would."

That made her smile. And inside, he did, too.

New York City
Afternoon

"There's something you'll want to see on Al Jazeera." Tanya Spencer leaned over Garrett's desk and worked the controls to pull up an enlarged Internet screen for the Arab news network and project it onto one of his TV monitors on the far wall.

He took off his suit jacket, pulled down his tie, and grabbed another cup of coffee while she worked behind his desk.

"Can I get you a cup?" he asked.

"No, thanks," she said. "I won't be here that long. And you'll be busy after you see this."

He watched her work, a somber expression on her face and efficiency to her hand movements. Tanya had worked with him for over ten years. An elegant black woman with a keen intellect, a quick wit, and timeless fashion sense. Her Southern drawl could ooze sex appeal or demand your attention with its commanding tone.

And Tanya knew how to wield both.

She brought up a column marked TODAY'S SCHEDULE on Aljazeera.net and scrolled down to what she wanted him to see. A dark screen filled the monitor with an arrow in the center. Once she clicked on it, the show would start.

A video.

In the wake of al-Qaeda evacuating Afghanistan, the movement and its various splinter groups had gone underground and launched greater efforts online. The Internet gave them a new lease on life. And they utilized a growing range of multimedia content, including video training clips, photo stills of victims about to be murdered, podcasts that featured testimonials from suicide bombers, and even movie shorts with dramatic music that romanticized life in the jihad and aided recruiting.

"I'll warn you now. This is disturbing," she said. Tanya gave him a look that got his attention.

"That's something, coming from you." He took a seat near the screen.

"No, really, Garrett. I mean it," she warned.

Without another word, Tanya dimmed the lights in his office and started the video. Shaky camera work and poor lighting made it hard to tell what was happening at first. Yet the recorded screams gripped him from the start. English-speaking men and women were yelling. Their voices were mixed with the angry demands of armed men in masks, speaking a dialect of Arabic. He didn't know enough about the language to understand it, but the AK-47s made their hostile intentions clear.

The video camera zoomed in tight on two women. Both looked terrified and were begging for their lives. The drama held him spellbound. And what happened next made him jump. A machete came from off screen. He would never forget the sound of the blade hacking into the woman's neck and hitting bone.

"Oh, my God." He'd never seen a beheading that close before. Blood sprayed the lens, and the video continued, but he'd seen enough. "That's it. Turn it off."

He'd spilled coffee on his dark slacks. The accident gave him an excuse to turn the lights on and compose himself as he wiped the stain with a napkin. In his lifetime, he'd seen enough death to lose sleep when certain memories surfaced. And he had certainly killed when it had become necessary, yet the level of brutality some men inflicted on others never ceased to amaze him.

"I tried to tell you," she said.

"I forgot. You're the queen of understatement." He set down his coffee and tossed the napkin onto his desk. "I'm assuming there's a reason you wanted to share this with me."

"My team analyzed the background and some of the faces. We did a facial recognition on a couple of them." She stepped behind his desk and removed the video from his monitor, replacing it with a news channel on mute.

"And?" he prompted.

"It's footage from Haiti," she replied. "A couple of faces matched the hostage list, including a nun who ran the missionary school. Sister Mary Katherine organized the fund-raiser that the terrorists attacked."

"She wasn't one of those women, was she?"

"No. And her body wasn't found at the medical-clinic siege either. We can only assume they still have her."

"Have you been able to trace the video upload?" He clenched his teeth and waited for her answer.

"Not yet. There's no guaranty we can trace it to a source, and they may be working through someone else. Chasing down all these angles will take time."

"Time we don't have. There's a hurricane bearing down on Alexa and her team." He slumped into his desk chair and swiveled as he thought. "I've been following the media on their Haiti coverage. The attack doesn't have the feel of al-Qaeda, yet that's what the talking heads are speculating. I think the authorities are being misled."

Tanya took a seat in front of him. "You have any ideas on who's behind this?"

"Not yet. But I think this video could lead us there. Kinkaid told Alexa that these bastards carried high-tech gear. GPS units, laptops, the works." He took a deep breath and stared across the room.

"They probably had cell phones that used the Internet, too. Those are not easy to trace," she added. "A person could have a New York City phone number, but calls made to that number would get routed through the Internet. Anyone with online access could use it. Chasing all this down takes time and manpower."

After a long moment, he brought up another idea. "What if I got you more help, someone who had mad skills when it comes to the computer? I have a feeling that discovering the source of this video will be vital. It might be worth a shot."

She raised an eyebrow. "Although I'm not sure I like bringing in someone from the outside, I have confidence in your judgment. You trust this person?"

"You know me. Trust doesn't come easy." He grinned. "Let's just say in the trust department, he'd come highly recommended. I'll arrange it."

"What's his name?" she asked. "You want me to do a background check on him?"

"Already done. I had the need to run one a few months ago." He gave her the details of where she could find the background check. "His past on paper is sketchy, but I've learned a great deal more about him since then. His name is Seth Harper, an acquaintance of Alexa Marlowe and Jessica Beckett. And as luck would have it, he's here in the city."

"How will you utilize his expertise? Outside our walls or do we bring him in? I'm sure you'll want to follow security protocols either way."

Implementing Sentinels' security measures would test Harper's sense of humor. A guy vacationing in New York would not expect to be hijacked into a covert operation with security measures, but that couldn't be avoided. He felt sure Seth would want to help Alexa.

"Certainly," he agreed. "I'll locate him and get back to you. Thanks, Tanya."

After she left his office, Garrett took the first step in locating Seth Harper in New York. And he had a pretty good idea where to start. Although Tanya and her team had the computer expertise to trace the origins of the video in time, the extra manpower wouldn't hurt. And recruiting Seth would give him a chance to see him in action.

A very convenient opportunity indeed.

New York City
Upper East Side

Jess knew enough about New York City to realize Alexa lived in one of the high-rent districts. The Upper East Side was a neighborhood in the borough of Manhattan between Central Park and the East River, sometimes called the *silk stocking* district because of the pricey real estate. Her new friend lived in a residential area off Lexington Avenue. Canopied storefronts were combined with small apartment buildings and elegant brownstone row houses.

Yep, this is so you, Alexa. Jess fought a smile as she took in the sights at a crosswalk, sipping coffee from a travel mug and finishing a warm bagel. She'd seen many new things since she moved east. And New York City had been a real departure from her Midwest roots.

Daytime hours in Manhattan were filled with the usual crush of humanity on the streets, locals and visitors from all over the world, everyone with places to go in a hurry. Jess had never gotten into the rat-race mentality. She walked at her own pace to take in the sights. And there was always plenty to see.

When New Yorkers ran out of acreage in Manhattan, they went vertical with the architecture. Over time, modern skyscrapers had been erected next to older structures, and she loved how the city had preserved a keen sense of history. Everywhere she turned, impressive historic buildings looked like a backdrop to a movie that could span decades. And another unusual nod to history was the odd wooden roof-mounted water towers on many of the city's buildings.

The sights, sounds, and diverse culture of the city infused her with energy as she carried her overnight bag slung over her shoulder and waited at the corner for traffic, the usual sea of yellow cabs, to come to a stop. When the light changed, she crossed the street with the rush of pedestrians and headed for the address Alexa had left on voice mail. Staying overnight would give her a chance to learn more about a part of the city she hadn't seen.

But she wondered why Alexa left town without much explanation. That only reminded her how little she knew of her friend and how private she was. Jess assumed the trip was work-related, something quick she was doing for Garrett Wheeler. That made her wonder all the more. Was this trip too important for a rookie to tag along?

And what was so vital that she left Seth in the lurch?

Seth. Thinking about him always brought a rush of emotions to the surface. And picturing him with Alexa made her stomach plummet, like free falling in a roller coaster. Since Alexa told her about him coming to town, Jess had had trouble sleeping. Even with New York City being so large, she *felt* him in her new world, a place she hadn't quite adopted. She missed Chicago and the roots she had there, but she had needed a break from the old and familiar.

Making the move to New York had been an escape. When she learned Seth was coming, his visit bridged the gap and reminded her how much she missed Sam Cooper and her old way of life—*and Seth.*

On a tree-lined sidewalk with a small picturesque park across the street, she spotted Alexa's apartment building up ahead. The architecture was classic, a timeless historical. The discreet four-story brownstone had a quaint exterior of lace-curtained bay windows with carved stone and wrought-iron accents. Molded newel posts with railings flanked stone steps that led to the main entrance, an elaborate wooden door with beveled-glass windows and a secured foyer. Very impressive.

Jess used the code Alexa had given her for the main security door and followed the signs inside to the manager to pick up the key left in her name. An old-fashioned elevator with a brass door was near the front entrance, but she opted for the marble stairs toward the back and headed for the third floor. Apartment 303 was toward the front of the building and probably over-looked the park across the street.

When she put the key in the lock, she heard water running. Noise traveled through ventilation and plumbing systems in older buildings, so she dismissed it. Yet when she got inside, she heard the water more distinctly. Someone was using Alexa's bathroom.

"What the hell . . . ?"

Jess dropped her bag near the door and pulled her .45-caliber Colt Python. She took a quick glimpse around the one bedroom. She smelled Alexa's perfume and noticed she had personal photos on the wall, confirmation she had the right place. Jess gripped her weapon, aimed it toward the bedroom, and followed the sound of the shower.

For an instant, she wondered if the noise was part of the maintenance Alexa had scheduled, but as she crept into the bedroom and looked through the half-closed bathroom door, she knew better. A naked man stood behind the opaque shower curtain, his back to her.

Nice ass, she thought. She nudged the door open,

slipped inside the bathroom, and raised both her weapon and her voice, "You better have a good reason for being here, Mr. Clean."

"Holy shit!" The guy jerked around and yanked back the curtain.

Seth Harper stood naked in front of her, his eyes wide and jaw dropping.

Wet. Sudsy.

And in all his glory.

CHAPTER 9

"Harper?" Jess lowered her weapon and her gaze. Self-control had never been her strong suit. "Nice to . . . see you."

"Damn it, Jessie. Turn around."

He grabbed the shower curtain and draped it over his hips. His shocked expression was priceless. But she wasn't about to tell him the see-through curtain gave her the equivalent of X-ray vision.

"Oh, right." She holstered her weapon and did as she was told—for once. Jess turned her back and knew he still wouldn't be happy. "Uh, Harper?"

"Yeah?"

She stared at his reflection.

"What is it they say about mirrors . . . objects may appear larger than they are?"

"Ah, Jessie. Cut me some slack, will you?" he pleaded. "Can a guy have some privacy?"

Seth was tall and muscular with a lean swimmer's body. An enticing sight. She'd always known he was beautiful. A guy with an angelic face and great eyes.

And now she got a peek at his other attributes and liked what she saw. Before he kissed her a few months back, she'd always thought of him as a kid. But that kiss had changed everything. And today, that boyish image had vaporized. Harper was a man with plenty to offer.

Steam fogged the mirror. She felt the heat—and hot water had nothing to do with it.

"Yeah, s-sure," she stammered. "I'll be out here. We probably . . . sh-should talk."

Jess rushed from the bath and closed the bedroom door behind her. She should have been mortified, yet when the reality of what happened hit home, she reacted. She burst out laughing. At first the whole incident struck her as funny, but before she saw Harper again, she had to get control. She was right. They had to talk.

What the hell would she say? That question had a sobering effect, and a bad case of nerves hit her.

In record time, Harper rushed to get dressed. She heard his loud rumblings behind the closed bedroom door while butterflies waged war in her belly. Amped on adrenaline, she paced the living room and wrung her hands as she thought about things to say. None of them worked. She felt unprepared to face him, and her time had run out.

When she turned, Seth was with her. His dark hair was damp, and he smelled like herbal soap and shampoo. He wore jeans and a pale blue Oxford shirt. His feet were bare.

And he looked . . . *amazing.*

"Hey, Jessie. How are you?" He nudged his head, real casual.

He acted as if nothing had happened. She took a deep breath. A better woman would have let him salvage his dignity, but *that* woman wasn't in the room.

"For cryin' out loud, Harper. I just saw you naked," she stopped herself. And after a long awkward moment, she nodded. "I'm good. Thanks for asking."

Seth blushed, and a lazy smile spread across his handsome face. Jess memorized every nuance of that expression. She wanted to remember it always.

"That wasn't my best moment in there." He shrugged and had trouble meeting her gaze.

"Not from where I was standing." She grinned.

"You're not gonna let this go, are you?"

"Would you?"

Harper finally gave in and chuckled. The sound of his laughter and the blush on his cheeks warmed her heart. It reminded her how much she missed him. And being alone with him, after going months without seeing him, had an overwhelming intimacy that was new and different. She should have felt self-conscious after what had happened, but she didn't.

"Seth, I . . ." Jess had no idea where to begin. She took a tentative step forward. And he did the same. Neither of them could look away.

"I thought you and Alexa . . ." She struggled with what to say next. " . . . I thought you guys had canceled your plans for this weekend. Why are you staying here?"

"She got called out on assignment. And she talked

me into staying at her place. So I canceled the hotel I booked. Why are you here?"

Alexa had set her up. And on purpose. *Maintenance, my ass.*

"A hotel?" She covered up her elation with a grimace. "You had a hotel room? That's . . . great."

"Not at four hundred bucks a night," he protested. "New York is expensive, Jessie."

"Oh, Seth, I know. I just thought you two were . . ." She couldn't admit that she'd assumed they were sleeping together. Saying it aloud made her feel foolish. And worse, it revealed too much about feelings she didn't understand.

"That we were what?" he asked.

She heard the hope in his voice as he closed the gap between them. And she found that she was holding her breath.

Images of him kissing Alexa still plagued her. *Strike one.* And normally, the cancellation of a hotel room would get no reaction from her, but *this* cancellation was significant. It meant her assumption about their physical relationship was off base, which made her strangely happy. *Strike two.* And the real kick in the teeth stood out more than the rest. Seeing Harper naked only made her want more. *A big strike three.* She had struck out on denials about her feelings for Harper, and the truth was staring her in the face with big soulful brown eyes.

Yet having feelings and acting on them were two different things. And years of abuse as a child left her feeling like she didn't deserve love or happiness—a heavy load of baggage to carry, much less overcome. She had ended her budding relationship with Payton Archer almost a year ago, using the distance between them as the reason. Alaska and Chicago were worlds away.

Now she had thoughts of doing the same with Seth after only one kiss. He'd been the reason she had left Chicago practically overnight to put distance between them. The patterns in her life were self-destructive. And even though she saw them coming like a train wreck, she felt powerless to stop history from repeating.

"Seth, I wish . . ." She stared into his eyes and took a deep breath until the ring of her cell phone made her jump. *Not cool.* She would have ignored it, but the sound had broken the mood.

"I'm sorry." Jess grabbed her phone and glanced down at the display. She recognized a strange series of numbers, even though there was no caller name. "I have to take this."

She hit TALK, and said, "Beckett."

"Jessie? This is Garrett Wheeler. I need to ask you a favor. I'm trying to locate your friend Seth Harper. Do you know where I can reach him?"

Jess looked up into Seth's eyes before she turned her back and grimaced, holding the cell phone to her ear in silence. She felt more than a little protective of Seth, especially with someone as powerful and crafty as Garrett Wheeler trying to locate him. It was one thing to work for the man—having a clever resourceful boss had its upside for her.

With Garrett having an interest in Harper, she pictured Hannibal Lecter asking if Seth was available for dinner. Whatever her new boss had in mind, he'd have to go through her first.

"That depends. What's this about, Garrett?"

As LaClaire maneuvered the boat closer to shore, Alexa scanned the beach and the wooded cliffs with her long-range binoculars. She had her gear on deck at her feet. And in the background, over the rumble of the boat engine, she heard her men preparing to disembark.

The beach was pristine. No footprints marred the surface of the sand. And there was no sign of civilization. On the one hand, she'd found a drop zone no one had traveled in a while, but on the flip side, this wasn't the spot the terrorists had landed with their hostages. They'd have to find their trail and track them another way.

The winds had picked up, and the sun had lost its battle with a bank of ominous dark clouds. Every swaying tree caught her attention as she looked for signs of danger. The impending storm had triggered her uneasiness and made it worse.

"Joe's ready to drop us off." Kinkaid's low voice interrupted her surveillance. She kept the binoculars working the shoreline and listened to the rest of what he had to say, "He'll take the raft to shore and stick close until we need him for our ride out."

"Sounds good. Let's hit it." She picked up her gear and turned to see Joe LaClaire at her back. He nodded, clearly wanting to have a private word with his boss, Kinkaid. She'd noticed the unspoken bond between the two men. But there was something else at play. LaClaire looked worried, and not only about the mission.

She met up with her team at the raft and took one last look over her shoulder, watching the two men at the bow of the boat. If Jackson Kinkaid hadn't been on the level with this hostage rescue, the lives of her team would be at risk. Crazed terrorists, one hurricane, and now Kinkaid had added a wrinkle that upped the ante.

You better not be keeping secrets, Jackson. She glared at Kinkaid one final time before she joined her men.

Joe pulled him aside. "I don't like this. Your skin is flushed. I bet that fever is back," Joe protested in a low voice thick with concern. "If you can't make it, contact me, and I'll pick you up. Let Alexa's people handle it. This ain't worth dyin' over—"

"Then what *is* worth dying for, Joe?" he interrupted. "Look, I don't have a death wish—"

"You could've fooled me," his friend interrupted.

"—but I can't let Kate down." Kinkaid kept his voice low, out of earshot of Alexa and her team, but hiding his anger was a different story. He glared at a friend he thought he knew as if seeing him for the first time.

"Who's this Kate person to you anyway?" Joe didn't wait for him to respond. "You and me, we got a good thing going. If you get killed doing this—"

"Then I'll be dead. And money won't buy jack shit in hell."

His friend stopped. *A wise move.* Their way of making money had been Kinkaid's idea. Stealing money from drug cartels and other criminals had become his private war. He hit them where it hurt most, and he knew they wouldn't complain to the law—the perfect crime if he could get away with the heist—and he didn't take orders from the Sentinels or anyone else. But when the scores got bigger, he'd needed a smart partner, one who could keep his mouth shut and hold his greed in check.

He had cut Joe in after the man had proven himself. And the money got even better. In no time, LaClaire saw how things would work. Their hits had run real smooth and regular as clockwork. They were a team.

But money made people crazier, even someone as solid as Joe.

Most days, LaClaire tolerated his penchant to play a modern-day Robin Hood because there was always more money coming in. He kept the greenbacks rolling, and Joe held up his end of their bargain. They were partners, even though LaClaire called him boss. Hell, he trusted the guy as much as he could trust anyone.

And until this moment, he thought his faith had been justified.

"Don't push me into making a choice between you and this rescue mission, Joe." Although Kinkaid meant what he said, the words came out harsher than he'd intended. He gripped the man's shoulder. "Look, I'll be okay. I have to do this."

Joe nodded. Stress still edged his face as he forced a smile. "After this, you and me are gonna take time off. We'll kick back on a real beach, maybe one of them topless ones. Somewhere with no one shooting at us."

Kinkaid crooked his lip into a smile. Joe was blowing smoke. They'd never taken time off together. When they needed a break, they went their separate ways. And his friend usually went on the prowl for love.

"You and me on vacation?" Kinkaid shook his head and grinned. "Face it, Joe. Male bonding is highly overrated."

His friend chuckled and shrugged. "You got me there. When I get time off, I'm usually looking for love in all the wrong places."

"Yeah, and your idea of romance usually means money changes hands and liquor is involved. But hey, nice try."

"Just don't get killed this trip . . . or I'm gonna be pissed."

"For your sake, I'll give it a shot." Kinkaid shifted his gaze toward Alexa. "I gotta go. Never keep an armed woman waiting."

Southeast Cuba
Sierra Maestra Mountain Range
Late afternoon

Alexa gave a hand signal for her team to take a break. Her GPS readings were off. Given the dense jungle cover, that was to be expected. She'd been using her compass and the map she'd studied last night. They were crossing the Sierra Maestra, a mountain range that ran westward across Guantanamo Province in southeast Cuba. The range rose abruptly from the coast where they'd put to shore, and the elevations were a secluded haven for terrorist training camps.

They'd already encountered one camp after they'd

heard the gunfire of training exercises. They had divided into teams and moved in closer to investigate until they'd seen enough and made the call to move on. It had taken time to rule them out as sympathizers aligned with the hostage takers—time they didn't have.

After they resumed the climb, they'd seen shanties with stone walls and rusted metal roofs dappling the hillsides. They weren't alone and would have to skirt the locals. In hostile territory, they'd have to remain alert.

She shrugged out of her pack and set it down before she sucked water off a tube from her hydration pack. Alexa held it in her mouth to quench her thirst and conserve her supply. Sweat was rolling off her body, and her hair and clothes were drenched. She had to keep hydrated to avoid muscle cramps or worse.

She crouched and peered through a break in the dense vegetation to catch a sporadic breeze. Below her position she saw clouds casting long shadowy fingers onto lush valleys as the sun flickered a sliver of light through the darkening clouds. The horizon was thick with haze, and the air smelled of humidity. The weight of the muggy air was oppressive. Gray tufts clung to the ridges ahead and obscured the view. They had more climbing to do before they'd reach a good staging area.

Alexa hoped they'd find something before the rain hit. Any rain would wash footprints away and force them to use other signs to find a trail to follow.

She had two men scouting ahead, looking for tracks and signs of movement. They'd report back soon. And she had two others standing guard while the rest of her team took a breather. Alexa stood and stretched before she rested against a boulder near the trail to drink more water.

The heat closed in. *And the damned bugs.*

Every member of her team had humped in a load and carried water, supplies, and munitions on their backs. She had done her part. And in the steamy jungle, the burden had taken its toll. They had stayed off the worn trails, fearing they might be booby-trapped, and trekked the steep climb running parallel to the narrow path. The going was slow. They'd covered only two klicks an hour. Fighting the underbrush had been tough. Lactic acid had built up in her muscles and made her legs burn, even as she rested. The mountainous terrain and the heat would normally be her first concern for the team, but the weather had her worried too.

And so did Kinkaid.

He looked grateful for the break. Keeping to himself, he pulled away from the others to down what looked like aspirin when he thought she wasn't watching. His skin looked pale and clammy—and not from the muggy heat. His normally alert eyes were sluggish and hard to read. Something was definitely wrong even though he was holding up his end of the bargain.

Carrying her Colt M4 Carbine assault rifle over her shoulder, she stood and walked to where he lay sprawled on a small rise with his back against a tree.

"You mind company?" she whispered.

He gestured an invitation with a hand and barely looked up.

"If we stick to high ground," she said as she retrieved insect repellent from her belt pack, "we get better reception for our GPS units and SAT phone. This dense canopy can mess up our readings."

While she talked, she sprayed bug juice on her clothes and skin.

"Yeah, that's good," he whispered with eyes closed. "Just don't get us caught on a ridge with our asses showing. We'd make easy sniper targets."

"How are you holding up?" she asked.

"I took a tumble off a ridge the other night. It's nothing. I'm good."

"Ah, thanks. That explains everything." She leaned her head back against the tree she shared with him and closed her eyes, her assault rifle across her belly. "And you're a lousy liar, Kinkaid."

Alexa waited for his sarcasm. When she got nothing except for a cloud of insects that buzzed her face, she settled back and dialed into her surroundings. Eerie sounds echoed through the jungle, the life-and-death struggle for survival. The ground smelled of decay, wet wood, and damp rich earth, a primeval odor that was all too familiar. And in the distance she heard the birds in the trees and the flutter of wings as they flew. Without opening her eyes, she pictured them from her memory and their sounds—brightly colored parrots, finches, and hummingbirds that hung motionless in the air.

When she slowed her heartbeat to doze in the heat, she heard Kinkaid's breathing. His easy rhythm signaled he'd fallen asleep. She imagined the two of them in another time and place on a lazy Sunday morning sleeping in. And it wasn't difficult to picture his bare tanned skin under white linens with those hypnotic green eyes luring her to bed.

She pictured sweat beading on skin, hands clutched together in a fevered pitch, and the grinding of two bodies in the throes of orgasm. Her breathing and heart rate escalated as she imagined what he would feel like inside her. With eyes closed, she fantasized about making love to Jackson Kinkaid on a warm Sunday afternoon when all they had was time. She fought the urge to smile and took a deep breath.

She'd had such thoughts before about him, and she understood physical need and the urgency of sexual attraction. But making a commitment to one lover—would she ever settle for a life like that?

And more to the point, would she ever want to?

"Marlowe."

She heard a male voice whispering near her. Hank Lewis wanted her attention.

"Yeah, Hank." When she opened her eyes, she saw the short muscular man with his burr cut crouched near her. "What is it?"

"Booker and Rodriguez are back," he told her.

Manny Rodriguez and Adam Booker had scouted ahead for the team. While one tracked and focused on the trail, the other flanked his position to keep watch. They rotated their assignments to keep their eyesight fresh.

"And?" she asked.

"Manny picked up a trail." Lewis smiled. "The tracks fit our head count."

She returned a grin and punched Kinkaid in the arm. "Wake up, sleeping beauty. Time to work."

If Kinkaid had seen distinctive footprints of the hostages and their terrorist captors, his memory would be put to the test. With any luck, the tracks her scouts had found would be the bastards who killed and abducted innocent civilians. Once they had a trail to follow, the chase would be on.

And when the team caught up with the men, they'd carry out their brand of justice.

The zing of a machete echoed past them and down into the valley below as the lead man cleared a path where the overgrown vines were too dense. Sister Kate and the other hostages had been climbing a tapering mountain trail since dawn. And although the exertion and the altitude made it hard for her to breathe, she knew better than to complain. She still had no idea where they were or where the men were taking them. They'd been ordered to keep their heads down and hadn't seen anyone else since they'd landed.

She caught glimpses of darkening clouds and noticed that the overcast sky had the smell of rain. And the wind had picked up. She felt the strong breeze most on the ridges they had crossed. And in the distance, she had seen the whitecaps. The ocean churned and had become choppy. A storm was coming.

By dusk, they made camp early, and bowls of food were handed out. At the bottom of rusted metal containers was a brown paste that they had to eat with their fingers. It smelled slightly rancid, but Kate forced herself to eat. The children did the same. And not one complained.

George had gotten worse. And no one had given him any food or water.

When she received her rations, she took some to him. The man lay sprawled on the ground under a stand of trees. His suit looked disheveled and filthy and was stained with his blood. Kate looked over her shoulder to make sure none of her captors were watching before she knelt by him.

"Here . . . you need this more than I do," she whispered.

She raised George's head to give him her share of water. The man looked into her eyes with a mix of gratitude and fear as he choked down the liquid. When she offered him food, he refused. His face had taken on a sickly gray pallor with spots of color where his skin was flushed with heat. A raging fever had stricken the poor man.

"I'll bring more when I can," she promised. "Now, let me have a look at this."

She peeked under the dressing pressed to his shoulder and decided nothing could be done. Parts of the makeshift bandage was stuck to the wound, and the bullet hole was still bleeding, a slow and steady ooze. She'd tried to keep the wound clean, but she didn't have fresh bandages, and infection had set in. The flesh around the bullet hole was red and swollen and hot to the touch. And foul-looking pus aggravated the injury and gave off a nasty odor.

Since there was no exit wound, she believed the

bullet was still inside. George needed a doctor. She knew it, and by the look in his eyes, he did, too.

"Thank you . . . S-Sister."

She dabbed the sweat from his forehead with a dirty cloth and felt the heat radiating off his skin. Raindrops pattered the leaves above George and fell onto his face. He was slow to blink them away. The man was getting weaker.

"Your fever is worse." She clutched his hand and felt him squeeze her fingers. "I wish there was more I could do."

"There is, Sister. My son." He cleared his throat and choked. His lungs wheezed with the effort. "If you make it home, please tell my son . . . that our last thoughts were of him. And that we will always love him." He tried to smile and didn't have the energy. "He got married last year . . . and they're expecting a baby. Our f-first grandchild."

He stumbled over the word "first," and she knew he was thinking of his dead wife. She wanted to comfort the man and tell him they'd all make it home again, but she knew that wouldn't be true. If George didn't get medical care soon, he'd be dead before help could arrive.

"Tell me about your son." She forced a smile and stroked his brow. "Where does he live?"

She listened to what George told her. He grew very still to focus on what he said. And for a brief instant, the pain in his eyes faded as the rain slid down his cheek and drained into his tears.

She committed every word to memory. If she lived

through this nightmare, she wanted to tell a son how much his father loved him. But before George finished, Kate felt a harsh jab at her back. When she turned, a young man holding a rifle aimed it at her and yelled words she didn't understand. He nudged his head, and she shifted her gaze where he pointed.

The terrorist leader stood in the clearing near the fire. The sight of him knotted her stomach.

"I'll be back . . . when I can," she muttered to George and squeezed his hand. "You rest now."

She glanced toward the children and they grimaced as they huddled in the rain. Being the oldest, Joselyne clung to the others. The girl's eyes welled with glistening tears, but she resisted the urge to cry out. Sister Kate forced a smile and nodded her reassurance, then stood and went with the armed young man.

Standing in front of the man in charge, she kept her head down and avoided looking into his fierce eyes until his silence forced her to look up. He stared down at her in disgust as if she were vile. Of late, every encounter between them had become a competition for him to win, as if he had something to prove to her. This she did not understand, not when he was clearly in charge.

"It is your turn to plead for your miserable existence." The leader raised his chin and looked down his nose at her. "And you will speak for the children. Their lives depend on you."

"How?" she asked.

"You will use my phone . . . and contact Jackson Kinkaid. He is a wealthy American businessman, and you are an American nun. He would pay for you, yes?"

The man looked at her with a smug expression, as if he had just revealed a secret of hers.

"Jackson Kinkaid?" Her eyes grew wide.

She counted Kinkaid as a friend, but not in the conventional sense. He was someone she had respected from the first time they met. And she understood what had mattered most to him and comforted him when he needed it. Beyond that, she never pried into his secrets. She accepted him the way he was, and he had done the same for her. Few would understand their bond—least of all the angry man standing in front of her now.

"I don't have a phone number for Mr. Kinkaid. I only have his mailing address. That's all."

"You are lying." The man yanked her by the throat and pulled her toward him. Her feet dangled under her, barely touching the ground. She felt the blood rush to her face.

"Please . . . I've told you all I know," she cried.

Kate heard the children screaming behind her. When she looked over her shoulder to find them, the man tore the veil from her head and threw it to the ground. He stepped on it and ground it into the dirt with the heel of his boot. And with his hand, he yanked her head back. He gripped her hair until her scalp burned.

"You will do this thing. Now!" he yelled, and fixed his eyes on her. His spittle mixed with the raindrops that struck her face and she winced.

"I can't. I've told you." She had no idea how much he understood, and she tried to explain. "The charitable foundation he set up is private. As far as I know, they don't advertise their good works. I only have his mailing address, I swear it."

"He gave money to the school." He glared at her. "And that party was in his honor. This I know from the news. And others here said he was at Dumont Hall and that you know him well."

"He's a contributor to the school, yes. And yes, I know him. But only as a patron to the academy." Most of what she'd said was the truth and not what he wanted to hear.

He stared at her and tightened his grip as the rain got worse. The pain made her wince, and she held her breath. He looked as if he were making up his mind about what to do next. Given the anger seething in his eyes, she wouldn't like the outcome.

"If you cannot reach him, then you are of no use to me . . . and neither are those children." He pulled a machete from his belt and yelled an order for the young man with the video camera to follow him.

The man dragged her by the hair into the jungle. She tried to keep up, but he moved too fast. She fell in the slick mud, and he didn't stop. Branches tore her tunic and exposed her legs to cuts. And she heard the roots of her hair pop as they were yanked from her head. He hauled her away from the others. And some of his men followed, cheering and hoisting weapons above their heads in victory.

And when they got to a small clearing, the man beat her with his fists. She crumpled to the muddy ground and curled into a ball, protecting herself from his kicks. It all happened too fast—the blur of images and her sudden rush of terror. She couldn't breathe.

Oh please, dear God. Not like this.

Grimacing in pain, she was hauled to her knees, yanked by her hair again. And the man with the video camera came forward and shoved through the bodies standing before her.

Her death would become a mockery recorded for the amusement of these cruel men. They knew nothing of her life, nor did they care. And all her sacrifices in service to God meant nothing. *Nothing!* Her passing would serve no vital purpose in this forsaken corner of the world.

Inside, she wanted to scream, until she heard the cries of the children in the distance. Their torment overshadowed any agony she felt for her own fate. In truth, she had let them down.

Now they'd have no one to look out for them.

CHAPTER 10

The sun glowed like a dying ember on the horizon, despite being smothered by a thick ceiling of clouds. And the rain had intensified. Although large drops pelted the trees, branches filtered the deluge and shielded them from the blowing downpour. The steamy heat had subsided, but the high winds and lightning posed a new threat. Alexa knew her team needed shelter to weather the worsening storm. And she'd seen a shallow stone overhang that might give them enough protection. They'd have to backtrack to make it.

Kinkaid wouldn't be happy. The man had followed the tracks Manny found with a frightening obsession. To convince him to retrace his steps wouldn't be easy, but she had to try.

"We can't stay out here," she cried, hoping Kinkaid heard her through the rain. But if he had, he ignored her. She yelled again, "We gotta find shelter."

Kinkaid had pushed ahead looking for the footprints he'd recognized. Now she couldn't stop him. It was getting darker, and the rain had obliterated the tracks. Any footprints had filled with rain and were submerged in puddles of mud. And their own tracks would trample what little remained. Kinkaid kept his head down and searched like a madman for signs that he was still on the right trail. And in weather like this, he could make a mistake and put them off the right path.

"We can make camp near here," she argued. "We'll pick it up in the morning, when we can see better."

"But the rain . . ." he yelled over his shoulder. "It's wiping out the tracks. If we wait until morning, the trail will be gone."

"My team is good," she countered. "We'll track other signs, Jackson."

He ignored her and staggered into the wind, holding up an arm to fend off the blowing branches. Alexa turned to see her men close behind. They were doing their best, but she knew what they were thinking. Kinkaid had lost his objectivity. She had to make the decision and do what was right for all of them, even if it turned him against her.

"You might be leading us the wrong way. And that could take us twice as much time to find their trail again." She stopped fighting the wind and stood her ground. "I'm ordering you to stop."

He shook his head. And when he stumbled and slowed down, she stepped into his path.

"Don't make me the bad guy." Alexa lowered her voice so only he would hear. She placed both hands on his chest, but that still didn't stop him. When he pushed by her, she yelled, "You know I'm right. What are you doing?"

Although Kinkaid finally stopped fighting, he didn't return her stare. He raised his face into the darkening skies and the punishing rain, his broad shoulders slumped in defeat. His hair and clothes were drenched, like hers, except he looked exhausted and beaten.

Something was terribly wrong.

"Talk to me, Jackson," she pleaded. "What's going on?"

She wanted to ask him about Kate, but was afraid what his reaction might be. The man didn't look stable. And when she finally got his marginal attention, he lowered his head and looked past her. He zoned out with a half-lidded gaze as if he'd forgotten where he was. His skin was pale, and he rocked on his heels, unsteady.

"Jackson?" She grimaced. "You're scaring me. And that's not easy to do."

It was the last thing she said before his eyes rolled into his head. His body fell hard to the ground in a backwash of mud.

Jackson Kinkaid had passed out at her feet.

New York City
Sentinels Headquarters

"I haven't been able to get through to Alexa." In his office, Garrett paced the floor in front of his wall of monitors. Even with all the technology available to him, nothing worked. "The edge of the hurricane has made landfall. The storm's interfering with communications."

"That's understandable. When did you last talk to her?" Tanya Spencer asked as she took a seat on the sofa.

"Two hours ago. I gave her an update on the storm and warned her to take shelter, but you know Alexa." He tried to smile and couldn't.

"What path are they projecting for the hurricane?" Tanya Spencer asked him. "Are Alexa and her team in its path?"

He stopped and shifted his gaze toward the weather channel. A swirling mass of radar projected hurricane Alex would hit Cuba. And even though there was irony in the fact that the storm had been named for a man—a name so similar to Alexa's—Garrett had a sinking feeling that this storm had her name written all over it.

"Well, the southeast part of the island isn't directly in the path, but it'll be close enough not to matter." He unbuttoned his shirt collar, yanked at his tie, and rolled up his sleeves. "The only saving grace is that she'll avoid the flooding if she stays in the mountains. She might find enough shelter there."

Wishful thinking was not his forte. He sucked at it.

"You said you wanted to talk about the terrorist cell who claimed responsibility a few hours ago," she reminded him.

He knew Tanya well enough to see she'd changed topics to get his mind off Alexa. And worrying about the weather did them no good.

"The group who claimed the kidnappings on the Internet was an outfit called the National Liberation Army," he told her. "They were originally a Marxist insurgent group based out of Colombia. They've been in existence since the mid-sixties, inspired by Castro and Che Guevara. They have terrorist cells training in Cuba."

"Why would such a group commit an act of terrorism in an impoverished country like Haiti, then take the hostages back to Cuba? For that matter, why take hostages from there at all?" she asked. "You'd think they would launch an attack where they could abduct vacationing tourists, people with money."

"Your instincts would be dead-on, but I think this was a training exercise. Whoever they are, I think they're preparing for something bigger . . . on turf where they feel comfortable." He shook his head and slumped in a chair across from her. "And as to why they took the hostages to Castro country, Cuba provides safe haven, medical care, and support for this group. And it's believed they have ties to Venezuelan President Hugo Chavez. Venezuela's involvement broadens their playing field. I think something else is going on here."

"You have a theory?" She narrowed her eyes.

"The National Liberation Army conducts hundreds of kidnappings for ransom in a year, and they generally target the employees of large foreign corporations. This broader focus doesn't fit the MO of the terrorist cell Alexa is tracking. The group claiming responsibility may be creating a smoke screen to cover up another agenda, or they're lying about who they are to throw off authorities." He leaned forward and rested his palms on his knees. "The tactics feel like Islamic Jihad, maybe a group out of Afghanistan in training for something bigger. Or maybe their goal is to aggravate an already strained situation between the U.S. and Cuba or Venezuela. America doesn't need another global distraction, not with a faltering domestic economy."

"Has this group asked for ransom money?" she asked. Before he answered her question, she posed another idea. "Maybe it's not about money. They've already posted one gruesome video that's getting attention. Perhaps they're after headlines in a global arena. These hostages could be nothing more than collateral damage to the cause."

He'd already leapt to the same conclusion until wishful thinking intervened.

"There have been no demands for money, but that might be due to the weather," he said. "They have no way to communicate until the hurricane passes."

The hopelessness of the hostage situation made him understand why Kinkaid had been so relentless, especially if there were innocent children involved, as the Haitian police had reported. And if his theory about this being a training exercise for a larger operation was right, Kinkaid's emergency call might thwart a more dangerous scheme geared for a higher body count. Gut instinct told him more was at stake for the terrorists than the lives of the hostages or any paltry ransom money.

"We need to track these bastards by other means. If we can find a way to trace their last transmission, that might provide us a clue. We could know what to look for when they post another video."

"What makes you think they'll post again?"

"They took a video cam with them for a reason. Groups like this crave attention." He nodded. "They'll post again. Each upload is a fucking victory lap."

His mind raced, formulating a plan and the logistics he'd need to pull it off. He got to his feet and went to his desk to jot down his thoughts.

"When we get through this storm, Alexa will need our help," he said, keeping his attention on the notepad as he continued, "If we know how to track these guys, we can give her an edge and have a backup team airborne to support her on the ground."

When his phone rang, Tanya stood and prepared to give him privacy. He glanced at the display and recognized the extension for security.

"I've got to take this, but stick around." He picked up his phone. "Wheeler."

A man from security informed him that his car service had arrived in the secured parking garage. His visitor was in custody and still wearing a blindfold. Jessica Beckett would be escorting the young man to his office.

"Can I send him up, sir?" the guard asked.

"Yes, immediately. And thanks." He hung up the phone and looked at Tanya. "Our visitor has arrived. Get your team ready. I want him to hit the ground running. Use your judgment and give him what he needs. He'll be under your supervision."

"Works for me." She left his office and shut the door behind her.

And for the first time today, Garrett smiled and meant it. "Great timing, Seth Harper."

* * *

"Bet this stop isn't in any brochure," Harper said. When Jess didn't answer, he yanked her chain again. "Not exactly what I had in mind when I came to New York. Sightseeing works best when you can actually . . . see, Jessie."

Seth walked slowly down a corridor with a blindfold covering half his face. He carried an overnight bag on his shoulder at Garrett's suggestion. Seth would be the guest of the Sentinels.

"Maybe we can put this blindfold to good use later, just you and me," he added. She heard the smile in his voice and pictured him with a devilish twinkle in his eye. "After all, I let you see me naked. The least you could do is return the favor."

"Thanks for the privilege, Harper. Next time you should charge admission."

"Next time?"

Jess held his hand and heaved a sigh with an eye roll she knew he couldn't appreciate. They were near Garrett Wheeler's office—an intimidating place she'd only been to once. Whatever was happening with Alexa, it had to be important for Garrett to bring Seth into their operation. She joked for Harper's sake, but she was worried for Alexa.

Seth let her lead him to the closed office door. He was having fun with all the security protocol. She only hoped he'd still have a sense of humor when this was all over.

Garrett had explained enough for her to appreciate that Alexa needed Seth's computer expertise, and time was apparently critical. When she presented the situation to Harper, he agreed to help without hesitation. She expected nothing less from a guy she'd grown to respect—personally and professionally—if computer hacking and online surveillance that bordered on criminal activity could be construed as "professional." The guy bent the ethics rules when it came to tracking criminal activity on the computer.

That could earn him a definite plus on his résumé— *or five to ten in prison.*

Jess let go of Seth's hand to knock on Garrett's door. She heard a man's voice inside, giving her permission to enter. When she led Harper in, Garrett wasn't alone. He had Tanya Spencer with him, his senior analyst and advisor.

Before introductions were made, Garrett exchanged looks with his analyst, and Tanya shrugged.

"Why is he still blindfolded?" her boss asked. "Once he was secured in the building, I thought you knew he could ditch the headgear."

All eyes were on her. Jess pursed her lips and avoided their questioning stares until Harper figured it out.

"Very funny, Jessie." He yanked down the blindfold and left it dangling around his neck. "You'd be a riot at a firing squad."

In truth, it wasn't a prank. She liked having Harper reliant on her for a change. And having a semi-legitimate excuse to hold his hand was an added bonus. The first time she put her hand in his, a rush of intimacy swept through her. She loved the warmth of his skin next to hers even though it made letting go harder to do.

Her new boss made the introductions and took great pleasure in shaking Harper's hand. Jess noticed Garrett's eye contact as he fixed on Seth with all the enthusiasm of a scientist testing a new lab rat. After everyone made nice, they sat and the briefing got under way.

Jess sensed that Garrett left key elements out of his update. He only named Alexa so Harper would understand why he had been asked to get involved. And he focused on details Seth would know from the news. Even Jess had heard about the incident in Haiti on CNN. She had no idea Alexa had anything to do with the aftermath of those tragic abductions. And with the added complication of the hurricane bearing down on Cuba, Jess understood why Garrett needed the extra help. Having Seth in New York had been a stroke of good fortune.

But Harper had his own thoughts on the subject.

"Yeah, I want to help Alexa, but why me?" Seth asked. "You've got all the spy toys and probably an army of computer wizards to work this. Why all the cloak-and-dagger to bring me in?"

Seth made his intentions known. He'd help for the sake of a friend, but he wanted Garrett to give him something, like a little more honesty.

"Bottom line, it takes time to hunt down the source of a transmission like this. And with lives at stake and the nasty weather, time is not on our side," Garrett told him. "My people could use the extra help. Do you have any idea how we can trace the source of this video?"

Seth furrowed his brow to form that endearing crease

she'd seen many times before. And in typical Harper fashion, he answered without hesitation, making the complicated appear simple.

"Yeah, I think I do. But you have to understand that terrorists use the Internet to avoid detection . . . or so I've heard," Seth began. "And there's a reason for that. Chasing online accounts can be next to impossible if the Internet service provider is international. Some countries aren't into holding hands, singing 'Kumbaya,' and doling out goodwill to all mankind. And if the terrorists are savvy, they buy phone service using Internet numbers that can be paid by wire transfer from someone using fake ID. So that becomes a dead end fast. They could also transmit through a handler who acts like a middleman, and we'd be chasing our tails."

Harper had Tanya's attention. The woman fixed her gaze on him and didn't waver. "So what do you propose?" she asked.

"I say we forget about wasting time with tracking down ISP addresses and dead-end phone numbers. Let's cut to the chase and trace high-density bandwidths. That video transmission upload takes some juice and the high-density bandwidth will stand out like a flare in cyberspace in that part of the world."

Garrett cocked his head and leaned closer to Harper. "And you can do this?"

"Well, yeah. Sure." He shrugged, as if the man had asked him if he knew how to ride a bike. "With a process of elimination, we can find the source of that transmission. And your satellite capability will allow us to triangulate the signal and track them. Once we pinpoint their position, we'll know what to look for when they transmit again."

"That just might work," Tanya agreed.

Garrett grinned. "Exactly what I wanted to hear. You've been reading my mail, Seth."

"No, but give me a little time, and I might." Harper nodded with a deadpan expression.

"He's only joking, Garrett." Jess forced a laugh and nudged Harper in the ribs.

"I've got a workstation set up for you, Seth. Whatever you need, you come to me," Tanya said.

"You'll report to Tanya," Garrett told him. "I'm sorry about interrupting your vacation. I'll make it up to you. I promise."

"No need, sir. Helping Alexa is good enough for me." Seth stood and shook Garrett's hand. Jess suspected Garrett was still sizing him up, but by the look on his face, she could tell he liked what he'd seen so far.

While Tanya cornered Harper, and they launched into geek speak about what he'd need, Jess took the opportunity to have a little one-on-one with Garrett.

"What do you need me to do?" she asked him. "I've got to do something."

"Stick with Harper. If he can pinpoint these bastards, that'll be crucial intel. And once I get a plan and clearer weather, you'll get your first assignment. Count on it."

She smiled. "Thanks, Garrett."

When another question lurked in her mind, she lowered her voice so Harper wouldn't hear. "How's Alexa . . . I mean, really?"

Up close, she saw the dark circles under Garrett's eyes, and that told her all she needed to know about how much sleep he'd gotten since Alexa left on assignment. And he didn't even bother to hide his concern.

Garrett sighed. "I wish I knew."

Southeast Cuba
Sierra Maestra Mountain Range

In a small clearing, Sister Kate wobbled on her knees, barely able to stay upright. She'd been beaten and shoved to the ground by the cruel man who held her by the hair and wielded a machete. He ordered his man with the video cam to record what he was about to do. She didn't have to understand his language to know what would come next.

Tears streamed down Kate's face. And she tasted blood from a cut lip and felt the heat from her swollen cheek.

When the camera lights came on, the glow cast eerie shadows onto the thrashing tree branches. And the blowing rain drenched her face and tunic. Armed men gathered around—a threatening horde backlit by the light—mocking her in a language she was thankful she didn't understand. They took turns spitting at her. And after her hands were tied behind her back, one young man earned cheers when he grabbed her breasts and squeezed. She winced with the pain.

But she kept her eyes on the camera.

Once the red light came on, she knew precious seconds would be all she'd have left. Time slowed to a painstaking crawl. She heard the beat of her heart, a relentless thud in her ears. The intensifying sound dulled the noise of the agitated men and muffled their insults. And when she felt the man yank her hair, she braced herself. He shifted his weight and tightened his grip.

That was when the red light flicked on.

And she shut her eyes.

CHAPTER 11

Southeast Cuba
Sierra Maestra Mountain Range

Alexa and her team searched for shelter with mounting desperation. The howling storm showed no signs of stopping and the winds were strong enough to knock a man off his feet. Carrying an unconscious Kinkaid made the climb exhausting and slow.

Steep ground had turned into rivers of mud and debris, making each step slick and treacherous. Her boots were caked in soppy clay that made them heavy. And her clothes clung to her body, drenched from the pelting rain. With the gear she carried on her back, Alexa felt like she was walking through quicksand. She leaned into the wind and, for every step forward, stumbled back and fought the storm.

A streak of lightning washed a bluish haze over the windswept trees and stone cliffs jutting from the mountainside. A stroke of luck. Alexa saw a dark shadow cut into rock. She knew she'd found the right spot, the one she'd seen before.

"This is it!" she yelled, waving her arm to show her men the way. She squinted into the blowing rain and wiped away the hair clinging to her face. "Get him inside."

It had taken two men—Lewis and Booker—to carry Kinkaid from where he'd fallen to a dugout carved into the side of a cliff. Even inside, rain leached through stone crevasses. And the interior of the cavern was like a sieve, with water following gravity and forming rivulets in the eroded sandy soil. The sound of the rushing water echoed in the dark chasm, magnifying the noise tenfold.

Getting out of the wind had made a big difference. Alexa flashed a light onto the walls to look for higher ground. Others on her team did the same. Beams strafed the inside of the cavern, and good fortune shone back again.

The cave was deeper than she first thought.

"Take him up there and find a dry spot," she told Lewis and Booker. And to the others, she said, "Let's make camp and start a fire. Looks like we'll have plenty of time to dry out. We're here until the weather clears."

She followed the men carrying Kinkaid and helped break out his bedroll and a pad to insulate him from the wet ground. This deep into the cave was noticeably cooler, which would help bring down Kinkaid's fever, but she'd need a fire to prevent the chills she knew would come. And although the area where they had him was cramped, she'd make it work.

"I'll check him over to see what's wrong. Set the rest

of his gear up here," she told Booker. "I have a feeling I'll need to search for those pills he was taking."

"You'll need a fire up here, too," Lewis offered. "I'll take care of that once we get one going below."

"Thanks, Hank."

Before he left, Hank Lewis told her, "You were right to pull him off the trail when you did, but I admire the guy. He's one fierce lunatic."

"Yeah, he is. And it scares me to hear *you* say that." She grinned.

When she was alone with Kinkaid, she switched on her flashlight again and set it on a rock ledge next to him, giving her a pale light to work under. She unzipped and unbuttoned his wet clothes, peeling them off layer by layer. Kinkaid was burning up. Heat radiated off his body. And he'd started to ramble and mutter nonsense with his eyes closed. He was already delirious.

When she got down to his T-shirt, she pulled out her knife and cut it off, the easiest way to remove the last wet layer. That was when she noticed the soggy bandage—soaked in blood, not rainwater. She peeled back the dressing to get a better look, then rolled him over to check his back. A bullet wound, and it had punched clean through.

"You crazy son of a bitch," Alexa cursed. To control her anger, she called over her shoulder, "Hank, get me the first-aid kit. Our boy's been shot."

While she waited for fresh bandages, she tugged at his pack and rummaged through his stuff. She found his iPod in an unzipped pouch and tossed it aside as she reached into the bottom of a side pocket, looking for the pills she'd seen him swallow. When she found them, she held the container toward the light and recognized the medication.

"Antibiotics. You thought you could hide this?" She wanted to curse at the unconscious bastard, but a part of her understood what he'd done. He was a brave man, driven to do the right thing. And with innocent lives in the balance, he'd chosen to ignore the dangers to himself.

That didn't excuse what he'd done. Kinkaid had lied to her. And worse—now he'd become a liability.

Hours later

Alexa jerked her head when she heard a sharp pop. She opened her eyes to see sparks from the fire spiraling into the roof of the cave. The sound had come from the crackling fire that burned nearby, the only defense from the chill of the cave. And the pale glow from two fire pits cast undulating shadows across the stone cavern.

Kinkaid was asleep next to her. She watched the rise and fall of his bare chest. His breathing was shallow, more like an agitated pant. When she reached over to place fingers to the side of his neck, she noticed his pulse was elevated. Not a good sign, but at least he was on the right side of the dirt for now. The meds she'd given him had allowed Kinkaid to sleep.

She had nodded off sitting up, too tired to care about her numb rear end and a rock jamming her back. Her men had traded standing watch and kept the fires stoked. The warmth of the fire and her exhaustion had caught up with her. And the steady drone of water in the cave and the rumbling of the storm made it real easy to fall asleep.

For much of the night, she'd been alone with her thoughts and old memories. A sane person wouldn't be here, but Alexa was where she wanted to be. The adrenaline rush of a mission was addictive, and the real juice came from wielding justice. She was making a real difference in the world—her way and without all the hoopla that came with media attention. The last thing she wanted was the media or the law second-guessing what she did for the Sentinels. Not many people would understand. Then again, not many did what she was trained to do.

No wonder she didn't have room in her life for a man who wasn't connected to all this—a man like Garrett Wheeler or Jackson Kinkaid. No one else would understand or accept the life she lived. And no one else would live as much in the moment.

That made her interest in Seth Harper all the more intriguing. What had made her turn the corner to pursue someone like Harper, a guy who would be completely invested in any physical relationship with a woman? He'd have expectations and needs. And she'd feel guilty not giving him what he deserved and had a right to expect. What the hell did that say about her? She wasn't sure she wanted to know. *You're a real piece of work, Marlowe*.

Alexa stretched and looked for a distraction to keep her awake. She saw the iPod pouch Kinkaid had brought with him on the ground near his pack. She'd tossed it there. It was too tempting to listen to his taste in music and find out why he'd brought it; but when she knelt over him to retrieve it, Kinkaid groaned and stirred.

She stowed the iPod in his gear and pressed the back of her hand against his forehead. Kinkaid's fever had gone down, but it was still there. And although getting him back on antibiotics had helped, the meds weren't a permanent fix. *Not by a long shot*. Being stuck in the mountains of Cuba with a raging infection and no medical attention didn't bode well for his future.

The damage had been done, and the infection would take its toll unless she got him to a hospital. Even then, it might be too late. His heart rate was elevated, and his breathing had turned shallow, even while he slept. Sepsis could turn severe and spread through his entire system and affect vital organs, causing irreparable damage.

Alexa poured water onto a torn section of Kinkaid's T-shirt. She pressed the damp cloth across his brow and down his neck and chest. When his eyes blinked open, and it looked like he might stay awake, she reached across him to retrieve his meds.

"Hey," he mumbled. "What h-happened?"

"You passed out," she said, keeping her voice low. "Here, take this." She raised his head and gave him water from his hydration pack to take with his pills. "When was the last time you took these?"

She held up the bottle of pills he had stashed in his pack. Kinkaid squinted at the label until she saw his recognition. Then he shifted his gaze and stared at her between sluggish blinks. Each time he closed them, she thought he'd go back to sleep. With his face silhouetted against the light of the fire, shadows made it hard for her to tell if he was still awake.

"I don't remember," he muttered. "Lost track."

"This is pretty strong stuff, but not enough to knock out the infection you jump-started." She narrowed her eyes. "What were you thinking?"

When he didn't answer, she grabbed his chin to keep him alert and ventured a guess. "You didn't trust us to get the job done. You couldn't sit back and let someone else take care of your friend. Is this about playing hero for a woman?"

"What?" He raised his head and winced with pain before he collapsed back. "What are you talking about?"

"Kate. What's she to you?"

"That's not important," he argued. "She's a . . . friend." Kinkaid wasn't in a sharing mood. The fever had made him surly. And his bad attitude had yanked her trigger.

"Why couldn't you let Garrett and my team handle this? You asked for our help. If you didn't trust us to do the job, why did you call in the first place?"

Even though she kept her voice low to avoid waking up her men, her venomous delivery made her point clear. She wouldn't put up with his macho attitude, not after he put her team and their mission at risk.

"I didn't call Garrett. Joe did." He tried to sit up again and grimaced with the pain. "Believe me. He'd be the last guy I'd call."

Garrett had warned her that he and Kinkaid had a history, and he'd refused to let her in on the story. Something must have gone terribly wrong. And from the look on Kinkaid's face, she wouldn't be learning the truth anytime soon.

Did he love Kate, the woman he had risked his life for?

Kinkaid was the kind of man who didn't open up easily. She knew that firsthand. Any woman who got under his skin would be special. Alexa felt a strange pang of jealousy toward a woman she'd never met.

For both their sakes, she needed a change of subject and a softer tone if she expected him to keep talking.

"So why did these men hit the fund-raiser? A Haitian missionary school event wouldn't be my first choice to find wealthy patrons worth ransom bucks. You have any theories?"

"Yeah, one. I think they were after me."

"What?" She had to admit his answer hit her between the eyes. "This I gotta hear."

He took a deep breath, and for a long moment, she wasn't sure he'd keep talking. Eventually he did.

"There's been an increase in drug-cartel hit squads. I thought it had something to do with payback. The terrorists called out my name at the fund-raiser and demanded to know where the American was. Maybe I brought this to Kate's door." The pained expression on his face told her he wasn't done with his explanation. "I raised my hands and was prepared to go with them to find out, but that's when things got crazier. And one of those bastards was gonna shoot a kid."

"Sounds like you did what you had to do." She reached over and touched his arm. "Those men brought AK-47s to a school fund-raiser. And you said it yourself. They might have known your name, but they probably were only looking for an American to take hostage. All of this is on their heads, not yours."

"Yeah, but what if those cowards were after me for another reason? This could be retribution for what I'm doing."

Ignoring the door he'd opened wasn't her style. She barged in with a question that was none of her business.

"And what are you doing . . . exactly?" she asked. "I mean, if you think they came after you for something, you must have a good reason to believe that."

Kinkaid didn't answer. His silence conveyed enough. Trust didn't come easy for her either. Although she couldn't blame him, a hollow feeling left her wishing he trusted her with the truth about the man he'd become and why. That would work for starters. He stared at her until his eyes slowly closed.

Before he drifted off, she had something to say.

"Look. If it hadn't been for you, these hostages wouldn't stand a chance. Now they have us. And we'll find them, Jackson." She tried to sound reassuring and had no idea if he was even listening. "You and me have ghosts in our pasts. And I swear, if I have any say, Kate won't be another one for you. We're here to help. I hope you believe that."

When she got to one knee, preparing to go, he reached for her hand and opened his eyes. "Thanks, Alexa. For what it's worth, I'm glad Garrett sent you."

Knowing Garrett, he probably sent her to serve his own agenda. He'd suspected her feelings toward Kinkaid when they'd first met. Whatever beef was between them, she had no doubt that Garrett had sent her with an ulterior motive in mind, whatever it was. None of that mattered now.

"Get some sleep," she told him as she pulled his sleeping bag over his chest. "I'll be close if you need me."

Alexa left Kinkaid to his demons and walked toward the mouth of the cave. She needed time to think through her next move. She had a big decision to make.

Her men were asleep, and she was alone, except for Booker, who was standing watch. The wind kicked up near the cave entrance and swirled dirt until the blowing rain scattered it. And lightning hurled flashes of light across the heavens. A real show, and she had a front-row seat even though the worst of the storm had moved on. She crossed her arms and leaned a shoulder against stone, melding her body into the shadows.

One thought had plagued her ever since Kinkaid had collapsed at her feet. Could she leave him behind in his condition?

She knew what Garrett would do. Weighing the interest of one man against the team and the mission would not be a tough choice. She couldn't spare a man to stay with him, especially since there wasn't much anyone could do. And even if she got him on his feet with megadoses of antibiotics, it would only be a matter of time before the infection would gain control again, and he'd be more of a liability.

Kinkaid could die alone in Cuba. And he'd have no one to blame but himself. *Damn you, Jackson. I told you what would happen if you screwed up.*

Blaming him gave her no satisfaction. It only compounded a heartbreaking tragedy that was far from over.

The rain had been steady and only a thick stand of trees blocked the wind. Under a slanted tarp that had been staked down, Joselyne lay on the cold ground, with the other children pressed against her. Puddles had seeped into the thin blankets they'd been given. Even as tired as they were, none of them had slept. She felt the tension in the other children's bodies because it matched her own. They jerked and held their breaths whenever the sky lit up from lightning and cracked with thunder.

And Sister Mary Katherine had not returned to protect them. Joselyne cried every time she thought of the brave nun.

Feeling sick to her stomach, she pulled the blanket over her head. When lightning cast a strange light through the trees, this time the light stayed, and she noticed it. She raised her head to see where it came from, and the other children did the same.

"What is it?" Andre whispered.

Like before when the sister had been taken away, the light from the camera glowed through the trees. Shadows of the bad men made them look larger than they were. And their angry cries made her cringe.

Were they killing someone else? Would she be next?

"I'm scared." Faye sobbed and reached a small hand for Joselyne.

Joselyne wanted to tell them that she'd protect them now, but she couldn't make a sound. She curled into a ball and wrapped her arms tight around her, wishing she were invisible. She couldn't help the other children.

She was only a child like them.

CHAPTER 12

Tanya had arranged a dormitory room in a secluded part of the Sentinels' facility for Seth Harper to work in. Four walls with a locked door and a bath; his meals would be brought to him while he remained there. His secured accommodations were functional and practical since he wouldn't be allowed to roam the below-ground complex without supervision. She wished that she could have done more for him, but Seth hadn't complained.

Jessie Beckett had planned to stay with him as he worked. Once he settled in, Jessie came looking for Tanya to tell her that Harper was ready to start and wanted to share his plans. Tanya brought members of her team and joined him in his room. When they entered the quarters, Seth Harper was sitting at the desk in front of a computer with the multiple monitors that they'd provided.

He swiveled his chair around and waved a greeting.

"Hey. Sit wherever you want." Jessie took a corner of his bed and the others crowded into the room.

"Would you mind if I downloaded music to work by?" Seth asked. "Maybe Lil' Wayne or Three Days Grace." His face was deadpan serious.

Jessie was the only one who knew what he was talking about. Although she had smiled and looked away, she was definitely entertained. Tanya liked her from the first moment they'd met months earlier.

"Whatever works for you, honey," Tanya said to Seth before she introduced her team. She'd brought them along for their cynical nature, to test Harper one last time before she turned him loose. "Now tell us what you have in mind."

"I'll focus my initial search on the high-density bandwidth that it took to upload the video. In that part of the world, it shouldn't be too hard to find. They've got to be using a cell phone to connect to the Internet. They wouldn't count on wireless in such a remote area. Once I know what I'm looking for, I can use a program to triangulate their position."

"What kind of program?" One of her techs looked skeptical.

"I've got something that operates like a fake cell tower," Harper began. "Cell phones in a specific grid are tricked into transmitting hardware serial numbers, phone numbers, and other information to law enforcement. In this case, it'll be me. The user won't know it's happening. And the program works long-range and off satellites."

"That's Triggerfish? It's nothing new," one of her team argued. "And I'd question how long-range it is."

"Plus you need a court order to use it with the phone companies. The Patriot Act requires one," Simon Bechtel, one of her senior shift supervisors, weighed in on the subject.

Tanya knew the Patriot Act had its share of controversy when it came to surveillance. The act was passed into law with overwhelming support from Congress as a counterterrorism measure to broaden law enforcement's authority to use wiretaps and other similar measures. And the debate on certain provisions raged on. Yet she had an appreciation for fighting terrorism by whatever means possible, even if it meant bending the law to do it. That's what her employer, the Sentinels, were all about— a vigilante group of international protectors who weren't hampered by laws when it came to dispensing justice.

She was interested to see how Seth Harper would handle the pushback from her team and the intimidating Simon Bechtel. Bechtel had an arrogant way of talking down to people, especially when he thought he had the upper hand, like now.

"You're right. Triggerfish is old news, but that's not what I'm talking about. And yes, the Patriot Act does require a court order when accessing phone records. You're right, sir, but hear me out." Harper fielded their questions with patience. "I'll be targeting a tight grid around Haiti to pick up the initial activity and follow it to southeast Cuba. At the risk of making a bad first impression, I'm not really a court-order-type guy. Back doors and sneaky shit are my specialty. And in the interest of full disclosure, I'll admit that I once ran with scissors."

Harper didn't wait for a response. "Not everyone plays by the rules. Shocker, I know. In this post-9/11 world, U.S. government officials in very high places have ordered eavesdropping on private calls and justify their actions in the name of national security. I'm not naming names, but certain enhancements were made to the Triggerfish concept to get around legal technicalities. And this new program has created a loophole in the law."

"My, you don't say. What loophole?" Bechtel turned toward her and rolled his eyes with a smirk. He had already dismissed the kid.

"If I can bypass the phone company altogether, technically I'm not breaking the law."

Her shift supervisor furrowed his brow and stared at Seth as if he had spoken in tongues. Jessie's friend really had a way of seeing things out of the box. And Tanya liked his unconventional approach—as long as he was working for them.

"No," the older man protested. "You can't do that."

"I didn't. Some other brilliant fringe dweller did." Harper leaned forward and rested his hands on his knees. "The Patriot Act became law in 2001. Sections of it deal with safeguarding civil liberties when it comes to 'Big Brother' accessing phone-company records, but prior to that, there was no law that covered location-tracking technology at all. A court order wasn't even needed before 2001 even though the technology existed. Ironic, huh? The Patriot Act gave us worthless protection against obsolete technology." Harper shrugged with a smile. "Some pretty big government types are operating under the same assumption I laid out. That's why this new program was created . . . or so I've heard."

"Where's the program? You didn't come in with anything except an overnight bag of your personal effects. You were searched at security." Bechtel turned to her again to make his case. "If he uses a program like that here, and it's traced back to us, it could prove to be a liability."

"I don't see that happening, but the call is up to you, of course. This is your house, and I'm technically on vacation." Harper stretched his long legs in front of him and slouched in his chair with arms crossed.

"I can confirm everything I've told you so we don't waste any more time," Bechtel argued. "This kid doesn't know what he's talking about. Let me make one phone call."

"Impressive." Seth shrugged. "The only thing I can get with one phone call is a pizza."

Tanya nearly lost it. "Where do you keep this program, Seth?"

"I store my programs online in multiple spots I like to call my 'cache.' That way I don't have anything in my possession. I've got them loaded all over. Some places might even surprise you." He crooked his lip into a smile. "My online activity runs through foreign ISPs and pings off other users, so it's hard to trace."

"Yet not impossible," Bechtel pointed a finger.

"No, I'd never make that claim, but I've got fail-safes in place to warn me if I've been compromised. And I figure you guys have an appreciation for tight security, too. Like I said, it's your call."

Tanya sat back in her chair and found it hard to stifle a grin. She had no idea if Harper had developed this software himself since he was cagey enough not to admit it. At a minimum, he had powerful connections that intrigued her.

"Do it, Seth. And, Jessie, call my extension when you two get something." Tanya stood and headed for the door. Although Bechtel would need his ego stroked, it had been worth it to see a young guy like Harper hold his own with the seasoned veteran. When her team left the room, Tanya stayed behind and winked at Seth. "I like the way you think, sugar."

Harper waited until the door was shut and locked behind Tanya Spencer before he turned toward Jessie, and said, "She called me sugar. Did you hear?"

"Yeah, you're a damned chick magnet." She grinned. "Work your magic, genius."

Jessie walked over to his desk and leaned down to kiss him on the cheek. "And thanks for helping Alexa, Seth."

"I haven't helped her yet."

"Yeah, but my money is on you, smart guy. Always."

His cheeks burned red, and he teetered between flashing a grin and avoiding her gaze with a shy blush. Eventually, he got to work.

Jessie loved watching him. The muscles of his long lean back moved under his shirt. After seeing him in the shower, she knew what he looked like under those clothes. She watched his hands as his fingers moved over the keyboard with confident, aggressive strokes. His intent expression never wavered from the computer monitor once he got started.

Jess knew it would be a long night. She called the in-house cafeteria and ordered plenty of coffee and munchies, the kind that would fuel Harper through the night.

She had a feeling he'd need it.

Southeast Cuba
Sierra Maestra Mountain Range

Alexa ordered her team to pack up and move out after dawn. They had no communication with Garrett for the moment. She hoped that would change soon. Her team was headed for the last known spot they'd seen the tracks from the hostages, the footprints Kinkaid had identified. He'd done his part. Now it was her turn.

Outside the cave, the air was thick with humidity after the storm. The excessive rain and high winds had ravaged the mountainside. Broken tree limbs had fallen onto the trail, and the lush vegetation had been flattened. Her scouts would have to find another way to track the movement of the terrorists.

They'd have their work cut out for them. And the clock was ticking for the hostages.

A steel gray sky cast a dull glow across the mountains and shed a glimmer of light on the damage left behind from the fierce storm. And a still, eerie calm put her on alert. There were no birds, and the normal sounds from the jungle were absent. She hoisted the pack onto her back and listened to the squish of mud under her boots as she navigated the slick ground.

Two of her men led the team out, and she looked over her shoulder one last time, thinking of Jackson Kinkaid lying unconscious in the cave.

Her doing.

"You did the right thing," Hank Lewis whispered, and patted her on the shoulder as he walked by her. "Don't beat yourself up."

She acknowledged him with a nod. It was too early for talking, and she wasn't in the mood. Alexa knew she'd burned a bridge with Kinkaid after what she'd done. The liberal dose of pain meds she'd given him would wear off soon.

He'd be alone in the cave with MRE food rations, first aid, water, and the tracking beacon she'd stowed in his gear to mark his position. She would extract him by helicopter after they'd rescued the hostages. Ironic that only hours before, she'd wanted his trust. Now she only hoped that after this mission he'd be royally pissed at her.

Pissed meant he'd be still alive, and that worked for her.

Alexa justified the decision she'd made. She only returned the favor after he'd kept the truth from her about his gunshot and jeopardized the mission. If she hadn't given him the extra pills, he'd try to join them, and she couldn't risk it. And who knows how far he would have gone to stay with her team. She owed it to her men to do what was right. And she didn't want a debate or a fight with one of the good guys in this business. Knocking Kinkaid out seemed logical under the circumstances.

Alexa kept in step with her men and shifted her attention back to the mission. *See you on the flip side, Kinkaid. For what it's worth, I'm sorry.*

In the dark bowels of the cave, Jackson Kinkaid opened his eyes and stared at rock crevasses over his aching head. Pitted stone faded in and out of blackness, spinning and shifting out of focus until he could see straight. The campfire was the only light in the cavernous space, with the entrance to the cave too far to make a difference. He forced himself to stay awake and winced as he sat up. His arms felt heavy and lethargic. And although his mind was foggy, he knew what he had to do.

He worked his tongue—a sluggish tedious process— to spit out the pills he had stuck to the inside of his cheek.

The meds had started to dissolve and take effect. That was unavoidable. He rolled and got to his knees before he made the effort to stand. When he got upright, he wanted to puke. He felt light-headed and weak, but he was banking on his brain clearing once he got moving. He had to catch up with Alexa and her team before they got too far ahead.

One foot in front of the other, Kinkaid. Keep moving.

He packed his gear and kicked dirt on the fire to put

it out. Time to go. When he hoisted his rucksack onto his back, he clinched his teeth to fight the pain. In his mind he pictured Kate, the only motivation he'd need. He headed for the entrance to the cave and squinted as he hit the muted light of an overcast sky.

When he looked down, he saw what he expected to see.

Unlike the hostages—whose trail had been washed out—Alexa's team would be easier to follow in the mud. He knew they would parallel the trail and that their footprints would be clear enough to track. And they wouldn't be expecting him. He'd keep his distance and watch, waiting for his opportunity to play the "fly in their ointment." He'd pick his spot so they wouldn't have a choice in taking him back. Or better yet, he'd hang back and let Alexa's trackers do all the hard work. Once they found the terrorists, he'd decide what to do next.

Being a team player wasn't high on his list of priorities.

He took one last gulp of water and looked across the horizon as he stood near the entrance to the cave. Thinking back to what Alexa had done to him, if she were hell-bent to get rid of him, he wouldn't have changed her mind. He saw her packing and suspected that she'd leave him behind when she hadn't bothered to wake him, except to dose him full of meds. And he saw no need to convince her at that point. Better for her to think she'd been clever to dope him.

In the back of his mind, he understood that she'd done it for the good of the team and the success of the mission—but it was hard to acknowledge her side when he felt so betrayed. He chose to ignore his abuse of the trust factor in not telling Alexa about his wound. The gravity of her transgression far outweighed his. If he had any doubts about whether he could trust her, she'd given him an answer and failed a very big test. Alexa could have confronted him and talked it out, but she hadn't.

Instead, she drugged him. The last time they'd talked, she even had the nerve to demand trust. *What a fuckin' joke!*

"You gotta earn trust, Marlowe. And you failed on all counts." His voice echoed into the dank cave as he left it behind and took off after Alexa and her men.

No one under Garrett Wheeler's command would have his back. *No one*. Alexa and her team could pull up stakes if Garrett ordered them to stand down and abort. Kinkaid knew that Kate deserved better than his one-man show, but right now he was the only one who really gave a damn.

And when he caught up to Alexa, he'd make sure she regretted leaving him behind.

CHAPTER 13

Southeast Cuba
Sierra Maestra Mountain Range
Noon

The mountain trail traversed a ridge with a valley on one side and sheer rocky cliffs on the other. The view gave Alexa a panorama of the devastation from the storm. The wider path led higher into the mountains and looked worn, but a narrower trail split and diverted toward the valley in a pattern of switchbacks. It wasn't clear which way her team should go, not after the ravaging storm had done its damage.

As Alexa had promised Kinkaid, they had picked up the trail that morning, using other means than the footprints that had been washed out. Her scouts had found a vague track of fresh machete cuts in the vegetation and other subtle signs. Although she knew they were on the trail again, finding the markers was hit or miss, and at times they had to retrace their steps. She ordered her men to stop at the fork and found a small clearing with good cover below the ridgeline to rest and wait until her trackers returned with news.

At this elevation, the thin air made it harder for Alexa to breathe, especially with the exertion of carrying a heavy field pack. Sweat and grime covered her skin, a fact she did her best to ignore. The bugs were drawn to her perspiration and would not to be denied, even near the summit. Tenacious flies as big as her thumb and a cloud of mosquitoes buzzed her, despite her wearing bug juice. Alexa swatted them as she rested on one knee next to Hank Lewis. She sucked warm water from the tube connected to her hydration pack and pulled out her binoculars.

"You smell the smoke?" she asked, keeping her voice low. "Someone burning wood."

"Yeah." He nodded and hunched next to her. "A few shanties across the valley. We're downwind." He pointed through the trees, and she caught a glimpse of the dwellings and the faint wisps of smoke hanging over the tree line.

Alexa tipped back her camo-colored boonie hat to use her binoculars. She peered down the gorge and checked for movement. Although the vegetation was too dense to see much, as the morning progressed, birds and other animals became more active and visible. And she saw no significant disruption—like birds being flushed from the trees in flight—to indicate that a group of men were moving hostages through the valley. She and her team were at a high spot, where noise would travel. They should see or hear hostages in the canyon.

But they had nothing. *Nothing*.

"Even though it's quiet below, that vegetation covers plenty," she whispered to Lewis.

"We've stayed clear of the locals . . ." he said, " . . . but with these bastards moving men, women, and children, they've got to have help. No one hauls warm bodies without stirring up the locals unless they've got allies. And with these mountains crawling in terrorist training camps, we'd be the odd men out if they knew we were here."

"Yeah, I've been thinking the same," she agreed. "When we shed these trees, let's make contact with home base."

Their SAT phone worked off low-orbiting satellites with minimal conversation delays. It was the only network that had coverage across the world, including the oceans, and the setup worked best with a clear line of sight to the sky. They'd have to find that.

Hank nodded at her order, looked over his shoulder and punched her arm. "Looks like Manny and Izzy are back."

Manny Rodriguez and Izzy Walker had been tracking since dawn, alternating between flanker and tracker duties to keep their eyes fresh. Manny was the real deal, but he'd been training his flankers, Booker and Walker, in the field.

"We found a few upturned rocks on the high road," her tracker whispered. "The dark side was up and hadn't dried yet. And the indentations in the soil were clean and fresh. Someone has been through here . . . and recently. I saw boot prints in the mud, with bent grass heading in that direction." He pointed a hand up the ridge. "But I didn't see the tracks Kinkaid identified the other day, up or down. *Nada*."

"You see anything else up there?"

"I found machete marks. Frayed and old. Nothing new."

Alexa listened to Manny as she kept her eyes alert, looking for any signs of movement in the brush around them. A creeping sensation had triggered her instincts. Nothing she could put a finger on, but she'd learned to pay attention to her gut. She wiped her palms down her BDU pant legs and rested a hand on her assault rifle, an edgy habit.

"What did you find on the low road?" she whispered. Her team huddled around Manny and listened. She cast a glance toward Hank, who caught the look and narrowed his eyes. He got her message that something else was on her mind.

"Not much," Manny said. "Terrain is rough going down, and there's high water below. They'd have trouble. We pulled a 360-degree sweep looking for tracks. Flooding was bad. No fresh signs."

"Give me the bottom line, Manny. Up or down?" She leaned toward him. "Your gut."

She could tell by his expression that the man carefully considered his answer. He'd make his best guess based on instinct, and she'd have to trust him unless she had a better idea.

"I'd take the high road and stick with the ridge. I definitely saw early-morning activity." He waved a hand toward the peak behind her. "Going up is rockier and harder to track, another reason they'd climb. It would be tougher for anyone to follow them and easier on the women and kids."

When she turned toward Izzy, he nodded in solidarity with Manny. The call would be hers to make. From what she'd seen earlier, the deep canyon showed signs of others living there, but no indications of hostage movement. It looked less likely that they would have taken the path down. The ridge held more appeal. It had a sheer drop on one side that would protect their asses. And trekking off the worn path below the ridgeline, they could avoid contact with locals while maintaining their good view below. They'd also have a better shot at making contact with Garrett if they stuck with the summit.

"We'll stay with the ridge for now," she whispered. "If we don't cross their path, we'll circle down into the valley and have a look around."

Her men nodded. They had a plan.

"Booker and Winslow will keep watch while Manny and Izzy rest," she added. "Hank? Let's talk."

After her team went about their business, she stayed crouched next to Hank. The man locked his gaze on her, waiting for what she'd say.

"The hair on the back of my neck is talking," she admitted. "I think we've stirred up local interest. Someone is watching us."

"Yeah, I've been feelin' it, too." He shook his head. "I don't like it."

"Pass the word to the others." She kept her voice low. "Stay alert. Bonus to anyone sprouting eyes in the back of their head."

"You got it." He grinned and headed toward the rest of her men.

They had a fifty-fifty shot at making the right decision. Some might like those odds, but she didn't. The storm had messed with their best chance at catching up to the hostages. Any delay in finding them meant someone might die.

No, she didn't like those odds at all.

Kinkaid crept low and steady through the underbrush before he came to a stop in a thicket off the trail. He'd gotten as close as he dared to Alexa and her team. Using his binoculars, he followed the movements of her trackers until they circled back. From experience, he knew they'd make an assessment on what to do next. The trail had split. They were looking for fresh tracks, and Alexa would make the final call.

His head ached, and the infected wound in his belly throbbed with heat. He took a gulp of water with more antibiotics while he waited for Alexa and her team to head out again. He didn't have to wait long. They took the ridge to the summit, and Kinkaid was ready to follow them.

But something caught his eye.

A glint of light flashed below. And something jostled a tree limb. By the time he turned to get a better look, the flash of light and the movement were gone. He blinked and wiped his eyes before he peered through the binoculars again.

Had he imagined it?

Kinkaid searched the canyon and didn't see anything out of order. Whatever he'd seen replayed in his mind until he made a decision. Alexa and her men were headed in the opposite direction. Their boot prints would be easy to pick up later, but he had to take the narrow path into the valley to make sure her trackers hadn't missed anything. If Alexa and her men got to the terrorists first following the ridge, they were equipped to handle them, and he'd hear the skirmish. If her team was headed the wrong way, he owed it to Kate to check out the road not taken, even if it was a risky proposition.

He stowed his binoculars and grabbed his weapon, an HK G3 assault rifle. With a grimace of pain, he stood and carefully made his way to the path down into the canyon. Although going alone into the gorge wasn't his smartest move, it was worth the risk. If he crossed paths with the bastards who'd taken Kate, he'd make good on his promise to pull the trigger when he got them in his crosshairs.

He wouldn't go down without a fight. A burst of gunfire from his G3 would be like sending up a flare. Alexa and her team would be within earshot to back him up. It would have to do.

The trail to the bottom of the steep gorge was a series of switchbacks, a narrow worn path cut through dense vegetation. The air was more muggy, and the bugs had multiplied. He kept his eyes alert and his G3 ready. His pace was slow and cautious. If he got ambushed, it would be on this path, when he would be most vulnerable. It was the only way down from the ridge.

Kinkaid crouched and moved through the tree line,

sticking to the shadows cast from the thick canopy overhead. He listened for sounds, searched for movement, and sniffed the air for anything that triggered his instincts. Near the end of the path, a bent limb caught his eye. Wind damage from the storm. He almost dismissed the shredded branch until he took a second look. When he got closer, he saw a white cut in the fallen limb. A clean slice. The kind of fresh cut from a machete. The sap had dried. By his estimation, it was no more than a day or two old. It was something.

His heart lifted for the first time that day.

When he reached the bottom of the trail, he hunkered down in a thicket to catch his breath and grabbed his binoculars. He peered through the trees and heavy underbrush. A slow-moving river had overrun its banks, flooding the ground and turning the land into a swamp. Although the clay soil had been saturated, shrubs and grasses protruded from the water, a good indication of where the riverbank had been.

On the air came the smell of death. He searched for the source and found the bloated body of a large rodent near an embankment. Flies buzzed the creature's swollen belly, and the stench carried on the faint breeze. With the intrusion of the flooding, the rotting smell of the dead rodent mixed with the stagnant odors of the jungle, but he found it hard to believe the foul stench came from one animal.

Something worse hung heavy in the stifling heat.

When motion in the distance caught his eye, it took him a moment to shift his binoculars for a better look. Eventually, he recognized what it was—a flap of a very large wing. The feathers were dark brown, the color caught in the dappled sunlight through the trees. He focused on the sight, unsure of what he'd found. Shadows huddled under a large tree. A dark horde moved as one until it broke apart into frenzy, tugging at flesh and something more.

Vultures were feeding on a carcass.

Slowly, he lowered his binoculars and fought the lump wedged in his throat. Kinkaid had seen enough. To make sure, he'd have to move closer. He wanted to believe the vultures were feeding on another dead animal, but he knew the truth.

Animals didn't wear black cloth.

CHAPTER 14

Southeast Cuba
Sierra Maestra Mountain Range
Afternoon

Excessive rains from the storm had caused the river in the gorge to overflow its banks. Kinkaid kept his eyes alert for any signs of danger as he headed for the far side of the canyon. Water looked knee deep on the fringes. He kept to the outer edge of the river and navigated the uneven marshy terrain.

He found it hard not to stare at the body lying under the trees ahead, covered with the feeding vultures that had claimed it. Normally, the birds fly high to spot their prey and circle above it. Nature's own cleanup crew. But the dreary dirty-looking predators were done flying and were now on the ravenous and greedy phase of their existence. Kinkaid gripped his assault rifle and made steady progress as he stuck to the shadows under the trees.

When he got close, the mounting drone of flies buzzed in a mind-numbing blur, white noise to a grotesque nightmare. Vultures covered the body with flapping wings in a feeding frenzy, brazenly feasting on decaying flesh with their bloodied razor-sharp beaks. The stench made it hard for him to breathe, especially with the muggy heat.

Kinkaid saw a black garment under the claws of the large birds, and his mind launched into images of Sister Kate wearing her nun's habit. Memories of the day they'd first met at the hospital raced through his mind. And even though those days were still a blur, he would never forget Kate. He clenched his jaw and fought the rage that welled inside him. None of this should have happened to her. It had been tempting to shoot his rifle at the scavengers, a release for his anger.

He couldn't do that. Not here. Not in hostile territory, with other lives at risk.

He crept closer and waved his arms, but the vultures had staked their claim and ignored his approach. He had to swing at them with the butt end of his rifle and kick a couple off before he saw the dead body. The vultures bounded away in lumbering and awkward hops. The birds stayed on the ground, only yards from the body, ready to pounce on the decaying corpse after he'd lost interest.

Kinkaid covered his mouth and nose with his arm and stared down at the beheaded body of a man dressed in a bloodied tuxedo. A swarm of large flies hovered over the corpse, and maggots writhed through shredded skin, adding the finishing touches to a nightmarish ordeal he wouldn't forget. He forced his gaze off the body and searched the ground nearby. The severed head was nowhere to be found, perhaps carried off by other predators.

He'd been relieved that it wasn't Kate and didn't want to think about how that reflected on him. The reality of the horrifying death this man had endured brought a rush of guilt and the powerless feeling that he'd laid this at Kate's door and been unable to rescue her.

He'd found one body. Would hers be rotting somewhere else . . . in a spot he might never find?

An overwhelming wave of nausea hit him, the result of the horror at his feet and a heady mix of antibiotics with too little food and too much heat. And he felt the fever under his skin. At this rate, the infection had an edge and would take him down. He had to keep moving.

Kinkaid wanted to bury the man, but the damage had been done. In an hour or two there would be nothing left except bones picked clean. There was nothing more he could do except look for ID. He winced in pain as he dropped to one knee to pat down the man's pockets. He found nothing on the body that would identify him. The man's shoes were gone and his belt, watch, and wallet were missing. His killers had stripped his body, the final degradation. He hoped they'd waited until after he'd been murdered, but he doubted it. Any man who would kill like this had no soul and no sense of morality. Only a solo cuff link remained on the corpse, picked at by the vultures until it reflected in the dappled sun filtering through the trees.

It was the glint of light he had seen earlier.

Kinkaid turned away from the body and shifted

his focus. Now it was time to help the living, and he hoped he wouldn't be too late. He circled the location of the dismembered corpse in a slow and methodical fashion, making a full 360-degree circuit to pick up any tracks leading away from the carcass. The storm made it almost impossible. Eventually, he found a recognizable boot print—a partial—one he'd seen near the beach in Haiti. The print had been sheltered from rain damage by the thick canopy of trees and hardened in the dried clay soil. He'd found the trail of the hostages again. And trampled grasses gave the direction he would go.

Before he headed out, he looked over his shoulder to see that the vultures had reclaimed their prize. An overzealous flutter of wings and snapping beaks reestablished their pecking order as they got back to the business of survival, leaving Kinkaid with a stark reminder of his own mortality. With the infection ravaging his body, he was living on borrowed time. If he died here, no one would know . . . and few would care. He could drop dead in the middle of nowhere, his body becoming nothing more than a host for maggot larvae and fast food for the ugliest bird on the planet.

Winding up as bird crap? If that didn't humble a guy, nothing would.

Clutching his assault rifle, he followed the tracks with a renewed sense of purpose and drive. His sliver of hope was only tainted by the fact that he was alone again. If he didn't find Kate and the hostages soon, Alexa and her team would be too far away to matter.

* * *

Joselyne ate with dirty fingers from a filthy bowl, scooping grainy mush into her mouth. Her eyes watched the men near the campfire, her lips hovering over the bowl as she ate. The food smelled bad, but she was too hungry to care. Her stomach grumbled and ached. She had to go again. Not more than twenty minutes ago, before the men gave them food, she had raced into the woods to potty. Two men with rifles followed her and watched as she squatted.

When they heard the embarrassing noises she made, they laughed and pointed at her. She didn't have to understand their language to know what they were saying. Without being able to clean up, she smelled bad from the thick brown dribble down her legs. She'd gotten some on her torn dress. After she came back and crawled under the tarp to hide, the rest of the kids had moved away and kept their distance.

All of the hostages looked scared. It wasn't just the other children . . . or her.

Their camp had been moved. After the storm, they had been forced to hike again. Only this time, they hadn't walked all day. Things were different. This time they joined another group of armed men who lived in a small village in the hills. And she saw they knew each other. None of these men seemed surprised that they were being held captive.

Being in a village, she hoped they would get better treatment. That didn't happen. They were forced to camp outside like before, herded to the outskirts of the village like goats. From under the tarp, she watched the armed men mix with the others. They ate cooked food that smelled better, and they laughed as if they were on holiday.

She hated them for taking her away from her family, her father.

At first she prayed like she'd been taught at school, but after a while she gave up. Maybe God didn't hear her prayers anymore, not after the men killed Sister Kate. She felt an ache deep inside when she pictured the face of the nun. Picturing her dead hurt as bad as the day her mother died.

And the sick man was gone, too, the one who had been shot. She remembered seeing the light of the camera on the night of the storm. And the next day, she saw the armed men do something she didn't understand until later. That was when she knew what they had done to the wounded man. They had done the same to the brave nun.

Thinking about Sister Kate and the man who'd been shot made her belly ache. And she was scared all the time now. The bad men kept looking at her. The way they looked at her made her feel dirty. She avoided their eyes, unsure that had stopped them from staring. She wanted her father to hold her and tell her she was safe, but with each passing day she thought that might never happen. She'd never see her father again.

"What are they doing . . . over there?" Andre whispered. All of them turned to see what he was looking at.

One of the armed men came to the leader, and they both headed to a pitched tent on the opposite side of their camp. They spoke again in words she didn't understand, but the man in charge was not pleased. He waved his hand and looked like he gave an order. Jose-lyne was certain she wouldn't like it.

Especially when the armed man came for her.

"No . . . please . . . NO!" she cried. Joselyne dug in her heels and made the man drag her in the dirt and through the mud puddles. The other children clutched at her legs, but none of them were strong enough to help her. She dropped her bowl of food and almost threw up. Everything slipped away, and the memory of her father faded into nothing.

In her moment of desperation, she found herself praying.

New York City
Sentinels Headquarters

"Jessie, wake up. Jessie?"

A voice edged her sleep and forced her to open her eyes. Jess squinted into the overhead light and raised a hand to block the glare, not registering what was happening at first. Seth knelt next to the bed and pulled a strand of hair off her face. His dark eyes came into focus, her first waking moment and a sight she could get used to.

"You with me?" he asked with a smile on his handsome face.

They were in a dormitory room at the Sentinels headquarters, with the smell of stale coffee and the remnants of cold pizza lingering in the air. Seth had worked through what had been left of the night. She looked down and realized he'd covered her with a blanket. And whatever tunes he had cranked while he was working earlier, a tinny hint of music came from the earplugs lying on the desk. He'd resorted to using them after she'd fallen asleep.

"Yeah, I think so." She propped herself up on his pillows and ran a hand through her hair. "What time is it?"

"I have no idea. In Harperworld, time is only a concept. We gotta talk, Jessie. I think I found it." Eagerness brightened his eyes, and his face glowed. No way he'd spent the whole night working. Harper definitely came from good genes.

"Found what?" She yawned. "I need to brush my teeth . . . get coffee."

"No, you need to listen this time." He grinned and pulled her chin toward him until her gaze locked on him. "I found a signal, Jessie. A high-density bandwidth in Cuba. It has to be them."

"You found the . . ." When his words finally sunk in, her eyes widened, and her voice raised an octave. "You did?" Before he answered, she leapt off the bed and hugged him. "Of course you did, Harper. Talk to me, tell me what's going on. Have you told Garrett and Tanya?"

"No, not yet. I thought you should have the honor." He leaned down and kissed her on the cheek. "But we gotta tell them now."

"Now? I thought once you isolated the signal in Haiti, you still had to triangulate their position and track them from there."

"Yeah, I did that. It took longer than I expected, and

I had to wait for them to transmit again. That's why I woke you. They're transmitting now. A fresh signal. If we can cross-reference the location of the signal with Alexa's tracking beacon, we can provide their coordinates and give her an idea how close they are."

"You're right. We gotta call Garrett and Tanya."

She grinned at him and cupped his face in her hands. Giving in to the moment, Jessie kissed him without thinking. A switch flipped in her brain, and she did what came naturally. She savored his lips and the warmth of his arms. His hands touched her body, and although she wanted more, it wasn't the time.

Rain check, Harper. A definite rain check. She didn't risk saying those words aloud. Maybe one day she would.

Southeast Cuba
Sierra Maestra Mountain Range

The armed man hauled Joselyne by the wrist and dragged her away from the other children to the far end of the camp. He yelled before he reached down to yank her hair. And when he tossed her under the tented tarp, he shoved her to the ground. Her knees were scraped, and they stung. And her eyes had to adjust to the darkness.

It was dusk, and nightfall would soon come. Only a glimmer of light shone through where the tent met the ground. It took her a moment to see. When she did, Joselyne cried. She crawled across the makeshift tent toward the body under the blanket.

The body of Sister Kate.

She barely recognized the nun's face. She'd been beaten. Joselyne reached toward the body with trembling fingers. Despite the heat, she touched lifeless skin that felt cool. The body reminded her of the day her mother was buried. But when the bloodied swollen face twitched, and a low moan came from the sister's throat, Joselyne jerked her hand back and cowered in the shadows.

Sister Kate opened her eyes and stared into the darkness. Her blank empty expression scared Joselyne. The life had gone from her eyes.

"Sister?" she whispered. "Are you . . . alive?"

Kate heard Joselyne's voice, and the sound brought her out of a stupor. The girl crawled to her in the dark, and she felt a timid touch on her cheek. When the child finally came into focus, Sister Kate felt the warmth of tears on her face. She opened her mouth to speak and choked. Her throat was parched. Joselyne vanished into the shadows and came back, holding something in her hands.

"Here . . . drink this." The girl held a cup to her lips and raised her head so she could drink.

"I've been worried . . . about you." Kate struggled to speak. She stared at the small girl edged in shadow, unsure if Joselyne were real or imagined. She raised a hand to the Haitian girl's face. Kate never thought she'd see her again.

"Me? You were worried about me?" The child's sweet voice did more to lift her spirits than anything she could imagine. When the girl sobbed, all Kate wanted to do was hold her, but she couldn't sit up. She wasn't strong enough.

"We thought you were dead, Sister. We never saw you after the night they took you away. And when we moved camp, you weren't with us. What happened?"

"I don't remember much. I was carried to a village by two of his men. I have no idea why he didn't . . ."

Kate stopped before she blurted out her true thoughts. She didn't know why he hadn't killed her. Memories of that night flashed through her mind, a blur of painful attacks. Her face ached in throbbing waves. And she could barely open one eye. Her lip was split and hurt when she moved her mouth. The girl dipped a hand into the water bucket and washed her face with small fingers, careful not to hurt her. Her tenderness broke Kate's heart. Joselyne made the rest of her pain fade.

"How are the other children?"

"They're scared . . . but okay."

"How is George . . . the wounded man? Is someone taking care of him?"

"He's gone, Sister." Joselyne shook her head. "I never saw them take him, but I think they . . ." The child struggled to tell her. "I heard them talking . . . after."

Kate ached down to her soul for George and his family. To endure two tragic deaths from violence was too much to bear for those back home. And she hated that Joselyne had seen such horror. No one, much less a child, should have to witness such cruelty.

"Tell me what you heard, Joselyne. Please." She reached for the child and tucked a strand of hair behind her ear. "I must know what happened to George, for the sake of his family."

"When you didn't come back, none of us could sleep," Joselyne whispered. "And after the storm came, we saw a light in the jungle. Those men. They were filming someone else. We didn't know who, but later . . . that's when I heard what they said."

"If this is too hard, you don't have to . . ."

"No, please." Joselyne grabbed her arm and squeezed it, pleading with her eyes. "They laughed, Sister Kate. Those men laughed at what he said when he died. They made fun of how he begged for his life . . . and talked about his son. And they stole his wallet . . . and other things. Why? Why did they do that?"

Kate not only saw the distress on the child's face, she saw her relief in being able to talk about it. The girl had seen things she did not understand. Kate didn't comprehend these brutal men any more than the child did. Being captive, none of them were allowed to say much to each other. Misery and fear got bottled inside. Kate knew what it meant to speak freely. She felt the same, especially if talking allowed her to console Joselyne.

"I'm sorry . . . for all of this." She kissed the girl's hand. "You shouldn't be here."

"None of us should be here." A tear rolled down Joselyne's cheek. "I miss my father."

"I know you do, honey." Kate opened her arms, and the girl collapsed onto her chest. "Your father loves you very much. And if I have anything to do with it, you will see him again. I promise you."

Kate knew she had no business making promises she couldn't keep, but when she had stared into Joselyne's eyes before, she had seen a child with a broken spirit. And she wanted to make things better, even if it required a goodly amount of wishful thinking for both of them.

"While it's quiet, and it's just the two of us, I want to . . ." Kate felt the sudden urge to tell Joselyne things that would die with her if they were never rescued.

Her stomach twisted with the knowledge that George had felt the same when he talked about his son. The man knew he was going to die and had come to accept it. Kate didn't want to delve into her own motivation too deeply. Talking to Joselyne felt like the right thing to do, but she had to find a way to talk to the girl so she wouldn't be scared.

" . . . I want to tell you about the dreams I've always had for you," she began. The little girl rose and cocked her head, looking confused, but she listened and didn't interrupt. "If I had a daughter, she would have been just like you."

The child finally smiled and nestled back into the nun's arms, laying her head on her shoulder. Kate talked about the future, the dreams she had imagined for Joselyne and the other children under her care. She wanted the girl to know that she could have choices in her life if she wanted them.

And woven into the story were her own hopes, her ambition to make a difference. Images of the young woman she had been flashed through her mind. Her family. The first boy who had ever kissed her. And her devotion to God when she knew what she wanted to do with her life. Kate had so much more to accomplish, but she had a sickening feeling that she'd run out of time.

"It's important to have dreams, Joselyne." She stroked the child's hair. "Do you have dreams, honey?" When the girl nodded, she said, "Tell me about them. I want to know everything. I want to hear your sweet voice . . . for as long as I can."

In the muggy heat of the tent, she listened to the child in the dark, ignoring the pain in her body. She imagined them both safe and far away from their ordeal, but on the edge of her mind she wondered why Joselyne had been allowed to see her. She closed her eyes and held her, stroking her hair and whispering reassurances in her ear until a chilling realization hit her.

One man had made the decision for her to see Joselyne. And she had learned his name after he'd beaten her the other night.

On the surface, permitting her to see the girl might have appeared an act of kindness on his part. She knew better. In the brutal world of Abdul Kabir Sayed, the terrorist leader, everything had strings attached and a price to be paid.

In her quiet way she had resisted him, and that made him more enraged. She saw it in his eyes every time she stood before him. He expected her to bend to his will and accept his control over her fate. Kate wasn't sure why her submission mattered to him, but it did.

And because the children meant a great deal to her,

they would become unwilling pawns in Sayed's mind game. Reuniting her with Joselyne had only been a first step in a battle of wills that she wasn't sure she had the strength to fight anymore.

New York City
Sentinels Headquarters

Without wasting any time, Jess had called Tanya Spencer, who directed her to take Seth to Garrett's office. Tanya had met them on the way. Behind his closed office doors, Garrett hit a button that opened a safe room near his private elevator. Inside that reinforced chamber, he had a bank of high-tech computers with a control panel, a futuristic-looking conference table, and a weapons room. She also saw food and water reserves, oxygen tanks, gas masks, first-aid and other miscellaneous supplies—a small self-contained command center.

"You're full of surprises." Jess stepped into the chamber, sliding her fingers across the conference table.

"Honey, you have no idea," Tanya said as she keyed data into a computer. "I'm putting in the coordinates Seth gave us for that video uplink."

A low hum echoed in the room—sounding like *Star Wars* light sabers—and the center of the conference table lit up into an array of glowing pixels suspended in space. The holographic shape cast eerie shadows onto the faces of everyone in the room.

"Oh, no way." Seth grinned and stepped closer to the table. He swiped a hand into the light and imitated Darth Vader. "Luke, I am your father."

Tanya ignored him. "Now I'm pulling in an overlay of a topographic map of southeast Cuba."

Holographic lights undulated and layered into the mountainous terrain of Cuba in a computer-generated mass. Jess joined Harper at the table, her mouth open like a kid on Christmas morning. A bright yellow dot of light glowed from a 3-D canyon to mark a specific location.

"Is that the bad guys?" Harper asked. He pointed to the glowing dot, pretending to crush them between his fingers.

"Yeah . . . your coordinates," Tanya replied without looking up.

Jess was impressed by the technology. When she glanced at Garrett, he had his jaw clenched, and he looked anxious to assess the situation. The light show was only a tool for him to make decisions. Real lives were at stake.

"When I located the high-density bandwidth in Haiti and tracked that signal to Cuba, I noticed other cell phones in the area," Seth told him. "That wouldn't have surprised me in Chicago, but in a remote area in the mountains of Cuba, all the cell traffic seemed out of place."

"That part of Cuba is host to a number of terrorist camps. And these groups have connections to their handlers in other parts of the world." Garrett narrowed his eyes. "Alexa is behind enemy lines and operating in a global fishbowl of piranhas. She's got to watch her ass and play it smart."

While Tanya worked the keyboard, Garrett continued,

"We haven't been able to contact her. The hurricane has disrupted communications. The storm shifted north before it hit land; otherwise, things would have been much worse."

"Yeah, but she's got a tracking beacon with her. Let's try that," Tanya pointed out. "I loaded her signal ID. It should be coming up . . . now."

A pinpoint of red light shone from the top of a mountain. It blinked in regular intervals, a live signal. That seemed to please Garrett. If he couldn't talk to Alexa, at least he could track her position. It was more than he had.

"Try her SAT phone," Garrett told Tanya. "If her tracking-beacon signal is strong, maybe her phone will come in now."

"Yeah, you got it." Tanya picked up a safe-room phone and gave an order to one of her people. "Contact Marlowe ASAP and patch the call into Garrett's safe room when you get the SAT connection."

But a faint light flickered in a valley below the summit. Jess was the first to notice it. "What's that? There's another beacon out there. Are they both from Alexa?"

"That's odd. She has more than one beacon for emergencies, but with a small team, I can't see her splitting up like that." Garrett's expression grew solemn. "That doesn't make sense."

"Why is that second beacon flickering?" Jess asked. "The signal looks weak."

"For two reasons. That gorge looks pretty steep," Garrett told her. "Mountains could block the signal, especially if the satellite is low on the horizon. And that part of Cuba is dense with trees. A tracking beacon works best with a clear view to the sky."

"Give me time to confirm that second signal," Tanya said, working the keyboard. Jess knew from her training that a Sentinels' tracking beacon would have identification embedded in its signal. It wouldn't take long to ID the property assigned to Alexa's team.

"Come on, Alexa. Talk to me," Garrett muttered as he glared at the light show in front of him.

Jess knew what he was thinking. He could mobilize a backup team to assist Alexa, but he'd have no idea which tracking beacon would be hers. And the signal locations were far enough apart to make a difference. If he picked the wrong one to launch his support and guessed wrong, it would expose his intentions too soon and make it worse for Alexa and her team. And as close as the faint beacon was to the terrorists, by the time he rallied help, any skirmish could be over.

They had to talk to Alexa. *Now.*

"If that's Alexa on the ridge, she's got ground to cover before nightfall. Whoever has the second signal in the valley, they're practically on top of those bastards." Jess shook her head, not taking her eyes off the holographic image in front of her. "But they're too far apart and out of position to launch a simultaneous strike. What the hell is going on?"

I sure hope you know what you're doing, Alexa.

CHAPTER 15

Southeast Cuba
Sierra Maestra Mountain Range

Jackson Kinkaid hunched behind a tree with his back to a rock cliff. He leaned against the hard surface to catch his breath. Fever had robbed him of his usual stamina. He shrugged out of his gear to locate his meds. And he palmed more antibiotics and sucked down water from his hydration pack.

Overdosing on antibiotics was the least of his problems.

He retrieved his thermal infrared binoculars to get a better look at the village beneath his position. Four armed men stood guard with AK-47s on the outskirts of a clearing, and a lone sniper had taken a spot on a ridge with a bird's-eye view of the canyon. Shanty houses were nestled along the tree line, with smoke curling from some of the stone chimneys. A communal fire pit burned in the center of the village, and makeshift tents made of worn tarps, cinder blocks, and corrugated metal were on the perimeter. Food preparation and the smell of burning wood wafted in the evening air as men with dark skin primed for a meal. Most of the inhabitants wore paramilitary gear, and so far he hadn't seen a woman in the camp. By the looks of the weapons and the setup, he'd found another terrorist training camp.

And the tracks he'd followed since the afternoon had led straight to the camp.

With his binoculars, he searched the shacks and tents for any sign of the hostages. The hovels on the edge of the village had the most potential. The armed guards concentrated their patrolling duties around a particular group of dwellings. For the sake of efficiency, he thought the hostages would be together.

Come on, Kate. Show yourself. Where are you?

Nightfall was closing in, and soon it would be too dark for him to identify the hostages. He'd seen enough to know these men held captives. A young girl had been hauled from a tent by a guard and moved to another hovel. She wore a tattered party dress.

He'd seen the girl before at the fund-raiser. Although he didn't remember her name, he knew she was one of Kate's students. And the guard had moved her to where more children were held. Since he'd seen Kate with four kids on the beach in Haiti, Kinkaid had little doubt that wherever the children were, the nun would be held, too. She was headstrong enough not to be separated from them. With confirmation of hostages, he worked on a rescue plan.

Alone, he knew he might not save them all, and that he'd have to improvise to do what he could. He didn't want to think about innocent lives snuffed out on his watch or be forced to leave anyone behind; but given the situation, that reality was a highly likely scenario.

With the sniper positioned on the ridge at nightfall, he figured the man had night-vision gear and had to be taken out first. And the guards nearest the children's tent would be his next targets. His assault rifle would be a weapon of last resort. Any killing would have to be done in deadly silence. He wouldn't get another chance.

Not knowing where Alexa and her team were, he couldn't count on them for backup. He'd be on his own.

Targeting the sniper, Kinkaid made his way up the hill and took the long way around so that the guards wouldn't see him. In his condition, the climb took longer. Sweat stung his eyes, and his vision blurred. And in the dark, his depth perception was off, a reaction from the infection. He wiped a hand over his face and blinked to clear his sight. His head ached, and a steady, incessant ringing in his ears hampered the use of his other senses. He was insane to attempt this rescue alone, but Kate and the other hostages had no one else. Not now.

On the ridge, Kinkaid stopped dead still when he smelled something on the muggy air. The sniper was smoking. To confirm his suspicions, he used his own surveillance gear and watched as the guard took another drag. A dull red ember glowed in the dark. The bastard had the nerve to smoke on duty.

His nasty habit would cost him.

Kinkaid set down his pack—grimacing with the pain—and ditched his gear close by. He slung his assault rifle over his shoulder, carrying the weapon only as a backup plan. When he slipped his bowie knife from its sheath, the blade whispered its lethal hiss, and he crept toward the enemy sharpshooter.

The man never saw him coming.

Sticking to her plan, Alexa had traveled the mountain ridge until her trackers saw no more fresh signs. Before it got too dark, her team had started to descend into the gorge with each man alert and moving in silence. She suspected the canyon had hostiles, and she'd given her orders. Rotating their duties, her men would launch a series of reconnaissance missions to locate their target. No fire. No food prep. No rest. They'd work through the night to make up for lost time. She sensed they were close and hoped luck would be on their side.

Her thoughts drifted to Jackson Kinkaid, and she pictured him alone in the cave, thoroughly pissed at her for leaving him and even more angry at her for drugging him. If he hadn't been seriously hurt and in need of a doctor, she might have smiled at the thought of pulling one over on such a cagey guy.

But their situation wasn't even remotely entertaining.

"Got a call from home base," Hank Lewis whispered as he caught up to her and handed over the SAT phone. "Urgent."

She gave the signal for her team to stop and take cover while she fielded the call.

"Martini One." She kept her voice low. "Talk to me."

It took a long moment for her response to make connection with the caller. SAT phones worked with a delay. She even heard the echo of her own voice.

Eventually the caller said, "We've triangulated the position of the target."   •

She recognized the voice of Garrett Wheeler. He gave her the coordinates, and she relayed the information to Hank.

"Confidence is high on this intel, but we're showing two active beacons. Can you confirm?" he asked.

She narrowed her eyes and thought about what he'd told her.

"Only one beacon active. X marks the spot for a pickup, with second beacon anchored."

"That's negative, Martini One. We show two beacons on the move. I repeat, two on the move." Although Garrett's voice sounded strained, he didn't break protocol to reveal too much on the transmission—or ask obvious questions.

When he gave her the coordinates, she shrugged at Hank and relayed the information. At first her mind reeled with what it meant; but if Garrett showed two tracking beacons moving, that meant only one thing.

Kinkaid hadn't stayed put. He was on the move, and that wasn't possible, not in his condition.

"What's going on, Martini One?" Garrett finally asked.

"We'll evaluate the situation and contact you when we know more. Martini One out."

Garrett wouldn't be happy with her cutting him off,

but her team had to move. If she knew Jackson Kinkaid, he'd be pissing in the wind of a real shitstorm. And from what she'd seen of his feelings for Kate, he'd have little regard for an exit strategy. On this mission, the guy hadn't backed down or compromised. He'd been reacting on pure instinct and showed no fear—as if he had a death wish.

"Damn it," she cursed.

"What's going on?" Hank knelt by her.

"I'm willing to bet our FNG is channeling Chuck Norris." Alexa used an acronym Hank knew well. Fucking new guy meant Kinkaid. "I think he's flying solo and found our hostages. Those coordinates will get us there."

"You got orders?"

"Yeah." She raised en eyebrow. "Let's give him a hand. He can't hog all the fun."

"Yes, ma'am." Hank grinned. To the men, he gave a hand signal, and they moved out, double time.

Alexa cursed Kinkaid under her breath and joined her men. She should never have left him behind. *Damn it!* If he weren't already dead when she got there, she'd be tempted to shoot him herself—if that weren't a waste of ammo.

A pungent smell filled Kinkaid's nostrils in the heat—and rightly so, it stayed. The blood of the dead sniper not only left its odor and stained his clothes. It marked his soul. The memory of the nightmarish moment would plague him in the days and years to come. And he had no doubt another face would haunt his nights.

He'd pinned the smaller man down with a hand over his mouth. The sniper bucked under his weight until Kinkaid plunged the blade into his neck. Warm blood gushed onto his hand, and arterial spray pulsated onto his clothes and face. It was over in seconds, and the man stopped struggling. When Kinkaid pulled his hand away, the guy's mouth gapped open, and his eyes stared at nothing.

An eerie stillness replaced his desperate last breaths after his lungs emptied for the last time.

Few would understand, but Kinkaid felt it was his duty to remember. Taking a man's life should never be easy, no matter what the reason. And forgetting or dismissing it would be an even greater offense.

Darkness had settled onto the gorge, leaving only a sliver of moon to cast its dim haze across the rock cliffs and trees. He crept down a slope toward the outskirts of the village. Digging his bootheels into the soil, he crossed the steep hill at a slant and braced an arm against the incline to steady himself. He avoided the dense underbrush and stayed clear of the established trail, fearing it might be booby-trapped.

When he made it to the canyon floor, he got a bad case of the shakes, and dizziness forced him to stop. He found a dark shadowy spot to hide and gulped more water, splashing some on his face and neck. The fever had gotten worse. His neck and shoulders ached, and sweat drenched his clothes. The infection seethed through his body in a constant clash between churning heat and a rush of chills. He chose to believe that the pain racking his body was only weakness relinquishing its hold on him.

Push through it, Kinkaid.

When he peered through the trees using the thermal infrared imaging capability of his binoculars, the tactical gear allowed him to see in the dark, and ghostly colored images were magnified. The village had quieted down. Not much foot traffic. And the fire pit in the center of the clearing had been reduced to glowing red ashes. No one tended it.

Kinkaid did a quick head count of the guards he'd seen before and watched their movements until he felt ready to go. He stashed his pack in a safe spot to retrieve later—alongside the weapon he'd taken off the sniper—and grabbed his HK G3 assault rifle before he headed out. He'd have to travel light to move fast.

Come on, Kate. Be there with the kids. He figured there would be only one reason Kate wouldn't be with the children. She was already dead. Kinkaid steeled himself for that reality. He'd know soon enough.

Twenty minutes later

Kinkaid dragged the dead man's body away into the brush, the last of the guards keeping watch over the hostages. He stashed the AK-47s with the two bodies. More armed men patrolled the camp perimeter. He'd have only a brief opportunity to speak to the captives and convince them to come with him.

Carrying his assault rifle, he crouched low and crept toward the hovel where he'd seen the children. If he found Kate there, he wouldn't have to persuade the kids to follow him. Kate would know what to do, and she could help with the other captives, too. When he got to the tent, he avoided the side facing the clearing. That side of the tent was too risky and would force him to turn his back on the other guards.

Instead, he moved to the rear of the tarp and used his knife to cut through it. He opened the torn flap and found the children cowering in the far corner. When he used a small penlight to see inside, the beam flashed across the terrified faces of the kids. They squinted and held up small hands to block the light.

The oldest girl shielded the others. Her eyes were brimming in tears. And even though her chin was jutted out in defiance, her lips trembled. The child didn't say a word, nor did she make a sound. Brave girl . . . and smart.

"Sister Kate. Where is she?" he whispered, and looked over his shoulder for any sign of movement. When the girl didn't respond quickly enough, he repeated his question in French.

At the mention of Kate's name, the expression of the oldest girl softened, and she whispered something to the other kids before she crawled toward him.

"Why are you asking about Sister Kate?" the girl questioned in English, letting him know she spoke his language.

"My name is Jackson Kinkaid. Sister Kate is my friend. I've come to rescue you . . . all of you." He craned his neck over the tent and looked into the clearing. A guard was edging closer. With three more tents to check out, Kinkaid was running out of time.

"Where is she?" he asked again.

The girl reached for his arm and tugged at his sleeve to bring him inside. And even though every move brought him pain, he followed her lead. She crawled toward the other side of the tent and pointed across the clearing.

"They have her there, the third tent to the left of the fire." She pointed a tiny finger, keeping her movement masked in shadows. "She is very sick. They beat her. I thought they'd killed her." The girl sobbed when a rush of emotions hit her.

He stroked her dark hair and kissed her forehead. "I'm getting you out of here. What's your name, honey?"

"Joselyne." She wiped tears from her face with a dirty hand and took a ragged breath.

"You're a brave girl, Joselyne."

He tapped her nose with a finger and forced himself to smile to put her at ease. Having the children and the other captives separated from Kate made things tough. He knew what he had to do, but the decision to leave Kate for last wasn't an easy one for him to make.

"I have to check on the other hostages. Which tents are they in?" he asked. After the girl told him what he needed to know, he said, "Stay quiet. I'll come back for you. I promise. Then you're all going home."

The word "home" struck him and brought unexpected and bittersweet memories. He hadn't had a real home in so long that the word sounded like a foreign language, but by the look in Joselyne's eyes, she knew what home meant. And he was determined to make it happen for all the children.

With reluctance, he left the kids behind while he made contact with the other hostages. Scrambling from tent to tent had taken time. After he'd gathered the others, Kinkaid kept them moving and quiet. He positioned himself between the captives and the remaining guards on duty. If they were spotted, he didn't want innocent lives caught in the cross fire. When they reached the children's tent, Joselyne had the kids ready to go. In silence, they crawled through the opening he'd made in the back of their tent.

He counted twelve hostages—men, women, and children. When he got them far enough away, he'd come back for Kate. *Lucky number thirteen.*

Kinkaid crouched on the edge of the clearing with his G3 aimed toward the camp. After he nudged his head and gave the signal for each hostage to move into the trees, he kept his eyes alert for the other guards and any signs of movement. One by one, the captives made their escape from the camp. And two of the men helped the children. When the last hostage crept by him, he backed away from the camp with his assault rifle leveled and melded into the shadows. He took a detour to retrieve the two AK-47s that he'd stashed with the bodies of the guards and joined the men, women, and children, who were waiting for him.

Under the cover of darkness and shielded by the trees,

the hostages huddled in a spot away from the camp and stared at him with expectant and scared faces. Dealing with dizziness and a queasy stomach, he knelt in front of them with clinched teeth to mask his nausea.

Kinkaid fixed his gaze on the three men in the group.

"Do any of you know how to use an AK-47?" he whispered, holding up one of the rifles.

When he pointed to Joselyne—and waited for her answer—the little girl finally broke down and smiled with a shake of her head. He winked and turned back to the men. Only one had raised his hand and nodded.

Kinkaid gave instruction to the men as he handed over the confiscated assault rifles. He had no expectations that these civilians would know how to fire a weapon or become marksmen after one quick lesson. His goal was simple. He wanted them to make noise if they had to and avoid killing each other in the process.

"Follow me single file. Do as I do and watch over the kids," he said in a low voice and looked into the eyes of each of his charges. "After we get going, not a sound, okay?"

He led them back to where he'd stowed his gear. The location was far enough away from the terrorist camp and had good cover for them to hide until he returned. He stayed off the path and navigated through brush. It made the trek slow, especially with the kids.

When they got to his stashed gear, he said, "I'm going back for Sister Kate."

Joselyne chewed a corner of her lip with a worried crease between her eyebrows. She didn't complain, but the little girl looked frightened.

"You." He pointed at her and shoved his pack in her direction. "Watch my stuff. I'm coming back for it."

Joselyne nodded with a fleeting smile. Her worried look had softened when he talked about returning. She took a step toward him and touched his arm, saying, "Please . . . find her."

He crooked his lip into a half grin and tapped a finger to her nose. "Whatever you say, sweet girl. Now go on with this nice lady here. I got something to tell these guys."

The men with weapons stayed put while Joselyne and the others pulled deeper into the shadows and hid. When Kinkaid knew he was alone with the men, he spoke in a hushed voice.

"All hell is about to break loose," he warned them. "Don't panic. Stay down until it's over. If I don't come back, this is what I want you to do."

There was only one reason he wouldn't be back, and by the looks on the men's faces, they understood what he meant. After he shared his contingency plan, he went back for Kate. From where her tent was located in the center of camp, he would need a diversion that made him look like an army.

He knew exactly what to do.

Alexa got a signal from Hank that they were getting close to the coordinates Garrett had given them. The location her boss had relayed for the terrorists was dead ahead. If she had any doubts about the validity of the locale or Jackson Kinkaid's whereabouts, her doubts vanished in a hail of bullets. She heard shots fired. And she recognized the sound of Kinkaid's HK G3 assault rifle. Downrange of her position, muzzle flashes lit the night sky and sent orange streaks through the trees. And the assault escalated when grenades erupted. Fireballs exploded with a thunderous boom that echoed off the canyon walls.

"Oh, hell," she cursed.

She used her night-vision binoculars to evaluate the situation and gave her orders through a series of hand gestures. Her men moved out like the well-trained team they were. With her men in formation, she cut through the brush and down a steep embankment, heading for the fight with her M4 assault rifle clutched in her hands. With enemy bullets ricocheting off stone and cutting through the trees, she stayed low and steadied her breathing, despite the pounding of her heart and the adrenaline rushing through her system.

Whatever happened now, they'd have to end it and get out. News of the incident would precipitate an investigation, and the world would soon know what happened here. If Garrett expected them to keep a low profile—to get in and out—she had no choice but to end it and have her team gone before morning, with no trace left behind.

But nothing would be that simple with a guy like Jackson Kinkaid.

* * *

Kinkaid felt the blowback off the grenade as the blast erupted. The fierce explosion radiated heat and a burst of hot air hit his body. Red embers spiraled into the night sky and sparks set tree limbs on fire. Shadows of men were silhouetted against the intense flames as they ran through the camp and into the hills. While they searched for cover, Kinkaid kept on the move.

He threw another grenade, which ripped apart a stone dwelling. A body in flames blew through the door and rolled into the clearing. And when shards of stone and wood splinters rained down on Kinkaid, he ducked and kept running through the billowing black smoke that drifted into a thick haze.

Heading for Kate's tent, he raced through the encampment firing his weapon for cover, tossing spent magazines and reloading on the run. Two men bolted from behind a shanty and fired their AK-47s. He felt the high-pitched whine of bullets whizzing by his head and fired back. His assault rifle bucked in his hands and jolted with every round as he fired on the run.

One man toppled to the ground after he was hit several times. Kinkaid shifted his aim and took out the other guy. As the rounds hit his body, the man jerked with every strike. His face went slack, and he collapsed to the ground.

More shots were fired and Kinkaid felt the burn of a bullet that grazed his arm. He dove for cover behind a shack made of cinder blocks and, with his back pressed to the outer wall of the hut, peered around the corner. Sweat stung his eyes, and another wave of nausea hit him.

Not now. Stay focused, lightweight, he chastised himself.

One man fired cover rounds as the other two raced by the fire pit. They were trying to surround him and put him in the middle of cross fire.

"Fuck that." He backed into the shadows and maneuvered until he got all three men facing the fire. With him staying in the dark, he would screw with their night vision. The advantage would be his for a split second.

It would have to be enough.

All three men fired at once, aiming for where he had been. Chipped stone flew into the air as bullets pounded the wall. Feeling cocky, the bastards kept firing. With smug expressions, they came out from cover firing. He waited until he had a clear shot at all three—and opened fire.

Everything slowed to a painful crawl. He was locked in the moment with three armed men. He kept on the move. Brass glinted in the firelight as his shell casings flew. His G3 assault rifle bucked in his hands in fierce recoil. The men turned to face him as he flanked them, but they were too slow. The first man was hit again and again. He staggered into the cross fire. And when bullets riddled his body, he died where he stood and dropped to the dirt. Kinkaid didn't stop firing, and he kept his feet moving. When he shifted his aim, his rounds pummeled the last men standing. And he didn't stop shooting until they hit the ground.

The firefight was over . . . for now.

With his ears ringing, Kinkaid knew time was running out, and he'd lost the element of surprise. He tossed his spent mag and loaded a new one. When he raced to Kate's tent across the clearing, he pictured her face. He wanted to see her . . . to see that first look of relief to know she'd been rescued.

"Kate!" he yelled as he got to her tent and flung back the tarp. "Kate, it's me. Jackson Kinkaid. I'm taking you home."

When he yanked back the tent flap, he looked inside. Behind him, the flames cast light into the dark—enough for him to see that the tent was empty.

Kate was gone. He blinked and stared into the empty shelter, his mind muddled by the fever.

"Damn it!"

He turned to look over his shoulder in desperation. Maybe he'd gotten it wrong. Seeing another tent, he ran for it and tore back the flap. *Nothing.* He tried the next tent . . . and the next. *Still nothing.* In frustration, he aimed high and fired a few rounds in a circle around him, bellowing like a madman.

"NO!"

He raced across the camp toward the hovels where the children and the other hostages had been. *Nothing.*

"Kate!" he yelled again into the night air. His voice echoed off the canyon walls, mocking him.

She never answered. Kinkaid took refuge in the shadows—staying clear of the light—and stood in the midst of the chaos he'd created. The terrorists had fled into the hills.

And Kate was nowhere to be found.

CHAPTER 16

As he hiked back to where he'd stashed the hostages, Kinkaid fought the urge to give in to the dark emotions he felt. He'd come so far, only to have Kate slip through his hands again, but now wasn't the time to wallow in self-pity or give in to doubt.

He had a lot on his mind as he reflected on his brushes with death over the last few days. They weren't the first ones he'd had, and they certainly wouldn't be the last. Although each near miss was unique, they ran icy cold in his veins. And cold sober, he had to admit they shook him up, despite his macho front to the contrary.

A normal man in another line of work might have sought therapy to deal with the trauma. His usual therapy was paying a visit to Dr. Jack Daniel's or his associate Dr. Johnny Walker. But here and now, he knew the next best thing. Having someone to protect or someone to hunt would be all the rehabilitation he'd need.

And lucky for him—*he now had both.*

That was what he was thinking when he came face-to-face with Alexa and her team. They had found the hostages and "disarmed" them. And no one had gotten killed in the process. He now had someone to deal with the captives, and he could track the bastards who'd abducted Kate without the trail turning cold. With the exception of Kate still missing, it had been a good day.

Alexa didn't look as if she agreed.

She glared at him and stood with arms crossed, blocking his path. And when she saw the bloody crease on his arm, she shifted her eyes back to his.

"What are you gonna do for an encore? Invade Afghanistan single-handed?"

He returned her glare. "You slipped me a mickey. And you left me behind." He shrugged. "I got bored."

"Next time I'll leave a deck of cards."

"There isn't going to be a next time, Marlowe. You and me? We're done." He heaved a sigh and ran a hand through his dark hair. "You have what we came for. Garrett can chalk up Kate to collateral damage and put this mission in the win column, mission accomplished. Take them home. I'm going after Kate." He turned his back on her and gathered his gear. "Have a good life. And thanks."

When he walked through the rescued hostages, men stopped him to shake his hand or pat him on the back. And women hugged and kissed him, calling him a hero. They reached their hands out to touch him as he walked by. He never thought of himself as a hero and found it hard to accept their gratitude, especially since they weren't out of danger yet.

But there was one person he wanted to see one last time.

Before he left, Kinkaid leaned down to kiss Joselyne on the forehead, and whispered, "I'll find Kate. This isn't over."

He headed toward the destroyed camp with his gear over one shoulder and his assault rifle in his hand. The terrorists had fled the canyon and escaped into the hills. And all he wanted to do was track them, but Alexa wasn't done. She stepped around him and stood in his path with a hand on his chest, shoving him to make her point.

"Garrett wanted to keep this mission low-profile. That means we clear out now . . . before morning. He doesn't want to see our faces on CNN or have to negotiate for our release from Castro."

"Neither do I. That's not gonna happen," he argued.

"You walk away now, and Garrett will cut off his help. You know it, and I know it," she threatened.

Kinkaid kept his mouth shut—his only answer. He was done talking. With his assault rifle and gear hanging off his shoulder, he stood with his arms crossed and his jaw tight.

"You leave me no choice." She mirrored his stance and her blue eyes turned icy. He knew from experience, the woman could be real dangerous when she got backed into a corner—one of the things they had in common.

New York City
Sentinels Headquarters
Hours later

It had been a long day. Garrett wiped a hand over his face in frustration as he sat behind his desk. He had taken a quick shower and changed into jeans and a light sweater, hoping to jump-start his brain with a fresh outlook. Alexa dominated his thoughts. And his fears for her magnified after he'd seen the latest on Aljazeera.net.

Two more videos had been posted online since the first grisly transmission. Tanya made sure he'd seen them. The posts stirred renewed interest in the Haiti incident. World media were focused on the tragedy again. The first new video was the beheading of an American named George Crowell, husband to the woman who had died the same way in Haiti. The video marked the tragic end to the philanthropic efforts of a remarkable couple, but why kill a wealthy couple like the Crowells if these men were after ransom money? The erratic behavior of the terrorists concerned him. They appeared more like ruthless killers using their fanatical beliefs as an excuse to butcher innocent people. Had money taken a backseat to bloodlust?

The second video piqued Garrett's interest more for a different reason.

A Catholic nun had been beaten in front of the camera. Watching the horror made him angry. And the outpouring of concern from the religious community—both online and in the global media coverage—had stirred a maelstrom of public opinion calling for action. They had run out of time, and the world was watching. The nun's captors were hooded cowards who demanded money. Garrett recognized the name of the American that these men expected to pay the ransom.

Jackson Kinkaid.

Unless Kinkaid had one hell of a vanishing act—and obliterated his personal history—he'd become the target of a media blitz he couldn't outrun. There would be no place for him to hide and no aspect of his life that would be off-limits. He knew enough about the man's past to recognize how devastating that would be. Kinkaid didn't have a covert international organization behind him to cover his ass like Garrett did.

And after CNN gave the name of the nun and her affiliation to the missionary school, it only took Garrett a moment to realize the truth. Sister Mary Katherine was the Kate that Kinkaid had cared so much about. The pieces to the puzzle were coming together, even though he still had no idea how Kinkaid knew the nun or why he would endure such an extraordinary rescue mission to save her. His people were doing their own digging, and he hoped to know more about Kinkaid's personal connection soon.

When he heard a knock on his door, he welcomed the distraction from his grim thoughts. "Come in."

"Sorry to disturb you, but I've got an update." Tanya carried a file and sat at a chair in front of his desk. "I had Seth Harper analyze old transmissions from another case that happened not too long ago . . . one we have more intelligence on. The MO was similar to the incident in Haiti."

"And you thought if we found a link to this old case, we might have an idea who's behind the abductions in Haiti?" he asked with a smile.

"Yes. I thought it would be worth a shot." All business, Tanya didn't wait for a pat on the back. "According to what Jackson Kinkaid told Alexa, this group carried high-tech gear. GPS units, laptops, the works. And their use of a video cam to post beheadings online is also distinctive. The MO in Haiti triggered something I remembered from an earlier case."

"Good." He nodded. "What did you find out?"

"I believe the terrorist cell Alexa is tracking is the same group who invaded a remote hotel in the British Virgin Islands and abducted five men on holiday. Three bystanders were killed. And Harper's analysis confirms similarities. He's found a link that ties this case directly to the Haiti incident. Here's a summary of that investigation." She handed him the report and continued, "A guy by the name of Abdul Kabir Sayed was believed to be the leader. He's making a name for himself, and he's after bigger and bigger headlines. Some believe he's got ties to Venezuelan President Hugo Chavez and that Chavez gave him a place to hide after the Virgin Islands incident."

"If that's true, then the Cuban connection makes sense. Chavez has forged links with Castro and modeled his government after communist Cuba," Garrett agreed. "And Chavez is one of America's newest adversaries. After he survived an attempted coup and a nationwide petition demanding his recall, the man has cultivated dangerous ties to terrorism. Chavez has got nine lives, politically speaking. He's been in power for ten years and the last referendum vote cleared the way for him to rule for decades like Castro. He's not going away anytime soon."

"Yes, and now the U.S. believes the Venezuelan government is issuing official documents to people who shouldn't have them," she said. "These documents could be used to obtain Venezuelan passports and American visas. They'd allow the holders to get past immigration checkpoints and enter the United States under false pretenses. It's one of the scenarios being investigated."

Tanya showed him an executive summary of a CIA threat assessment and the Venezuelan connection to known terrorist cells. "You said before that you thought this Haiti attack had been training for something bigger. You still feel that way?"

"Yeah, I do," he said. "Someone like Sayed could be planning a major incident on U.S. soil. And with help from big brother in Venezuela, it looks like he might have the means to enter this country legally."

"Are you planning to inform the CIA or Homeland Security of your theories? It's one thing for our organization to rescue these hostages and stop Sayed in Cuba, but a guy like this is only a cog in a wheel. Others will follow. This threat won't go away if Alexa and her team just take him out. We need to question him and advise the CIA or Homeland Security of the possible threat."

"Yes, I know. I've been thinking the same thing." He steepled his hands and rested his chin on his fingers. "The CIA is most similar to our organization, at least their covert arm. And we have solid inside connections there."

"Why do I hear a 'but' coming?" She narrowed her eyes and waited for his answer.

"This could turn into a political circus, and we'd lose control, especially with a new administration coming into power. I had hoped with this new president that the CIA would get restructured . . . that the covert operatives would do their jobs under the guidance of the Pentagon rather than reporting through the president. If that happened, the Sentinels could breathe easier on the domestic front."

"I'm not following." She shook her head.

"The CIA has gotten bad press over the years, bogged down by politics. If they were under the Pentagon, it might be a different story. They'd do their jobs without some bureaucrat second-guessing their moves. Covert activities shouldn't fall under any U.S. president. CIA analysts could remain part of the executive branch to advise the president, but there's too much temptation to play God on a global scale with the covert branch part of that same package. As it is now, the CIA gets constant interference from a revolving door of armchair quarterbacks sworn into office every four years. They contend with presidents who either don't have the guts to make decisions or who think they can flex their political muscle for their own agenda like it's a game. I hate breaking in a new administration." He looked her in the eye. "I'll figure out a way to pass the word after our mission is over and we cover our tracks."

"I take it that's why our organization was formed. Members of the Sentinels were tired of business as usual in Washington and wanted results."

"Makes sense, doesn't it?" He nodded, implying she was right.

But he knew the truth.

The Sentinels had been around much longer than

the United States. And even though he'd been sworn to secrecy about their covert activities and their agenda when he became leader, he believed in their cause and would do anything to defend and perpetuate their rich history. His knowledge of the Sentinels' past was limited to what he'd studied in the archives and had been told by those who came before him. Yet he knew enough to realize that the powerful men and women behind the Sentinels had a proud lineage and would carry on long after he was gone.

The weight of his responsibilities often forced him to make decisions that went against his personal beliefs even though they were for the greater good. And many times he had agonized over the outcomes. Any covert agency would go to great lengths to defend its own country's interests, but how far was too far? In a dangerous world of underlying political agendas stemming from greed and the seductive temptation of power, a coalition of countries aligned for a common purpose made sense. Yet Garrett understood that power of this magnitude was a slippery slope, no matter who or how many were at the helm.

Who would oversee those in control?

So far he hadn't come up with a good answer to that question. And in all their years of existence, neither had the Sentinels. They sought control and gained ground with each passing year.

When would it be enough, and what was their ultimate goal? Others would make that call.

"You look a million miles away." Tanya's voice pulled him from his thoughts. "Are you worried about Alexa?"

Tanya was one of the few people within the organization who knew of his personal history with Alexa. He didn't mind the woman knowing about their past, but the part he'd played in the annihilation of any future he might have had with Alexa—and his feelings on the subject—were off-limits.

"I just want to know what's going on." He sighed and looked toward the active TV monitors along the far wall. "It's been hours since our last communication. A lot can happen."

"Let's get an updated reading on those tracking beacons," she suggested. "And I'll check with Seth Harper to see if he's recorded any more transmissions from the terrorists."

While Tanya got on the phone to obtain her electronic updates, Garrett opened his safe room and activated his holographic map of Cuba. Within minutes, Tanya joined him and keyed in the new coordinates. When the 3-D image projected onto the conference table, communications interrupted with an incoming call from the field. Hank Lewis was on the SAT phone. And Tanya had the call redirected to Garrett's safe room phone.

"Moonshine Two reporting." The voice of Hank Lewis crackled onto the line with a staggered delay. "School's out and mission accomplished, sir. We targeted a baker's dozen, but are coming home with twelve. We're at the rendezvous point now and will be gone before daylight."

A baker's dozen meant thirteen. One hostage was missing or had been killed.

"Copy that. And good work, Moonshine Two. Any casualties?"

"None, sir." When Hank didn't elaborate on the last hostage, he knew there was something the man was about to tell him or had left out.

He watched the two tracking beacons on his holographic map of Cuba. One signal was stationary and located near the shoreline. The other was positioned farther north. Hank Lewis wasn't done reporting, and Garrett had a bad feeling he wouldn't like the rest.

"I'm tracking more than one location," he prompted. "Where's Martini One?"

There was a hesitation on the line. For a moment, he thought that he'd lost the connection. Eventually, Hank replied.

"Martini One is after our last target. And the FNG is tagging along."

Hank conveyed more before he concluded his report and ended the call, with Garrett gritting his teeth. Kinkaid and Alexa were after the last hostage. And a tidy operation had turned messy.

To complicate matters, Kinkaid's involvement had already been made public online with the ransom demands of the terrorists who held Sister Mary Katherine. If Cuban officials caught him during his rescue attempt of the nun, Garrett couldn't be sure that Kinkaid wouldn't drag him or the Sentinels into his mess.

And even though a rogue mercenary in league with drug cartels would make a handy scapegoat if things turned ugly, the same couldn't be said for Alexa's involvement. If she were taken prisoner with Kinkaid, Garrett would have explaining to do. And disavowing the operation could get complicated unless he found a way to exploit it.

But Garrett had confidence in his ability to manipulate the situation in his favor. With finesse, Alexa could serve as his pawn, and Kinkaid would make a convenient sacrificial lamb. His actions would be completely justified if he protected the interests of the Sentinels.

"Dig up everything you have on Sayed," he said to Tanya. "With Alexa still on the ground in Cuba, maybe we can spin this to our advantage. I've got an idea."

Southeast Cuba

Alexa worked under the pale light of the moon. Kneeling beside Kinkaid, she had bandaged the bullet graze on his arm and was now putting a fresh dressing on his belly wound. Kinkaid had stretched out on his sleeping bag with his shirt off, wearing only his BDU camo pants and boots. His chest glistened in the sweltering heat, and his skin was warm to the touch. She had no doubt his fever had returned. Lying on his back, he was propped on his elbows and stared into the darkness. When he tried to pretend she wasn't there, she reminded him with a move Florence Nightingale wouldn't have approved. It made him wince.

She hated being ignored.

Kinkaid hadn't said much since she forced him to take her along on his mission to save Kate. They trekked into the hills and found good cover against a rock face surrounded by trees and a trickling stream nearby. Muggy heat closed in, and the bugs had no respect for their fatigue. They'd continue their search for Kate after they got a few hours to sleep.

On the surface, Kinkaid would have appeared angry and sullen, but she knew exhaustion fueled his distant mood. And his unrelenting fever hadn't helped.

"I'm taking first watch. No arguments," she whispered, having no intention of waking him to spell her. The guy needed sleep. "When was the last time you took your meds?"

"I'm good," he said. When she was done playing nurse, he lay back and stared into the night sky with an arm under his head. "And . . . thanks."

Instead of rolling over and going to sleep, he turned toward her, and she caught a glint of light in those green eyes of his. Jackson Kinkaid always had an effect on her, but in the dead calm of night, his low voice and quiet gentle ways made her forget the usual rift between them. It made her wish that they'd never met on the job. Things might have turned out differently if they had been introduced in a less complicated way, as just a man and woman.

"You didn't have to come with me," he began. When things got personal, men often chose a convoluted way to say what they really meant. Kinkaid was no different.

"You're welcome." She forced a weary grin and stretched out next to him on her sleeping bag. Braced on an elbow, she looked down at him. "You could barely stand, hotshot. I'm just returning the favor."

She pretended to adjust his arm bandage, wanting an excuse to touch him. "You got those hostages out on your own," she added. "Very impressive."

"I thought you were long gone," he said. "Or maybe you were watching to see if I got my ass kicked."

She saw him flinch with a smile. With Kinkaid it was hard to detect the difference between amusement and outright hostility.

"Depending on who was doing the kicking"—she grinned—"I might pay top dollar for a ringside seat." She told him about the tracking beacon that she'd stowed in his gear.

"You stuck a tracking beacon on me?"

"Yeah. I wanted you easy to find for a rescue mission after we got the hostages," she admitted. "It's still in your gear. In the bag where you stow your iPod. I figured you'd never leave that behind. The beacon made it easy to find Waldo."

Kinkaid only shook his head, and they fell into a comfortable silence. Since the mission had started, they had not been alone much to talk. She felt the distance between them, but the rescue was the main objective, and she'd let it go. Now they had a quiet moment together, and she didn't want to waste it—even if she ticked him off.

"What happened to you?" she asked.

The sudden shift in topic took him by surprise as she had hoped. His faint amusement was gone, replaced by definite hostility. In truth, his shift in gears turned her on. He had an edge that scared her—and she liked it.

"Rumor has it that you work for South American

drug cartels. You go wherever the money is best. When we worked together before . . ."

"That was a long time ago, Alexa. Ancient history." He narrowed his eyes and pulled the boonie hat off her head and ran his fingers through her hair. If he was trying to distract her, the man had hit the bull's-eye dead center.

"We all have choices in how we live our lives. I thought you were one of the good guys." She reached for his hand and stopped him from toying with her hair. Taking his hand in both of hers, she entwined her fingers with his. "Working for the highest bidder doesn't strike me as your kind of gig, especially drug cartels, Jackson. That's why I gotta know. What happened to you? What made you change?"

"Whatever you think you know . . . you don't." He stared into the dark and heaved a deep sigh. "It's complicated. And I'm working things out . . . my way."

"It's just that I'm worried . . ."

"I know you are," he interrupted. "I can see that, but let it go."

Kinkaid had changed. She saw it in everything he did. He'd lost the peaks to his valleys and was content to drift through life like a ghost, unfettered by real emotion . . . even joy. She rested her hand on his arm. The intimacy felt natural between them, and he didn't object. The feel of his hard muscles brought a new rush of heat to her cheeks. And when he fixed a languid gaze on her, she forgot to breathe. Heat radiated off his skin, and she felt a primal urgency take hold. From the hunger in his eyes, she knew he had the same urges.

She didn't have to wait to find out.

He trailed a finger down her cheek and neck. And with his touch, she closed her eyes, and a suggestive gasp escaped her lips. Grasping the back of her neck, he pulled her to his chest and explored her mouth with his warm, wet tongue. Her nipples reacted to the feel of his hard body through her damp T-shirt. She straddled his leg and felt the rush of desire as adrenaline surged through her.

She knew this was wrong. This wasn't the time or the place to give in to the craving she felt for Kinkaid, but her tongue had a mind of its own. She pictured unzipping him and taking what she wanted. His low groans of breathy intimacy sent a message that he wouldn't protest.

But a second later, they both stopped and locked gazes as if they were reading each other's minds.

"Wait a minute," she gasped.

"We can't do this," he said in unison.

"I said it first." She brushed back her blond hair and rolled off his chest. It took a moment for her to regain control.

What had happened with Kinkaid left her stumped. She understood the physical need, and the chemistry had always been there between them, but his feelings for Kate confused her. It was obvious he had strong feelings for the woman, enough to risk his life for her. Yet he'd just kissed another woman as if he meant it. His sudden display of sexual need made her wonder. Was Kate the real deal for him, relegating her to play the role of a handy "friend with benefits"?

And since when did *that* bother her?

She understood the need for a man to release sexual tension, and normally she'd be happy to oblige, but being around Kinkaid on this mission had messed her up, and she wasn't sure why. Maybe it had started when she questioned her motives for wanting to play "tonsil hockey" with Seth Harper.

What the hell's happening to me?

"I have to ask you something." She fought to steady her breathing. "Don't shoot me, okay?"

"I wouldn't shoot you, Alexa." Without a smile, he shrugged. "At least not here. Too loud."

"Tell me about Kate. What's she to you?" When he looked as if he would object, she reasoned, "I'm risking my neck for her. You owe me an explanation."

"You're risking your life because it's the right thing to do," he argued. Anger flared in his eyes. "What's between me and Kate shouldn't matter. And it's none of your business. Wake me for my watch."

With effort and a groan, he rolled over and turned his back on her, leaving her with pent-up sexual tension and unanswered questions. She grabbed her weapon and found a spot to stand watch. Kinkaid's feelings for Kate mattered to her. She wasn't sure why—but they did. *He* mattered to her.

And that left her wondering—what the hell was wrong with her?

Beyond the canyon, Abdul Kabir Sayed crouched in the dirt and glared into the dark heavens, unable to sleep. He was still seething from what had happened. Only four of his men had survived the attack on the terrorist camp. And they had left gear and supplies behind. His handler would have to provide him a name, someone local who could give him safe haven and replenish what he had lost.

After the humiliation he had suffered, that would not be easy.

The other men from the camp had scrambled into the hills like cockroaches scurrying for cover. They distanced themselves from him, knowing the attack had been his doing. He'd brought trouble to their village, and word would travel. He would be blamed unless he could turn the insulting incident to his advantage.

At least he still had the woman.

He stared at her now. His men had bound her hands and feet tightly and hung her from a sturdy tree branch with her feet dangling as punishment for her part. The weight of her body would cause the ropes to burn and cut into her skin. And breathing would be difficult, especially with the gag stuffed in her mouth. He heard her pathetic gasps for air, and her struggle for survival grated on his nerves like the incessant whine of an insect buzzing at his ear. She would pay for what had happened. All that remained was for him to decide how.

To redeem his name, she would be made an example. And the world would soon know his purpose.

Sayed had not expected to be attacked in Cuba, a country that allowed him to operate in anonymity and train his newest recruits. His men had been careless, and some had paid the price for their mistake. Their deaths had saved him the trouble of killing them himself. And given what he'd learned tonight, he now knew that he'd been followed from Haiti—and by a man that the white woman claimed not to know well.

Jackson Kinkaid.

She had lied to him. *LIED . . . to him!*

He ground a fist into the dirt beneath him, barely aware that his knuckles stung and were bleeding. After the attack, the voice of Kinkaid calling her name had echoed in the canyon and taunted him. In shock and anger, he had turned toward the white woman as they fled the explosions. He saw in her eyes that she recognized the man's voice even though she'd tried to hide her reaction.

She knew Jackson Kinkaid better than she had admitted. The wealthy American had come to save her, and that would not have been the case if they were merely acquaintances. And an even greater insult, the rescue of the other hostages by Kinkaid and his men would be blamed on him. Those who envied his sudden rise in power would seek to undermine his authority, but since he still had the white woman, perhaps he could redeem himself. He still held the most valuable hostage, a woman this American hero had risked his life to save.

Only a weak man would do such a thing for a mere woman.

And Sayed vowed to use Kinkaid's weakness against him. He did not understand how a woman's life had value, not even if the woman had the honor of giving birth to him. A woman would always be made to serve men in that way. It was their purpose in life. But if Jackson Kinkaid valued this woman enough to come for her once, he would do it again. And this time the American would face him, not skulk like a coward in the dark.

Kinkaid and this woman would pay for what they had done to him—and the world would witness his triumph.

He stood and walked toward her. With eyes wide, she trembled and shook her head as he came closer. Useless tears streaked her battered face. She was a stupid woman. *Insignificant*. And her fear only made him stronger. It fed his need to lash out and quenched the thirst of his rage. She pulled at the ropes, and her body swung in and out of shadows. Blood from her wrists trickled down her arms. The dark streak marked her pale skin. He took his knife from its sheath and let the blade catch the moonlight, enough for her to see what would come.

He would not wait until morning to inflict his punishment.

CHAPTER 17

Southeast Cuba

Dawn cut the dark horizon with a jagged edge of steel gray. Yet even under a mantle of darkness, the jungle came alive. Animals foraged for food, and birds stirred in the branches over Alexa's head. The world had its own clock, its natural order. Even the humidity had tapered off enough for her to notice.

She watched Kinkaid sleep. His bare chest rose and fell in a steady rhythm now, but rest had not come easy. She heard him toss and turn during the few hours he had to sleep until he retrieved his iPod from his gear. The volume was too low for her to hear what he played, but as soon as he plugged the sound into his ears, he settled into a deep sleep where he barely moved.

Jackson Kinkaid was like an engaging foreign flick, only he didn't come with subtitles. What she saw in him made her yearn to know more, but without a deeper understanding, she knew she was missing something major. Some men were open books and easy to read.

A guy like Kinkaid would never be.

"Damn it," he grumbled as he rolled to one side and ran a hand through his dark hair. "Why didn't you wake me?"

"You needed your beauty sleep way more than I did," she smirked. "And from where I'm sitting, you still do."

"More snooze time won't fix what's wrong with me." He curled a lip into a half smile. "And your looks don't need improving."

"And here I thought your idea of foreplay was a rousing argument," she countered. "Don't play nice, Kinkaid. I won't know how to act."

She covered her reaction to his compliment with attitude, but in the quiet of morning, his deep voice had raised goose bumps across her skin. His voice had the warm bite of a fine Cognac—sweet, potent, and addictive. And the charm of his flattery took her by surprise, especially given how abrasive he'd been through their mission. She did her best to ignore what he'd said, but inside she was smiling.

"Today we gotta make up time," she said. "I smell rain. We can't let the trail get cold, or we'll lose them. You better be up for this."

She ignored the shadows under his eyes and the fevered look of his skin. And she did her best to overlook the sluggish way he got off his bedroll. Giving him a hard time for pushing himself would do little good now. Neither of them could do anything about it. She had to press him for all he had left. Anything less would jeopardize them both.

Kinkaid was getting worse. She knew it and suspected he did, too.

"How are you doing on meds?"

He didn't hesitate. "I'm good." His stock answer.

Kinkaid wouldn't have told her otherwise. As he gathered his gear, she remembered hearing him take pills last night. Judging by the soft rattle of an almost depleted bottle, she knew he was running on empty— in more ways than one. As an operative, she understood what Kinkaid needed. He wouldn't respond well to coddling or a nursemaid, not when he had a personal stake in the mission. The best medicine would be to keep him focused and on track.

What they both needed was to rescue Kate as soon as possible. She hoped that when they found her, it wouldn't be too late for Kinkaid.

New York City
Sentinels Headquarters
Hours later

"Jessie." When Seth saw her at his dormitory door, he grinned and his face lit up as if he'd flipped an internal switch. "Tanya busted me loose. I'm confined to this facility until someone escorts me back to Alexa's place, but no more locked doors. Check it out."

He closed the door behind her and opened it again to prove his point with a wave of his arm, acting like a magician with a new trick.

"You're easy to amuse." She smiled. "When are you leaving?"

"I'm not. Not until I know Alexa is safe." The mischievous glint in his dark eyes vanished when his expression grew somber. "I want to be here in case they need me."

Jess was relieved to know he wanted to help and would be around if Garrett needed him. Having Seth part of the team that would bring Alexa home made her feel better, especially when she had news of her own to share.

"What's the matter?" he asked. "Did something else happen?"

Jess wiped her palms on her jeans and took a deep breath.

"I'm heading out soon. Garrett is sending a team to help Alexa, and I'm on it." She looked him in the eye. "I wanted to thank you . . . for everything."

"Even for the peep show in the shower?"

"Especially for that peep show." She grinned and enjoyed the blush on his cheeks.

She'd forgotten how comfortable he always made her feel. Even when life felt like a kick in the teeth, Seth Harper could usually make her smile. Still, Jess knew her life wouldn't be an easy fit with his. It had been another reason why she'd resisted letting him into her heart any more than she already had.

She'd never found a man with staying power. And even if Seth had real potential, she knew not to expect much, but not because she thought he'd deliberately hurt her. She was a card-carrying member of the walking wounded. She couldn't expect him to accept her the way she was. That was too much to ask of anyone. And when she finally had to let him go, it would be too painful.

Seth would leave an empty crater in her heart—in a place where only *he* would fit.

He stared at her a long moment. He crossed his arms and didn't take his eyes off her until he finally spoke again.

"I know this is what you do. And there's a chance you might . . ." He held back the rest. "I'm proud of you, Jessie, but that won't stop me from worrying. A man's gotta do what a man's gotta do. I hope that's okay."

"Yeah, Mr. Macho. I think that'll be okay." When she stepped toward him, he held her in his arms and rested his forehead on hers. She closed her eyes and breathed deep, taking in the intoxicating smell of his skin. With the warmth of his body next to hers, she felt safe . . . and loved.

It was good to have someone to lean on, even for a little while.

Southeast Cuba

Trailing the men who had Kate had been slow, especially with Kinkaid in his condition. Alexa did most of the strenuous tracking, leaving him to flank her position and be on guard against an ambush from the men they were chasing. After last night, the bastards who had Kate knew they were being tracked, making them more dangerous. And since they had home-turf advantage, the terrorists knew where they were going, which put her and Kinkaid at an even greater disadvantage. They also had to stay off the main path. That left them drudging through thick vegetation at nearly twice the distance.

Alexa looked over her shoulder to see Kinkaid behind her with weapon in hand and eyes alert. Even as sick as he was, he was a big man and still looked formidable to anyone who didn't know him—but she knew better. His movements were more languid than usual, and the steely glare in his green eyes lacked his usual predatory gleam.

When she got to good cover, she caught his eye to signal him to stop. He joined her and dropped to a knee. Drizzle pattered on her boonie hat, a reminder they were still at the mercy of Mother Nature.

"Take a break," she said as she shrugged out of her pack and pulled out a map. "We've been heading north. I think these guys are making a beeline for the only nearby town, Baracoa." After swatting at a cloud of gnats, she pointed to a spot on the map on the southeast coast of Cuba. "We missed most of the hurricane, being in the mountains, but Baracoa is at sea level. There will be flooding, and we'll have to deal with the aftermath of the storm."

"Only one road in?" Kinkaid asked.

"Looks like it, if it's not flooded. The road will be watched. We'll have to find another way in." She folded the map and took a drink from her hydration pack. "These bastards must have connections in town. Why else would they risk taking a hostage there?"

If Kate is still alive, she almost said. She knew the little Haitian girl had told Kinkaid last night that Kate was still alive, but there were no guarantees she'd be breathing today. And even though they both knew the odds of his friend surviving her ordeal, neither of them talked about the worst-case scenario.

"They know we're coming." Kinkaid wiped a hand across his face. "They'll be ready this time. We can expect more men. And we won't know who to trust in Baracoa."

Alexa knew they'd stand out in town. And for every contact they made, they'd have to expect trouble and be more guarded. They couldn't trust anyone.

"You speak the language?" she asked.

He nodded. "Yeah."

"Good. That'll help."

If the rumors were true about Kinkaid having links to regional drug cartels, she had a pretty good idea he spoke several languages fluently. His unsavory affiliations would pay off in Cuba.

"I'm going to call home base." She retrieved the satellite phone from her gear and pointed. "I'm heading to that ridge. It's not far. You can keep an eye on me from here."

"Be careful," he replied.

Alexa took her assault rifle to look for higher ground and better reception for the SAT phone. As she headed up the slope in the rain, she dug her boots into the dirt and pulled through the heavy brush, looking for a clear shot at the sky. The climb was short, but strenuous. Sweat trickled off her neck and down her back. Following the terrorists had brought them to a lower elevation, and the muggy heat was back. The air was downright steamy with the rain. And if it was possible, the bugs had gotten worse.

Near the ridge, she found good cover with a view below to Kinkaid's position. She caught his eye and he waved to let her know he'd keep watch. Within minutes, she had Garrett on the line.

"The Home Shopping Network is sending you a package." Garrett gave her an estimated time of arrival in code. "Give my regards to the bounty hunter."

In cryptic fashion, Garrett had informed her that help was coming, and Jessie would be a part of the backup team. Alexa suspected that Garrett hadn't been pleased with her decision to help Kinkaid find Kate, but to his credit, he hadn't mentioned it . . . so far.

"Copy that."

Between the voice delays inherent in a satellite phone, she gave him a brief report on their plan, purposefully sticking to protocol and communicating in code when necessary. When she was done, Garrett surprised her with information on the terrorist leader they were chasing. Their target's name was Abdul Kabir Sayed. Using the man's name had violated procedure. Garrett had taken a risk to get her the information she'd need to track the bastard when they got to Baracoa.

Kinkaid would be pleased that he would have a name.

"Thanks for the ID on our target. I'll contact you . . ."

Before she finished, Garrett interrupted her.

"We need Sayed alive, Martini One. Do you read me?"

In a hostage-rescue mission, the priority was to save

innocent lives. Extracting the hostage had priority over the lives of the captors. And with Kinkaid along, she had a feeling the mission would be search and destroy—with extreme prejudice. Any man who had taken his Kate would pay.

"I read you. And we'll do our best," she acknowledged, but Garrett wasn't done making his point.

"This is imperative, Martini One," he insisted. "This isn't a request. Consider it an order. Even if the pawn is at risk, we've got more at stake. The pawn is expendable."

Alexa narrowed her eyes, not believing what she'd heard until he clued her in on why he was ordering a change in plans. Although he only spoke briefly, what he told her broke protocol. That couldn't be helped. He knew she'd need more reason to go against her instincts.

Risking the life of the hostage they were trying to save made no sense. Garrett was asking her to place more importance on taking the terrorist leader into custody than in saving the life of the hostage Kinkaid had risked his life for. Her mission would be at odds with Jackson's personal stake in all this.

What the hell would she tell him?

When she had remained silent too long, Garrett clarified, "If there's a choice, the nun is collateral damage. Is that clear?"

Alexa wiped the beads of perspiration from her lip. "Say again, sir?"

What nun?

All she heard was static. She didn't know if the SAT

phone lost its link, but she stayed on the line, hoping Garrett would explain. *Kate was a nun?* Had Garrett known all along? He'd sent her on this mission because of her past with Kinkaid. He owed her an explanation, especially now that he'd complicated things with a new directive. If Garrett were standing in front of her now, she'd be in his face, demanding to know more. Why Kate was expendable compared to the despicable coward who had waged war on innocent women and children?

Garrett's voice finally came on the line. "He hasn't told you about her?"

"No. Not a word."

"She has a direct line to the Almighty . . . and the uniform to match. They met at a hospital outside Boston. Years ago."

"A hospital?" she questioned. "Was our boy wounded?"

She watched the rain roll down her arms and waited for his answer, not fully realizing she was holding her breath. There was a long stretch of silence before Garrett came back on the line.

"A psychiatric hospital, Martini One. Our boy was a patient there."

CHAPTER 18

Alexa's throat tightened as she turned her gaze down the hill and spotted Jackson Kinkaid staring up at her. Garrett's words replayed in her head.

The nun is collateral damage. He hasn't told you about her?

They met at a hospital . . . years ago. A psychiatric hospital . . . our boy was a patient.

She tried to get more out of Garrett, but sharing details over the SAT phone was not the way to do it. Even though she had a feeling that her boss knew more about Kinkaid's hospital stay, Garrett wouldn't say any more about it. She had ended the call with more questions than she had answers. For her to think that Kinkaid's mental state was part of his feud with Garrett would be pure speculation.

If she wanted to know more, she'd have to pick the right moment to get it from Kinkaid—even if she didn't have the right to ask.

"What happened to you?" she whispered under her breath as she watched him through the rain.

The life they both led certainly wasn't for the faint of heart. All operatives had their own reasons for the choices they made. And each mission tested their ability to live with what they did. She understood that. But for a guy as mentally tough as Jackson Kinkaid, what would have driven him over the edge and forced him into a psychiatric hospital? And what did a nun have to do with his mental breakdown?

As she headed down the slope, Alexa thought back to her initial infatuation with him. They'd had chemistry from the start, yet despite her wanting more, he never let the attraction go anywhere. They shared a few missions for the Sentinels, but after a while she lost track of him. And since he never talked about his private life, she didn't know much about him beyond the job.

She slid down the bottom third of the hill and wiped her hands on her BDUs as Kinkaid joined her.

"What did Garrett have to say?" he asked.

"He's got a team coming. They'll make contact when they get here," she told him. "And he gave me the name of the man in charge of the terrorist cell, the one who has . . . Kate."

Kinkaid fixed his gaze on her. "Who is it?"

"Abdul Kabir Sayed. You know him?" she asked.

Kinkaid thought about it for a minute and shook his head.

"No. Name's not familiar." He narrowed his green eyes. The glint of the predator was back. "But I can't wait to meet him."

Alexa could have shared what Garrett had told her about taking Sayed alive for the sake of the greater good. Interrogating Sayed was imperative. Kinkaid would have understood her new directive—if Kate hadn't been the one who was taken and the woman's life wasn't still hanging in the balance.

No, Kinkaid wouldn't listen to reason. She'd keep the information about Sayed to herself for now and deal with Kinkaid later, when she had a team to back up any decision she might be forced to make.

"Let's get moving," she said. "We've got ground to cover before this rain gets worse."

Alexa had a hard time looking him in the eye.

Baracoa, Cuba
Dusk

On the horizon loomed a recognizable landmark that Alexa remembered from her map, a distinctive plateau named El Yunque. Normally, Baracoa was a quaint colonial village surrounded by secluded beaches and a pristine rain forest, but it had become a virtual cesspool in the wake of the hurricane. The annihilation the storm had brought looked more dismal in the waning hours of an exhausting day as Alexa accompanied Kinkaid through the carnage.

Neither of them spoke. They couldn't. No words would describe the devastation.

The overcast skies stole the last remnants of light, and the drizzle had been unrelenting. They were drenched and waded cautiously through knee-deep dark water as they followed a side street into town. To the right, churning seas brought whitecaps into the already flooded shoreline, with spindly trees protruding from muddy waters. The salty smell of the ocean mixed with the stench of raw sewage. Alexa found it hard to breathe.

Even at this hour, scantily clad survivors were still sifting through rubble in search of anything worth saving. Soggy mattresses, damaged but usable furniture, and clothing were piled high along the road, ready to salvage for those desperate enough to need it. And heaping piles of splintered wood, corrugated metal, and sandbags were stacked to create a barricade against high water. The refuse had been pulled from the wreckage of shops, office buildings, and dwellings in preparation for cleanup.

They had trailed Sayed to Baracoa, and their search for him would take top priority even though Kinkaid looked dead on his feet. Alexa feared Kate wasn't the only one out of time.

"You holding up?" she asked.

"Yeah. No worries." He avoided her gaze.

"Liar," she muttered as she returned the stares of locals watching them from a distance.

She had stowed her assault rifle in her pack so she wouldn't draw attention. Kinkaid had done the same, but they both kept their handguns in reach and under cover. Although most residents would be focused on recovering from the storm, Alexa knew there would be men who had other priorities.

Opportunistic men.

Sayed would seek such men for different reasons.

"We should get to higher ground. This water is filled

with sewage," Kinkaid said. "Our target will be looking for a safe place to hide. If there's a Muslim connection here, he'll find it. His food. His culture. His people.
That's what we'll hit first, as soon as we find a place to
stash our gear."

"Preferably a place with a hot shower," she added.
"Not that I'm complaining. I've gotten used to sweat
and bug juice. It makes a heady bouquet."

"Don't get your hopes up." Kinkaid gave her a sideways glance. "Hot water may be too much to ask."

"A girl can dream."

Kinkaid pointed left. Wedged into the hillside were
buildings that had fared better in the storm. The structures looked as if they might have escaped the flooding.
And with downed power lines, some streets were dark,
but other places had electricity. They headed for high
ground and the light. Once they got past the flooding,
Baracoa's cobblestone streets were lined with single-
story buildings with roofs of weathered red tile. The
brightly colored structures were jammed next to each
other. Despite paint peeling from the heat of the sun,
remnants of the town's colonial charm remained.

It took them an hour to find a functioning motel with
an available room—one room. Kinkaid took it without
asking her opinion. And judging by the looks of the
place when they opened the door, he had cultivated his
low standards to an art form.

They dropped their gear on the floor and stared at the
room in stunned silence. Two bulbs were out, making
the place dark. But from where she stood, that was a

blessing. The old carpet had a musty stench to it, made worse by the muggy stale air. And the bed was rumpled. Who knew when they had last changed the sheets? The walls could have used a good coat of paint . . . ten years ago. And behind the curtain, the annoying buzz of flies pinging off the window capped off the ambience.

"Promise me," he said.

"What?"

"No matter what happens. Don't let me die in this fuckin' shit hole."

She sighed and cocked her head.

"Not funny, Kinkaid." *Not funny at all*.

Near Baracoa, Cuba

Blood loss had made Kate weak. Last night, Sayed had cut into her skin with his knife and torn clothes from her body. She knew parts of her were exposed. The air that hit her bare body made her skin prickle. And her tunic was shamefully dirty and tattered, making a mockery of her faith. If his intention had been to humiliate her, he had succeeded.

She had no idea how severe her wounds were. No one had tended to her. And she tried not to move. Moving opened the gashes and started the bleeding again. Without stitches, she would have no way to stop it. And infection would set in soon, but she had a feeling she wouldn't live to see that happen.

She still had no idea where she was. They'd brought her to this new place with her head under a black hood.

Sayed and his men were the only voices she heard until they locked her into a cell, tied her up, and yanked off the hood.

Her hands were bound above her head with rope, and her body hung from the ceiling under a stark light. In these conditions, she would not sleep. And to punish her further, Sayed had not given her water or food since the night of the raid—*just like George*. With her body depleted, she knew this did not bode well for her survival, but she was beyond caring.

Except for one bright moment of hope—Jackson Kinkaid. She was still shocked that he had risked his life to save her.

Apart from the friendship they shared, Kate knew he could be a dangerous man. She figured that out after their many talks at the hospital. And between each confidence he shared was the underlying pain, the sadness that would never leave his eyes. To this day she saw it. He'd never gotten his life back, not after what had happened. But he had come to rescue her, giving her hope until—

Kate heard footsteps echoing down a hall outside her cell. She gasped at the sound. And her heart thrashed in her chest as a deep ache clinched her belly. When the footsteps grew louder, she knew they were coming for her.

A key slid into the lock, and the door opened with a creak. She blinked her eyes to clear her blurred vision. A dark-skinned man stood in front of her. Sayed had come for her, the man who had taken such pleasure inflicting pain with his knife.

He had a tall glass of ice water in his hand. Taking his time, he drank and watched as she licked her lips, unable to hide her thirst. Her throat was parched, and her lips were so dry, they were cut and bleeding. She felt the sting of peeling skin and tasted the tang of blood every time she moistened her lips with her tongue.

"Ah, refreshing." He grinned as the ice settled back into his glass. "I was very thirsty from the trip, but soon I will be enjoying a feast fit for Allah. My host, who is a man of my faith, has been most generous. He is preparing a banquet to celebrate my great victory. Curry chicken, roasted rabbit, olives, pomegranates, succulent sweet dates—these foods remind me of my home." He narrowed his eyes, and his face turned into a scowl. "The fact that I am here with you is a true insult."

Without warning, Sayed threw the glass across the room in a sudden fit of rage. The glass shattered against the wall, and the shards splintered. Pieces flew and glinted in the light. She hid her face on pure instinct. When she turned her head, he grabbed her chin and forced her to look him in the eye. For a long moment, he glared at her as his fingernails dug into her skin.

"Jackson Kinkaid. You must think him a hero, yes?" he said.

When she didn't answer, he leaned closer and intimidated her with his intimacy. She felt his warm acrid breath on her face.

"Your hero was responsible for many of the hostages getting killed in that cowardly raid of his." He nodded and glared at her. "It's true. I was after ransom money, completely. These people would have been returned to their families . . . in time, but not now. Now, is too late."

He stepped around her, where her eyes couldn't follow. Having him behind her made her skin crawl. Her body tensed. And she held her breath.

"And as for your precious children, would you like to know who will not be going home?" He grinned and she heard the sick satisfaction in his voice. "Perhaps I will save this for another time. You are not worthy to know such things . . . unless I decide to tell you."

He headed for the door to her cell, but turned at the last minute.

"Do you still think Jackson Kinkaid is a hero?" Sayed sneered. He left her alone again and locked the door.

Debilitating grief mixed with blind rage. Her eyes welled with tears, and her body fell slack. She wouldn't have the strength to survive much longer. She wasn't worth saving if the cost meant others would be killed. Kate wanted this to be over, and she no longer cared how that would happen. The faces of the children flashed painfully through her mind. Why had God forsaken her to this merciless man? And why had he allowed so many to be killed? Doubting God hurt far worse than anything Sayed could have done to her—and the wound had been self-inflicted.

Before dinner, Sayed went to the guest room he'd been given. He looked at his watch and calculated the time in his head. He had waited long enough. Back home in his country, his handler was an early riser.

Sayed had made a video of his own words and would transmit the uplink now. His teachings would be posted for the world to see. And this time, he would not hide behind a mask to gain deserved attention for killing his enemy. He would convince his handler to post his personal message to followers he was sure would soon know his name. Raising money to fight the oppressors of his people had value, but others were more suited to pursue this endeavor. He had a different calling. A much greater purpose. Of this he was certain.

And soon, others would know it, too.

New York City
Sentinels Headquarters

After Jessie left for her mission, Seth knew he'd go stir-crazy, worrying about her. He needed a good distraction—one that might help her in the process. He got Tanya to relocate his workstation to the main control room where her geek squad worked. Across the room, the cavernous space was dark, and the faces of analysts were cast in eerie shadows, with a kaleido-scope of colors coming off the screens. Tanya's people looked like the remnants of a bad acid trip or an MTV video gone amuck. The fancy setup was intimidating at first, he had to admit.

The massive room filled with high-tech toys nearly gave him a woody.

"Garrett . . . you and your people sure know how to roll," he muttered as he sat at his new workstation, a half-moon-shaped desk with plenty of elbow room. He had state-of-the-art technology at his fingertips, three large computer monitors, and a cool ergonomic chair that had more adjustment buttons than a TV remote.

Although the setup was impressive, it was almost wasted on him. He didn't need all the fancy bells and whistles to help Jessie and Alexa. He got to work, initiating the tracking program he had stashed at his cache sites.

Everything in the room around him faded to black. The voices were tuned out. And nothing existed except him and his program.

While he waited for the terrorists to use their SAT phone again, he adapted instructions for the program to track where the call went. Locating the origination point was easy now that he knew what signal to look for and had narrowed the search parameters in Cuba. And since he already had a sample of Sayed's voice from the British Virgin Island kidnappings, he could use the man's voiceprint to specifically target any similar voice patterns coming from southeast Cuba. Voice recognition would trigger his trace program faster and allow him to capture vital location parameters sooner.

Tracing the call to the handler would be another story. Success would depend on the duration of the call and how fast his program worked. If he built upon the trace data piece by piece, his modification might give Garrett a good shot at isolating a part of the terrorist network that was higher up the food chain.

But as he was putting the finishing touches to his

program, one of his monitors flashed a warning. A new trace had begun.

"Holy shit. Here we go," he whispered, his gaze fixed on the screen. He worked the keyboard as fast as he could.

"Damn it!" He nearly forgot to breathe. Colors off the screen flashed across his face. And his heart pounded like a sledgehammer as his fingers moved on instinct. He barely noticed the crowd of analysts who rushed to his workstation and stood behind him.

"Come on," Seth pleaded under his breath. "Stay on the line. Please!"

Baracoa, Cuba

Alexa had showered and changed in record time. She didn't want to be in their motel room any longer than necessary. To blend in, she shed her BDUs in favor of more casual civilian attire, jeans and a T-shirt. Kinkaid did the same. Before he put his shirt on, she helped him re-dress his belly wound and watched as he sat on the edge of the bed and took the last of his antibiotics. He tried to hide that fact from her, but in the reflection of a mirror on the dresser, she had noticed and didn't say a word. *No point now.*

She turned and placed her hand on his brow and moved her fingers down to his cheek and neck.

"You're burning up. I've got aspirin." She retrieved the pills from her first-aid kit. "Maybe we can find a doctor in town."

"No, we don't have time." He shook his head. "And doctors ask too many questions."

For his sake, she wanted to argue, but he was right.

"Then let's get moving," she said as she stashed the SAT phone into her fanny pack.

"Wait," he said as he stood. "We gotta do something first."

As a precaution, Kinkaid stashed the assault rifles and their valuables behind a removable ceiling tile before they left their room. If anyone broke in, searching for something to steal or their identification to learn who they were, they wouldn't find much.

When they hit the streets of Baracoa, Alexa was impressed with Kinkaid. He was indeed fluent in Spanish. As promised, he spoke the language like a local. And she did her part by keeping her mouth shut—not an easy feat. Despite its isolated location, Baracoa had a burgeoning tourist business, so no one asked too many questions about why they were in town. When they did, Kinkaid claimed they were freelance reporters covering the hurricane damage.

People were more willing to talk to a reporter, especially after the storm. Kinkaid got the layout of the town in short order, narrowing their search to likely places for Sayed to hide. He avoided obvious tourist traps, figuring a terrorist on the run with a captive would do the same. Their search was focused on places frequented by locals.

"I've got someplace else," he said. "It's tried-and-true . . . and not far."

"Where's that?"

"You'll see."

"You're a man of secrets, Kinkaid. A real puzzle." She smiled.

While they walked, Alexa took advantage of the opportunity to question him.

"So tell me about Kate. How did you two meet?"

At first he looked surprised by her question. He shifted his gaze and stared straight ahead, not really focusing on anything. His mind was clearly in the past. The mounting silence made her believe he might not answer her. Eventually he did.

"We met at a low point in my life. I was like a drowning man, going down for the final time, but Kate wouldn't let that happen." At the mention of Kate's name, Kinkaid smiled. It was a distant expression, an odd mix of sadness and amusement. "She's stubborn, but in a gentle, persistent way, you know? She got me through some dark days. I consider her a good friend."

Alexa wanted him to go on, but he stopped. And he purposefully left out any reference to his meeting Kate at a psychiatric hospital. She'd have to find another way to keep him talking.

"She sounds like an interesting woman. Did the two of you ever . . . get together?"

He lifted a corner of his lip into a lazy smirk.

"Get together?" he questioned. With him staring at her, she felt her cheeks blush with heat until he said, "No, it's not like that between us. She's got a . . . significant other in her life. She's pretty devoted to him. In fact, she worships him. The guy walks on water as far as she's concerned. Like I said, we're friends. That's all. Why are you asking all these questions about Kate?"

"Just making conversation, that's all," she lied.

"Uh-huh."

Alexa gritted her teeth and avoided his eyes. *The guy walks on water, my ass*. Kinkaid was playing her and having fun doing it. She ignored the fact that she was toying with him, too. Prying personal information from him was more like . . . intelligence gathering. It was practically her job, for cryin' out loud.

No matter how she justified her curiosity, Alexa knew her interest in Jackson Kinkaid had become personal. The man intrigued her. She'd become obsessed with learning more about his connection to Kate and his stay at the psychiatric hospital.

Given their mission, she couldn't afford to alienate him by pushing too hard. If she admitted knowing that Kate was a nun, he'd realize she got that from Garrett. Whatever beef Kinkaid had with her boss could drive a deeper wedge of mistrust between them.

With her thoughts focused on Kate being a nun, Alexa found it ironic when she saw where Kinkaid had taken her.

They stood at the front steps to the Immaculate Conception Catholic Church, a cathedral near their motel and a focal point to the main part of town. It was a massive stone structure with a bell tower and had an arched entry of double wooden doors with an impressive stained glass display over the doorway.

"Do you think we should split up when we get

inside?" she asked as she stared up at the stained glass. "If lightning strikes, both of us won't get whacked."

He cocked his head and raised an eyebrow. "Just give up the idea of salvation and embrace the dark side, Princess Leia. Works for me."

"That explains a lot, Kinkaid."

When they entered the church, Alexa felt the weight of her .45-caliber H&K MK23 at the small of her back under her T-shirt. And even though none of the parishioners paid them much attention, she still knew she didn't belong. She felt like there was a sign over her head in flashing neon that read—*OUTSIDER!*

"What are we doing here, Kinkaid?" she whispered.

No matter how quietly she walked, her footsteps echoed on the tile floor, but her companion didn't bother with subtlety. He stomped down the center aisle as if he had a perfect right to be there. He headed for the altar, his eyes searching for something.

"I'm looking for a priest. Just follow my lead."

"Have at 'er, big guy. I'm not sayin' a word."

"That'll be a nice change of pace," he sniped.

Before she could slay him with a clever comeback, a priest came through a side entrance and walked toward the confessionals with his head bowed. He was short and pudgy with full cheeks and thinning gray hair. He wore the usual uniform, black with white collar. When Kinkaid called to him in Spanish, the man stopped and greeted them in his native tongue.

Kinkaid introduced them both and launched into his usual banter in a language she didn't understand. And as he and the priest spoke, she watched the other parishioners. The priest must have noticed her lack of attention, because he eventually stopped his conversation with Kinkaid and focused on her.

"You do not speak Spanish?" he asked in English. When he smiled warmly, she did the same.

"Unfortunately, no," she replied.

"My name is Father Ignatius. Welcome to my church." He extended his arm down the side aisle. "Please . . . come to my private office. We can talk more and not disturb my parishioners."

When they both nodded, the priest ushered them back the way he'd come. He took them into a cozy room that was more of an antechamber to a private residence than an office.

The room had a desk with stacks of dog-eared papers on it and a basket piled high with old magazines on the floor. A wall of bookshelves was behind the desk and along one of the walls. Alexa expected to find religious books, and there were plenty of those, but it surprised her to see so many books on cooking, art, and architecture. And there were original oil paintings displayed on one wall under special lighting—landscapes, still lifes, and monastic settings.

Father Ignatius was a true Renaissance man.

"Are these your paintings, Father?" she asked.

"Yes, I find painting relaxes me. It's a hobby."

"You're quite good." Alexa admired the artwork up close. "Very impressive."

Before they sat, a petite woman with gray hair and striking blue eyes joined them. Under her apron, she wore dark slacks, a pink blouse, and had a string of pearls around her neck.

"Can I get anything to drink for you and your guests, Father? Coffee?" she offered with a sweet smile. "And I have gingersnaps."

"This is Mrs. Torres, my housekeeper." Father Ignatius made the introductions. "She's an excellent cook," He patted his stomach. " . . . as you can see."

"I'd like coffee if you don't mind," Alexa said.

"Nothing for me." Kinkaid shook his head and flashed a rare smile.

When the little woman disappeared into the next room, she left the door ajar, revealing the private residence of Father Ignatius. Alexa wouldn't have been so nosey, but when she saw a home theater with a big-screen TV, she almost burst out laughing.

Oh, God. This is my kind of church, she thought.

After Mrs. Torres served coffee and a plate of gingersnaps, the woman closed the doors to give them privacy, allowing Kinkaid to take over.

"I've had to resort to some colorful ways to find information on a local man. We don't know whom we can trust, but I won't lie to you, Father," he began.

As he paused for effect, she wasn't sure what he'd say next.

"We're freelance reporters. And we're looking for a despicable man," he told the priest.

Alexa resisted the urge to roll her eyes. And she clenched her jaw, waiting for lightning to strike as he lied to a priest.

"You don't say. Please . . . tell me more." Father Ignatius steepled his hands and narrowed his eyes, completely enthralled by Kinkaid's story.

"This man is taking advantage of those devastated by the hurricane. He takes money from desperate people and has no intention of fulfilling his obligations to salvage and rebuild their homes. And we believe he should be held accountable for his actions."

"How terrible. Do you believe this man is part of my church? Is that why you've come to me?"

"No, he's Muslim, Father. He wouldn't belong to your church," Kinkaid reassured the priest. "Right now, he's hiding from the press. And we think he's staying with a local man, someone perhaps with criminal connections himself or links to terrorist organizations. His benefactor might even be a weapons or drug dealer. Can you help us find anyone who might harbor this man?"

Before the priest answered, Mrs. Torres entered the room. In her hand she held a piece of paper. She avoided looking at them this time and handed the page to Father Ignatius, then left the room without a word. The priest seemed to expect her interruption and stared down at the paper in his hands, reading what was printed on the page.

"How curious," the priest remarked, before he pursed his lips and looked at Kinkaid, giving his request full consideration. The man remained silent for a long time, with only the steady tick of a clock filling the void. When he finally opened his mouth, what Father Ignatius said surprised Alexa.

"I might be able to help you. I have been in Baracoa for many years, but I am curious." The priest shifted his gaze toward her. "You've been very quiet, my dear. What do you have to say about all this, Martini One?"

When the priest used her call sign—the one she'd been assigned specifically for this mission, a name known only to those at Sentinels headquarters in New York City—it was as if he'd struck her in the face with a two-by-four.

"Father, pardon my language, but . . ." She stood and leaned across his desk. " . . . what the hell did you just call me?"

CHAPTER 19

Immaculate Conception Catholic Church
Baracoa, Cuba

"I'm rather partial to martinis myself. I give them up for Lent, but I can assure you I will explain all this cloak-and-dagger business straightaway. Please. Sit, my dear." With a benevolent pious face, the so-called priest gestured with a hand.

Alexa noticed his English had improved, and his pronounced Hispanic accent had faded. And although he used British terms, like "straightaway," she couldn't be sure if that wasn't another diversion. The man was an imposter and a damned chameleon.

"If you don't mind me asking, what did Mrs. Torres bring you?" Alexa asked.

Father Ignatius smiled, folded the paper in his hand, and shoved it into a pocket of his cassock before he said, "She ran a facial-recognition program on both of you when you first entered my church. Standard operating procedure."

"Presbyterians do that, too," Kinkaid added.

The clergyman ignored him, and continued, "When we got a hit, I made myself available, to see if you'd make contact. And you did."

"He works in mysterious ways." Kinkaid shot a sideways glance at her.

"So I've been told." Father Ignatius sat back in his chair, his fingers locked over his belly. "You didn't lie about your names, only what you did for a living . . . and about your target. That will be ten Hail Marys by the way." The priest swiped his hand in the sign of a cross.

"The night is young. Hold off on the penance, Reverend. I'm only gettin' started." Kinkaid's sarcasm was on full throttle.

"Don't you see? I had to know if I could trust you. The information we have on both of you is a bit sketchy—for most good operatives, that's the way it is—but it seems we have mutual allies. And that was good enough for me."

"What are you talking about?" Kinkaid looked annoyed. "Good enough for what?"

"Good enough for what I'm about to say. I hope you appreciate that I'm taking a risk to reveal how I obtained the name of Martini One. I could have listened to your cover story—very clever, by the way—and been very sympathetic before I sent you away without any help at all. But it appears time is of the essence . . . for all of us." Father Ignatius reached for a cookie. "I love gingersnaps, don't you?"

Kinkaid glared at the man. "If you're not a priest, who the hell are you?"

"I'm the man capable of delivering divine intervention. That's all you need to know. As I see it, you could use the hand of Providence." The priest dunked the cookie into his coffee and tossed it into his mouth. He chewed as he spoke.

"If you ask any good Catholic in town, I minister to the needs of my parishioners. I have a rather daunting schedule of baptisms, marriages, confessions, and funerals, and I conduct masses. I'm rather a jack-of-all-trades, you might say."

Alexa knew there was more pressing business to discuss with this faux priest, but she couldn't resist asking the obvious.

"If you're not ordained, how can you misrepresent yourself as a priest? You're marrying people under false pretenses . . . listening to their confessions?"

"Who said I wasn't ordained?" Father Ignatius cocked his head in question. "Being a priest has its moments. I quite enjoy it most days, but what I do for my employer is my true calling."

No matter how this man justified what he was doing, Alexa didn't buy that he was a real priest. And she didn't miss the fact that he never actually admitted to being ordained either. The best undercover agents were the most convincing when they believed their own lies.

"And what exactly is it that you do for your . . . employer?" she questioned.

"I monitor the region and maintain Echelon III," the man said. "I intercepted your SAT-phone communication and eavesdropped, I'm afraid. *Mea culpa*."

"Echelon is a surveillance program, isn't it?" Kinkaid

slumped back in his chair. He didn't look happy at being taken in by this unassuming guy, especially not after the man saw through his lies.

"It's much more than that," the priest argued. "It's an entire network that provides vital information to support national security, military operations, and law enforcement. Such intelligence is at the heart of the world's struggle against terrorism. And the intel we obtain can also act as a deterrent against serious crime."

Alexa sorted through her memory for details on Echelon. Run by four agencies within the United Kingdom and counterparts within the U.S., Echelon III was an updated version of a global network of computers that automatically searched through cell-phone calls, satellite transmissions, faxes, and e-mails, acting like a massive vacuum cleaner.

The program intercepted messages and funneled the gathered data through state-of-the-art computer processors in a network of stations, looking for key-words that generated an alert. And each station had its own Echelon "dictionary" that was merged with all the keywords for the four agencies. The interactive array would disseminate the analyzed data, filtering a wealth of raw information down to a manageable report for further oversight.

If this priest monitored the region, he maintained the local "dictionary," which stored extensive data on specific targets, including names, topics of interest, addresses, and phone numbers—a database of key surveillance parameters for this part of the world.

"If you manage Echelon"—Alexa furrowed her

brow—"that means you're a spook undercover. Who do you work for? The NSA? GCHQ?"

The Government Communications Headquarters was the U.K.'s version of the NSA.

"That doesn't really matter. We're on the same side. And besides, you have limited options." The priest took another cookie. "If you hadn't come to me, I would have sought you out. From the first mention of Sayed's name on your SAT phone, a red flag went up. Abdul Kabir Sayed was involved in an incident in the British Virgin Islands that my people investigated. This fellow has been making a name for himself. He's ambitious enough to become the next Bin Laden. So it would appear we both have an interest in him."

"I have only one interest in that bastard. He abducted a friend of mine. A woman. And he still has her," Kinkaid said, leaning forward. "We've tracked him to Baracoa. You have any idea who he'd go to for help?"

"Yes, I have a pretty good candidate," the man told them. "Jamal Ghazi is an arms dealer with connections to al-Qaeda. He lives in a compound north of Baracoa. Only one road runs north out of Baracoa. It will take you straight to him. He's well armed and has a small army working for him."

Father Ignatius not only provided the address, he gave them a sketched layout of Ghazi's compound, including his best guess on where captives might be held. He told them that since Ghazi had been under his surveillance, he had such information readily available.

"If Sayed is looking for a place to hide, that's where he'd go. But you'd better have more than just the two of you making a house call."

Alexa almost told the priest that she had a backup team coming, but she resisted the urge to share the intel. In her line of work, trust had to be earned. And there was too much at stake for her to blindly have faith in a wily stranger like Father Ignatius.

"Tell me, what will you do with him once you find Sayed?" the clergyman asked her, then shifted his gaze to Kinkaid. "You look as if you fancy yourself a cowboy. Will it be a gunfight at the O.K. Corral?"

"That's none of your . . ."

Alexa interrupted Kinkaid. "Thanks for opening up to us . . . Father." She stood and shook the man's hand. "And we appreciate the intel."

"God's speed." The clergyman nodded.

Alexa left the church with Kinkaid and pondered what the priest had told them. Dark scenarios ran through her head, especially if Father Ignatius had ulterior motives for sending them into a firefight. The man could be in league with local terrorists or be looking to disgrace U.S. operatives on foreign soil.

Neither of them spoke until they got far enough away from the cathedral and had made certain they were not followed. Without asking, she knew Kinkaid was heading back to the motel.

Her backup team would arrive soon. And they had a siege to plan.

"Do you trust him?" she asked as she kept pace with his lengthy strides.

He thought too long about his answer to give her any real comfort.

"He's all we've got."

New York City
Sentinels Headquarters

Garrett heard the insistent knock on his door and knew who stood on the other side. Tanya had called earlier and said she had something urgent.

"Come in, Tanya."

She entered his office with a file in her hand and Seth Harper at her heels. Harper wore navy slacks and a white dress shirt, but under his shirt he wore something else. The clear image of a Jerry Springer T-shirt was visible. When Garrett saw it, a smile tugged at his lips.

"What do you have, Tanya?" he asked, and gestured a hand toward chairs in front of his desk. "Please. Have a seat."

"Harper found something. I'll let him explain." She winked at Seth and handed him the file.

"Sayed uploaded another video, and he used his SAT phone again," Seth began. "Since I narrowed my search pattern to southeast Cuba and had his voiceprint, my program alerted me when he made a call. I traced the origin right away."

"And? Do you know where he is?" Garrett asked.

"Yeah, I think so." Harper opened the file and spread a satellite overview of Cuba on his desk.

"You think so? How sure are you, Seth?"

"That depends on how much you trust the intel on the British Virgin Islands abductions, sir. If Sayed was behind those kidnappings, then yes, the voiceprint matches."

When Garrett looked at Tanya, she nodded, and said, "That investigation was solid. I think we've got Sayed, thanks to Harper."

Garrett looked down at the map on his desk again. "Where is he? Do we know what this facility is?" He pointed to a spot on the map that had been marked.

"Yeah, and you're not going to like it." Tanya reached across his desk and pointed to a road. "There's only one way going in and out of Baracoa. And that facility north of town belongs to an arms dealer, Jamal Ghazi. He's been linked to al-Qaeda. He's one nasty son of a bitch."

"Dig up all you can on Ghazi and get it to Alexa and Hank Lewis as soon as possible. What's the ETA for Hank's team?"

"They'll be in Baracoa in ten minutes," Tanya told him. "But there's more. Seth, tell him."

"It was easy to lock on Sayed's call at the origination point, but I adapted my program to expedite the trace to its destination. Sayed was calling someone in Afghanistan. Tanya thinks it's his handler. If that's correct, we may have someone deeper into his network."

"Good work, Seth. Both of you." He smiled. "Tanya, I want to contact Alexa and Hank ASAP. We need our hands on Sayed and to get our people out of Cuba . . . tonight."

"Yes, sir," she said. "I'll have dispatch make contact immediately. They'll route the calls to you."

Garrett watched Tanya and her new charge leave his office. With Tanya's sharp thinking, they had worked as a team to identify the target and expedite the online hunt. And Seth Harper had adapted and improvised to isolate a significant thread tied to a terrorist network. As pleased as he was with the good news, Garrett knew the most dangerous part of the mission still remained. Cornering a terrorist cell led by a treacherous leader like Abdul Kabir Sayed could be deadly, especially if their objective was to take the bastard alive.

His thoughts turned to Alexa, a woman who had a place in his heart—and had *always* deserved better.

Offshore Baracoa, Cuba

As Joe LaClaire's boat sped toward the shore, its hull hit the tops of waves and kicked up a fine salty mist that covered Jessie's face. With LaClaire at the helm, she stood in the bow of the boat and held on, staring dead ahead at the only lights on the horizon. This would be her first mission with the Sentinels. And even though it had only been a short time since she'd last seen Alexa, it felt like ages. Worrying about a friend wreaked havoc on her sense of time.

In the wake of LaClaire's boat followed another craft, carrying the rest of her team. Being a rookie, she had been assigned to stick with Hank Lewis until the teams were split between him and Alexa, their team leaders. Hank was a man of few words, but she'd liked him immediately, which was unusual for her. She normally didn't take to strangers that soon. Maybe her respect for Hank had something to do with his treatment of the rescued hostages—the men, women, and children who had been abducted from Haiti. Hank had filled the team in on what had happened.

With Alexa still in Cuba, they couldn't afford to have the world media's attention on what remained of her mission, but the rescued hostages needed tending. Hank had arranged for medical attention and also had the Haitian families join their rescued loved ones in a private location, away from the media. It had been a humane outcome that served the objectives of the Sentinels as well as the needs of those rescued and the people who loved them. She admired Garrett for arranging it.

Soon they would land in a harbor near Baracoa, Cuba, and join Alexa and Jackson Kinkaid, a man she'd never met. That would happen shortly. Her team leader had already made contact with Alexa.

Their rendezvous and transportation had been arranged. As their boat neared shore, Hank's SAT phone rang, and he answered it.

"Moonshine Two. Talk to me, home base."

Although Jessie only overheard Hank's side of the conversation, she understood enough to know they now had a specific location to find their target. And she knew Harper had worked his magic to find the terrorist in Baracoa. Despite her adrenaline rush for the mission ahead, she couldn't help but smile when she thought about Seth.

"Way to go, genius," she whispered.

*　*　*

Father Ignatius had waited for his guests to leave before he slipped into his private residence. Behind his home theater—a personal eccentricity—he had a safe room that stored his high-tech equipment and link to Echelon. While Mrs. Torres had puttered around the room with a feather duster, he observed Jackson Kinkaid and Alexa Marlowe by surveillance cameras as they walked from the cathedral.

When he knew for certain that they had gone, he got to work.

He searched for more details on the backgrounds of Kinkaid and Marlowe to do a proper search. His efforts took time, but the results were worth it. What he found only gave him more cause for alarm. They were too experienced to attempt an assault on the Ghazi stronghold without help and resources. And although neither of them had mentioned they'd be working with an assault team, he had to assume they wouldn't be alone. If they attacked Ghazi, they had a strong chance at succeeding with their mission to save Kinkaid's friend—and killing anyone in their path, including Abdul Kabir Sayed.

He considered his next step carefully before he acted. But act, he must. After weighing the consequences of his decision, he picked up the encrypted phone he had in the safe room and made a call. A man answered on the second ring.

"You'll soon have company." The priest told him what he knew. "As a precaution, we must get Sayed out tonight. He's vital to our cause. We have no choice now."

He ended the call as his loyal housekeeper and confidante came into the room. She had a service of tea and a snack.

"Mrs. Torres, you'd better shed the apron," he told her. "I'll be needing your services."

CHAPTER 20

North of Baracoa, Cuba

Alexa and Kinkaid had arrived at the harbor in two SUVs they'd misappropriated from a rental-car agency for their rendezvous with Hank and his team. This time of night, the vehicles wouldn't be missed. In the wake of the hurricane, Baracoa was dead, with the harbor deserted. When they met the backup team at the dock, Jessie had gifts from Garrett. Uniforms, full assault gear, and body armor. Everything a woman would need.

After the bounty hunter grinned and tossed a bag of gear onto the pier in front of her, she stuffed black BDU pants into her arms.

"Guess this makes us a twisted version of the *Sisterhood of the Traveling Pants*."

"It would take magic pants to get either of us at a chick flick." Alexa returned her smile. "Good to see you, Jess."

"Yeah, you, too." Jessie shifted her gaze toward Kinkaid, who was changing into the gear Hank brought him. With a concerned look on her face, she asked, "Is that the FNG?"

Before Alexa could answer, she added, "Who knew Gerard Butler had a doppelgänger? He's fine with a capital 'F,' but is he okay? He looks . . . sick."

"Yeah, bullets tend to do that." Alexa changed as she talked. "He's runnin' on empty, Jessie. I don't know how long he'll hold out, but he's determined to see this through . . . if that infection doesn't kill him first."

"Then we better get moving." Jessie had accepted what she'd said and didn't ask questions. She only wanted to help. It reminded Alexa why she'd wanted her as a partner.

They split the teams between the two vehicles and loaded up the gear. Heading north on the only road out of town, it didn't take them long to find the private residence of Jamal Ghazi.

From a safe distance, Alexa used night-vision binoculars for a sweeping look over the arms dealer's compound. The sprawling estate was a fortress bordered by a formidable stone wall. Security lights made it a beacon amidst the darkness. And men patrolled the grounds at regular intervals. The sketched layout from Father Ignatius closely mirrored what she saw below. Having the advance intel made her more comfortable with their strategy, but all the lights and activity on the grounds gave her reason to be concerned.

"A lot going on down there," she whispered to Hank and Kinkaid. "You think they're expecting us?"

"Hard to say," Hank said as he looked through his binoculars. "Maybe recon will have something."

Alexa had sent two teams to scout the perimeter. While she waited for more intel, she laid out preliminary plans for the assault. She would lead a team of seven, including Kinkaid and Beckett. Hank Lewis had the same number and would focus his attack from the front of the compound. His timed diversionary assault was intended to draw Ghazi's men into the fight. That left her to cover the back. And in stealth mode—after Hank had initiated the action—her team would infiltrate the estate, looking for Kate.

For the assault, they would use the wireless communication links Garrett had sent. The links were voice-activated and would work effectively as long as her team stayed within distance of each other.

When the scouts returned, Alexa used their input to come up with a final assault plan. She gave the order to get into position. As she moved in the dark with her team, Alexa was aware of Kinkaid next to her. He was a force she found hard to ignore under normal circumstances, but with him along, this mission hadn't been normal from the start. And now—given her orders to bring Sayed in alive regardless of what happened to Kate—she felt as if she'd turned against him.

With any luck at all, she wouldn't be forced into such a choice. Still, the notion of betraying him weighed heavy on her conscience. When she got to her spot, she communicated with Hank through her com unit.

"Martini One in position."

"Copy that, Martini One."

They had a plan and would go in only after Hank

initiated his assault. Alexa watched her team settle into their locations. And Kinkaid crouched by her. When he took off his com set and fixed his eyes on hers, she did the same.

Whatever he had in mind, he wanted privacy.

They were alone for one last time before the attack began. She saw in his eyes that his fever had gotten worse, but something else lingered there. He wanted her. *Needed her.* And for one brief moment, he was hers. Around them, whatever was about to happen faded to black. All that remained was the two of them. And everything that she felt for him welled inside her, breaking free in an impossible rush.

He pulled her to his chest and lowered his lips to hers. With his taut body pressed against her, she closed her eyes and surrendered to the moment as Kinkaid held her. He kissed her as if he had invented it. And the smell of his skin was intoxicating. His hands on her body left her jonesing for more, but the toe-curling heat ended way too soon. When he pulled back, she was breathless, stunned, and utterly speechless.

"What? Nothing to say?" He grinned, an expression she hadn't seen in a very long time. "If I knew that's all it would take, I would have kissed you more often."

Alexa looked into his eyes, wondering if she'd misread his meaning for the sudden affection. If Kinkaid had a death wish, his kiss might have meant—

"What was the kiss for?" she asked.

"It's not good-bye. It's just . . . because I had to."

Alexa narrowed her eyes and slapped him. The smack was only hard enough to get his attention.

"What the hell was *that* for?" He grimaced and rubbed his cheek.

"That's a reminder"—she raised an eyebrow—"for you to be careful."

"How thoughtful. I'll try and remember."

When she turned away, Kinkaid grabbed her arm.

"You and your men don't have to do this." He had trouble meeting her gaze. "They'd be risking their lives to save one person. I'd understand if you changed your mind."

His timing wasn't the best, but it took guts for him to stop her like this. If their mission had been purely to save one life, Alexa might have reconsidered and planned to go with Kinkaid on her own. She would have been concerned for the lives of her men, too. His honesty made her realize he deserved the truth—even if it cost her his trust.

"I want Kate rescued. I know how much she means to you. You've risked your life many times since this whole thing began, but don't worry about the commitment of my team. With Sayed behind this abduction, we've got more at stake. We're in this together."

She hoped he would have accepted what she'd said at face value, without question. No such luck.

"What do you mean?" he asked. "There's something you haven't told me. I thought you didn't know much about this son of a bitch."

With Kinkaid's trust issues, she knew telling him the truth wouldn't be easy, but she had to do it. And although she knew Garrett wouldn't have approved, that didn't matter now. Kinkaid had to know.

"We need to take Sayed alive. We think he's planning another attack on U.S. soil similar in magnitude to 9/11. If that's true, there's more to this mission than one life."

"So . . . you've really been after Sayed all along, not Kate. Is that it?" He tightened his jaw and glared at her. "Garrett's behind this, isn't he? He gave the order. How sure are you that your boss is telling the truth?"

The truth? Alexa hadn't even questioned what Garrett had told her. She trusted him. And if she doubted intel from her own boss, it was time to quit. Kinkaid knew that. Under normal circumstances, he wouldn't have argued the point—but nothing was normal about this mission.

"We're going to rescue Kate. Are you in or out?"

She forced the issue, knowing his only real choice was to join them. Kinkaid clutched his weapon and put distance between them without saying a word. That was the only answer she'd get.

When Alexa turned, she found Jessie watching her. Her new partner had slipped closer when she'd been distracted by her argument with Kinkaid. The bounty hunter had a concerned look on her face.

"If you know what's good for you, you'll mind your own business, Beckett," Alexa said.

"Since when have I *ever* known what was good for me?" Jessie smirked, with a hand covering her mouthpiece, then whispered, "Come on, Hank. Let's get this show on the road. I'm no good at waiting."

Jessie got her wish. She didn't have to wait.

The night sky lit up like a Fourth of July in hell.

A rocket-propelled grenade struck the front gate and blasted it apart. Armed guards were blown off their feet. Their bodies hurtled through the air like macabre and broken dolls. Using more than one RPG launcher, Hank's team fired two more explosive warheads from their shoulder-launched weapons and struck the main house. Ghazi's men scrambled for cover, taken off guard by the sudden and vicious attack.

With precision, Hank and his men engaged the remaining guards, drawing fire. The assault had begun. And Alexa had a bird's-eye view.

"Martini One . . . on the move." Alexa spoke into her com unit and headed out with Kinkaid and the rest of her team.

Her sniper, Manny Rodriguez, had found a sweet spot on a ridge and would provide cover for their retreat if they needed it. The rest of her team moved from the shadows behind the residence and headed for a locked metal gate built into the stone wall. To breach the obstacle, Adam Booker shaped C2 plastic explosives on the lock and inserted a detonator. It would do the job and cut through the metal without the noise of C4.

"Executing breach," he warned the team before he triggered the blast.

When the gate blew open, Alexa's team charged through. They dodged the security lights and stuck to the shadows as they made their way to the back of the residence.

Booker crept behind a guard who appeared at a side entrance and dispatched the armed man with his knife. The guy never made a sound. Her scout gave a hand signal, and the team closed ranks. In stacked formation, they entered the residence and shuffled through a hall with their weapons raised. Although the priest's schematic seemed accurate, the real test lay ahead.

Without a sound, they moved toward a stairway that led belowground. According to Father Ignatius, Sister Kate could be held in a cell one level down.

They'd met little resistance so far. The real war was happening out front. Alexa heard the staccato sound of gunfire from automatic weapons. And RPG rounds sent a wave of tremors through the walls. The explosive repercussions bellowed down every hall. Dust and debris drifted through the air, made more apparent when the electricity flickered out and her team turned on the lights mounted on their assault rifles. The beams captured drifts of smoke and dust particles as the team moved down the stairs and through an empty hallway below. Eerie swirls of smoke played tricks on their eyes and made every shadow look threatening.

The lower level wasn't much, only one dead-end corridor with four cells and a long hallway that led toward another set of stairs. Each cell had a locked door with a barred window that would allow them a look inside. Booker stood watch while Kinkaid led the search for Kate and was joined by Jessie. Using extreme caution, they glanced into the rooms and flashed a light. They shook their heads when they came up empty. After the last room, Alexa knew Father Ignatius had either guessed wrong about where Kate was being held, or Sayed had moved her.

Hell! For all they knew, the nun was already dead.

That thought made her sick to her stomach. After what Kate had been through to survive, Alexa didn't want to imagine her dead now. With all her heart, she wanted the woman to be alive, but she had a mission beyond the rescue of one hostage. Her thoughts shifted to another objective—Abdul Kabir Sayed. She had a bad feeling that wherever they found the terrorist, they would also find Kate.

And her worst nightmare could happen, where she'd be forced to make a choice.

When her team turned down the longer hallway, two shadows emerged from the far stairs. The guards raised their weapons, but never had time to shoot. Booker and Jessie were the first to fire. They had no choice.

In the dark, confined space, the muzzle flash from Alexa's M4 Carbine nearly blinded her. And the intense sound of gunfire reverberated off the walls and dulled her hearing. Bullets pummeled the men who tried to stop them. Their bodies jerked where they stood until they dropped to the floor.

Alexa and her team backed down the corridor and headed out, the way they'd come. They didn't want to be trapped on the lower level.

"No hostage below. We're heading for the first floor," Alexa communicated to Hank and the others. "We unzipped our fly. They know we're here. Honeymoon's over."

Alexa and her team swept the first floor, taking out pockets of Ghazi's men as they confronted them room to room, using frag grenades. In tight quarters, frags left no place to hide, and the concentrated blast shredded the enemy. Although Hank still waged war out front, the resistance they met inside had been scattered. And Hank's diversion masked most of the sounds her team made. It wasn't until they entered a large ballroom on the north wall of the compound that they finally found their target.

And the terrorist looked as if he had expected them.

Across the room near a large doorway with stairs, Abdul Kabir Sayed stood next to a well-dressed man in a suit. It had to be Jamal Ghazi. And three of his armed guards dressed in camo BDUs glared at them, clutching weapons and ready for a firefight. Sayed had the nun by the throat with one hand, prepared to slice her with a knife he had in the other. Even though the men around him brandished automatic weapons, Sayed had chosen a knife. A vicious slash across the throat carried an element of drama that the bastard couldn't resist.

Her team fanned out and kept their weapons raised. When they closed the gap between them and the terrorist, Sayed was first to speak.

"That's close enough." He ordered them to stop. One by one, he glared at each of them. It didn't take long for him to settle on Kinkaid.

"In my world, Islam has become a religion of fear. With fear comes respect. What I do, I do with honor," he justified his despicable acts with faint amusement. " . . . for my people."

"You make war on innocent women and children," Kinkaid began. "What you do, you are a man without honor."

Sayed gritted his teeth and clinched his knife. The nun trembled, her eyes on Kinkaid.

"Are you okay, Kate?" Kinkaid asked the question, but it was obvious she'd been severely beaten. The battered nun didn't need to reply. And she wasn't a stranger to Sayed's knife. Her skin was cut. A few gashes needed stitches. And her clothes were slashed, exposing her body. If Kate survived this ordeal, she'd need medical attention pronto.

"Please . . . I don't want anyone else to die, Jackson. Promise me," the nun begged.

"I won't lie to you, Kate. No can do." Calm and cool, Kinkaid fixed his eyes on Sayed and aimed his assault rifle at the man's head. "Some people are a total waste of gray matter," he said under his breath.

"You must be Jackson Kinkaid. At last we meet." Sayed tried for casual and in control, but he came off nervous. He shifted his gaze from Kinkaid to the others in the room, and a bead of sweat trickled down his cheek.

"This isn't how I imagined it," Kinkaid said, not flinching a muscle.

"Oh?"

"Yeah, in my scenario, you weren't breathing."

Sayed tightened his jaw, and his lips twitched.

"This woman . . . she lied about how she knows you. Yet you killed my men to rescue her. How do you think that makes me feel?"

"A man like you? You don't give a shit about your men, Sayed."

"So . . . you know who I am." The egotistical terrorist smiled. He had ignored Kinkaid's insult and only heard his own name.

"Yeah, we know who you are," Alexa intervened. "And you're not leaving here . . . unless you let her go."

"I refuse to deal with a woman." Sayed shot Alexa a dismissive glance and glared at Kinkaid. "What kind of man are you, letting a mere woman speak for you?"

"That 'mere woman' can kick your ass. And I, for one, would love to see her do it. What kind of man uses a woman as a shield? You're a fuckin' coward."

For the first time, Kinkaid faltered. He lowered his weapon a hair and blinked. He looked pale, and Alexa noticed sweat across his brow. He looked as if he would pass out, and she hoped Sayed hadn't seen the same thing.

"You dare to insult me . . . when I have your friend?" Sayed gripped Kate by the throat. When he pressed his knife to her face, the nun gasped. Her eyes bulged wide as she stared at the blade. The sharp tip inched toward her eye socket.

"While we argue, I will carve out her eye." Sayed smirked. "Then we will see who wins. Or maybe I cut out her tongue. What will you do then?"

Tension filled the room. And Kinkaid hadn't come back with a smart-ass remark. Wheels were turning in his head, and Alexa wasn't sure she'd like what would come of it. He already didn't trust Garrett, and, by extension, that meant her, too.

"You cut her . . . and you die. And I'll personally wrap your dead carcass in pig's skin for the big send-off." Alexa capped off her threat with a religious slap in the face.

The standoff was electric. Anyone in the room had the spark to ignite a firestorm. Sayed and Ghazi were ready to blow. Kate's lips trembled and moved in silent prayer, and Kinkaid was about to pass out. Sweat trickled down Alexa's back and crawled like spiders down her spine. And with every burst of gunfire outside, she felt the urgency for something to happen.

"I've got the shot. Just say the word." Jessie clenched her jaw and aimed her weapon at Sayed's head. "I can drop him before he even knows he's dead."

Jessie knew their objective was to keep Sayed alive. She was only bluffing, making the man feel the pressure of others in the room. But if Alexa gave the order, she had no doubt Jessie wouldn't hesitate to crack open the man's skull like a ripe watermelon.

"Take me. You don't need to hide behind that woman. Take me instead." Kinkaid said it, and there was no going back. His offer was on the table. And for good measure, he embellished his convincing argument.

"You said it yourself, I killed your men. And if it's money you want, I can get it. But the nun is freed unharmed. That's the deal."

"Kinkaid, you have no authority to do this," Alexa argued, keeping her eyes alert and her rifle on the target.

"You're in no position to make deals. I decide," the terrorist yelled. Adrenaline pumped through his body and made him jumpy. " . . . but what you say . . . I agree." After consideration, the terrorist nudged his head at Kinkaid. "Drop your weapon and walk toward me . . . slowly, with your hands up."

For once Kinkaid did as he was told. He laid his rifle on the floor, unsheathed his knife, shed his handgun, and took off his com link. Kinkaid had given up his store of weapons, but he was lethal without them. She only hoped he'd get a chance to demonstrate.

"Jackson, please don't do this, not for me," Kate pleaded with tears in her eyes. She reached for him, but Sayed twisted her arm and made her cry in pain.

"You sorry son of a . . ." Kinkaid lunged for the terrorist, but Ghazi sucker punched him in the gut with his rifle, cutting off his attack. When Kinkaid doubled over in pain, Alexa saw blood drop to the floor as he gripped his belly. He was bleeding again.

"Jackson, please . . ." Alexa wanted to help him, but the best way to do that was to keep her cool. "We could have worked it out. This didn't have to happen. You should have trusted me."

"I still have faith in you, Alexa," Kinkaid said. "You'll find Waldo. You always do."

Sending her a message, he stared at her with his mesmerizing green eyes one last time. He'd given her the same look before he kissed her. A lifetime of regrets swelled to the surface and gripped her heart. She had a strong feeling this would be the last time she'd see him.

The exchange was made as Kate stepped toward one of Alexa's men. Adam Booker grabbed the nun and pulled her behind him.

"And Kate?" Kinkaid called out to her. "Put in a

good word for me with the man upstairs. I'll need all the help I can get." He forced a beleaguered grin and winked. His gesture brought on more tears from the exhausted nun.

"There's nothing more I can tell him about you that he doesn't already know, Jackson." Kate wept. "God knows your heart. And that's what matters."

Before he could say anything, Kinkaid was yanked backward toward the doorway. Sayed had traded his knife for a gun and had him by the neck, with the weapon pointed to his head.

"If you try to follow us, he dies," the terrorist warned.

Along with three armed guards, Sayed and Ghazi hauled Kinkaid up the stairs. Alexa searched her memory of the schematic that Father Ignatius drew of Ghazi's compound. They were headed for the rooftop, but she had no idea why. What was up there?

And what the hell was happening?

"I've got activity on the roof, Martini One." The voice of Manny Rodriguez, her sniper on the ridge, came on the line. "Not enough light to see."

"Our target released the woman, but he's got a new hostage. Our FNG is with him," she told him. "What's happening? Talk to me, Lone Wolf."

She ran toward the stairs that led to the rooftop and peered around the corner, half-expecting to hear a burst of automatic gunfire aimed at her head. When that didn't happen, she crept up with her eyes alert, taking a step at a time. Jessie and two more from her team followed. The others stayed behind to watch her back.

Alexa had her rifle clutched in her hand, ready to shoot. At the first landing, she crouched low and looked up the next flight. She heard a door close above her, but she resisted the urge to run toward the sound. Moving in too fast might get her killed. As she made her way up the next set of stairs, Manny came back on the line.

"The rooftop is lit up now. They've got a helicopter." His voice sounded more urgent. "And they're ready to take off. What's your order, Martini One?"

Sayed had too many armed men with him to make this an easy play for a sniper. And with Kinkaid as a hostage, she didn't have much choice but to say, "Stand down, Lone Wolf. I repeat, stand down."

At the sound of the helicopter engine revving up, Alexa hit the last flight of stairs with Jessie and the others close behind. She rammed a shoulder into the metal door and dropped to a knee, taking cover by a mechanical housing unit. Jessie ducked near her and aimed her weapon. The helicopter sat on a helipad in a circle of lights. A sturdy brick wall near the aircraft gave them cover. That was why Manny hadn't seen what was going on.

Why hadn't the priest told them about the helipad?

When they realized they'd been followed, two of Ghazi's men turned to fire. One dodged right and the other dove to the left. Alexa and her team opened fire as the rotors of the helicopter ramped up speed. The craft kicked up a stiff breeze and blew dust into her face as she returned fire. Sayed and Ghazi loaded Kinkaid into the helicopter. She had no idea how many were already on board, but the two men shooting their weapons had been left behind.

The helicopter lifted off the helipad. In seconds, it was airborne.

"Damn it!" she cursed.

Gunfire had them pinned down until Jessie wounded one of the gunmen. When that happened, the other man stopped firing and gave up. He raised his hands and shouted his surrender, but it was too late. Jessie and her team rushed by her to subdue the two men, leaving Alexa alone to watch helicopter lights fade into the distance.

She ached inside with frustration. Jackson had felt the need to control the hostage situation because of his lack of trust in her. And she had no one to blame except herself. Alexa understood him wanting to protect Kate at all cost. Had their roles been reversed, she might have felt the same, but comprehending his actions didn't make the pain go away or the guilt disappear.

Kinkaid was gone. And her best hope of rescuing him alive had vanished too.

CHAPTER 21

The rooftop had been dimly lit until a brilliant display of lights blinded Sayed. High beams switched on and blazed in a circle beneath a helicopter with its rotor blades in motion and its engine whining. He had kept close to Jamal Ghazi, outpacing the men behind them. As they neared the craft, two of Ghazi's men had opened fire. Sayed scrambled into the helicopter and hauled Jackson Kinkaid in with him at gunpoint. Only one of Ghazi's personal bodyguards remained with them. With bullets whizzing by Sayed's head, he ducked and used Kinkaid as a shield.

"Hurry," he remembered screaming at Ghazi. "We have to leave . . . Now!"

Inside, Sayed cowered in the shadows with his gun still on Kinkaid. When the bodyguard shut the compartment, Ghazi yelled an order for the pilot to take off, then found a seat and buckled in. Sayed slammed the butt of his gun against the head of his captive until the man blacked out. He didn't want to bother with restraints. He knew Ghazi's man would secure Kinkaid once they got under way. Sayed rushed to a spot next to Ghazi and fastened his seat belt. He heard the bodyguard do the same.

As the helicopter lifted off the ground and lurched forward, bullets hit the fuselage. Rounds battered metal in a series of thuds. He ducked for cover. The sound reverberated through the passenger compartment, dulled by the roar from the turbine engine and rotor blades. When the assault from the ground ceased, he breathed a sigh of relief.

He had narrowly escaped. Allah had been with him. It was a sign. After several minutes, he took a deep breath and smiled at Jamal Ghazi.

"Where are we going?" He raised his voice to be heard over the noise.

"I have another place outside Havana." The arms dealer gestured with his hand. "I've instructed the pilot. He knows where to go."

Sayed nodded and allowed himself to relax. His heart had finally slowed, and he got his breathing under control as he wiped the sweat off his face with a sleeve. But when his thoughts turned to the Christian woman he'd left behind, he gritted his teeth, and anger stirred his blood. She had brought him bad luck. And after today he vowed never to talk of her again. Ghazi had not heard the full story of what happened. And since he was the only one who had gotten away, no one would know he had failed.

Besides, he had a better prize unconscious on the floor behind his seat. Abducting a wealthy American like Jackson Kinkaid would earn him more respect, and imagining what his handler would say made him smile. Sayed settled into his seat and crossed arms over his chest. As he stared through the dim lights of the cockpit, he fixed his eyes on the horizon and watched the calm movements of the pilot and copilot.

He had no doubt now. Allah had provided exactly what he had deserved.

North of Baracoa, Cuba

Even though Kinkaid was missing in action, Alexa found comfort in the fact that none of her people had been killed. They had a couple of minor injuries, but nothing life-threatening.

Ghazi's men who were left behind were taken prisoner and weapons were confiscated. After the helicopter departed, his men didn't resist. Now most of them knelt on the grass in front of the estate with their hands bound by flex cuffs behind their backs. While Hank and his team made a final sweep of the rooms inside, Alexa had her people stand watch over the prisoners and tend to the wounded.

Being in a foreign country, Alexa wouldn't stick around to see the men punished for harboring Sayed. And without Jamal Ghazi to lead them, his men wouldn't cause trouble for them with the local law. Everyone would break even and walk away—all except the dead. Ghazi's men would free themselves eventually and get help for their wounded comrades before they crawled under a rock or surfaced in another criminal operation. It was a fact of life she had to accept.

Alexa had other things on her mind.

"Track that beacon, home base. It's our best chance at finding . . . our target," she said over the SAT phone after she had briefed Garrett on the outcome of their assault on Jamal Ghazi's estate.

She had wanted to say Kinkaid's name instead of using the word "target," but Alexa wasn't sure how her boss would react. For Kinkaid's sake, she had to keep Garrett on task without the personal distraction. Ironically, if they were successful in finding Sayed, it would be entirely due to Kinkaid and his reference to finding Waldo. Without tipping off Sayed, he'd found a way to remind her that he still had her tracking beacon. She'd stowed it with his iPod, something he kept with him and would never leave behind.

Now that tracking beacon was his only lifeline.

"Copy that, Martini One. Already on it," Garrett said.

She ended the call as Hank reported back. He gave her the thumbs-up. It was time to leave. Alexa loaded her teams into the two SUVs, and Kate came with her. As they headed back toward Baracoa, Alexa held tight to the wounded nun. The woman made the sign of the cross and closed her eyes while her lips moved. Alexa figured she was putting in a good word for Kinkaid. Even though the woman was completely exhausted, she prayed for her friend.

When Kate noticed Alexa staring at her, she said, "God had tested my faith. I thought He had forsaken me when I needed him most. I failed, but Jackson didn't." A tear rolled down the nun's cheek.

"I don't understand," she said. "What do you mean, Sister?"

Alexa had never been a religious person. She believed in death, and she'd seen true evil. A person didn't do what she did for a living and not believe in real evil, but putting stock in God was another story. To believe a Supreme Being existed—and let atrocities happen under his watch—made the world more hopeless than she wanted it to be. She preferred to take action and wage war against bad guys. That made more sense to her than passively having faith that a higher power would take care of those she loved. Kinkaid would understand that.

"Jackson was the answer to my prayers. God had acted through him . . . to help me. I had lost my faith, but Jackson helped me find it again," she sobbed. "I owe him more than just my life. He can't die now. I have to tell him . . ."

"If I have anything to do with it, you'll get that chance, Sister," she promised. The odds weren't good for Kinkaid, but Alexa saw no need to overdose the nun with reality. She'd had enough of that to last a lifetime.

"Tell me. What happened with the children? Sayed told me that some of them . . . didn't make it. He said many of the hostages were killed the night Jackson came to rescue me." Kate's eyes welled with tears as she clutched Alexa's arm. "I know how Jackson is . . . especially if children died. That had to be unbearable for him."

Kate pressed a tight fist to her lips to hold back her sobs.

"No one died, Sister. Jackson rescued everyone . . . single-handed. And I think little Joselyne has a mad crush on him," she reassured the nun. "That rat bast . . . I mean, Sayed, lied to you. He was only messing with your head."

"Oh my, God. She's alive. My dear sweet Joselyne and the others," she cried. "Praise the Lord . . . sweet Jesus." Not holding back, Kate let her emotions go—a strange mix of joy and a final release of all her fears. "My dear, sweet Jesus. Thank you."

Alexa put her arm around the weeping nun. She understood regrets, and she knew what it felt like to run out of time. Regret made her angry. If she had known Kinkaid was wounded before the mission, she might have made different choices. He could have gotten medical help before the infection poisoned his body. And now he was in the hands of a madman, a terrorist bent on humiliating his enemy by killing him in a public way online.

But Alexa dialed back her frustration when she imagined what Kinkaid's reaction would have been if she'd left him behind. He wasn't the kind of guy who sat on the sidelines. The decision to risk his life had been his all the way.

For right or wrong, this was the real Jackson Kinkaid—a guy who knew loyalty and risked his life when it mattered most. She'd had misgivings about him at the start of the mission. But no matter what he did for a living now—for whatever reason—the real Kinkaid hadn't changed. She knew that now.

Why had she ever doubted him?

Twenty minutes later

On the ride back to Baracoa, Kate had fallen asleep with her head on Alexa's shoulder. Sitting in the shadows of the SUV and holding the nun, Alexa replayed the siege at Ghazi's compound in her mind. For the most part, she knew they'd been lucky. Kate was safe, and no one from her teams had died.

Yet the hypnotic green eyes of Jackson Kinkaid haunted her, and guilt twisted her gut. If she had been more truthful with him from the start, maybe he wouldn't have felt the need to play sacrificial lamb in order to free Kate. But placing the blame for what had happened was a distraction neither of them needed. As long as Kinkaid was alive, there was hope, and she'd fight to save him.

Alexa shifted gears to focus on something more productive. No matter how she reran the assault scenarios in her head, she kept coming back to one thing.

The priest hadn't told them everything about the layout of the estate. He'd left out critical information that he should have known if he'd investigated the arms dealer like he said. The helipad would have been more visible during daylight hours. He should have seen that. And if he left out the helipad, what else had he lied about? Sayed had seemed ready for their raid. The terrorist had Kate out of her cell, and he appeared to be waiting for them with a planned exit. Had the so-called priest tipped him off? The more she thought about it, the more she filled with rage.

Damn it! Anger gripped her, but she had her priorities.

Right now, she had to wait for Garrett to trace the tracking beacon and locate Kinkaid. If she found him fast enough—while he was still alive—she had no doubt Sayed would be there, too.

Plotting revenge while holding a sleeping nun would have played on the conscience of most people, but Alexa wasn't wired that way. Lives depended on her stopping Sayed—and not just Jackson Kinkaid's life. This mission had become personal.

Kinkaid made it personal.

But when she fulfilled her obligation, she vowed to pay a call on Father Ignatius. And this time his slick talk and white collar wouldn't protect him.

From the corner of his eye, Sayed watched Ghazi. The man gazed out the far window of the helicopter, looking below. Only a short time into the flight and Sayed had almost nodded off until the arms dealer punched his arm.

"Something is wrong," Ghazi yelled at him before he turned toward the pilot. "Na'il, why are we flying over water? I told you we were heading to Havana."

Ghazi reached for his seat belt to unbuckle it, but it wouldn't release. He punched the button and tugged at the belt. It wouldn't budge.

The silhouette of a gray-haired man emerged from the cockpit. And he held a gun. "Na'il didn't make it, I'm afraid. Rest his soul." The man made the sign of a cross, a Christian ritual. "But fear not, I have supplied my own pilot. She is delightful . . . and a good cook, too."

"What is the meaning of this?" Ghazi demanded. "How dare you! Do you have any idea who I am?"

"Yes, of course. That's why we're here." The man had a distinctly British accent.

"We?" the arms dealer asked.

The bodyguard stood and aimed his weapon, but not at the foreigner. Ghazi had been betrayed by one of his own. And without a word, the man frisked them and took their weapons. Sayed glared at the arms dealer before he turned his attention to the gray-haired foreigner.

"Who are you?" Sayed asked. "Why are you doing this?"

"Think of me as a savior of souls. And we shall be well acquainted by the time this is all over."

After holstering his weapon, the bodyguard bound their arms behind them with duct tape. He did the same with their legs and placed black hoods over their heads. When Sayed was unable to move, the man jammed a needle into his neck. The injection burned like acid under his skin.

"What the hell are you doing? What was that?" he demanded.

"You will know soon enough, dear fellow."

In Cuba, Father Ignatius went by one name, but in his inner circle of spooks, he was known as the Deacon. Waiting for the drug to take effect with Sayed and Ghazi, he knelt beside the unconscious American and checked for a pulse. When the Deacon stood, he had greater motivation to do what must be done.

He had injected his two captives with an experimental drug that affected the hypothalamus, a portion of the brain that was about the size of an almond. It linked the nervous system to the endocrine system through the pituitary gland and regulated four basic biological needs in all animals, including human beings. The basic needs were often called the "*Four Fs*" and involved evolutionary biology—an animal's basic instincts—fleeing, feeding, fighting, and fornication.

The drug had been designed to take quick effect and would heighten the fear response. His captives would be compliant and more apt to talk in an interrogation.

"They say confession is good for the soul," the Deacon said. "For your sake, I hope they're right." He racked the slide of his weapon and pressed the gun to Sayed's head. "Let us pray, shall we?"

East of Cuba
Over the Atlantic Ocean

When Sayed felt the gun pressed to his head, an overwhelming sense of panic took hold as if his body were possessed. Fire churned under his skin like a thousand pinpricks, and fear knotted deep in his belly. With his chest heaving, he heard the loud thumping of his heart inside his head—an amplified incessant pulse that fueled an intensifying frenzy. He felt like a drowning man in the middle of a vast ocean, flailing and unable to swim. As he gasped for air, the black hood sucked over his mouth and threatened to suffocate him.

He couldn't breathe.

He couldn't see.

And his own body assaulted him.

Sayed heard a whimper, a pathetic mewling sound. It took time to realize the cry came from him. And that terrified him far worse. From under his hood, he heard sounds around him.

Something was happening.

"In the interest of fair play, you both shall be given the chance to live," the Englishman said, "but only one of you will earn that right. It's my version of musical chairs . . . only this time, the loser shall be thrown out over the Atlantic."

To make his point, the helicopter door opened. The engine sound magnified. It blocked out everything. And a rush of air pummeled his body. Sayed screamed and pushed back. His body grew rigid with terror. When a man spun his chair toward the opening, Sayed felt a warmth in his pants. He had wet himself.

And next to him, Ghazi cried out, a muffled scream. They had done the same to him.

"We will start with you, Sayed," the Englishman said. "Tell us the name of your handler and where he is located. It's a simple thing, really. One name. One location."

Sayed shook his head, too scared to refuse aloud.

"And we want to know what you have planned. We have proof you are staging a terrorist attack on foreign soil. We want details, my friend."

"No, I cannot." Sayed yelled this time. And spittle ran down his chin. "I'm not a traitor."

"Then you admire loyalty, is that right?" Before Sayed could answer him, the Englishman added, "If

you wish to save the life of your loyal friend, Jamal
Ghazi, you will tell me what I want to know. If you
don't, I will shove him from this craft into the ocean.
The decision is yours."

Sayed heard Ghazi scream again. He had no idea
what was happening. The hood cast him in darkness,
as dark as the Atlantic below. The thought of drowning terrified him. He couldn't swim. And bound in duct
tape, he wouldn't have a chance.

"What's your answer, Sayed?" the man demanded.

He shook his head, but this time, it wasn't good
enough. "Speak up, Sayed. Let Jamal know your
answer, you gutless wonder."

"No, I won't do it. And if Jamal were in my shoes—
given such a choice—he would do the same. I am not
a coward."

He held his breath, waiting to see what would happen
next. Surely these men would not do such a thing.

He got his answer soon enough. Sayed heard a scuf-
fle and someone was shoved against him. Before he
could ask what was happening, he heard the paralyz-
ing scream of Ghazi. The man's muffled cry echoed
within the aircraft, then died away as he was thrust
from the moving craft. They'd thrown Ghazi from the
helicopter.

"No! What did you do?" Sayed heard the fear in
his own voice. His throat was parched with it. "Please.
Don't do this."

"It's already done. Your friend is gone. And you are
next," the Englishman said. Sayed was moved closer
to the open door as the man continued, "If you do not

tell us what we want to know, you are worthless to us. Talking will save your miserable life."

Sayed had run out of options. His body trembled, and tears drained down his cheeks. No one else would speak for him or save him from what was about to happen unless he did it himself. But before he could speak, from nowhere he felt a sharp pain in his leg, a gut wrenching agony. He cried out, unable to hold back. Someone had stabbed him. The burn of the gash traveled up his body. When he doubled over, he smelled a coppery sweet odor and felt warm blood drain down his leg.

"Why? Why do you do this?" He struggled for his English. In pain, he wanted to cry out in his own language, but he knew the man who tortured him wouldn't understand.

"Your blood will draw the sharks," the man yelled into his ear. "You won't know they are there until you feel the first tug at your body."

Sayed sobbed now. He couldn't hold back.

"What does it say in the Qur'an about the Day of Judgment?" the Englishman asked. "The body and soul are reunited, is that right? After sharks tear you apart, there won't be much left, I'm afraid. Now last chance . . . what's your answer?"

The image of sharks ripping into his flesh in a feeding frenzy started Sayed talking. Everything he knew or thought he knew came spewing from his mouth, the voice of a stranger. He spared nothing. By the time he got done, he was exhausted.

Sayed had lost all sense of time. His body felt weak

and depleted of strength. To curl up and sleep was all he wanted. He was so exhausted, when he felt a second needle in his neck, he didn't cry out or move. The world became as black as the ocean's depths.

And as far as he knew, he died—a drowning man.

As he stared down at the unconscious terrorist—slumped in his passenger seat, bound hand and foot—the Deacon yelled an order to Raul Soto, the inside man who had served him well within Jamal Ghazi's organization.

"Pull him up."

Using a wench, Raul hoisted Jamal Ghazi back into the helicopter. When the terrified arms dealer got shoved back into his seat with his hood yanked off, his eyes bulged from his head. And after the gag of duct tape was ripped from his mouth, he screamed and ranted in broken English with sweat and spittle streaming off his face.

The man smelled of urine and far worse.

"Now it's your turn, Jamal," the Deacon yelled loud enough for the man to hear above the engine noise. "Sayed came to you for help, and you gave it, yet he betrayed you. He didn't think twice about saving your life. I wouldn't stand for that if I were you. Tell us what you know. We'll see that he pays for his treachery. And you'll be the one to live."

Pumped full of liquid fear, Jamal Ghazi didn't need the added motivation of revenge against Sayed. The man was more than willing to talk now. The arms dealer knew the reality of being thrown from a helicopter. The sudden jerk of the tether that kept him alive had served its purpose. It was a reminder of what could still happen if he refused to cooperate. The intel acquired from Ghazi would be gravy. The Deacon had only intended to question Sayed. Anything Ghazi gave them now was an added bonus.

And with Sayed wearing a hood over his head, the terrorist never saw the tether harness attached to Ghazi and never knew the arms dealer had his mouth gagged with duct tape. The Deacon didn't want Ghazi to tip off Sayed.

His deception had worked. The terrorist had shared plenty for now. Contact names, locations, means of communication, money transfers, and bank accounts. More interrogations were planned on solid ground. His makeshift plan had gone off without a hitch, thanks to the diversion of the Americans and their rescue mission.

"We have a stop to make before we drop off our cargo, Raul. I hope you'll indulge me."

Being a man of few words, Raul Soto simply nodded as he took care of their prisoners. The Deacon rather liked that about the man. It certainly allowed him more than enough opportunity to dominate the conversation. And as his pilot, Mrs. Torres, changed course, the Deacon made peace with his God and put in a good word for the American.

It was the least he could do.

CHAPTER 22

Hours later

Back at the harbor in Baracoa, Alexa waited for a call from Garrett. He'd promised word on the tracking-beacon location. She imagined a moving target in a helicopter had made his job tougher, so she had to remain patient—a skill she hadn't acquired.

In the few hours before dawn, her men used their two boats as a place to care for their wounded. They had first aid and bunks on board to get sack time while they waited. Kate got patched up, and after a quick shower belowdecks, she'd changed into clean clothes that she'd borrowed from Jessie, who was about her size.

Too anxious to sleep, Alexa sat alone in the wheel-house with the SAT phone close at hand. She stared at the moonlight reflected off the water. And with the undulating motion of the boat, she was lulled into an overload of thoughts centered on Jackson Kinkaid. Her mind flashed back through dozens of memories she didn't want to forget, yet the man still remained a mystery.

Why did it take losing him to realize how much she . . . ?

"Do you mind company?" A gentle voice intruded on her misery. When she turned, she saw Kate in the cabin doorway.

"No . . . please, come in." She waved a welcome.

"Any word on Jackson?" the nun asked.

Alexa shook her head.

"I can't stop thinking about him," Kate admitted. "He's in here . . . and here." The nun touched her head and placed a hand over her heart.

"Yeah, I know what you mean, Sister." Alexa forced a smile. She wasn't in the mood to talk, but having Kate with her felt as if she had a connection to Kinkaid. "Once he gets under your skin, he's a hard man to shake. Damn near impossible."

"Yes. Very true." The nun sighed. "He's such a good man. He deserves to be happy."

Kate had opened the door for her to ask about Kinkaid's past. Alexa could have tricked the nun into revealing how they'd met by using a ruse she employed in interrogations, where she pretended to know more than she did. But she had too much respect for Kinkaid and Kate to do that. And no matter how much she wanted to know why Kinkaid had been in a mental hospital, she knew that should come from him.

He was a deeply private man. And knowing he had secrets, Alexa had to be careful, too. She didn't want to reveal too much of his covert life or tell Kate of her suspicions about where he got his money. Even though the nun was a good enough friend for him to risk his life for, Kinkaid wouldn't have let Kate know everything.

But one question had plagued her from the start. She decided to begin there.

"What happened to him, Sister? He's not the same man I knew years ago."

Kate avoided her gaze and stared onto the water, adrift in the past. Alexa got the feeling the nun was considering how to answer her question without violating her confidence with Kinkaid.

"Something broke inside him a long time ago," the nun began. "And a light simply switched off. You can see a void in his eyes even now. I've prayed for him, but his salvation must come from inside him. He's got to want it for himself. And he's got to feel like he deserves joy in his life again."

"This whole hostage ordeal started at your missionary-school fund-raiser, where he was your guest of honor?" Alexa posed her remark more like a question and smiled at the thought of Kinkaid on display at a charitable affair.

"Oh, he hated that part." The nun chuckled. "But he loves the children. He donates quite a bit of money to my school. And he's very generous with many others, too. I've seen it. His Lost Angel Foundation does God's work on earth."

"He's got a foundation?" Alexa asked.

A drug cartel mercenary with his own charitable foundation? And donating to children's causes?

Alexa wondered if Kinkaid appeased his guilt over what he did for a living by donating to charity. And maybe *he* was the lost one. *Kate's lost dark angel.* More secrets from the man with many faces. And she had no doubt he'd kept the source of his funds from his good friend Kate.

Before she could ask more, the SAT phone signaled a call coming in, and she picked it up.

"I'm here. Talk to me."

"We've traced Waldo," Garrett told her.

This time, they had deliberately avoided using Alexa's handle of Martini One and relied on voice recognition. She was concerned Father Ignatius and his Echelon program might key off that name, triggering unwanted attention on the transmission. Their communication would still be searched by Echelon for keywords, but using different coded phrases would buy them time and stall outside interference. Garrett informed her they'd traced the tracking beacon to a local residence in Baracoa. As he gave her the address and a general description of the area, Alexa envisioned another compound similar to Jamal Ghazi's place.

How could Sayed escape in a helicopter, only to be tracked back in town hours later? She didn't like it, but she had to check it out.

"I'll update you when I can." When Alexa ended the call, she fixed her gaze on Kate, who looked miserable with worry. "We've got a fix on Jackson. Keep praying, Sister. We could use the help."

Alexa rounded up Hank, Jessie, and others who volunteered to go. They loaded an SUV with weapons and gear. She expected another firefight like they'd encountered at the estate of the arms dealer, but in her gut she feared the worst. For the signal to be coming from a local residence made no sense, not when she'd seen Kinkaid taken away in a helicopter by a crazed terrorist.

If he'd been separated from his tracking beacon, Alexa had a bad feeling they'd never find him. And she had no idea how she'd live with that.

Dawn

A dark silhouette of rolling hills masked the edge of sunrise, and fire tinged a bank of clouds with a hint of the world awakening. The early-morning hour would work in Alexa's favor, but only marginally. Dressed in camo with full assault gear, her team would have to execute their breach quietly and without a shot fired. If they failed and drew attention to their raid, the local cops might shoot first and ask questions later.

Alexa hoped it wouldn't come to that.

Unlike Jamal Ghazi's estate, the residence where they'd traced Kinkaid's signal was more of a ranch on the edge of town, without armed guards patrolling the grounds. A dirt road led through an open stone archway and up to a hacienda surrounded by barbed wire and pastures with cattle. Two cars were parked in front. The picturesque setting left her even more confused as to why Kinkaid's signal would be coming from there.

Using scrub brush for cover, they crouched low and moved along the fence line, making their way closer to the main house. She had a scout and a flanker working ahead of her team. When she got close to the residence, she used hand signals to communicate her order to stop as Manny and Booker returned.

"One man in the kitchen. He's making coffee," Manny whispered. "And there's an open window in back. A man and a woman are sleeping, but I heard a strange beep . . . like some kind of machine. I never saw it."

"Could the beep come from a security system?" she asked.

"I don't think so. I've never seen security work like that."

"What else?"

"There's a back porch with entry into the house and windows off this side." Manny motioned with his hand. "We'll have to watch those. Someone could slip through. No upstairs and no lower level."

"What's your read?" she asked in a hushed voice.

"This looks like a private home, and there's one guy awake," her scout said. "Closest neighbor won't be a problem unless there's gunplay. I say we hit 'em hard and fast in front with a 'bang and clear.' Another team sneaks in the back. No explosives. No weapons unless we have no choice." Manny's flanker, Adam Booker, nodded in agreement.

Alexa gave her order to split up. Hank led his men toward the rear of the main house. Manny and Booker got positioned to maintain surveillance on the side windows, leaving Alexa and Jessie and two others to hit the front door. Walker would execute the breach, and Winslow would be first through the door.

Alexa crept toward the front, careful not to cast a

shadow across a window. She stood with her back near the doorjamb and gripped her weapon. Jessie scrambled to the other side of the door with her assault rifle ready and her eyes fixed on Alexa.

Walker hustled toward Jessie, holding a tactical Ram breaching tool in both hands. He swung the heavy black cylinder backward, then shoved it hard against the door lock. On impact, wood splintered with a loud crack. When the door blasted open, Winslow rushed through it with weapon drawn. In a bang-and-clear operation, the team followed in stacked formation and swept through the front half of the private residence. They cleared rooms and looked to subdue anyone inside the house.

The man her scout had seen in the kitchen would have heard their entry. Alexa knew he'd be their priority. With the kitchen dead ahead, she noticed there were two ways into the room. She signaled for her team to split up.

Expecting trouble, Alexa entered the room with her assault rifle aimed. Walker was close behind her. When she saw a man at the kitchen table, drinking his coffee, she narrowed her eyes but didn't lower her weapon.

"Good morning," he said, and raised his coffee cup.

Jessie and Winslow eased into the room, not saying a word. They waited for Alexa to confront the man. But before she could, Hank joined them. He had a man and a woman with him. His prisoners were dressed in pajamas and looked as if he'd rousted them from bed.

"The rest of the house is clear. Found these two in a rear bedroom," Hank told her as his men herded their captives toward the living room. "But you gotta see this."

When she cocked her head in question, Hank insisted, "Come on."

"Put him with the rest," she ordered, and nudged her head toward the man drinking coffee in the kitchen. Alexa lowered her weapon and followed Hank down a hallway toward the back of the house.

When she got to the end of the hall, Hank swung open a door and she looked inside. A lump wedged in her throat, and fear gripped her belly.

Jackson Kinkaid lay unconscious on a bed, surrounded by hospital equipment. He was hooked to a heart monitor—the beeping sound Manny had heard earlier—and had an IV in his arm. A bag of clear liquid hung by his bed. And a fresh bandage covered his wound.

He looked as pale as the gauze wrap. She'd never seen him so sick.

"We can still search the grounds, looking for evidence Sayed was here, but I doubt we'll find anything. That bastard never would have left him like this," Hank said in a hushed tone. After a moment of awkward silence, he added, "You want a minute?"

"Yeah, I do. Thanks, Hank."

"Sure." He left her alone with Kinkaid.

Alexa stepped into the bedroom that had been turned into a makeshift hospital. She stood by his bed and laid a hand on his bare chest, watching and feeling him breathe. He didn't wake.

His breathing was rapid and shallow. And his skin was hot from the fever he hadn't shaken. Someone had cleaned him up, but perspiration beaded on his forehead and chest.

"Jackson?" she whispered his name, but he didn't move. "Oh, God. What's happening?"

He had a bruise on his stomach where Ghazi had struck him with his rifle. And she saw stitches on his forehead. She had no idea how he'd gotten those, but she had a good notion that Sayed had something to do with it. For all he'd been through, he was finally getting the care he needed.

As he slept, she saw the child he must have been. Despite the fever, his face was at peace, and his inherent sadness had vanished. Gone was the stern-faced man with the defiant green eyes who had become adept at hoarding his secrets.

Lying here, he was vulnerable.

Lying here, he could die.

She brushed a strand of his dark hair off his forehead and stroked his cheek, taking advantage of the fact he wasn't aware she was doing it. Kinkaid wasn't the kind of guy who appreciated coddling, but in the past there were many times she'd resisted the urge to show the tenderness she felt for him.

"You better not die on me, Jackson."

He was battling the infection now. And whatever damage had poisoned his system, it could spread to other organs and do more harm. He had known the risks and took a chance anyway—to save Kate's life. But she found it hard in hindsight to accept his choice now, especially if it meant she might lose him.

Alexa gritted her teeth and funneled all her frustration into getting answers. It pained her to leave Kinkaid alone, but she had questions, and the residents of this house held the key. When she got back to the living room, Hank had their prisoners sitting on a sofa and chair. The two dressed in pajamas were nervous. The woman held the hand of the man sitting next to her, probably her spouse.

But the odd man out—dressed in dark slacks and a Cuban Guayabera shirt—didn't look anxious at all.

"The two having a pajama party own the place. This is Eduardo Gomez and his wife, Marisa." Hank made the introductions. "Eduardo is a doctor."

Alexa nodded, and asked, "How is he, Doc?" She hoped the man understood her.

"His body is fighting off a severe infection," Dr. Gomez replied in perfect English. "I've got him on strong antibiotics, trying to get him stabilized. He's not out of the woods yet. And if he survives, he still might have permanent damage from the infection. It's too soon to tell."

She considered what Gomez told her. If she hadn't seen the doctor's care firsthand, she might have doubted that he was telling her the truth. But no one would have gone to so much trouble to harm Kinkaid—not now and not like this.

"And that man says you know him," Hank said.

"Yeah, I do. And I haven't figured out if that's a good thing." Alexa glared at the gray-haired man sitting in a chair across the living room. He had a cup and saucer in his hands. "You've got some explaining to do, Father Ignatius. Start talking."

"Certainly, my dear. But can I get you some fresh coffee?" He raised his cup and smiled. "I brewed it myself. I used to prefer tea, but Cuban coffee is an acquired taste."

Alexa rolled her eyes and sighed. The priest had his own clock and wouldn't be rushed. She had to focus on what he'd tell her about Sayed and Kinkaid. She had a job to do, and her team needed a hasty clean departure from Cuba, under the radar of the local law. And the clock was ticking.

But she'd already made up her mind. No matter what happened, she wasn't leaving Jackson Kinkaid.

CHAPTER 23

Once they were given their freedom, Dr. Gomez and his wife offered breakfast and coffee to their guests. Hank accepted if he and Adam Booker could cook. That allowed their hosts time to change out of their pajamas and join them without lifting a finger. Alexa left three of her men on guard duty as a precaution. And she took a walk outside with Father Ignatius to have a few words alone with him.

They headed toward rolling foothills and walked down a dirt road. The morning sun brought heat and had burned off the clouds she'd seen at dawn. If she hadn't been worried about Kinkaid, she might have appreciated the beautiful day. They walked in silence, something she hadn't expected from a man who venerated the spoken word, especially coming from him.

"You're an artist, Father Ignatius," Alexa began. "But your rendering of Ghazi's estate didn't include a helipad. For a guy with an eye for detail, I found that odd. I hope you gave yourself at least ten Hail Marys for your lie of omission."

"Ten? You drive a hard bargain, but ten it is." He smiled. "I wasn't sure who you worked for, my dear. I'm still not clear on that point." Father Ignatius clutched his hands behind his back and squinted into the sun when he looked at her. "That gave me no choice. I left off the helipad for a reason. I had to intervene."

"And how exactly did you do that?"

"You might be curious about that point, but it's really not very important in the bigger scheme of things. Let's cut to the chase, shall we?" He winked. When she nodded, he continued, "I had an opportunity to question Sayed and Ghazi. And they were most cooperative."

"They must have seen the error of their ways." She raised an eyebrow. "Did you threaten them with eternal damnation?"

"You might say that, yes." He chuckled. "Sayed wasn't keen on being dismembered. Can't blame him actually. I'm not too keen on it myself."

Alexa grimaced at the man. She had a hard time picturing what he meant by "being dismembered." A part of her didn't want to know, but he never gave her a chance to ask.

He told her about Sayed's plot to explode a radioactive dirty bomb near Chicago using spent nuclear fuel rods stockpiled at one of the larger nuclear plants in the area. The terrorist had planned to enter the United States using phony documents issued by his Venezuelan government contacts. And he had members of his terrorist sleeper cell working in security and other critical operations within the targeted facility.

Alexa had heard about such a conspiracy theory

before. Each year, spent fuel rods were removed from nuclear cores and stored in pools to cool down. It took years for that to happen. Eventually, the waste would be encased in concrete or glass and consigned to dry storage before it got transported to a long-term facility—in theory.

But without resolution on the issue of developing a longer-term storage site, nuclear waste across the country had been stockpiled for years. Until a year ago, the Yucca Mountain Repository in Nevada was the proposed storage facility for spent nuclear-reactor fuel and radioactive waste. Given the delays in upgrading the site and the most recent withdrawal of government budget dollars to develop it, that left nuclear facilities across the country with no place to store waste.

If not controlled on a very tight basis, nuclear waste could be stolen by domestic or foreign terrorists. The homegrown material could be fashioned into a dirty bomb. She knew stringent controls were in place to protect against such a thing, but this was a case where not one single failure could be allowed. There'd be no such thing as being wrong once.

And if Sayed and his men had been successful, the full extent of the damage would be hard to assess. The blast radius would be an immediate concern for casualties and damage. And depending on how much radiation would be present, only a limited area would be directly impacted, but the long-term aftereffects could be more demoralizing. Exposed individuals would have a greater potential for developing cancer in time. And buildings and land would be unusable for years.

"I turned Sayed and Ghazi over to my local counterpart in the NSA. And I've provided details of my interrogations. We have Sayed's funding sources and other key contact information. And arrests are being made as we speak, from what I've been told," he said. "We built quite a case against him with his abductions and killings in the British Virgin Islands. And between his offenses toward your country and mine, I'd say his days of freedom are over."

If she believed what he'd told her—about working with the NSA—that meant the so-called priest worked for Britain's GCHQ, the Government Communications Headquarters. It made sense.

"I hope you don't mind, but I'd like a name at the NSA to confirm what you've told me. No offense," she said.

"Oh, none taken, my dear. I completely understand." He stopped and looked her in the eye. "If you'd like, I could call our operation a joint effort. Your government should know that if it weren't for you and your young man in there, we never would have tracked down Sayed. He might have slipped through our hands and not surfaced until it was too late."

"I appreciate the thought, Father Ignatius. But no, recognition isn't necessary. And I'm sure Kinkaid would feel the same. I'm just glad Sayed was stopped . . . and most of the hostages were rescued." Her thoughts turned to the dead. And she hoped Kinkaid wouldn't be added to that list.

"Yes, I thought as much," he said. "I admire quiet heroism . . . yours and the people who work with you.

For most, freedom and democracy are taken for granted. Yet every day, there is a price to be paid by a brave few. I make my contribution to the cause, but not like you. You risk your life, and yet you're content to operate in anonymity. People in your country, and dare I say the world, will never know your name or see your face."

"With any luck they won't." She felt an uncomfortable rush of heat to her cheeks, caused by his unnecessary praise. "But if you're looking for the real hero in all this, he's lying on that bed in there. If it hadn't been for him . . ." She fought to stay in control, but the catch in her voice gave her away. " . . . many more people would have died."

"It never gets any easier, does it, my dear?"

She took a deep breath and stared into the foothills to regain her composure. And the priest let her do that, without feeling the need to fill in the void in conversation.

"No, it doesn't, but I've got a favor to ask."

Given what Father Ignatius had shared about Sayed—something he didn't have to do—she felt comfortable trusting him to a point. Although she'd have to verify what he'd told her through Garrett, she'd need a favor and someone local to help.

"As soon as I make a call, I'm sending my team back, but I'm staying with Kinkaid. I can't leave him in his condition."

"Yes, I wondered about that," he said. And as they made their turn to head back to the hacienda, he added, "I'll be happy to provide my car . . . and anything else you require while you're here. I would consider it an honor."

The only thing Alexa really needed was out of her hands. She'd never thought of herself as religious or even spiritual, but with Kate putting in a good word for Kinkaid, she hoped a few prayers couldn't hurt.

It didn't take long for Alexa to place the call to Garrett from the Gomez hacienda to confirm the story from Father Ignatius. She cut Hank and the rest of her people loose, and they made arrangements to go, but Jessie was reluctant to leave until Alexa convinced her. She had explained that the Sentinels preferred to minimize their presence on foreign soil, and their success relied upon their continued anonymity. And she finally had to admit to her new partner that her need to stay had become personal.

But before Jessie got in the SUV, she had something to say.

"Thanks for arranging Seth's visit to New York City. Apparently you knew before I did. That guy can grow on you . . ." She grinned. " . . . like a wart." When her smile faded, she said, "It's always been hard to know what's good for me. I never learned that skill. My whole life, I feel like I've been whacking myself in the head with a hammer. And someday, it's gonna feel real good when I stop."

"Self-destructive behavior. I get it. Good analogy." Alexa nodded. "Mind if I use it sometime? I've gotten pretty good at swinging my own hammer." She shook her head. "But I had a hunch about you and Harper. He's . . . special. And you deserve to be happy."

Take your own advice, Marlowe.

Jessie had made the assumption that Harper's trip had been solely intended for her benefit. Alexa didn't consider herself *that* altruistic. In hindsight, she'd let her libido do her thinking when she asked Harper to make the trip. The idea of taking on a younger lover had driven her to extend the invitation, but she was thankful that she'd forced Jessie to make a choice one last time before she crossed the line. For once, she'd exercised restraint, and it had paid off in a way she hadn't expected. She felt closer to Jessie, like a big sister.

And although being with Kinkaid on this mission had opened her eyes to how things could be with someone she really cared about, the reality of her feelings scared her. She wondered if she could open her heart to a man like Kinkaid, but maybe it was already too late.

"You seem to have some history with Jackson Kinkaid," Jessie said. " . . . like he was the one who got away."

"So far." Alexa raised an eyebrow and smiled, hoping she looked more confident than she felt. "See you stateside, partner."

"Call me if you need to talk. Anytime, day or night." Jessie reached for her shoulder, but Alexa opened her arms for a hug.

"Yeah, you got it. And thanks, Jess."

After her partner got into the SUV, Alexa waved good-bye to the rest of her team. They drove from the

Gomez hacienda, leaving her with a growing emptiness deep inside. Whatever was about to happen, she'd have to face it alone.

She hoped the ache she felt wasn't a premonition of bad things to come.

Hours later

Dr. Gomez and his wife had offered her a bedroom. A very kind gesture considering her team had held them at gunpoint only hours ago. After thanking them for their hospitality, Alexa turned down the invitation. She wouldn't leave Kinkaid's side, even if she had to sleep on the floor.

If something happened, she didn't want him to die alone.

She pulled up a chair next to his bed and held his hand until she got antsy and made herself useful. As the hours went by, she cooled his skin with compresses. She wiped his brow and ran a damp washcloth over his chest and down his arms.

Touching him. Helping him. It was all she had left.

She whispered to him and told him things she never would have said if he were awake. Intimate things she felt for him. He never woke up. She watched the sun set through a window, but as darkness settled in the room, she didn't turn on a light. She let the shadows close in and swallow her.

Alexa sat with Jackson in the dark and listened for every breath he took.

She must have fallen asleep, because when she awoke,

it was nearly midnight. Someone had draped a blanket over her shoulders as she laid her head next to him on the bed. And a small lamp shone its light into the room, cutting through the darkness.

Kinkaid's IV drip had been changed, too.

Alexa stretched and took a quick break. The house was dark and quiet. The doctor and his wife had gone to bed. And she noticed the priest had taken off, leaving his car parked in front as promised. When she got back to Kinkaid's room, she saw that his clothes had been cleaned and folded on the dresser next to his tactical gear. And the pouch where he kept his iPod and the tracking beacon was there, too. When curiosity got the better of her, she walked toward the dresser and pulled out his iPod and searched through it.

She had expected to see his play list, but that didn't happen. Only one recording was listed, and she found it odd. That alone intrigued her. The iPod was intended for multimedia use—music, videos, and electronic downloads of all kinds. It had a capacity for thirty-thousand-plus songs and hours of video.

But Kinkaid only had one recording on it.

She plugged the iPod into her ears and listened to his only song. From the sounds of it, someone had made a special recording for him. There were voices and muffled laughter. And a contagious giggle that made her smile.

"Come on. Talk now, silly," a woman prompted. "Just like we practiced. Remember?"

In the background, there was a garbled sound of a microphone brushing against cloth, but eventually a little girl's voice came on.

"This is *my* song . . . for you, Daddy." The child couldn't have been more than five years old. "I miss you, Daddy."

"Daddy's little angel insisted on playing this for you, honey. She knows it's one of Mommy's favorites," a woman said in a playful voice. And in a more intimate tone, she added, "I miss you, too. Please come home soon. I love you, Jackson."

The haunting melody of "Angel," a song by Sarah McLachlan, began to play.

Her smile vanished. And Alexa felt her heart beat faster when the song talked about second chances. At first, she felt like an intruder into his life until anger bubbled to the surface. Why hadn't he told her that he was married . . . and that he had a child? She looked at his reflection in the mirror as if seeing him for the first time. And a flood of memories and quiet conversations rushed through her mind as the song played.

Had she seen the signs and ignored them? Or had he deliberately lied to her and kept his marriage a secret? She couldn't reconcile Kinkaid earning money from drug cartels and going home to his sweet little "angel." Did his wife even know what he did for a living?

She fixed her gaze on Kinkaid through the mirror and forced herself to listen to the whole recording. The sad lyrics conjured a pervasive loneliness. And with nothing but her solitary existence ahead, she felt exhaustion bleed from her veins. Her fatigue made it easy to imagine that he'd somehow betrayed her.

And she wondered if he even knew the story behind

the song. It had been written for a drug-addicted key-board player who had overdosed on heroin. The angel in the song referred to the drug that eventually killed him.

This time when she looked at Kinkaid, a tear slid down her cheek. She didn't know him at all.

New York City

When Jessie got back from Cuba, the first thing she did—even before she went home—was to break Seth out of Sentinels headquarters. The trip back to the States had only been tolerable because she thought of him every minute. And she couldn't wait to see him.

At headquarters, Jessie raced through the computer analysts' bullpen. When she didn't see him, she ran for his dormitory room. This time of night, he'd probably crashed after the long hours he'd put in. She knocked on the door to his room with her heart doing the cha-cha-chá. And a marimba band was knocking around her belly with a mounting impatience that made her skin tingle.

When he opened the door, she almost laughed at the big grin on his face when he first saw her. His sweet dark eyes lit up. And his tousled hair looked as it always did, like he'd just gotten up. Jessie felt like a kid, open-ing the best Christmas present, meant only for her.

"Let's blow this place," she said. "It's time we saw New York City. What do you say?"

Before he answered, she leapt into his arms and kissed him. Their bodies fit in all the right places. And she breathed him in like a drowning woman taking a gulp of air for the first time. In his arms, she felt loved. And if she hadn't been so happy, she might have cried like a baby.

His lips were perfect. Insatiable hunger fed their first touch, but that melded into a savory slow burn of intimacy that could have gone on forever. He nuzzled her neck and her ear. And his tongue sent a ripple of chills over her skin.

"I don't want our first time to be . . ." she whispered into his ear. " . . . here."

He pulled away enough to stare down at her, and he laughed. She loved the sound of it.

"Knowing these sick Sentinels' geeks, they'd record us on surveillance and we'd go viral on *YouTube*."

"Not exactly what I had in mind." She chuckled.

"Then show me what you love most about New York City, Jessica Beckett." He grinned, still holding her in his arms.

"Now why didn't I think of that?"

While Seth packed, Jessie thought of places to take him. She'd been too busy with training to explore. In truth, she'd always wanted to share these places with someone special. Even though it was late, they took a boat ride around Manhattan, a private charter trip that Seth had sweet-talked a proprietor into making and had paid for dearly.

The neon lights of New York shimmered on the water. A real-life postcard she never wanted to forget. And the Statue of Liberty gleamed like a beacon, an unforgettable image. The air off the water dropped the temp, and she rubbed her arms to stay warm. Seth didn't miss a thing.

He wrapped his arm around her and held her hand. And for the rest of the trip, they kissed and talked.

When they got back at the dock, Jessie grabbed a cab, not wasting another minute. She took Seth home to her place on the Lower East Side. In the past, whenever she had sex, she turned out the lights to hide the scars on her body. They were constant reminders of the horror of her childhood. And even with Harper, she felt the same anxious urgency to undress in the dark. Her shame had become a part of her, but for him, she wanted their first time to be different. She let him undress her, piece by piece. And they bathed together by candlelight. Seth kissed her jagged scars with such tenderness that it brought tears to her eyes. And they made slow sweet love for the first time . . . and the second . . . and the third.

Jessie fell asleep in his arms, listening to the beat of his heart. She'd never felt so cherished.

When she woke the next morning, Seth was up making breakfast. She put on her robe and joined him in the kitchen.

"You're ambitious." She grinned as he handed her a cup of coffee and kissed her on the cheek. "You might get invited back if you keep this up."

"Keep what up?" He winked with a devilish look in his eye.

"I've created a monster." Jessie laughed. "My kind of monster."

He served her fresh-squeezed orange juice, her favorite kind of bagel with cream cheese, and a bowl of fruit. After they sat down, he brought up his news.

"Garrett offered me a job. He wants me to work for him. In Tanya's group."

"Oh, my God. That's great. So . . . when are you moving? I can't believe it." She didn't have to think about it twice. She reached for his arm and grinned, but when he didn't return her smile, she asked, "What's wrong? You're not telling me everything."

After a long moment, he told her the rest.

"He gave me the choice of working here . . . or in Chicago."

When he had a hard time looking her in the eye, she knew what he'd decided before he even explained.

"I don't want to disrupt my dad," he told her. "His doctors are in Chicago. And with dementia like his, changing his routine could be devastating. I can't do that to him. I've accepted Garrett's offer, but I'm staying in Chicago. I hope you understand."

She wanted to be happy for him, but she couldn't. She didn't know what to think. Everything had happened so suddenly. It had taken her a lifetime to feel she even deserved happiness, but owning that feeling and sustaining it were too very different things. She needed time. Time she didn't have.

"This is my last day in New York. I've got a flight out late today," he said.

It took a moment for his words to sink in. As happy as she'd been with him in New York, she had been just as heartsick to know he'd be gone by tonight. Jessie had to remind herself that she still had feelings for him. That hadn't changed, but a growing ache in her stomach left her empty inside.

"You still want to see New York City?" She tried to smile, but only gave it half an effort.

"With you? Yes."

After they ate breakfast, she took him to Central Park. They had a picnic in the grass, took in an exhibit at the Met and looked over Central Park from the rooftop of the museum. They had a quiet dinner at a restaurant on the Upper West Side, but all too soon their time together had ended.

After he had packed, she called him a cab from her place. When it arrived, she stood with him on the curb and they kissed. And after they pulled apart, she said, "After today, what I love most about New York City . . . is you in it. I miss you already, Seth."

Her eyes welled with tears. And when she looked up, she saw he wasn't immune to the moment. The trail of a tear glistened on his cheek, and he didn't bother to wipe it away.

"I want you in my life, but I won't force you." When he kissed her on the cheek, he said, "I love you, Jessie."

No man had ever told her that. The moment was wonderful and terrifying at the same time.

Without waiting for anything from her, Seth slid into the cab and waved good-bye. Dumbstruck, she stood on the sidewalk and watched as the taxi rolled forward and merged into traffic. He told her that he loved her. And it scared the hell out of her.

When he was gone, she whispered, "I love you, too."

Gomez Hacienda in Baracoa, Cuba
Morning
Days later

It had taken days for Kinkaid to get back on his feet.
Alexa had stayed to help him. She wanted to make sure
he'd pull through the worst of it, but the strained silence
between them had become palpable. He was too weak
to notice at first, but eventually he did. And when they
were alone, with their hosts gone for a few hours, he
pressed her for answers.

"What's going on, Alexa? You haven't said much
lately."

"Never thought you'd complain about that." She
forced a smile as she stood near the kitchen.

Moving slower these days, he walked into the living
room, dressed in jeans and a navy T-shirt. His dark hair
was wet from the shower. She had brewed coffee and
been waiting to cook for him.

"Are you hungry?" she asked.

"Not really. Coffee works."

Kinkaid's body had taken a beating, but there was
nothing wrong with his eyesight.

"What's this?" He pointed toward the front door and
narrowed his eyes. "You leaving?"

He noticed her gear packed and behind a chair
near the entry. Whatever time they had together had
run out. She had already made arrangements to leave
Cuba that day. She felt like a damned coward, but she
had to remind herself. There was nothing real between
them. All they had were old memories and her gullible

notion of a road not taken. He had never promised her anything. And the attraction and feelings she believed they shared hadn't been there at all. Their emotional connection had been a one-way street, driven by her desire to make a change in her life—and wanting it to be with him.

"Yeah, life goes on," she said. "Didn't you get the memo?"

Her words came out harsher than she had intended. Or had they? Anger colored her mood. She was leaving, acknowledging that she'd been wrong about him, but he'd lied to her.

And that hurt, damn it!

"Why didn't you tell me that you're married, Jackson . . . and that you have a kid?" She couldn't hide the hurt in her voice. It made her sound like such a . . . *girl*. The last thing she wanted. "I never figured you for soccer games and PTA meetings."

"What?" He glared at her. She'd crossed a line, and she had no idea how. "Did Garrett tell you about them? I'm surprised he had the nerve, the bastard."

What did Garrett have to do with Kinkaid's wife and child? Heat rushed to her cheeks, along with the cold realization that she was treading on dangerous turf and going in blind.

"No, I listened to your iPod. That's all."

"And that's enough." He raked a hand through his hair and turned his back on her. With a loud sigh, he stuffed his hands into his pockets and let the silence build a wall between them.

When he finally spoke, she barely heard his voice.

"My wife and little girl are dead. That recording I have . . . it's the last time I heard their voices."

Alexa felt as if she'd been sucker punched. She had barely gotten used to the idea of his being married. Now to hear his wife and child were dead ripped her heart out—for him. A guy like Kinkaid lived to protect. He'd been trained for it, but the instinct came naturally. It was in his genes. For him to love someone enough to marry her and have a baby, his wife had to be a very special woman. And a father should never experience the death of his little girl. *Never.*

Alexa ached for him and knew he was hurting. She had no doubt grief had been the reason for his stay in a mental hospital. For him to lose it like that would have been devastating for a take-charge guy like Kinkaid. She waited for him to say more, but he didn't.

"When did it . . . happen?" she asked.

"After the last mission I had with you. Nearly five years ago. They were murdered, Alexa. And I was the one who found them."

"Murdered?" Alexa was numb with shock. "Who would have killed them, Jackson?"

"It was a professional hit. Police didn't even get close to finding out who did it." When Kinkaid turned, his face was flushed. "Garrett had a security detail on them, but something went wrong. After what happened, I called it quits with the Sentinels . . . and Garrett. If I'd stayed, I would have been too tempted to kill your boss."

"Since your family was under Sentinels' protection, did it have something to do with a mission?" she asked, but didn't wait for his answer. "Why didn't Garrett conduct his own investigation? When one of his own comes under fire, he'd be the first one to . . ."

"Look, that's not how it went down. And I've said too much already. I don't need you involved in this."

"Why didn't you tell me? Any of it." She hadn't meant to ask that, but the words were out before she could stop. And there was no reining back the heartache she felt inside.

He shook his head. "I kept my wife and kid a secret from everyone. In our business, having a family makes you vulnerable. And they meant too much to me. I couldn't risk *anyone* knowing, not even you. And after they were killed, I wasn't exactly thinking straight."

But Garrett had known about Kinkaid's family, she thought. *Garrett was supposed to keep them safe*.

A stab of fear gripped her stomach, making her wonder what had really happened. And she had a feeling Garrett would have nothing to say, not about the death of Kinkaid's wife and little girl. Alexa didn't know what to believe. She respected both men and had feelings for them too—*very different feelings*.

"Kate mentioned you had a charitable foundation." She changed the subject, wanting to understand. "What's that all about? You work as a mercenary for drug cartels, siding with the highest bidder. That doesn't fit the image for . . . what's the name of your foundation?"

She tried to recall the name. When he filled in the blank, saying, "Lost Angel," she suddenly knew.

The foundation had been named for his daughter. *Daddy's little angel*.

"Oh . . . I'm so sorry, Jackson. I didn't know. And you don't have to explain. Not to me."

"You're right about one thing. I *am* taking money from drug cartels. It's just not what you think. Let's leave it at that." He sighed and fixed his gaze on her. "My wife and kid are dead, Alexa. And I'm getting on with my life . . . my way."

"Are you?" She cocked her head. "Who are you trying to convince?"

"Look, this is none of your business."

"Yeah, I finally see that," she said. "Thanks for the eye-opener." She headed for the door.

"No, you don't understand. This is too . . . personal. Having a kid, it wasn't like anything I've ever felt." He stopped her with the emptiness in his voice. "Love at first sight can be a powerful and consuming feeling. I never believed in it until the day my daughter was born, and I held her for the first time. That moment was so . . . perfect. Even now, I can smell her skin and feel her move in my arms."

Tears drained down his cheeks. She knew he was in another place and time, and he'd taken her with him. Alexa felt his gut-wrenching pain and experienced his profound sorrow.

"It was going to be the three of us," he said. "And all I wanted to do was protect our baby girl, but when it counted, I couldn't do that."

Kinkaid shut his eyes and lowered his head. She'd never seen him so lost. All she wanted to do was hold him, but out of respect for his grief and the family he had lost, she kept her distance.

"Some roads you've got to go down alone," he admitted. "And I'm not ready to let go. I can't." He looked her in the eye. "Not even for you."

The truth had finally surfaced. And she knew it would take time for her to accept it. She could only imagine the horror of what he'd been through. Living with the reality of such an atrocity would be hell on earth. And even if he wanted to remember them alive as he listened to their recorded voices, he'd been the first one to find their bodies. That cruel memory would haunt him—a merciless torment he didn't deserve.

"I'm not asking for you to let go. Only you will know when it's time to do that," she said. "I just wish you could have trusted me with the truth."

Alexa knew that he trusted her with his life, but beyond that, real intimacy was a precious gift that had to be earned. She wasn't sure she deserved that kind of trust from him, but that didn't stop her from wanting it—or needing it.

She had to accept that Kinkaid had chosen a life detached from others, and nothing she said now would convince him to change how he felt about her. And only time and her taking stock in her life would prevent the same isolation from eventually happening to her. It was a slippery slope and an easy trap to fall into in their line of work. She picked up her gear and carried it to the door before she turned one last time.

"Kate wants to see you," she told him. "Anything you want me to tell her?"

"No, nothing."

"You're not going to see her again, are you?"

"She doesn't need me in her life. Hell, she's better off without me. She always was. I'll still support her school, but she won't know the money is coming from me."

"What about you? Walking away from a friend like Kate . . ." *And me*, she wanted to say. " . . . that's not good. It's hard enough to do what we do. Doing it alone only makes things . . . worse. You know that, don't you?"

"I never wanted to go it alone, Alexa, but shit happens. Getting too close to me isn't good for your health, or haven't you been paying attention?" He shook his head and grimaced, unable to meet her gaze. "This shouldn't have happened to Kate. *None* of it should have happened. Why did they . . . why did anyone have to die?"

Alexa wasn't sure if he was talking about Kate and the hostages anymore.

"I don't know, Jackson." Her eyes brimmed with tears. "But Sayed was responsible for what happened to Kate and the others, not you. It's why we stopped him . . . together. How long will you beat yourself up over something you had no control over?"

"For as long as it takes."

She wished what he said wasn't true, but she knew different.

"Good-bye, Jackson. I hope you find . . ." She struggled for words. *Find what?* Kinkaid was a guy who *had* found happiness once—*and lost it.* "I hope you find whatever it is that you're looking for."

After a long moment, Kinkaid nodded, and said, "You too, Alexa."

She walked out the door, fighting a lump in her throat, a knot of emotion that she would deal with in the days and months to come. A part of her would always love Jackson Kinkaid. She knew that now. Yet there would be a part of him that she could never have—and that wasn't good enough.

She needed more than he had to give. And if Kinkaid were any example, time wouldn't heal *all* wounds.

And now
a special early look at the
next title in the Sweet Justice series

Reckoning for the Dead

Coming 2011

From Jordan Dane and Avon Books

Outside Ciudad Juárez, Mexico
Dusk

The footsteps of Ramon Guerrero echoed as he stepped closer to the hostage. A dark silhouette of a man was backlit from the only barred window in the cell. His prisoner had been stripped of his clothes. Completely naked, he sagged by the weight of his own body as he hung from a metal bar. Ropes cut into his wrists and blood drained down his arms. Dark bruises mottled his ribcage, an aftermath of the beatings he had survived.

"Why are you here in my country?"

The man did not hesitate. "I'm here to kill a man."

Guerrero burst into laughter at the man's gall. "And how is that going for you?" Without waiting for an answer, he shook his head and said, "We know who you are."

"You don't know shit. Go to hell."

In the stifling heat, Guerrero punched the hostage in the gut. *Once. Twice.* The prisoner clinched his stomach muscles and took the blows without uttering a sound.

"We shall s-see ... " he panted, " ... h-how long your arrogance lasts."

His cartel boss had demanded to see the prisoner. It was the only reason Garrett Wheeler was still alive ... *for now.*

Dressed in gray slacks and black cashmere sweater, Alexa Marlowe sipped coffee as she looked out her apartment window, located on the third floor of a brownstone on the Upper East Side off Lexington Avenue. For the last week, she'd been restless and sleep hadn't come easy. In her line of work that was a hazard of the trade, but she had another reason to worry. And after getting a call from Tanya Spencer yesterday and arranging for an early-morning meeting at her place, she wondered if the Sentinel's analyst had been losing sleep for the same reason.

When she heard the soft knock on her door, she rushed to answer it.

"Good morning, Tanya." She forced a smile. "Please . . . come in."

"Thanks for accommodating my crazy schedule."

Even before dawn, the woman was impeccably dressed in a navy Burberry blazer and a pencil skirt. Her black skin looked radiant with only a hint of the flawless make-up she wore. And her southern drawl could melt butter. That voice had calmed Alexa on many covert ops missions when she had needed analytical support . . . and a friend.

"Sorry to get you up this early, but I thought we should talk somewhere away from headquarters. And your place was on my way to work."

"No trouble. You've given me a jump on my day. Can I get you coffee?" Alexa asked.

"Yes, please."

Alexa had already made a pot. She served Tanya a cup and they sat in her living room.

Being a covert agent, Alexa viewed the world differently than most people. She looked for ulterior motives and conspiracies under every rock. It was how her brain worked out of necessity. Her survival sometimes depended on it. And since Tanya Spencer had a similar background—having worked many years with the privately funded Sentinels and as Garrett Wheeler's right hand for the last decade—Alexa figured the woman's cryptic words meant she was only playing it safe.

"So tell me what's on your mind, Tanya."

"I'm not sure if I should be saying this, but . . . " the woman began. " . . . I haven't heard from Garrett in almost two weeks. And that's not like him." When Alexa didn't act surprised, Tanya said, "What's going on? Do you know anything about this?"

"No, I don't, but I've noticed the same thing." She heaved a sigh. "I thought it was me. After I broke it off with him, our relationship changed. It had to, but I haven't heard from him either. And that's got me losing sleep."

Tanya was one of the few people within the Sentinels who knew about her personal relationship with her boss, Garrett. She considered the woman a trusted friend.

"Isn't anyone else concerned about this?" Alexa narrowed her eyes. "He's head of our organization. What's he been working on?"

Tanya had been Garrett's senior analyst and advisor

for the last ten years. She usually kept close tabs on him. And he trusted her with every aspect of what he did. They were a team.

"That's just it. I don't know." The woman shook her head and put down her coffee. "And it's got me worried sick. He's never done this, Alexa. He'd always involved me with anything he touched. That's why I wanted to talk here, at your place. Something's been going on and I've been cut out of the loop. The people Garrett answers to have to know something, but they're not clueing me in."

"So who's in charge with Garrett gone? I've never seen him work with anyone in particular who could step into his shoes."

"Yeah, I haven't either, not with the secrecy above his level. But this can't go on forever. If Garrett is AWOL, someone's got to assume his duties."

"You have any idea who?"

Tanya only shook her head. She was normally unflappable, but seeing the grimace on her face told Alexa all she needed to know about her concern.

"We'd have to be careful looking into this. We could blow his op and put him in danger if we barge in without knowing what's going on."

"Does that mean you and Jessie will be looking into this?" Tanya asked. "I've tried tracking Garrett, but I've got nothing. Maybe if we trace other movements within the organization, we'll have better luck."

Tanya was right. If Garrett was involved in a covert op that excluded his top analyst and his most trusted agent, it had to be really big. But that also meant Sentinels' resources would be dedicated to the operation.

And if Alexa could handpick someone to dig through the veiled secrecy of the Sentinels—an organization of international vigilantes who operated off the global grid to dole out their brand of justice—she would have Tanya Spencer at the top of her list. The woman had connections in and out of the organization. And with her internal systems knowledge, she could slip through virtual backdoors without anyone noticing.

"I'm meeting Jessie later for breakfast. She's pretty new to how things work within the Sentinels, but we'll see." Alexa sat back on her sofa and crossed her arms. "If we do this, we'll need your help."

Tanya nodded and said, "Count on it."

Alexa knew that what she was planning to do—using the organization's resources to trace a covert operation involving her boss and former lover—would not be sensible. It could turn into a career ender at best. Or a death sentence at worst. And to involve her new partner, Jessie, would not be wise either—especially for Jessie's sake.

Relying on gut instinct, she'd have to make that call when she talked to Jessie. If she read anything in her that raised a red flag, she'd let it slide and go it alone with Tanya. But one way or another, she'd take the risk for Garrett—because he would do the same for her.

New York's Lower East Side

The ringing of a phone early in the morning was never a good thing.

Jessie Beckett pulled the bedcovers off her face and fumbled for the light switch. And after she flicked on her lamp, she squinted at the alarm clock on her nightstand.

"Six twenty? Who the hell—?" She winced, grabbed the cell phone off her nightstand, and flipped it open without looking at the caller's number. "You better have a damned good reason for breaking into my beauty sleep."

The sun had barely made an appearance. And that meant she didn't give a rip about winning Miss Congeniality.

"Jessie? It's Sam."

She recognized the voice of her best friend. Samantha Cooper was a vice cop in Chicago. And she had better sense than to call her at this hour if it wasn't important.

"Sam? What's up? Is Seth alright?"

Her worry barometer worked double-time when it came to Seth Harper, a guy who had nestled into her heart and made a home. The whacked-out computer genius had a habit of getting into trouble, and not only because he knew her. The boy had a serious way of attracting it himself. And with his recent recruitment into the Sentinels for his mad skills with a keyboard—the same organization Jessie worked for—Seth had more than doubled his gift for luring trouble.

"No, Seth is fine, I guess. I haven't seen him lately, but I was calling you about . . . something else."

"Oh?"

Her friend cleared her throat and stalled, which wasn't like her.

"Spit it out, Sammie."

"Chicago PD received a bulletin from a sheriff in La Pointe, Wisconsin."

"Where the hell is that?"

"It's at the northern tip of Wisconsin. On Madeline Island in Lake Superior, to be exact. I looked it up on a map."

"Thanks for the geography lesson." Jessie ran a hand through her dark hair. "Explain why I should care about this?"

Sam cleared her throat again. Definitely stalling.

"You should care because the sheriff was working an old cold case. A pretty gruesome murder that happened over twenty years ago."

"Twenty years. We were both kids back then. Why are you calling me about this, Sam?"

Jessie didn't like where this was headed. Twenty years ago she was a child in the hands of notorious pedophile Danny Ray Millstone. At least, that was what she believed. She was too young to really know the truth about how she ended up with him—or maybe she'd blocked it out. And insult to injury, after she was rescued by Detective Max Jenkins of the Chicago PD, no one from her family stepped up to claim her. Not even the national media coverage afterward shed light on what had happened to her. That aspect of her past had remained a black hole. And she'd given up trying to find where she'd come from.

Looking into the details of her childhood nightmare had always been too painful.

"Yeah, well, back then DNA wasn't used to solve

crimes like it is now," Sam said. "But an old case caught the eye of this sheriff. And he sent in evidence he had stored in archives to the state crime lab. When the lab ran its findings against the CODIS and NCIC databases, the sheriff got two DNA hits—and his first new lead in over twenty years."

Jessie's mind worked quickly, thinking how a DNA test would link to her. The FBI maintained both the Combined DNA Index System and the National Crime Information Center. The first held DNA profiles in a database while the other was a repository for specific criminal records on known fugitives, missing persons, stolen property, and other details. Such database information was available to state and federal law enforcement types and was meant to share information across jurisdictions. Since she'd been a missing person as a child, her gut twisted with the implications of where Sam might be going with this.

"Got two hits . . . on what?"

"Since you were a missing kid, your DNA is on record, Jess. The Wisconsin crime lab got a hit on your DNA. It puts you at that crime scene over twenty years ago."

"What?" Jessie grimaced. "I don't understand."

"I didn't either. That's why I called that sheriff. His name is Tobias Cook. I only asked questions and didn't tell him anything. I wanted to talk to you first," Sam told her. "Apparently the DNA hit on you was a dead-on match, but that's not all."

"Oh, great. The hits keep coming."

"They found more DNA that suggests you were with

a family member. The second hit showed a 95% probability match to your DNA."

"What does that mean?"

"You were too young to be alone. That second DNA sample came from a family member. Your *real* family, Jessie." Sam let that thought settle before she landed a second shocker. "Besides the DNA, the sheriff has reason to believe . . . that you might have been with your mother."

"My mother? How would he know that?"

"I tried getting that out of him, but he wouldn't say."

Hearing the word "mother" always flashed her back to a haunting memory that had been with her since she was a little girl. She recalled a sunny day with fall colors and a woman's smiling face. She held those images close to her heart, of a woman playing with her in a park. She must have been someone very special because the memories always made her happy. Although she still couldn't be sure the woman in her dreams was really her mother, Jessie needed to believe she once had someone who loved her like that.

She'd always fantasized that if she saw the woman again, she'd know it. Something in her eyes would give it away. At least, she'd always hoped that would be true.

"But . . . our DNA was found at a murder? This isn't the family reunion I was hoping for." She shook her head, grappling with the idea that her real mother might have had a connection to a murder. "Was my mother . . . a witness? Or was she the one murdered?"

She had a hard time saying the word "mother," but had an even tougher time considering what dark scenarios had put her at that crime scene.

"The sheriff didn't say. He only said he wants you to contact him."

"Wait a minute." She shut her eyes tight, feeling the start of a major headache. "Does he consider her a suspect?"

"Don't know, but if your mother had been connected in some way to a murder, that would explain why she never came forward after you were rescued."

What Sam said made sense. It had always pained her that no one had claimed her after her ordeal with Millstone, especially with all the national media coverage. Given the scant memories she had of a woman she believed to be her mother—a child's wishful thinking— Jessie didn't want to even think about the woman being involved in a killing. The life she led before Millstone had been an abyss until now, but maybe this sheriff could fill in the gaps. Jessie would have no way of knowing anything for sure unless she contacted him.

"So now what?" Sam asked. "People here at CPD know we have a connection. They're letting me handle this bulletin request for information, but I can't stall them."

"No, and I don't expect you to." Jessie chewed the inside corner of her lip. "I'm flying to Chicago as soon as I can arrange a flight. I'll call you when I get there."

"You want me to pick you up?"

"No . . . I'll get Harper to do that. But I'll call you, okay?"

"So what are you going to do?"

"I'm driving to La Pointe. You can tell Sheriff Cook that I'll see him face-to-face. I've got to know what evidence he has on that case. And why he's looking for someone he thinks is my mother."

"Look, Jess. I know this is hard for you, but if you need to talk, call me."

"Thanks, Sam. I will."

Her past never went away. For the first time in her life, Jessie had a future and prospects working for the Sentinels. She wasn't just a bounty hunter drifting from case to case living in a crappy apartment on the fringe of society in Chicago. And since Seth Harper had nudged his way into her life, she also felt good about herself. He had known about her past and accepted her. The scars she carried on her body and soul weren't an issue with a guy like Harper.

So why now? Why did this damned cold case in Wisconsin have to bite her in the ass now?

It scared her to think that her only memory of someone who might be her mother may have been wrong. Was she ready to kill the only good thing she remembered of her past?

"I can never catch a damn break," she muttered as she got out of bed.

Dressed in a tank top and boxers, Jessie trudged into her living room and logged onto her laptop to look for a flight to Chicago that would work. She had breakfast plans with Alexa Marlowe that she could still make on her way to LaGuardia. Her new partner would need to be in the loop that she was leaving town, but Alexa didn't need to know everything.

Very few people knew the details about the nightmare of her childhood ordeal and she preferred to keep it that way.

Two hours later

Norma's restaurant in Midtown West was packed. Bright and bustling, the place had high ceilings, wood paneling, and silver-edged tables that gave a modern yet comfortable feel. It was a popular cafe for breakfast and lunch, located in the Parker Meridien Hotel lobby. Norma's was too expensive and trendy for Jessie's taste, but Alexa knew her partner had suggested it for her sake. Being a former bounty hunter, Jessie had dealt with the dregs of humanity and would have been satisfied with any hole-in-the-wall greasy spoon.

When she arrived, she noticed Jessie had gotten there early and scored a table, a small carafe of coffee, and two shot glasses of the restaurant's complimentary smoothie du jour. After her partner waved her over, it didn't take Alexa long to notice the carry-on luggage under the table.

"Planning on staying the week? The blueberry pancakes are good, but come on," she joked to cover up her surprise . . . and disappointment.

"I'm heading for the airport. Going to Chicago. Something personal has come up." Dressed in a T-shirt and jeans, Jessie leaned across the table. "I know this is short notice, but I don't have a choice."

Alexa narrowed her eyes and dropped her smile. "Anything I can do?"

"No, nothing." Jessie shook her head. "I've got it covered."

Jessie had hesitated enough to tell Alexa her trip to Chicago wouldn't be for pleasure.

"And I'm guessing you probably don't want to talk about it."

"Bingo." Jessie grabbed her coffee cup and hid behind it.

Her partner was a woman with secrets and Alexa respected her privacy. The scar over her eyebrow had a story behind it, one she'd never been privileged to hear. Even though not too long ago Alexa had gotten a glimpse into something Jessie had barely survived as a child, her partner had never confided in her and she hadn't pushed.

And Alexa also guessed Jessie had feelings for computer genius Seth Harper. Maybe her trip had something to do with Harper. The guy was a new recruit for the Sentinels, but he'd opted to stay in Chicago rather than move to New York so he could stick close to his mentally deteriorating father who lived in a nursing home. That had been her first thoughts about Jessie's trip, but with her partner she might never know for sure.

"How long will you be gone?" she asked. "I mean, in case something comes up."

"Maybe a few days. Not long."

"Okay." She nodded. "Will you call me if you need anything?"

"Yeah . . . I'll do that. So what's good here?" When Jessie flipped open her menu, her eyes grew wide. "Oh my God! They have a lobster and caviar omelet for a thousand smackers. Who the hell are they kidding? That's just . . . insane."

As fast as Jessie stuck her nose in the menu and changed the subject, Alexa knew her partner would never take her up on her offer. Jessie had a tough, independent streak. It was one of the things she liked most about her, but sometimes that made it hard for anyone to get inside. As a partner and a friend, Jessie was an acquired taste.

But with Jessie going out of town—completely distracted by her personal agenda—Alexa knew she'd be working with Tanya alone. Once her partner got back and could focus, she might ask for her help, but for now Jessie was out of it. And there was no sense telling her anything about Garrett. She had enough going on in her life without adding the guilt trip of leaving her in the lurch—because that's exactly how Jessie's mind worked. She'd feel guilty over something she had no control over.

As if she'd read her mind, Jessie looked up from her menu and said, "You look tired. You getting enough Zs?"

Alexa ran a hand through her blond hair and heaved a sigh as she propped her elbows on the table.

"I'm doing okay." She lied and forced a smile before she shoved over her empty cup. "Now dose me up and pour me some coffee, will ya?"

And as she expected, Alexa turned her thoughts to Garrett. Something was terribly wrong. As an experienced operative, she sensed it in her bones, especially after talking to Tanya and hearing that Garrett's top analyst hadn't heard from him either.

When they were together, he had been an attentive, aggressive lover and had quickly become her obsession. He had unleashed an insatiable need in her and the passion they shared had gone beyond love. Garrett Wheeler had marked her soul. And no matter how hard she had tried to move on without him in her life, she knew that she'd never forget him.

Where are you, Garrett?

Outside Tampico, Mexico

"Is it . . ."

"Is it . . ."

". . . him?"

A woman's voice filtered through the fog in his brain. Her words overlapped like undulating ripples across still water, mixed with the faint, distant echo of a child's laughter. The sounds nudged his faltering consciousness or tapped into his memory. He didn't know which. And he had to concentrate to hear anything at all. He didn't know where he was or how he got there. He barely remembered his own name as his body drifted through the shadows from where he'd come.

When he felt a cool velvet touch on his fevered cheek, he heard a moan, unsure if the sound came from him. He forced his eyes open a crack and caught a glimpse of light. Shadows eclipsed a dim glow, but he was too weak to move. With the drug still too strong in his system, he wavered on the razor's edge of darkness and took the only comfort he could. He imagined the woman's voice he had heard morphing into a more familiar, sultry one and pictured running his fingers through a soft tumble of blond strands as he gazed into pale blue eyes.

His lover's throaty voice stirred him and her haunting eyes lingered along with a trace of her perfume. He felt her kiss and her whisper in his ear as she trailed a finger down the bare skin of his chest and onto his stomach. Her touch made him flinch and his body reacted.

He wanted her.

He needed her.

And when he willed the beautiful woman to stay— *she did.*

Next month, don't miss these exciting new love stories only from Avon Books

Mad About the Duke by Elizabeth Boyle

The Lady Elinor Standon needs to find a new husband, quickly. When she hires a solicitor to help her land a lofty lord, she never imagines she might fall for the man! James Tremont, the Duke of Parkerton, hadn't intended to let his little charade go this far, but now he just can't help but wonder if he can win the lovely widow without divulging his title.

An Accidental Seduction by Lois Greiman

When Savaana Hearnes agrees to impersonate newly wed Lady Clarette Tilmont, she imagines it will be an easy way to make money for a fortnight. Until Sean Gallagher, a ruggedly handsome Irishman with a secret of his own arrives, and Savaana's plans are shattered by desire.

The Dangerous Viscount by Miranda Neville

To escape the reputation of her noble but eccentric family, Lady Diana Fanshawe is determined to make an impeccable match—which is why she *will* marry Lord Blakeney, though she'll never love him. But when the brilliant but unconventional Viscount Iverly kisses her and then steals her heart, will Diana choose love or respectability?

Lord Lightning by Jenny Brown

Unrepentant rogue Lord Hartwood is infamous for his outrageous behavior, and amateur astrologist Miss Eliza Farrell is not at all the sort of woman he amuses himself with. But when demure Eliza becomes entangled in his latest prank, sparks fly with an electric passion that threatens to transform them both.

Visit www.AuthorTracker.com for exclusive information on your favorite HarperCollins authors.

REL 0910

At Avon Books, we know your passion for romance—once you finish one of our novels, you find yourself wanting more.

May we tempt you with . . .

- **Excerpts** from our upcoming releases.
- Entertaining **extras**, including authors' personal photo albums and book lists.
- Behind-the-scenes **scoop** on your favorite characters and series.
- **Sweepstakes** for the chance to win free books, romantic getaways, and other fun prizes.
- Writing **tips** from our authors and editors.
- **Blog** with our authors and find out why they love to write romance.
- **Exclusive content** that's not contained within the pages of our novels.

Join us at
www.avonbooks.com

AVON

An Imprint of HarperCollins*Publishers*
www.avonromance.com